A DEEP GREEN WAR

The Second Mill Meacham Story

A
Carson A. Pierce
Novel

The characters in this novel are entirely fictitious and bear no resemblance to anyone living or dead. Character names were checked to make sure none used in the book represent actual people working for the agencies mentioned. Certain living and deceased historical figures are included to give the novel verisimilitude.

Library of Congress Cataloging-in-Publication Data is available from the Library of Congress

ISBN 978-0-9827537-2-9

Acknowledgements

A Deep Green War would never have been completed without the invaluable support of friends and family. Blending mystery, adventure, crime, and light satire was a real challenge for me--one that I would not have met without significant help from others.

My wife, Cheryl, is my constant source of insight and encouragement. She served ably as idea checker, proof reader, and editor.

Neil Hoopman gave me invaluable support in working with complex software and book design. Eloi Hoopman gave me expert medical advice.

Forest Service Law Enforcement Officer Ted Rainville gave me useful insights into the equipment used by Forest Service law enforcement and how he and his colleagues conduct operations.

Several people read the book in draft and provided me useful edits and comments. These caring critics include: Frank Caplan, Allen Gibbs, Bruce Parker, Ted and Christine Rainville, Jim Van Loan, Victor Rozek, and Kathleen Williams.

My profound thanks to everyone.

Message from the Author

Is *A Deep Green War* a gritty crime story? A mystery-adventure? A love story? Is it about a young woman painfully coming of age? About agencies and their cultures? About environmental politics and conflicts? Is it a narrative? A commentary on good and evil? On conflict and dispute resolution? Humor? Poetry? Satire?

Maybe it's all of these things, a spicy cocktail blended for readers who want their literature to shake and shock them, to inform and intrigue them and, if they choose, to educate and uplift them.

Read! Enjoy!

Cap, 2010

Dedication

To
all
Forest
Service
people, past
and present, the
best natural resource
professionals in the world,
I pray you the best in all ways,
always. *You readers there!* Lift your
glasses! Here's to wild places and to the
wild things that live in them! And here's to the
people who care for those wild places and things!
The best ever!
Now
drink!

Table of Contents

Chapter 1

Miller's Gold

A flash catches Clarence "Bud" Miller's eye, a bright, sunny wink against the old forest's dark-day bronzes and greens. Through a slight break in the forest canopy overhead, a pencil-thin beam of sunlight streams into the clearing from the east and ignites the gold-circle flash again..

Bud walks over, his eyes widening as he gets closer. "My God, it's a coin," he says aloud, "A gold coin hanging by a gold chain right out here in the middle of nowhere!"

He hefts the coin with his right hand. It covers half of his big, rough palm.

He untangles the chain from a slender branch with his left. Once free, he holds the coin close to his face for inspection.

Even without his "old man" glasses, he sees the words "South Africa" and "Krugerand" on it. Smaller letters state "102 Fine Gold" and "1975." A beautiful antelope figure adorns one side and a guy's head peers out from the other.

He weighs the heavy coin and says, "I wonder how this beauty could have gotten here? 'Fine gold' means 'pure gold' maybe? Wonder what its worth?"

"Some fool hanky-headed hiker must have lost this," he mutters.

"But, why would a hiker have been carrying this in these woods and how did it wind up in the middle of a timber stand hanging from a twig?"

Bud shakes his head.

This makes no sense.

He wonders if he should just stuff the coin in his pocket and keep it.

But, an honest man, Bud figures he'll turn it in to Forest Service Law Enforcement and see if it gets returned to him later on. It's the right thing to do.

This thought is his last.

In the next instant, Bud Miller dies.

Chapter 2

Baby LEO

Millicent "Mill" Meacham waits in her warm Forest Service Law Enforcement rig for her supervisor, Patrol Captain William Zumo, to arrive.

Windshield wipers beat intermittently against the light rain.

A laptop screen glows.

Radios crackle and mutter with far-a-way calls.

Mill doesn't think a crime has been committed here, but she had cordoned off the scene of Bud's death with yellow-and-black striped "Crime Scene Do Not Cross" tape anyway.

Mill took other precautions to protect the site, too. She feels satisfied that they worked. The few people visiting the site earlier did little trampling or disturbance apart from the area within a yard or so of Bud's body.

Hours ago, before any site disturbance took place, Mill had measured the area with the help of the Medical Examiner and his assistant.

And when the widow-maker tangle was moved to reveal Bud's body, they shot photographs, and then examined and removed him.

The whole sequence was in Mill's digital camera. She logged notes to accompany each shot.

Early that morning, Bud had been declared overdue by Bud's boss, the Mapleton District Ranger. The Siuslaw Deputy Forest Supervisor, en route to a meeting in Coos Bay from Corvallis, responded to the "be on the look out" radio call and drove up to the timber-sale site. He found Bud's truck and, a few minutes later, saw Bud's boots....

The Forest Service is built like a four-layer cake: executives at the top in Washington, DC, middle managers and staff at nine regional offices and the 120 or so national forest offices, and nearly a thousand local ranger district offices.

Within the layer-cake, the Deputy Forest Supervisor is a middle manager. He usually works "in town." In contrast, Mill is a district grunt, delivering services to people in wild places.

The badly shaken Deputy Forest Supervisor left soon after Mill arrived. He waited only long enough for her to take his statement.

His words seemed to catch in his throat, "Boots...I saw his boots. Under there...."

He started to giggle compulsively and shake his head. He moved quickly away once Mill suggested he go and looked back at her gratefully as he backed his white Forest Service Dodge Durango off the log deck.

The Medical Examiner and his assistant arrived shortly after the Deputy left. In less than an hour, they left too, on their way back to Eugene taking the body of Bud Miller with them for autopsy.

ME told Mill, "Look, the cause of death is certainly clear. Widow-maker caught him. But I can't be sure until we get autopsy results."

He looked at Mill and shook his head, "I never can figure how something like this can happen to an old woods rat like this guy, Bud Miller. I mean, how long has he been cruising timber?"

Mill also shook her head, "It doesn't figure to me either, but I guess anybody can have an accident in the woods. Even when you've been out here 30 years like Bud."

The ME grimaced, "It's my experience that old-timers keep an eye on what's above them. Still, I guess anyone can get a little too confident."

They chatted a few minutes longer. It was hard to fathom Bud not being more careful, but they agreed accidents happened out here too often.

The ME made motions to leave.

He turned back and touched Mill on the shoulder. "Look, Officer Meacham, you probably know this already, but you told me you're new. Don't talk to anyone until the County Sheriff's office made the autopsy results known officially. I'll call you or Zumo know as soon as I have the results, but please let the Sheriff do his part before going public on your end. Okay?"

Mill nodded in agreement.

After getting her agreement, the ME had smiled appreciatively at Mill's fit beauty, shooed his assistant into their four-wheel-drive van, and drove away.

Mill is two months out of the Federal Law Enforcement Training Center or FLETC in Glynco, Georgia, on her first assignment in law enforcement with the Forest Service.

Confronted by Bud's death, a man she hardly knew except by his huge reputation, she feels every bit the rookie. She had always felt smooth confidence during her years as a field-going fisheries biologist, but that swagger is gone now that she totes a gun as a new law enforcement officer, or "LEO" as they are called.

Mill thinks briefly about Special Agent Armando "Manny" Suemez who had been such a help to her in Alaska and inspired her to become a LEO.

She muses, "Wonder what Manny would think of me sitting here on

4

my butt instead of chasing bad guys? He'd tell me 'a LEO's life is either routine or rodeo...just do your job and everything will turn out okay.'"

She drums her fingers impatiently. She would like to leave this place but she has to wait for her boss to clear her..."just do your job...."

She smiles at the memories of the bad guys Manny'd battled for her, some of them in law enforcement. A tough guy, Manny, and one who'd openly admired Mill's toughness...birds of a feather, he'd said.

Mill pulls her thoughts back to the present.

When confronted with Bud's death, only her natural toughness and LEO training had prevented her from having chattering teeth and stuttering speech like the Deputy Forest Supervisor's.

She smiles a tight smile at her reflection in the windshield.

Bud left behind two grown kids and a work-at-home wife, his loss painful to think about.

"Uncle Sam'll give her a good pension and a big cash pay-out for accidental death on the job," Mill thinks, "but the government doesn't issue new husbands, fathers, or grandfathers."

Chapter 3

Woods Rat

About an hour before his death, Clarence Miller had cautiously parked the Forest Service pickup on the old landing where logs from previous timber sales had been decked. Bud made sure to miss the large potholes and soft spots that dotted the site.

Because of budget cuts, the Siuslaw National Forest road crew had not plowed and re-graveled the site for several years. And, nearby timber sales had not come along to pay resurfacing costs.

Bud's work today might change that. He was there to lay out a timber sale.

The landing sat just off a rough logging road high up in one of the prettier Oregon Coastal Range watersheds, a few miles northeast of the town of Lakeside near Kentucky Falls. The landing Bud used as a parking area was one of the few flat spots this far up the river--a place where you could park and be well off the road.

Eroded by rains and snow runoff in some places, the landing's once durable rolled-gravel surface lay dotted with potholes. The sandy clay under-soil got pretty slick when soaked with rain. Bud had found it damned hard to get out of when it was also disturbed by spinning tires.

Snaking among the potholes, Bud parked the rig and got out.

He could smell the sea breeze. He imagined he could faintly hear the Pacific surf far away. He pictured the windy Oregon coast, surf pounding spray into the air, a light mist surrounding the rocky horns thrust up and out of the creaming water and sand.

A tall, grey man, slightly bent by his years of public service, Bud loved to beach comb after a big storm had tumbled the trash and treasure of the Pacific onto jetty and sand.

Walking to the rear of the truck, he grabbed his timber-cruiser vest, filled with tools for tree measurement and marking.

Because he was alone today, he pulled out his paint-spattered aluminum hardhat instead of the hokey yellow plastic one issued by the government. Just like his solid metal lunch bucket, his "tin pot" had been with him longer than his boss, the Mapleton District Ranger, had been out of diapers.

No one was going to tell Bud Miller what to wear in the backcountry, particularly when he was a long way from his boss and working alone.

He laced up his caulks, boots with spikes in the soles to hold him steady on slippery surfaces.

He settled his pack and gear.

Finally, he picked up his walking stick and a spray can of marking paint and headed over to a nearby timber stand.

Before him, a beautiful mixture of cedars and Douglas fir filled the stand. He could see that many of the sale trees would go to forty inches in diameter or larger. With high timber prices, this meant plenty of money for the U.S. Treasury when the trees sold at auction in a couple of months.

Earlier in the month, Bud had decided to work this small sale alone. Big sales took a marking crew, but these small ones he could handle by himself. He knew he could squeeze more timber volume out of a stand than his less-experienced employees and that meant more and better trees going to local mills.

Besides, he enjoyed the time away from the sharp-tongued girl Ranger, the office, the computer, and the paperwork.

A pre-sale crew had already marked the sale boundaries. Bud stepped inside their line of tree tags and orange flagging and entered the area where trees could be cut. He began to measure trees and spray paint to show the loggers which ones to cut and which to leave standing.

As he pulled the trigger on the paint gun, Bud knew this sale would be the last in this watershed for decades. Through a bunch of dunderheaded agency decisions and losing court cases, areas had been set aside to protect marbled murrelet nest sites.

The murrelet was a small sea bird that nested in big old-growth trees along the Oregon coast. The set-aside lands also buffered the many salmon-bearing streams that flowed through the area.

Old-school Forest Service, Bud believed in industrial forestry, in getting the most timber yield from each acre. He hated the restrictions on timber harvest that had weighed down the agency over the past many years. Long gone were the heydays of clearcutting hundreds of acres in one big block.

His job had made a difference back in those days, helping people build houses and providing local communities with jobs.

Bud and the Forest Service were respected then.

Now Bud was marking a "partial harvest" timber sale, an idea laughed at by private land forest managers in the Siuslaw area. The Forest Service sale planners required him to leave about half the trees on the site after it was logged, and many of them big, commercially valuable trees.

He knew that the "leave" trees would create more habitats for the murrelets and other plants and animals. But he chafed at the idea of leaving half when taking all the saleable trees was much more economical and provided that many more jobs in town.

Didn't people count for more than a few ferns, birds, and critters?

The biologists over on the Willamette National Forest even talked about protecting a jumping slug!

That's what the world needed more of, jumping slugs!

Good God what a crazy idea!

Although not well-educated in the college sense, Bud was intelligent, well-read, and well-organized in everything he did. People knew him as a hard worker on and off the Forest Service payroll.

So, while he complied with the new order of things on the job, off the job Bud served as an outspoken advocate for timber cutting and timber jobs.

And people listened to him. Over the past ten years, Bud and a few others from around Lane County had organized the Oregon Coast Timber Coalition. The Coalition attracted many followers from among loggers, timber mills, and supply businesses.

And, once the Coalition really got going a few years back, plenty of money flowed in from the timber industry and other developers to propel their message out to the public and to lawmakers. They'd even gotten support from conservative professors at Oregon State University and other schools. The combination of business and scientific support meant a lot to the credibility of the Coalition and its impact on politicians.

At first, Bud regretted having the "suits" and eggheads show up. But you couldn't argue with the success they'd brought with them. The Coalition had gone from being a little squirt outfit with big ideas to a force to be reckoned with.

With the added resources, they had become a major a major national voice. The big DC lobbyists and the Republican Congress were clearly listening.

And, against all logic and common sense, the woods-savvy Bud had somehow become the voice and face for the movement. He spoke and others listened.

No amount of shushing or threats by Bud's Forest Service superiors or pleas for cooperation by environmental moderates was having any effect on Bud's talk or the Coalition juggernaut. A significant rollback in environmental protection laws might be coming and soon. Congress might finally mandate that the highest dollar returns should guide all decisions on the national forests and other public lands.

Bud found the prospect very exciting and long overdue. He smiled at the thought as he continued to measure and mark trees for harvest.

It also didn't hurt Bud's feelings that the Coalition went from beer and hamburgers at monthly board meetings in Eugene to fat cigars and single malt scotch at Washington, DC, receptions.

Now, that was fun. He'd never had a hundred dollar cigar and a hundred-dollar shot of scotch before, let alone both at the same time and free refills whenever he asked for them.

He smacked his lips and smiled at the memories.

Bud marked another large Doug fir with blue paint and moved forward towards a small clearing, thinking about taking a break and sampling the coffee in his Thermos.

And then he noticed something odd.

It turned out to be a big, gold Krugerand, hanging almost in front of his face....

———————————————//———————————————

At the moment Bud's moving the coin into his pocket, a massive, loose branch, called a "widow-maker" by woods workers, drops from the wind-battered, broken-branched, "snaggy" tree above. It lands directly on Bud's head and right shoulder.

The widow-maker slams him down and hides his upper body. Small branches and debris knocked free by the widow-maker shower down and hide the rest.

When the debris settles, only his feet can be seen in the tangle, tightly laced into his caulks. Knocked loose, Bud's prized tin-pot hard hat lands 30 feet away in the clearing, the aluminum deeply dented, glowing dully in the momentary sun.

Fine pieces of needles, bark, and duff swirl damply in the air. The lightest dusty pieces blow away on the gentle breeze.

A later autopsy in Eugene will show Bud died instantly of a compressed skull fracture. The blow also crushed three of his neck vertebrae and the bones of his right shoulder.

Bud Miller never knew what hit him.

As the damp dust settles around Bud's prone body, a bulky figure rises up from behind a nearby tree--a tall, narrow, shaggy pile of what appeared to be leaves, moss, and lichens. The figure slips out of from behind the tree moves with a loose-limbed, flowing, Big-Foot-caught-on-video quality. Large, wide feet like snow shoes propel it along, with just a hint of legs under the loose shaggy surface.

The figure is a person dressed in a ghillie suit, a shaggy camouflage outfit worn by military snipers and bow hunters. This ghillie closely matches the surrounding green, grey, and brown forest colors as well as many of the local plant shapes and textures. Any person wearing it is essentially invisible when they crouch down by a tree or stretch out flat on the forest floor.

Rigged like snow shoes to the wearer's feet, big smooth-bottomed slippers leave little disturbance and no clear foot prints on the mossy ground and vague, muddy game trails that cross the area.

Ekos moves to the base of the snaggy tree where Bud lies and, reaching behind the tree, loosens the nearly invisible wires that had held the widow-maker's radio-controlled release mechanism high up in the snag.

After a few well-practiced tugs, the apparatus falls to the ground, a small tangle of wires, pulleys, padded steel jaws, and metal angles. The killer quickly smooths and sorts the tangle into a coil and shoves it into a camouflaged backpack along with its radio trigger.

Ekos peers into the tangle for a moment to see if the gold coin can be salvaged from under the debris, but decides that too much would have to be moved to reach the coin in Bud's pocket.

Ekos' colleagues had counterfeited the "Krugerand" out of gilded pot metal, so it represents no real loss. Still, Ekos hates to leave any evidence at the site. Doctrine says that a kill site should be clean and clear when an assassin departs.

Undecided, Ekos hesitates for a long moment, then shrugs, turns, and heads out of the timber stand and directly away from Bud's parked rig. Slippers pad silently along the little muddy deer trail.

Ekos walks a mile in the ghillie suit and slippers before removing them. Then, in boots, hikes ten miles more to a stolen, battered '77 Ford pickup parked in a brushy area in the next watershed. Along the way, Ekos never breaks cover. Eventually, one of Ekos' colleagues would drop the thoroughly sanitized vehicle at a busy mall in Portland with the keys in the ignition.

Ekos had designed the dead-fall trap personally. It worked flawlessly.

The intel from Ekos' colleagues was exact as to the day and hour Bud would mark the timber sale; and correct that he would be working alone.

The dead-fall's impact site, with its snaggy tree and large previously fallen branch, was a happy find.

The modified hunter's tree stand that served as the drop platform was easy to strap into the tree and camouflage from view. Getting the heavy widow-maker up and into position was a strain even for many pulleys and Ekos' strong, tough body.

And getting Bud to stand in the five-feet-square impact zone proved to be the most challenging. But that, too, had worked by baiting the zone with the Krugerand.

Another Strike for Ekos!

One dangerous agency slug down and dead!

And only one small clue left behind.

No matter.

Ekos grins in triumph.

Chapter 4

Mill Searches

Mill stares out of the Expedition's windshield at the fluttering flagging that borders the accident site. Her boredom is becoming infinite.

Feeling suddenly mortal, she shifts her government-issued body armor around to make it more comfortable. Called a "ballistic vest," the armor feels as thick as her two-inch camping mattress and feels about as stiff.

The vest would stop the rounds from the smaller handgun calibers but anything larger, like the high-powered hunting rifles common in Oregon's backwoods, would pass through. Mill is not sure that the trade-off between the loss of mobility imposed by the vest and the small improvement in protection is worth it.

For cops in the city where handguns were often used, yes, but out here? Still, the Forest Service requires the vest and she wears it religiously.

She hopes that it will at least slow a 30.06 round before it reaches her skin.

Mill's slender, muscular build and disproportionately large breasts make the armor's fit loose around the shoulders and mid-section and tight across the chest. Dressed in her green uniform shirt over the vest, she muses that she looks like a green pumpkin above the waist.

That's it, a green pumpkin stuck on a fence post.

What a mess! She's a regular Forest Service feminist fashion plate. She smiles a little at the thought—one she's had before.

She can hardly wait to save up the thousand bucks or so to get a thinner, better ballistic vest--one more tailored to her shape and designed for freer movement. The one she prefers had lumpy ceramic plates in it to protect vital organs.

"I'll still look like Hell," she muses out loud, "but a better kind of Hell--still a freak of nature but less of a pumpkin...damned uniform."

In her several years as a field-going fish biologist in Alaska she never wore the uniform. But now as a LEO, she finds herself stuck in one because it's mandatory. And the other "accessories" that come with the LEO job are the lumpy, ugly tools of her newer trade.

With a bigger smile, she thinks, "Hard to make the case that a Glock, Taser, pepper spray, flashlight, and handcuffs add anything to the uniform or my sex appeal."

Of course, with everything else off and just the cop belt on, she might attract a certain amount of favorable attention.

That idea makes her grin. "Nothing like dissing the ol' uni-form and thinking about sex to cheer a girl up," she dimples.

Suddenly feeling a little guilty about smiling at a death site, she pulls her mind back to the grim scene in front of her.

The instructors at FLETC had drilled into her, as she summarized it, the need for "self-control, situation-control, and evidence-control." With this in mind, she tries to bring to mind all her evidence training.

She closes her eyes to concentrate and then opens them. She's now refocused on the site and the deadly event that had happened there.

Through the lens of a lifetime as a Forest Service brat running the woods and later as a field-savvy "fish squeezer," Mill sees nothing that seems unusual or out of place. The impact site had been disturbed by the removal of the body but otherwise the surrounding soil and vegetation bear little sign of trampling or disturbance.

Outside of the impact area, ground-covering mosses are slightly flattened here and there but essentially unbroken. The small, more fragile forest understory plants—ferns, salal, huckleberry, and a little Devil's club-- show a few broken, hanging twigs and stripped leaves.

But that's all.

Mill thinks, "About what you'd expect from deer or elk coming through and grazing a bit, maybe resting a while before moving on."

Probably few elk came through here regularly, though, because they had a reputation as "six hundred pound vacuum cleaners" when it came to eating up forest vegetation. With their big feet and eating habits, she'd expect to see a lot of hoof prints and grazing signs if they'd been here long.

Besides, elk preferred the plants and habitats found around more open sites like nearby clear cuts rather than the denser growth of this older forest.

A lightly trod game trail winds away from the impact area, opposite from where she sits in the parked LE vehicle on the log deck, about 30 feet from Bud's rig. Maybe she should look around some more.

Mill steps down from the big white and green Expedition, leaving it running.

The Expedition had so much electronics aboard--LEO essentials that had to be left turned on during duty hours. Under that load, even the double set of deep-cycle batteries could be run down to nothing if the engine was turned off.

She had discovered this fact when she shut the rig off while assisting with a search-and-rescue a week ago.

She had also found out how embarrassing it was for a rookie girl LEO to ask her fellow officers for a jump start. Several of the boys just "trying to help" offered to "give her a jump," she remembered with a slightly sour but appreciative smile.

In response to their leering offers, she said, "So boyish, so obvious... so unprofessional. So, no chance...too close to home...not my cup of tea... so sorry...get lost, wieners!"

Today, as she walks forward towards the tape, she savors her verbal triumph again. She dusts her hands together as if to say, "So much for them."

She circles the crime scene area. The yellow and black boundary tape blends oddly with the orange flagging along the boundary of the timber sale. She finds the scene disturbingly colorful against the dark green, brown, and grey forest background, a bit like a circus tent pitched in a graveyard.

Mill moves slowly down the trail about 100 yards. She uses the bright beam of her LED flashlight to cast back the rainy gloom and illuminate anything odd or out of place.

The trail shows a few vague deer tracks but little else. She knows that rain on the sandy soils quickly obliterates any animal track unless the tracks were very fresh--and no fresh sign of animals today.

Then just as she is about to turn back she notices a tangled, greenish piece of cloth hanging by a thread from a broken-off twig. It appears to be cotton, perhaps torn from a handkerchief.

She looks around her carefully. She sees some scuffed needles and leaves ahead on the trail but nothing that indicates anyone had walked this trail recently. The frayed scrap could have been here for months, she thinks, the loss hardly noticed by someone hiking through.

Still, as she examines the scrap, she feels a slight chill move up her neck. "Just a wet breeze from the shore," she reassures herself. Still, her intuition tells her that the scrap is out of place, odd.

It had been hanging precariously from the twig in such a way that a strong breeze would have easily carried it to the ground. So perhaps it caught here more recently than she first thought, maybe even today. Still, she's seen no other sign of human presence or passing.

Mill shrugs. She re-searches the area more slowly, flashlight probing under the brush and higher into the trees. No other sign of anyone's being here comes to light, just the scrap of cloth.

Without thinking more about it, she puts the scrap into an evidence bag, dates and initials it, and then puts it into her dark-green rain shell's pocket.

As the bag disappears into her pocket, she hears the sound of a high-revving motor, a truck in low gear. Her hand-held radio blares with her supervisor's voice asking for her "20."

Mill walks back to her rig. As she goes, she gives directions to Patrol Captain Bill Zumo and guides him from the logging road to the accident site.

After parking, Bill steps down from his rather fantastic looking pickup.

A few months ago, Zumo had set up his rig with a rack for carrying a four-wheeler All Terrain Vehicle, or ATV, for work on the Oregon Dunes National Recreation Area. Now the ATV juts high over the cab like a metallic ant with four headlights for eyes.

Most of the Siuslaw's crime and craziness happened on the Dunes. The ATV made it so Bill could get his job done quicker...serve the public faster and better. It didn't hurt that he loved to ride the fast four-wheeler over sand and trail either.

As he walks towards her, Bill calls, "Hey, Mill," loud enough to be heard above the sounds of their fast-idling engines.

She replies "Hey."

She knew he was mildly interested in her, a little intrigued with a fifth-generation Forest Service employee, daughter of a Regional Forester or something-or-other big-guy pooh-bah.

She thinks he is a little too government-cop geeky, too ready to emphasize filling out forms and databases, and then play "can you top this" about incidents in his past.

"A typical guy," she had thought after they first met, "So ready to talk about himself, so slow to listen."

Still, he is a boss who knows the ropes. He seems always willing to share what he knows.

On balance, a good guy.

He, in turn, finds her bright and curious, well-trained at FLETC and comfortable in the woods and on the water.

He thinks she missed being beautiful only by a slight irregularity of her features and a face that almost always carries a slight frown even in repose. When her grin occasionally breaks out through that frown, it's like Oregon Coast sunlight, rarely seen but instantly welcome.

Her oval face holds three slight dimples, one on her chin and one in each cheek. And, when she laughs, the dimples deepen, her eyes nearly close, and laugh lines make two nested parentheses around her mouth. Her laugh's clear tones peal up like a bell ringer playing four joyful notes.

Today, her dark hair is short but fashionably cut, the style most female LEOs wear--women who have to deal with hats and helmets, exercise programs, and hair-grabbing bad folks. And even the ballistic vest and awkward uniform she wore could not conceal her ample-busted, trim, athletic figure.

He knows she has a female roommate but she doesn't come across as a lesbian, a sexual orientation common enough among women in law enforcement and corrections.

Thinking of how attractive she is, Zumo realizes that he's surprised she hasn't yet entered his sexual fantasies. He's resigned himself to the idea that someday she would.

But though he might daydream a little about her, Bill knows he would never act on whatever fantasies he built. The job and their professional relationship are way too important for that kind of energy to intrude.

He studies the accident site while he thinks a little more about Mill and her development as a LEO. For now, he wants to see if she has a cop's smarts and guts.

He didn't know whether she could see past people's cons, keep a cool head with angry people in her face, or back him up in a tough spot—with fists, baton, or bullets if necessary.

She definitely had potential. After watching Mill's woods-wise moves on search and rescue incidents, being outshot by her on the combat pistol range, and getting pounded by her black-belt martial artistry in the gym, things look good in the "Mill's got Bill's back" department. Still, Bill has no way to tell for real until he sees her in action--when fists or bullets started to fly their way--a tough and dangerous time to test Mill's true mettle.

Bill knows that the wait can't be avoided, and that the test of Mill's nerve would eventually come. Zumo lives a cop's life—days and weeks of routine unpredictably punctuated by minutes of adrenaline-soaked danger. In a cop's life, everyone gets tested—cop, family, friends, and, for sure, the cop's LE partner.

Refocusing to the here and now, Bill asks, "So what'd the ME find at the site?"

Mill replies, "Nothing that would show that Bud's death is anything more than an accident."

A small lump comes into her throat as she once again touches the loss Bud's family and friends had sustained.

She quickly swallows the lump down, a little irked with herself for being soft. She hopes Bill can't guess her feelings.

Bill responds, "I really need the specifics, Mill."

His slightly annoyed tone makes her flinch a little inside. This is not the first time he has shown a little anger with Mill's tendency to summarize rather than recite the facts in detail.

He is exacting in every aspect of his work, from fueling an ATV to bagging and inventorying evidence. He wants to hear it all, in order and delivered precisely.

He waits for that now.

Mill smiles a flat smile of understanding.

She walks over to the Expedition's driver's door, opens it, and takes out the list of items she and the ME's assistant had compiled. Walking to the back of the vehicle, she opens the lift gate and pulls out several evidence bags.

She and Bill go down the list. They open the unsealed bags, and check each item. Then, in turn, they seal each bag and initial it. Every item is consistent with Bud's presumed activity on the site until they come to the gold coin and chain. It's mixed in the bag with his wedding ring, pocket knife, keys, and change.

Pulling the coin out by its chain, Bill asks, "What was he doing with this, do you think?"

Mill replies, "Beat's me. It's bright and not beat up as it would be if it had been in his pocket or out in the weather long. It's mounted in a ring with the chain attached. I can't see a guy like Bud wearing it around his neck. Could it be a gift, a pendant for his wife? Or, lucky gold piece maybe? If so, the luck's run out of it today."

Bill thinks for a moment, "You picked a couple of good possibilities, Mill, a gift or a good luck piece. He may also have been doing some buying and selling on the side. A lot of Forest Service folks here have some sort of small business to make extra money."

He looks closer at the coin, "I can't imagine he just found it on the way here, but I suppose that's a possibility, too."

He looks at her, "To my way of thinking, the gold piece's out of place with his other belongings. So, bag it separately. It'll be in evidence for a while, at least through Bud's inquest."

He looks at her more closely to see if she is following. She is.

She slips the coin and chain into a new bag, seals it, and initials it. She finishes the notations on the evidence log, dates it, and passes it to Bill for his sign off.

He continues, "When you get a chance, take it over to Bud's wife and ask her if he had a reason to give her a gift, or if he carried a lucky gold piece. Also check with his timber-sale crew. Work the small business angle with them, too."

She nods and makes a note on her patrol log.

Bill turns back towards his pickup.

Over his shoulder, he adds, "Radio the Forest and tell them its okay to send a couple of guys out to get Bud's rig and bring it in. I'm headed down to an accident at the third beach parking lot in Winchester Bay. Two idiots topped Biscuit Dune at the same time, going like Hell…one East and one West…so, one of them is critical and the other one's dead. How's that for luck? Douglas County deputies are down there handling it, and I need to check in with them. See you back at the shop. Call me on the Tac channel if you need me."

With a tight smile and a wave, he backs out and is gone.

She knows she wouldn't need to call him on the secure "tactical" radio channel, but he always said it when they parted. And she knows he really meant she could call him, too.

Still, she wants to be independent, as much as possible stretching and loosening the baby-LEO leash that Bill had her on. So, she'll try to call him as little as possible.

Mill knows she has to accompany the forest safety officer and the Office of Safety and Health Administration accident investigator back to the site the next day. So, before leaving, she checks to make sure the crime scene tape is secure and unlikely to blow down if a squall comes in from the sea.

Then she jumps back in the warmth of the idling Expedition, and heads for home, lurching and wallowing down the rough logging road.

Chapter 5

Home

Mill reaches U.S. 101 in about 30 minutes. She turns the Expedition north towards the town of Florence.

She'd not thought much further about the events of the day as she battled ruts and washboard down the mountain. But, now that she's on pavement, she gives full attention to some of the thoughts and questions that had been floating around in the back of her head.

"Why DID that 'ol moss-back Bud have that gold piece in his pocket?" she wonders out loud.

It seems so out of place and character for him.

And something seems funny about the coin itself. She would have thought that a big gold coin like a Krugerand would weigh more. Even though the coin is heavy, it doesn't seem heavy enough for solid gold.

But then what does she know about gold?

The heaviest gold thing she'd ever held was a pair of 14kt earrings. But, the question lingers in her head, a small mental itch that wants to be scratched.

She tunes her radio to Tac 4, picks up her radio mike, and keys it. "Zumo...Meacham ...Zumo...This is Meacham," she radios Bill using the Forest Service call pattern. After two more calls, when Bill doesn't answer, she stops trying and says flatly into the mike, "No contact. Meacham clear."

She had been going to ask Bill if she should have the coin checked by a coin dealer. But, she could just go ahead and do it, too, discussing the results with him later.

Checking the coin would be a minor item, just routine evidence procedure anyway. He has often told her to use her initiative, so she would.

The evening is late now as she approaches Florence. Her house is on the south side and secure parking for Forest Service vehicles is well to the north. Mill decides to park at her house for the night.

Although she was authorized to park at home anytime she needed to, she doesn't want neighbors or people driving by to get the impression that she abused her privileged use of a government vehicle. So, she rarely parks it at home. But it works for tonight.

She would stop by the Mapleton District office the next day to fuel up, drop off the evidence in her safe, and get her report started.

And, sometime during the morning the OSHA rep would show up. The forest safety officer would want to get out to the site of Bud's death.

She decides she will brief them at the District office first, complete with a slide show from her new digital camera. That way, she will get a little practice with downloading photos from the camera and using the projector. And the guys will get a good idea of what's out at the site before venturing into the rain and cold.

She parks in the driveway of her house, a nice little place with a neat appearance. The house was recently re-roofed and got painted within the last two years. The landscaping around the foundation is attractive and well-tended. Mill has a few calluses to prove it.

A split-level with a split-foyer entry, the house has about as much upstairs space as down. Two big bedrooms upstairs give her plenty of quiet space. The basement holds two smaller bedrooms, one of which she uses as a home office and another as a weight and work-out room.

The previous owner had built the two-car garage to be extra tall and deep to accommodate a mid-sized RV. He added extra lighting in the bays to help him park his boxy RV. He put even more lights in the shop area to light up his hobbies and repairs. With all that space and light, the garage is a great place to spread out bigger craft projects and to hang tents and other camping equipment after a weekend in the wet.

Lights glow in the windows and next to the front door of Mill's house, welcoming her home to what was once her cozy safe haven...

Not so cozy anymore.

Chapter 6

Mill and Till Fall Down Hill

Popcorn, Tilly Cocoran's white puffball of a bichon frese, meets Mill at the door, barking happily. Popcorn's stub of a tail wildly wags her whole body.

Tilly had named the dog Popcorn. The moment Mill met the dog, she had mentally added (Fart) to her name.

Mill unhooks her belt and gear and lifts them onto the wall rack next to the door. She removes her Glock .40 caliber handgun and "safes" it by removing the cartridge from the chamber. She leaves the magazine in place, ready, if called upon, for lethal force.

She carries the Model 23 Glock, a compact version of the standard Model 22 and one built for people with smaller stature.

She picks up the tiny Popcorn (Fart) and cuddles her. Although she finds the dog adorable, Mill also knows she's also a spoiled pest, constantly seeking attention and trying to mooch tidbits. And guests got leg-humped far more often then you'd figure a girl dog would want to do.

Tilly walks in from the kitchen, slightly flushed from standing over the stove. The smell of frying onions and Italian spices comes into the room with her.

She tentatively approaches Mill for a kiss. "Welcome home, sweetheart."

Mill kisses her passionately, signaling that they would have sex that night. Tilly grimaces slightly, shows a hasty pout, "Are you sure?"

Mill replies firmly, "Yes. Definitely."

Tilly reluctantly bobs her head in submission, a flash of resentment in her eyes. She turns on her heel and retreats back into the kitchen. Mill walks slowly towards the living room.

Matilda and Millicent.

Tilly and Milly.

Till and Mill.

Mill had often thought that their names seemed to entwine like those you find in a nursery rhyme, "Till and Mill went up the hill" or "Tilly and Milly were ever so silly."

Their life together had begun with passion and intimacy. But now, after more than a year together, the two are more than roommates but less than a couple. They maintain frequently spend the night together in Mill's big queen-sized bed, but maintain separate bedrooms.

Something, once whole, has broken.

Even back in their first days together in Alaska, Tilly wanted Mill to be her's exclusively and said so: friends in public, lovers at home.

At the time, Mill was ending her days as Wild Girl Hunting, desperate to stop bingeing on sex and drugs and to find a lighter, more peaceful life with someone. So Mill agreed. Commitment seemed to fit them together so naturally. And even during the long months of Mill's LEO training at FLETC that followed her time in Alaska, the two stayed close, exchanging cards, calls, and monthly visits.

Then, after Mill's return from Georgia, something profoundly jarring had occurred between them.

Mill gradually withdrew from Tilly.

Although Mill's hurt happened months before, it's still so fresh... glass shards in tender feet....

———————————————//———————————————

Mill's living room had served as the snug refuge where she and Tilly gathered after work. Sometimes they read the mail and newspaper together or ate dinner there; sometimes they made cozy love there, too.

A fireplace framed by wood bookshelves serves as the room's centerpiece. Wood floors match the warm tones of the bookshelves, covered by highly patterned area rugs in natural greens, rose, and buff.

The walls are painted eggshell on three sides. On the wall opposite the fireplace, a darker, cherry-tree-bark color frames the entry to the dining room.

Mill and Tilly decorated the walls with mahogany-framed prints from artists of the 19th century Hudson School. The prints bring an old-timey, bucolic, and slightly mystical character to the room.   The lines and coloring are reminiscent of Audubon's work but, instead of birds and wildlife, the artists gracefully capture landscapes, horses and riders, and long-ago agrarian lifeways in the Hudson River Valley.

The extra deep and long light-brown leather couch stretches along one wall, matched by two reclining easy chairs that face the fireplace. Colorful and patterned pillows match hues and lines from the area rugs. They lie scattered across the couch and the chairs. A few are piled on the floor near furniture legs. Casual wooden end tables and tallish warm-grey ceramic lamps complete the space.

One Friday evening in early April Mill tossed the night's newspaper to the floor. She reached for Tilly and began kissing her.

Tilly first resisted, saying she wanted to shower and make dinner before sex. Wine-reckless, passion pulsing between her legs, Mill overcame Tilly's initial resistance with forceful kisses, caresses, and murmured endearments.

They stood up from the couch, kissing. Mill gently, quickly undressed Tilly, preparing her with light and practiced touch from hands and lips.

Mill gently pushed the naked Tilly down to the couch, pressing her shoulders back. Kneeling on the floor, Mill leaned her head towards Tilly's waist, attempting to press her thighs apart with her hands on Tilly's knees.

Now propped against two pillows and almost prone on the couch, at first Tilly stiffly kept her legs together. Mill wondered if Tilly resented Mill's taking the lead in making love and was not going to cooperate.

But after Mill pressed harder with her hands, Tilly relented, opening her legs fully. With a small murmur, she lifted her hips to Mill's lowering mouth.

Mill pressed her mouth into Tilly. She began sucking and tonguing Tilly gently, giving her increasing pleasure.

And then Mill realized she tasted something bizarre...impossible.

Her mind first denied it...refused it.

Then the shock of recognition hit fully.

"I taste semen!!" her mind screamed, "Semen...what...how?"

For a moment, although she did not pull her head away, Mill stopped pleasuring Tilly.

Her heart thudded.

Her mind veered wildly, questing for a rational perch, an explanation where it could stand.

Nothing.

After the moment's hesitation, Mill continued her caresses. She had to think this through. Could she be wrong?

Several minutes later Mill brought Tilly to a strong, lengthy orgasm.

Mill moving like a zombie as they reversed positions.

Mill began to accept the same attention from Tilly. But Mill's head was whirling. She felt nothing...numb. She tried to pull her thoughts and feelings together.

There was no doubt about it. Mill knows that taste. It wasn't something else.

Tilly had been freshly fucked by some guy that day, perhaps just before coming home to Mill's arms!

What the Hell was this?

Tilly was the one who had wanted an exclusive relationship.

Yet, here she had opened herself to a man with no protection! She was risking disease or pregnancy.

Even more exquisitely painful to Mill, she had placed her relationship with Mill in grave jeopardy.

Why would she behave so recklessly, so irresponsibly, so wickedly?

Mill's feelings flew from panic, to fear, to rage, to self-recrimination.

Was Tilly a liar and cheat by nature?

Had she cheated before?

Was it something she had always done and never been caught?

Had Mill done something to trigger this infidelity? Was she so bad as a friend, a roommate...or worse, as a lover?

What would happen if Mill confronted her? What would happen if she did not?

Was their relationship over?

Was Tilly getting ready to leave her...abandon what they had together?

Mill had no answers to the onslaught of questions and doubts that overwhelmed and seared her, that pulled her out of the moment and into a painful, abstract world.

She writhed a little at her inner turmoil.

From Mill's movement, Tilly got the entirely wrong idea that Mill was responding favorably to her intimate caresses. So she increased the intensity of her loving touch.

She pulled more strongly on Mill's hips. She pressed her face and tongue deeper into Mill.

Though misguided, Tilly's extra effort was beneficial.

In her numb turmoil Mill had been slow to respond to Tilly's lips and tongue. But Mill now felt her passion rise. She gradually reached and melted into her orgasm, momentarily thrusting anger and hollow doubt aside in the rush of a thigh-burning release.

Tilly withdrew her mouth. Knowing Mill's preferences, she blew gently on Mill's throbbing parts. She patted Mill's inner thighs as her orgasm peaked and faded.

Afterwards, the two lay curled together. Mill's breasts touched

Tilly's back, skin-tight, warm-to-warm. She gently touched places on Tilly's body--intimate places that Tilly said were exclusively Mill's--places that someone else had invaded today.

Facing the back of Tilly's head, Mill felt tears running down her face.

She made no sound. She would not allow the sob she felt in her chest to surface.

Her heart beat tight--broken and sad.

Mill's heart already knew this place of doubt and pain.

Little Milly was seven. Her mother had been gone for days with no word about her whereabouts or possible return.

Mill knew that her mother must have left her only daughter for something or someone who was worth much more. Back then, little Milly almost disappeared into herself at the thought.

And now, who could Tilly have found who would be worth much more than Mill?

_____//_____

That night, Mill sat alone on her bed grimly facing the devastation Tilly had brought into their lives.

Mill had allowed Tilly to be closer to her than anyone had ever been before. But, as Mill reflected, she admitted to herself something that she had been pushing aside for some time.

Their relationship had been changing and not for the better. Something shared and purposeful had been slipping away. What had begun as joyous sharing had become a life of tensions and tedious chores.

In the beginning of their love making in Alaska, Tilly had been tender and tireless. But over time, their passionate couplings had fallen off to a kind of genial companionship.

Before, they had dropped everything to satisfy the other sexually. Now, there was no intimacy between them unless Tilly initiated it. She blocked Mill's advances with a blend of rejection, allusions to aches and pains, and a packed personal social calendar that left her without time or energy for love making.

When Mill pressed for more, Tilly added Mill's long, and sometimes irregular, hours at work to her list of reasons why they had lost love's labors and joys.

Once their love had been dessert served on the dinner table, now they scarcely ever made love even in Mill's warm, feather-topped bed.

If Tilly had cheated with another woman, Mill's reaction might have been different. Mill had known casual girl sex personally.

She knew that kind of love could be quick--first strong and then infatuation gone.

As a college sophomore, Mill had been seduced by a charming, strong-minded dorm assistant. A tall athlete with a quick smile and bright brown hair and eyes, Sally had loved Mill for eight months.

Sometimes they found each other between classes for a moaning tryst in the shrubbery. Once they'd done it standing up behind an open classroom door, quick fingers bringing pleasure. When they could, they made love all night sprawled across sturdy dorm furniture or close together in a narrow dorm bed.

They kept their infatuation a secret from the world.

When they were together overnight, the visiting lover, usually Mill, left for her own room before sunrise. And as further cover, both women had continued dating boys, and occasionally sleeping with them.

Mill had found that some of the boys just wanted to screw her and disappear. Others looked for more intimacy with her.

But Mill was too distracted by Sally to experience anything other than the fun and pleasure the boys brought her. On dates, and in bed, she had found it hard even remembering the boys' names.

Mill's thoughts and emotions struggled to keep up with her experiences. In Sally's embrace, she could picture the boys' strong hands and erect members. When Mill was next in bed with a boy, she would think of her next tryst with Sally, craving her touch.

So, as she moved from lover to lover, pleasure to pleasure, bed to bed, Mill's mind whirled around on an emotional merry-go-round. It was all so exhilarating but dizzying.

A little exhausting, too.

Then after Sally and Mill left for summer break, Sally stopped calling. Her infatuation had run its course. She'd grown impatiently tired of Mill.

Mill made a few tentative attempts to remain in touch but stopped, confused. She was first hurt, and then a little relieved, when her calls and notes to Sally went unanswered.

As the "after Sally" summer unwound, Mill realized she had grown by the whole cycle of being desired, seduced, loved, and then dropped. More than simply adding spice to Mill's sexual stew, the sexual merry-go-round gave her greater sexual self-confidence. Mill realized that whole thing had been a huge challenge...one she met.

So, as her junior year approached, Mill was still confused about her sexuality and love relationships. But Mill had learned that a label of "lesbian" or "straight" did not apply to her very well.

Sally and the boys had given her Pandora's gift: everything sexually good and bad was out of the box and available to her. She could be with anyone, everyone...but maybe, probably...always with someone.

Being so free felt good. But her past behavior came at a cost.

Mill had been almost continually stressed by the pretense of acting straight with boys while having sex with another girl. So, she pledged to herself that she'd not conduct her love life burdened with secrets anymore.

She'd keep everything up front and simple. If she herself wasn't exactly straight sexually, she could at least keep her sexual relationships straight.

She also pledged to stop being so promiscuous. Her sophomore experience with its sexual jumble had been exciting and enlightening. But she'd decided being bounced *in* bed was good but bouncing *from bed to bed*...bad.

Mill would also make sure that, no matter how many or few lovers she might have at any one time, they would fit well with all the other things going on in her life.

And, she would know lots about them, including their names. She would at least admire them for something before inviting them into the warmth of her embrace or body.

As she let go of labels and social constraint, Mill also knew that she had lost something--the comfort of the clear, conventional social choices conveyed to her in her mostly sheltered Forest Service youth. But, she had really lost her secure sexual cocoon when she was fourteen.

However honest and forthcoming she would be with her future lovers, Mill would have to be publicly guarded and private with her personal life as long as she stayed in the cloistered and conservative Forest Service world.

By the end of that summer of reflection, Mill had learned that she could not sexually define herself. But she did know that, sexuality aside, she wanted to continue the process of finding her strength and integrity. Her confusing sexual urges and actions would just have to develop along with the rest.

Mill went back to school.

Chapter 7

Finding A Footing

A few weeks after Mill caught Tilly cheating, she reached some conclusions.

No, Tilly's infidelity was nothing like Sally's self-centered fickleness. Sally never really pretended that her relationship with Mill was anything more than lust mitigated by social niceties like dating boys or making casual conversation before jumping into bed.

Mill was painfully aware that she had slipped away from her junior-year commitment to clear and honest communications with lovers. She hadn't confronted Tilly about the fractures in their intimate life. And when Mill discovered Tilly's deceit, she remained silent.

So much for honest communication.

Mill searched Tilly's room and found Tilly's birth-control pills, hidden in her bureau drawer. The pink package looked new but it was hard to tell. But one thing for sure, if Tilly was taking the pills, she did so in the privacy of her room, not with her orange juice and vitamins at breakfast every morning.

But the simple presence of the pills told Mill more of the sad story. Tilly was making secret sexual choices, long-term ones, outside her relationship with Mill.

After she mourned her losses for a time, Mill found that there was a certain upside. Tilly's betrayal gave her a kind of freedom. Mill could change their relationship or move on.

Was this an out that Mill had been unconsciously seeking? Did she have to be so hurt before she could end things? Could that be what Tilly was signalling, too, blowing up their relationship in a crude sexual way to gain her own freedom? Mill had no experience with commitment or the end of it, so she simply didn't know.

Finally, frustrated, Mill realized that the whole business of trying to figure these relationship things out was getting too twisted for her to deal with. She would get nowhere guessing at secret motivations or convoluted emotions that might never be expressed or understood.

Mill also thought of something far more satisfying. For as long as their relationship lasted, Mill no longer had to compromise between lust and intimacy.

She could be more sexually forceful with Tilly. And, as long as she was getting what she wanted, Mill told herself that she no longer cared what guy Tilly was screwing.

Otherwise, things didn't have to change much for life to go on.

She mostly meant it, but she was wrong.

Things had to change...did change.

Now Mill insists Tilly shower before love-making. And when Tilly is ready, Mill bores in quietly, fiercely, secretly competing with her invisible male rival, daring him to do better, driving Tilly through multiple orgasms that leave her spent and limp.

On her part, Tilly finds that sex has suddenly become uncomfortably frequent and mechanical. Mill's eager tenderness has been replaced by some sort of orgasm scorecard. Love making between them is more probing and metallic than touchingly organic.

And, once out of the sweat-clingy embrace of the bed covers, Tilly can sense the uncompromising glow of anger within Mill. Mill's impatient eyes avoid Tilly's. Her curt remarks cut off talk. Cold pauses stretch into long, achy, silences.

After days of living in this cold shadow of Mill's contempt, Tilly asks Mill if something is driving them apart. Mill simply replies, "Yes."

But then in response to Tilly's tearful questions, she refuses to name the "something."

As Mill watches her betrayer cry and quietly beg, she thinks, "Tilly, can't you guess? Confess your secret. Ask forgiveness. Maybe there's a chance for us."

Mill wills her to speak the words, to end the deadlock. But Tilly does not catch Mill's thought. She does not confess her secret or ask forgiveness. And so, she goes unforgiven.

After a long, resentment-filled pause, Mill tersely describes what will be. About the shift in control over their sex lives. About the distance coming between them.

Mill tells Tilly it will have to do. Mill will give nothing else.

They both cry.

Seeking comfort from the familiar, the two make love tenderly.

But after, Tilly crawls out of Mill's bed and goes back to her room.

Mill feels her bed grow cold.

That night, Mill struggles through a dream that has haunted her for years. Sometimes the details are different, but the twisted sensations and emotions are always the same.

Mill finds herself somewhere in her house, or in a dark forest or, horribly, in a totally dark, musty crate. Maybe a casket.

She's bound tightly in soft but unyielding cords or vines.

She's cold, and for reasons that are not clear, deeply ashamed.

She has done something very, very wrong. And whatever the wrong she's done, it's all her fault. No one else's.

Mill struggles against the cords. They become tighter. And as they tighten, her shame deepens.

She writhes and whimpers, but no one comes to set her free, to help.

This night, with Tilly gone from her bed, Mill writhes, sweat-soaked, twisting. She wakes up screaming...a whimper.

Chapter 8

Green Milly in Dark Green Places

Milly Meacham is fourteen.

She is about five feet two inches tall and still growing. Nature is filling out her flat spots with curves.

She's a smart and pretty girl, quick to smile, determined and tentative all at the same time, never quite sure where she fits in her world.

She makes and keeps a few good friends easily. She gets along well with almost everyone else, adults and kids alike.

She has good grades in spite of running with a wilder bunch--kids who had been her friends and surrogate brothers and sisters for her years in Idaho.

Her father, W. A. Meacham, is District Ranger at Summit District on the Targhee National Forest, west of Grand Teton National Park.

Having raised Milly by himself for the last seven years, he's well aware that Milly is growing into a pretty young woman. And, worse, she's somehow still a tomboy, running all around town and in the woods with every wild kid from town and the Forest Service compound.

As Milly matured, W. A. has grown increasingly distant from his daughter. Some of the wild things she's doing make him very concerned. His women colleagues and lovers advise him that, "Milly has a good head on her shoulders. She'll grow out of it once she's a little older and discovers boys."

However true or likely, if these well-meaning words are intended to reassure him, they don't. Milly's burgeoning womanhood poses problems that he can't quite understand. Somehow she represents a bunch of vague threats and challenges to his manhood and to his carefully manicured career.

The whole Milly-growing-up business makes him very uneasy.

On Milly's part, W. A.'s complaints and concerns about her conduct are confusing. Until recently W. A. had told her to "get out of the house and have some fun" so he could spend time drinking with his friends, playing at Forest Service politics, and pleasuring his lovers.

Now, he is telling her to stop seeing the scruffy friends she has spent years having fun with. Milly wonders where his crappy craziness has come from. Has she done something wrong? Everything seems the same. It's a mystery to her why W. A. suddenly wants her to be girly-girl and hang around home.

After W. A. confronted her several times, a defiantly teenaged Milly had told him he was crazy and to leave her alone.

Whereupon he got mad, real mad. He had told her she was "a little bitch" and "not too big to spank."

Subtly erotic to W. A., the spanking threat blatantly menaced Milly's fragile adolescent dignity and something weird about his eyes gave her clear warning. So, after W. A. yelled this intention at her, Milly stayed well clear of his reach until he calmed down.

As their conflicts grew, a red-faced W. A. often told her in a loud voice, "You better stop hanging out with those punks or you're headed for trouble. Every one of them had been in trouble with the law for some mischief or other. You'll get pulled in to some craziness and wind up in jail. If you do, don't expect me to come down and bail you out. You deserve what you get."

Or he would say, "I can't have you ruining my reputation in this town and all around the Forest Service, so cut it out." They went around and around but nothing altered Milly's cautious defiance or W. A.'s angry threats.

Except that Milly has started hiding her adventures from the bullying W. A.. She tells him "I'm going to the library to study" or "I'm going over to Tracy's to watch TV." Cover lie told, she'd head for town or the woods and meet her rascally fun friends.

She knows he'll be even madder if he finds out she's deceiving him but, really, he has no right....

After all, it's not like her wild bunch are really wild. When they meet, they mostly just hang out, play music, and talk trash, silly stuff. When the mood seemed right, they play one of the many games they had played for years—games they made more elaborate and interesting as they grew older.

They had always played some version of "war." As little kids they chased each other around in screaming packs, tumbling over jungle gyms, and wrestling on top of downed trees to see who was "King of the Hill."

Now in their teens, they play a more complicated war game, called "POW tag." It's based on what they'd seen on TV about how prisoners of war were captured and treated in Viet Nam, Iraq, and places like that.

On this day, they decide to play POW tag in one of their favorite hangouts, a large, treed site near town. In this game, they split up into two teams.

Each of the teams has a designated camp. From the camps, the teams fan out in the woods and quietly hunt their "enemies." Hiding and ambushing one another, players tag one or more of their enemies who become "prisoners of war" and are led back to camp.

The teams have a rule that prisoners can't try to escape on their way to camp. The only exception is if the captors are ambushed and tagged. Then the captors become the prisoners and the former prisoners go free.

Once at camp, prisoners are hooded with a burlap sack and have a stout stick pushed between their elbows and back. Then they have their hands tied in front of them with the rope across their bellies. Their arms loop around the stick at the elbow—just like in the movies. The bonds are gentle but secure with loops around each wrist, the stick snug against the back.

For a while, they'd tried forcing prisoners to kneel or squat but those positions got too painful too soon and they'd let that idea go. Now each team lets their prisoners sit back to tree, resting more comfortably than not.

Sometimes the prisoners are guarded. But because everyone wants to hunt for enemies and there's lots of territory to cover, mostly the prisoners are left alone. After all, where will they go, tied up and blind, unable to break their fall if they trip?

Occasionally, a team would raid the enemy camp to free their friends. This is risky because they can easily be ambushed when going to such an obvious place.

But, done right, it could work. Milly has led several such raids with great success, using a diversion to pull the guards away and quick hands to bring freedom to her friends.

Once captors go back to the woods, prisoners might escape if they can free themselves. But freeing oneself is almost impossible alone so prisoners mostly help one another get free.

Milly had gotten away several times by working blindly with her captured teammates. She thought it delicious fun to work frantically, fumbling at knots and cords one-handed and giggling with urgency, listening with half an ear for returning enemies.

And, once free, Milly had scampered off triumphantly to the safety of the forest, discarded bonds left behind to mock her enemies.

The teams' "Generals" were the older, bigger boys. In turn, the most able kids, or the general's favorites, held other "boss" jobs.

Occasionally, a kid nobody liked would try to hang out with them or a regular player would offend a General. When these offenders are captured they're given the regular prisoner treatment, hooded and bound. Then, they're "pantsed" with their shoes and jeans forcefully removed.

The victims sit in their socks and underwear until the game ends.

They're teased and humiliated by their captors.

In the past, many of the pantsed boys knew Milly was watching. For some of them, the fact that a teasing girl was a part of their humiliation made their anguish deeper. When freed, many of these boys left crying or cursing.

Most of them never returned for more.

As Milly had started to fill out, a couple of the boys made comments about her curves or tried to grab her breasts. Milly slugged those boys solidly.

Wearing a few bruises, the boys became more cautious in what they said or did. If they teased her at all, they made sure to stay several steps away with their feet aimed along a good escape route.

Once several girls had run with the pack of a dozen or so boys. Now, only Milly is left.

So, to preserve her status as a team member, she covers up with bulky flannel shirts and loose jeans. She complains very little. But mostly she shows her teammates that she can hold up her end of the games.

Milly's in that ambivalent teenage-girl place where she can see that being a girl made her life easier in some ways but where she also doesn't want special treatment. She really didn't want to accept the changes. But she also did have to admit that they were inevitable.

Girl or not, Milly's teammates like having her around. Quicksilver at eluding others in a foot race, good at hiding, and able to skillfully dance out from concealment to tag her enemies, she's agile and crafty as a woods nymph. When she moves through the forest, it's as if the forest opens pathways just for her, while underbrush and tree roots seem to reach up and trip her clumsy pursuers and brambles claw at their clothes to slow them down.

She has a way of crossing nearby deep Cottonwood Creek with enemies hot on her trail. She runs along a single log, dances madly between branches and then, across and a few hundred feet on the other side, invisibly goes to ground.

In the past, several boys had tumbled into the creek trying to follow her. Now, no one tries to chase her down.

Not only was she too fast and agile on the log, but her hideout location is also so well concealed that, once across the creek, no one can find her. Only her friend and teammate Philip knows the location of her hideout, finding out only after she led him teetering across the log to its location.

Her den's up under the root wad of a large tree that wind and snow had tipped over. It lies high along a bank, the den hole dry and out of sight.

On this day, with enemies hot on her heels, she dances over the limber log above Cottonwood Creek, darts down a faint deer trail, and slips into her hideout. There she waits for a few minutes, listening for her pursuers.

Hearing nothing, she hugs herself and gloats a little...

But then, what's that? A muffled noise as something slides down the bank near her.

She freezes, barely daring to breathe. "Stupid boys couldn't have found me. Could it be a coyote...or worse, a bear?" she whispers, a little chill of fear on her neck.

She edges towards the back of the small hole.

Then, she hears footsteps. Voices whisper.

Damn it! Boys! Probably enemies!

She stays very quiet, willing the voices to move on, to miss her.

She hears a small scuffling noise, heavy breathing. A hand grabs her ankle. A loud boy voice yells, "Got you, Milly! You're our prisoner."

Damn! How could they have known where she was, or worse, that it was *her* snug hideaway? Of all the rotten luck.

They lead her away. All she can think about is how she will wipe the smug looks off their faces. That's it, she'll escape and rub their faces in that!

They make her wade across the creek at a shallow spot. Her jeans and boots get soaked.

What a pain, when crossing the log would have kept her dry. But, of course, fat, clumsy boys can't do that!

The day is a little cool, but not cold. Getting wet does not matter much to her. She begins to plan for a quick escape on the other side.

Once at the enemy camp, Milly sees that she's their first captive. Her captors drop her off and quickly run away, looking for more of Milly's team.

Bill Moon, the older of the two boys at the camp, puts a stout stick between her elbows and back, ties her hands firmly in front, and pulls a burlap hood over her head. Moon uses a string woven through the burlap to make the neck opening snug but not tight.

Knowing her ability to escape, Moon ties the bonds carefully. Although she was hoping Moon would leave the knots loose enough to let her work her way free, Milly appreciates the snug-but-not-tight cords. Sometimes captors tie too tight, leaving marks or making hands tingle and go numb.

As soon as the hood goes on, Milly's nose begins to tickle from the rough, dusty, smelly cloth with its frizzy threads. She sneezes once and then again, harder.

Not knowing where her captors are, she yells, "Hey, guys, get me another hood will you? This thing's nasty."

Someone move towards her from her right. One of the more bullying Generals, Moon says, "Prisoners have to be quiet. No talking, Milly. Shut up."

"Bill, damn it, this thing's nasty. Just get it off me and give me another one."

Milly begins to shake her head back and forth, trying to get the hood off.

Unexpectedly, Moon grabs her and snarls, "Okay, Milly, I told you to shut up. For a regular smart ass, you sure complain a lot."

Milly begins to protest again but Moon'll have none of it.

He snarls, "I'll teach you to disobey me."

He hooks his leg in front of her shins and pushes Milly forward. She falls to her knees hard, just able to keep herself from falling forward onto her face.

"Bastard," she yells, "I'll kick your ass, Bill Moon, as soon as I get loose."

"Yeah, sure you will," says Moon, shoving her again.

This time her whole body thumps the ground.

"Ooof," Milly gasps as her stomach lands on an exposed tree root and the wind goes out of her.

Moon puts his knee in the small of her back to hold her down.

He says to the other boy, "Jake, we're going to pants this little bitch. Help me get her boots off."

Jake replies, "Bill, I dunno. Milly's nice. She's a girl. Doesn't seem right."

Moon yells, "You get her boots off or I will smack you shit-wise right now."

Grumbling a little, Jake gives in to Moon's bullying. He throws his body across Milly's calves, unties her wet boots, and pushes them off.

With a practiced hand, Moon reaches under Milly and loosens her belt and the top button of her jeans. Feeling Moon's hand, Mill begins cursing a blue streak. She starts kicking her legs frantically up and down to try and stop Jake.

Jake tries to grab her pants' cuffs but misses her flailing ankles. Moon yells, "Try harder, you piece of shit!"

40

After several tries, Jake finally catches hold of first one and then the other. Pulling hard against the fabric wet-tight to her skin, Jake rips the jeans off her body.

"You sons a bitches," Milly gasps under Moon's weight, "I will just kill you both."

The friction of the pants coming off has forced Milly's underwear down a few inches, exposing the top half of her bottom. She feels Jake quickly pull her panties up.

Through her tears, she murmurs, "Thanks, Jake."

Maybe little Jake isn't a complete monster moron after all.

Tears of pain and frustration start from her eyes.

This is betrayal beyond her understanding. What had she done besides ask for another hood?

She has been these boys' friend since they were children and barely allowed to leave their yards. And now this, this monstrosity, this crushing humiliation, this outrage.

She is a girl! She is their friend! What are they thinking?!

Grief and embarrassment settle over her.

She sobs. Her tears wet her face and the burlap.

Bill moon looks down at her. She's been pantsed and lies passively crying, so Moon stops leaning his big ugly fatness on her.

"Stop being such a baby, Milly, you ain't hurt," says Moon, lifting her to her feet. "Sit over here and stop blubbering." With his hand guiding her, she walks slowly and blindly to a spot next to a tree and sits down.

As a prisoner, she would normally have sat cross-legged, back against the tree. But now wearing only her panties, she feels too vulnerable and exposed for that comfortable position. So she tucks her feet under her and leans a shoulder against the tree.

An uncomfortable thought suddenly strikes her. Milly can't remember which panties she had worn that morning. How weird that what panties she had on somehow matters to her.

She recalls that they might be the blue ones with the rainbow across her rear. Her face burns with the thought of how childish those panties seem now, a symbol of little-girl tastes so shamefully exposed to a couple of teen jerks.

Then Milly wonders what the boys think when they look at her without her jeans. Did they see a skinny girl or a woman? Much worse, were they attracted to her?

She shudders with that horrible thought.

She can't see them but she just knows they're watching her. Their eyes crawl over her, looking at places they shouldn't see. She loathes them for looking at her, staring at her. She sobs, frustrated, self-conscious, mourning her loss of privacy.

Then, another horrible possibility occurs to her. What if they tried to remove more of her clothes? What if mean Moon tried to pull off her panties?

Fear and rage shake her.

She would kick and kick, until he left her alone.

Maybe she could kick his face. She would break his nose. Or maybe she would bust his balls.

If Moon went for her flannel shirt, she'd wait until they loosened her hands. Then maybe she'd grab the stick that held her arms and beat him silly. That would serve him right, the drooling fool.

Milly starts to feel a little stronger, more prepared. She grows a little defiant.

She hopes they're getting a good look. No matter what they do or how nice they are in the future, they will never have a chance to look at her this way again. She's done with Jake and Moon after today.

Her mind gyrates around in this fashion for a time, from awful fascination to painful modesty to angry revenge and back around again. But little Jake and big Moon do not approach her. Instead, she hears them move off to her right. The sound of their footsteps quickly fades as they go on their way to stalk more enemies.

Gone and good riddance!

Milly begins to think about her next moves. She knows that the enemy team will make plenty of fun of her when they came back. They'll laugh at her and tease her, sitting here in her socks and panties.

She grins a tight smile, "I can handle those bastards, but this is the end. No more hanging out with these bozos. Never. Not even if they apologize on their bellies in an elk wallow."

She tests her bonds. Moon has done his job well. She can't free her hands by herself. But maybe the hood will come off or rip if she scrapes it against the tree. If it did and she could see, she could maybe wiggle back into her pants somehow, or at least push her feet into her boots, and run away to freedom...to town. There she could find some girl's helping hands to untie her.

She rubs her head against the tree, hooking the burlap on rough bark outcrops. But, although she pulls firmly, the sack does not come off or rip.

42

Moon tied the sack around her neck with a firm knot. The fabric too tough to tear in only the bark's grip.

Milly grimaces in the stuffy gloom. It's no go. She settles down to wait.

Her mind wanders. Thoughts of hope and doubt come randomly. What if one of her other school friends came by? After all, they're not that far from town. That would be bad and very embarrassing, but once released she would be quickly dressed and gone.

Or, maybe her team would raid this camp and set her free. Boy, would she be glad to see them. But that would be even more embarrassing, having them see her bare legged in her blue kid panties.

Time ebbs by. Frustrated and impatient, she waits for the game to be over and her embarrassment to be made complete.

Then Milly hears footfalls to the left, coming her way from the opposite direction the boys had gone to hunt more prisoners. Were Moon or the other boys coming back with more of her team?

She doesn't hear voices so she can't be sure.

But she soon realizes only one person approaches. The sound of heavy boots and brush scraping against cloth moves closer.

The boots scuff to a stop a few feet away. She hears a low whistle. She sees a shadow on the burlap hood. Someone id kneeling next to her.

Without warning, a hand roughly fondles her left breast through her flannel shirt. Startled, Milly flinches back and snarls, "Bill Moon, keep your fucking hands off me. If you touch me again, I'll kill you, you son of a bitch!"

She clumsily tries to free her legs from under her to kick Moon as hard as she can. But a strong hand grabs her left shoulder and presses her back against the tree. Milly senses a head near hers.

A voice quietly hisses, "Shhhh" in her ear.

She smells the distinct odor of snoose or chewing tobacco. She stiffens at the scent. At least as far as she knows, none of the boys dip or chew. So, this bastard is not one of the boys! Who can it be, she wonders?

Then, Milly hears a click. A sharp knife blade presses against her neck just below the burlap. She feels just enough pain to wonder if the blade has cut her neck. She tries to pull away, but her head just presses harder against the tree.

The man's voice says, "Shhhh" again.

Milly realizes he wants her to remain quiet or he promises to cut her or maybe kill her.

Milly whispers, "Okay, okay, just don't hurt me."

Fear races through her and her heart thuds painfully. Milly realizes that whoever holds the knife has become a lot less important than what he plans to do with it.

The man takes the knife away. She feels him unbutton her flannel shirt. Cool air flows down and across her stomach.

He grabs the front of her bra and pulls it out from her chest.

Knife cold touches her skin.

Milly's heart pumps wildly. Thinking he's going to stab her, she almost screams.

But, with a quick move, he cuts the front of her bra between the cups. Her breasts fall free.

After a moment, rough hands touch both breasts and fondle them for a time. His scratchy touch is painful. She gasps aloud when he pinches her nipples but she does not move.

As he touches her, Milly keeps her mind blank so she won't cry out and get cut...so she won't have to think about someone touching her breasts without permission. Although she's daydreamed about romance, she's never had a boyfriend, or even kissed a boy, let alone undressed for a boy or allowed him to touch her there.

Milly loses track of time as the man crudely squeezes and rubs her. Then he lets go, leaving her shirt unbuttoned from neck to waist. He again presses the knife to her neck, hissing, "Shhhh."

Relieved that the breast squeezing has ended, she nods carefully to signal that she'll remain quiet and cooperative.

Milly hears the man walk to her right. She hears him fumble through the prisoner-of-war materials, mostly sticks, cords, and burlap bags stacked between two big trees. She'd seen them piled a few feet away from where she now sat when she'd arrived at the camp.

Then the man walks to her left, towards Cottonwood Creek where several large windfallen trees crossed one another like giant jackstraws.

The noise of his movements fade. Maybe he's left!

She frantically tests the strength of the ropes that hold her. No go.

She pulls hard against the stick across her back. It doesn't break.

Maybe she should stand and try to creep away in stocking feet, blindfolded. Again, no go. Even if she could move away without falling, how would she ever conceal herself?

Then, far off to her left, she hears the sound of branches breaking. He hasn't left.

44

After a wait, she hears his boots plod back towards her. In less than a minute, they scuff to a stop next to her again.

Grabbing the stick behind her back, the man pulls her quickly to her feet. His arms slide under her legs and shoulders and lifts her easily into the air. The rough cloth of his shirt scratches her bare legs. His strong arms hold her tightly captive.

She flails her legs a little in panic, whimpering involuntarily. Next to her ear, the man hisses, "Shhhh."

She stops kicking and making noise. He begins to walk over the uneven forest floor, wobbling a little under her weight..

Blind, bound, and moving through the air, Milly feels like she's falling from a great height. She suddenly craves the feel of the earth under her feet. She tries to fill her body with energy to twist free, blind or not, before the man can reach the abyss she senses ahead. She's ready to drop, land like a cat, and race away.

But she doesn't twist free. She can't speed away. Milly shudders with dread, her breath shallow, wrapped in his grip.

At first, Milly had been confused when the man picked her up and carried her away from camp. Is he going to fondle her breasts some more? Is he going to kill her?

Milly is panicky but hopes that he'll not harm her. She reassures herself that he could have killed her when she was seated by the tree.

But then she realizes that by carrying her away from camp, he could kill her and conceal her dead body in the tangles of the forest. There, she might never be found except by scavengers. A surge of fear makes her breathe quickly and shallowly again. Her head begins to swim.

Even filled with dread, Milly relaxes a little when she hears the calming call of Cottonwood Creek not too far off. She judges they are a few hundred yards away from the camp and close to the creek. If only she could reach those waters, so helpful before in blocking her pursuers. Somehow she might get away.

Now the man's rough pace and movements, and the sound of breaking twigs and branches under his feet, meant that they were among the jackstrawed, blown-down trees. She knows she will not get free and run to Cottonwood Creek from within this jungle.

After staggering and sliding over a few logs, the man stops. He puts Milly down.

Hands on her shoulders, he turns her away from him. Taking a firm grip on the stick tied across her back, he pushes her forward until her shins

45

and thighs touch a big log. Then he bends her face-down across the log, with her feet on the ground and torso curled over the top.

He shoves her forward until her bottom and head are at about the same height. Milly can feel the rough touch of burlap along her thighs and the deeper roughness of the bark under the burlap. A tree knot presses painfully into her side. She squirms away from it.

With his rough boots, the man pushes her feet wide apart, wider than her shoulders, until her ankles meet the splintery stubs of tree branches. Using a rope, he ties her right ankle securely.

Realizing he wants to immobilize her, Milly panics and squirms up off the log. She tries to move her untied foot out of his grasp, to stand.

Almost instantly, she feels the point of the knife against her left side. She hears, "Shhhh" once again. She resists until he presses it harder.

Flinching against the pain, she bends back down across the log. He pushes her left ankle to the other shattered branch and ties it firmly, too.

Her ankles now secure, the man presses down on the stick. She can only move her head a little left and right; the rest of her body is immobile.

His cold knife slips up under the right side of her panties and cuts the cloth through. Then the left side. The back of her panties falls away. He pulls them out from under her.

Before, when Moon and Jake pantsed her, she felt cold and exposed. But then, like a bathing suit, the fabric of the panties had somehow been a shield that protected her from prying eyes. Now that the panties are gone, she feels utterly exposed and vulnerable.

And any illusion she had about what the man intended dropped away with the panties.

She's heard the word "rape." But now its grotesque threat and ugliness seems poised to rip into her life. A cornered-rabbit whine catches in her throat.

Unexpectedly, she feels a wet-cold touch on her labia and bottom. Reacting to it, Milly pinches her bottom together and curves her back upwards in protest. The man roughly shoves her down by a hand on her neck. His knife blade presses into her right hip. He hisses, "Shhhh" again.

She nods, resigned. When he removes his hand from her neck, she stays down, relaxing her bottom.

As his touch continues, Milly smells the light scent of Corn Huskers lotion, a product used by many woods workers to treat their chronically chapped hands. The man's fingers push it into her vagina and up and down her crease.

46

His fingers linger and his breath is hoarse.

Then she hears the sound of his zipper and the faint rustle of his clothes falling.

She whispers, "Please, please, no…not in me…no baby, please don't, I don't want this…to get pregnant…no, no."

Not acknowledging her words, he takes her hips firmly in his hands. He pulls Milly a few inches towards him.

She goes numb with fear.

He enters her, slowly thrusting against the resistance of her body until he's fully in her, his hips pressed against her bottom. He begins to thrust in and out.

At first, numb with dread and distraction, Milly feels nothing.

And then, suddenly alive and in the moment, she feels *everything*.

His rough hands pinch into her hips.

A sharp pain boils in her abdomen. A virgin, she's stretching… maybe tearing. The pain sears through her. She grits her teeth against it and breathes harshly through her nose.

He seems huge within her. As he thrusts, the sharp pain gradually eases, replaced by an ache like a strong cramp. He maintains a steady rhythm against her immobile body.

She can breathe more easily but can't relax her jaw.

She mentally begs him to stop…hurry..anything.

Time drags by…minutes…hours…she can't tell. She just wants him out of her.

But then, shock! She knows this growing sensation. Although she's a virgin, she often touched herself under her covers at home. In response to his thrusts, an orgasm is building within her!

Until now, for all the pain, she has been apart from his violating contact, forced to act but somehow uninvolved because she was bound and unwilling. But with the growth of the orgasm, somehow she's becoming a part of this terrible violation.

Her body seems bent on betraying her, connecting her to the acts of this horrible, coarse, snoose-stinking man. She wants him out, out of her… before her body can betray her with binding, involuntary pleasure.

Outrage fills her. She hates and loathes him.

Out…OUT! But even with her revulsion unchecked, the perverse pleasure still builds within her. She has a mild orgasm. A despairing sob cleaves her throat. Then, a moment later, another stronger orgasm shakes her.

Under the burlap, pain forgotten, her cheeks flame red from shame. In this moment, she hates herself and loathes her lack of control, her weakness, and this, this unholy *bond* with her rapist.

He begins thrusting harder and harder. The, he leaves her body, groaning, moving urgently.

She feels hot fluid scatter across her legs. Spent, he falls forward across her. His naked thighs and rigid penis touch her. Pressed down by his body, she shudders with nausea and disgust.

The pain drops to a throb between her legs. Milly cries quietly. Shame and revulsion still color her cheeks.

After a few moments, the rapist lifts himself off her and steps away. She hears the scratchy sound of his clothes as he sits back on a nearby log.

"Please, please," Milly whispers, "Let me go. I won't tell anyone. I won't."

He steps back towards her and pokes the knife point into her hip. "Shhhh."

Flinching away, she nods and waits, head down across the log. Tears drip off her runny nose, blotted up by the smelly burlap.

After a time, Milly hears him move. His hands grip her hips again.

She thinks to herself, "Maybe it won't hurt as much this time."

She clenches and sets her jaw anyway, readying herself for renewed pain. With a quick tug, he pulls her towards him.

But, this time his target is her bottom. Taking her completely by surprise, he thrusts quickly and fully into her.

Pain like a giant wave rolls up her back and engulfs her. She squalls once in protest and then clamps her jaws together.

In a spasm, she throws herself up against his hands, one now clamped firmly on her neck and the other on the stick. Her hips are pressed tightly against the log as he moves within her.

She holds her breath against the pain, grits her teeth, back rigid, and almost blacks out. Waves of burning pain keep rolling in. Milly gasps for air.

Time has no meaning to her.

Milly gets no pleasure from this violation.

She doesn't feel his frantic thrusting or his eventual orgasm inside her.

She only feels the uneasing pain.

But when he leaves her body, the pain lingers as she lies, afraid to move, breathing desperately across the log, tears and pain-sweat dripping off her face.

Drawing back, the rapist pats her bottom.

She thinks distractedly that his pat seems almost affectionate. Her mind grabs at this simple action like a drowning person's hand grabs a life ring.

Why a pat instead of the knife or a slap? What did this mean? Did he care about her somehow? Were rapists nice to their victims after abusing them? Was he done hurting her? Would he set her free?

She hears him pull up his pants...the slide of his zipper. He's done with her.

Remembering his sharp knife, Milly's brief hope fades. She wonders, "What will he do with me now? Will he kill me?"

She pleads with him again, whispering, "Please don't kill me, don't..." As she whispers her plea, he moves.

But no hurt comes. He puts his hand firmly on her back. Milly feels the knife first cold against her right ankle and then against the left as he cuts her feet loose from the branches. Turning her around, he lifts her by the waist and sets her down on the burlap bags draped over the log. Milly winces from spikes of pain in her violated parts.

Grabbing her neck from behind with his left hand, the rapist puts his knife to her neck hard enough to draw a little blood. He says "Shhhh" again and shakes her a little for emphasis.

She nods vigorously, sobbing. She tenses, waiting for the knife to cut into her neck or stab her chest.

She feels him saw on the ropes holding her hands but they don't come free. Then he picks her up again, turns her, and puts her over the log on her stomach again. Her bare bottom is in the air and her head is low.

Is he going to rape her again?

Milly doesn't know if she can stand another violation. Even though she knows the cost of raising her voice would likely be her life, she almost screams.

Holding her breath to stifle the scream, she trembles violently...and waits.

Chapter 9

Footwork

Mill gets back from the field visit with the OSHA inspector and forest safety officer. Taking the coin out of a locked cabinet, she drives it to the Gold Bug jewelry store in Florence. There, she asks the proprietor to examine it.

The tall man removes the coin from its setting and chain and holds it under a loupe. Weighing it first in his hand, he then places it on an electronic scale and notes the reading.

He looks at Mill appraisingly, "Know anything about counterfeits, Officer Meacham?"

Not too surprised by his words, Mill responds, "Only a little bit, Mr. Singh. So, this is a counterfeit?"

He nods, "And a very good one, to be sure. Without further testing, I cannot tell you exactly of what metal it is made. But I am very sure it is not of gold and it is not ferrous or magnetic."

His slight Indian-British accent and musical intonation gives the serious subject a lighter quality. But Mill can tell he is intrigued by the coin's mystery and wants to help her.

Gesturing at the coin, he continues, "If you would allow me, I would scrape the gold surface, a tiny scrape only you see, and I could then guess what metal lies underneath. Otherwise, I would suggest that the most excellent State Police crime lab would be the place to have more work done."

Mill replies, "No, I'm afraid you can't be scraping or testing the coin any more than you've already done. But thank you for sharing your professional knowledge with me."

He smiles and says, "You are indeed most welcome, Officer."

"You know, because of the setting and chain, I would say this is just a piece of costume jewelry except only for a few things. The quality of the minting is most excellent. The obverse and reverse of the coin look quite genuine. If it is plated, the gold is most ably applied. And, the edge of the coin is milled, just like the real coinage."

"These things would be unnecessary if it was simply an imitation made for the jewelry trade. So, I conclude it is a counterfeit deliberately made and simply mounted in the setting for someone's convenience or to make jewelry of it."

He pauses and then looks at her quizzically, "Officer, for you to be here in my little shop, this coin must be connected to a crime. May I know which one?"

Mill keeps her face neutral, "No crime that I know of. This was turned in to us and we are just checking it out. You know, value and all that."

Mr. Singh nods, "It has no real value so, absent sentiment for it, no one may come looking."

He goes on, concluding their discussion, "Well then, I will leave it to you to contact the Secret Service about this coin. Counterfeit American currencies must be reported immediately to them, but this is a foreign coin, and so, unless someone was trying to use it for commercial chicanery, I'm quite at a loss of what must be done."

Mill tells him she would call the Secret Service later in the day, thanks Mr. Singh again for his kindness, and leaves his shop.

As she drives the Expedition towards Bud Miller's home, Mill exults, "So, the damned coin is counterfeit!"

She smiles, "Girl, did I call it or what?"

But then what did the coin's being a fake mean? As weird as it was for there to be a big gold coin in Bud Miller's pocket to start with, she is even more confused as to why he would have had a *counterfeit* coin at all. He wouldn't have carried jewelry for his wife into the woods either, let alone doing it in the same pocket with his keys and his pocket knife.

No sense to it unless he just stumbled over it somehow on his way to the timber sale site or out in the woods. And, what the hell would the coin have been doing in some donut shop parking lot or, more crazy, out there in the woods anyway?

She spends only a few minutes with Bud's widow, Helen, a pleasant, chubby lady who looks like she could command cakes and pies to leap into pans and cook themselves up perfectly.

Helen Miller had already been visited by the Siuslaw Forest Supervisor and his Administrative Officer as soon as Bud's identity was confirmed. Her grief yesterday had been profound but composed.

Today, Helen is still very sad and yet very courteous. In her motherly way, she's also visibly concerned that Mill has to deal personally with the circumstances of Bud's death.

Mill's touched by her strength and compassion, a fleeting question passes through her mind about how her own mother might have reacted to this situation, a thought followed by regret that Mill would never know.

Helen gives Mill nothing she can use to unravel the coin's mystery or anything else about Bud's death. No, there's no birthday or celebration coming up, no business on the side.

Helen remarks with a rueful smile, "As Bud used to say himself, he wouldn't know jewelry from jerky. His presents to me were always dinner out at Sizzler or something for my kitchen like a new mixer. If I wanted something nice for myself, I got it myself."

She smiles a little more, "If he had tried to buy me jewelry or clothes, I'm afraid of what he might have dragged in here. I never minded though. He was a wonderful husband even though he had no taste except for what was in his mouth. And I kept him very happy there."

Hearing her own gentle mockery of what they had been to each other, Helen's face falls. Tears start in the corners of her eyes.

Touched, Mill stands and hugs Helen awkwardly, constrained as she is in her ballistic vest and new-LEO shyness. Releasing her and saying a gentle good-bye, Mill leaves the Miller's snug little home, heading towards the Mapleton District office.

There, Mill gets the same news from Bud's timber crew. Forest Service crews that worked together a long time tended to be close-knit and crusty towards outsiders, even towards Mill just trying to do her job.

In as few words as possible, they tell her they know of no celebrations coming up and no business on the side.

Mill asks gently if there could have been any girlfriends out in the wind somewhere. Taken by surprise, the crew guffaws.

One of them drawls, "Bud Miller with a girlfriend? Bud drank coffee, ate sardines for lunch, and dipped snoose all day. Bud's breath could knock a buzzard off a shit wagon! I can't imagine any self-respecting woman getting within arm's length of him."

He pauses, considers his remarks, and gets embarrassed. Then he adds somberly, "Except Helen. Helen's a saint for sure."

The group clouds up and looks thoughtful, also a little embarrassed they might have revealed something uncomplimentary about one of their own, particularly their dead boss.

They talk a little more. Then Mill heads back to her office near the front door to the building, waiting for Bill Zumo's return.

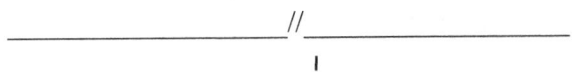

Zumo pulls in around quitting time and comes directly to Mill's desk. It's not hard to do since they're crammed together into a windowless former storeroom. The lack of a window is a little suffocating on warm days. But, on balance, it works okay because it means that they can maintain security for their weapons, files, and evidence that much easier.

Zumo plops down in Mill's visitor chair, sighs, and stretches out his legs. His feet and uniform trousers are damp in places and sandy.

He asks, "So what did you find out about the coin?"

Learning from the last time he'd asked for information, she pulls out her patrol log and starts down through each of her notes, from Mr. Singh at the Gold Bug to Bud Miller's crusty crew.

She concludes, "Bill, the only thing I can figure is that he found it somewhere on his way to the sale or once he got there. Nothing else stands out."

Bill looks at the ceiling for a moment, "Well, I think you're right. Unless something else comes up, we'll put the coin back in evidence. We'll wait to see if the Lane County Coroner needs it or any other evidence for the inquest. I'm betting he won't."

Looking a little puzzled and concerned, he adds, "Something else odd with this case has come up. It's nothing really but it's out of the ordinary. Makes an old LEO wonder."

Mill looks at him with a question in her eyes.

Bill says, "The secretary for the Assistant Special Agent in Charge in Portland called me and asked for the evidence to be sent in as soon as we can clear it. Normally, they'd leave the evidence here until OSHA and safety are done and we're ready to archive it. Then it would go directly to the archives. Or, if there was going to be a higher-level safety investigation, the request would come through the Regional Safety Officer, not law enforcement. It's just different to have the ASAC's office ask. So I got a little suspicious."

Mill asks, "Any chance they're checking up on us, on whether we followed procedure or whatever?"

Bill shakes his head, "No reason to for a routine accident investigation. If there were politicians, drugs, or lots of money involved, it'd be different. Plus, the ASAC would never have let us handle this if it was an important case, at least not without some Regional Office rat tailing us around."

He smiles at his own words, nods reassuringly at Mill, and goes over to his desk to get on his computer.

A few weeks later, they testify at the Coroner's inquest into Bud Miller's death. The Coroner's jury finds the death to be accidental and cites no suspicious circumstances. Bud's death is just another unfortunate woods-worker loss.

Mill and Zumo return Bud's personal effects to his widow. Then, they load all the remaining evidence, including the coin, into a sturdy cardboard archival box, adding their reports along with photos of Bud's personal items before sealing the container. They both sign the sealing tape. Mill sends the container up to the ASAC.

Mill puts a complete file of the case documentation along with a storage chip with the photos into the locking cabinet near her desk. To the file she adds the scrap of cloth she had found down the trail from the impact site, something she forgot to mention to Bill.

She can see no connection to the accident, but since she had found it in the area, it seemed like the right place to keep it.

She'll tell Bill later if the subject comes up....

Chapter 10

Rebirth

Young Milly lies naked across the log strangling the scream in her throat, struggling for sanity and control.

She hears her rapist's heavy boots scuffle away off to her left.

Is he moving away for good?

A warm hope surges back into her.

Her compulsion to scream fades.

Around her silence settles save for forest's murmurs.

For a time, Milly listens for the man's return.

Her fear recedes and then returns.

Her mind races wildly from recent memories of pain to fearful thoughts of freedom and movement.

What if he simply lurks a little ways away, watching her, ready to come back and kill her if she moves? But, as she had done before playing POW tag, this could be her chance to escape. She could run, find safety in the forest, and walk warily home.

For a moment she lies paralyzed with indecision. Then her fighting spirit kindles saying, "Take the chance. Do it now before he comes back!"

Milly jerks upright.

She slides a foot or so down the log.

Her feet hit the uneven ground. Wobbly legs let go and she falls blindly. She lands on rough bark and small branches, which poke and scrape the backs of her legs and her bottom.

Ouch! Damn it!

As Milly struggles to roll over, her hands suddenly come free. The rapist must have cut the rope almost all the way through. The strands have parted against her clumsy, frantic movements. Milly shakes off the ropes and lets the stick behind her back fall to the ground.

Reaching up, she finds and unties the drawstring on the damned burlap hood. She pulls the smelly suffocating thing off.

For the first time in hours it seems, she can see and breathe!

She can run!

But...but...first.... Looking around wildly, Milly searches for her blue panties. Into her racing brain comes the thought that if she could only find them and put them on, maybe everything would be all right. In her pain and humiliation, the scrap of cotton has somehow become a symbol powerful enough to renew her virginity...or at least restore her modesty.

Then Milly remembers the blue panties are cut, spoiled, and useless.

She's naked where she had once been clothed. Injured in ways she never expected. And she can't see the panties anywhere. She will have to let them go.

She bows her shoulders and sobs, hands over her face. She cries for a long time, first weaving slightly on unstable legs and then, grief stealing her strength, leaning back against the log.

As her emotional storm ends, Milly wipes her tears and nose viciously on the arm of her flannel shirt. She pulls the flannel tails of the shirt down as far as she can to help cover her nakedness.

Looking around, she picks up a stick and prepares to use it as a walking stick, or as a club to defend herself if need be.

She peers grimly around the blown-down tangle.

In agony that she might be seen raped and half-naked, Milly walks as quickly as her unsteady legs and stocking feet will allow back to the camp. She leans on the stick when the going gets rough or she gets dizzy.

Back at camp, she quickly finds her boots and jeans where Moon and Jake had stripped them off. Someone had draped her pants over a tree branch to dry—"nice Little Jake" she imagines with a sob, his kindness so touching after her experience with brutality.

Milly yearns to get dressed and run away. But she is so dirty and bloody, bruised and used, that she just *has* to wash off before dressing.

Lovely Cottonwood Creek gurgles and flows just over there. A short walk and Milly can undress behind the screen of willows along the bank and sink into the rushing waters.

She thrusts her feet into her boots. Wrapping her jeans around her like a skirt, Milly walks as quickly as she can towards the creek.

Her wounds smart at every step.

As she passes the site where she had been raped, she grips her walking stick even tighter. Eyes averted, her mind avoids the ugly memories squatting in that place.

On the bank of Cottonwood Creek, Milly quickly drops the jeans. She kicks off her boots, pulls her shirt over her head, shrugs the ruined bra off her shoulders, and uses her toes to shove ruined socks off her feet.

Then she steps in against the cool current and sits down. She feels the slight shock of the water against her skin and abused flesh. At first, her cuts and abrasions complain about the water's touch like small crying babies.

She digs her fingers into the sandy bottom. But after a moment, the little pains numb and their cries still.

Milly takes handfuls of sand. She rubs herself gently to get the dirt and blood off, careful with her most tender parts.

She dunks her head under quickly. When she comes up, she wipes sweat and tears from her face. The water swirls around her, carrying harm away.

Milly lies back against the current until her body parallels the bottom, her feet and fingers just touching there. Her face bobs above the moving water.

Sunlight gently covers Milly's body through the water. Current and riffles join light and water together, and bright, transparent, crystalline shapes slide across her.

Along the opposite bank, cottonwood and willow leaves dance in the light wind, reflecting the sunlight. The leaves flash like small mirrors and send coded messages her way--tree secrets about life and wholeness-- messages she can't quite comprehend.

Milly sinks a little. She lets the stream arch over her face and carry away more of her tears. There, near the surface, she sobs through clenched teeth. Bubbles rise with her sobs and flow away down the creek.

For a moment, Milly thinks maybe she should just follow the bubbles, let the deep creek take her...carry her away, to a soft, quiet place where all her pain and shame and humiliation would be gone. She could ride the creek away from the loss of her mother. Away from her angry Dad. Away from horrible Bill Moon. Away from that horrible, snoose-stinking man and...rape.

Acting on that impulse, she rises to the surface. She takes another breath and submerges again.

Digging her fingers into the sandy bottom, she lifts her legs and torso into the creek's flow. She wills her fingers to let go. Her hands drag along the bottom. Aaahh, she's moving downstream towards the tall, steep waterfall and the deep, secret pools below it.

But then, as if acting independently, Milly's fingers drive deeper into the sand. She is instantly annoyed at her fingers.

Why won't they pull free of the sand? They seem set in mortar, not lightly sliding lightly through the shifting sands and pebbles as they had before.

She wills her arms to take control of her fingers and lift. Her arms try to obey but they can't free her fingers either.

Milly stays put.

Finally, breath spent, intention fading, Milly sputters her way back to the surface. She lifts her face and body into warm sunlight. The radiance forces her eyes closed. Senses overwhelmed by water and light, she rests on the creek's surface.

The water begins to feel alternately warm and then cold. She shudders when she feels the water's touch grow cold. She relaxes and cries when it warms.

Deep breaths filled with sobs come and go.

Awash in sensation, Milly's body slowly reweaves itself from broken pieces into a whole.

Milly sits up. She scrubs every inch again. This time, she touches herself even more gently than before.

Done at last, Milly rises from the creek. Water streams from her. She rubs her hands along her body to send the excess back into Cottonwood Creek.

Still fragile and stiff, she climbs the bank carefully.

She takes her damaged bra, wads it up, and throws it into the creek. She watches it float out of sight, a quick white speck. Then gone.

Milly dresses as quickly as she can, struggling to pull dry cloth over wet skin.

Stepping away from the willows screening the creek's banks, Milly looks around warily. She sees and hears no one. Relieved, Milly moves quickly towards home. She fervently hopes she will not meet anyone along the way.

But, a few hundred feet down the trail, she runs into her friend, Philip. Where could he have come from?

She becomes immediately shy when she sees him. Her eyes fall to the ground. Her cheeks turn pink with embarrassment. What is he doing here, she wonders? Why isn't he playing tag with the rest of her team?

At first, Milly won't let him come close to her or touch her. She thinks Philip is looking at her oddly, appraisingly, even slyly—as if he knows the secrets of her last hour.

Had Philip seen her washing up in the creek or…worse…bent over the log?

Philip is shocked, too. He sees that his friend's hair is wet although her clothes aren't. She has cuts on her wrists and neck. She walks as if each step hurts. She has been crying, probably for a long time.

Philip asks quietly, "Milly, what's wrong? Are you hurt? Did you fall?"

Milly shakes her head strongly. Eyes filling with tears again, she yells at him, "Just leave me alone. Get out of here. I don't want you here."

Philip steps back in shock, "Milly, the least you can do is let me walk you home."

She looks down and then, realizing that he will keep asking her questions and delaying her unless she agrees, Milly nods. With her arms hiding her breasts, she turns and walks away on fast feet.

Philip walks quickly to catch up. Reaching her side, he looks anxiously her down-turned, teary face, "Milly, please tell me what's wrong."

Milly shakes her head "no" again. Giving him a glance both hopeful and defiant, she moves even more swiftly down the path.

Catching up again, Philip clumsily tries to put his arm around her shoulders.

She shoves him away, calling him "a stupid, fucking bastard." Then, her strength lost to the shove, Milly slumps forward and almost falls.

Philip steps in, half catching her in his arms. She rests her face in the curve of his neck and cries bitterly.

Philip can only guess about Milly's distress from past talks they'd had, from words spoken on lazy childhood days, heads close together and feet dangling down from fence tops or benches.

So, Philip asks, "Is this about your Mom? Are you missing her a lot?"

Face against him, Milly nods strongly.

She sobs harder, recognizing with mild surprise how accurate his guess is. Philip's question has opened her heart. Milly knows that she has never missed her mother more than this day.

When her worst tears subside, she leans away. Without speaking, they turn towards home.

Philip awkwardly holds her hand all the way there. He gives her a clumsy hug before she turns to go into her house, to face W. A.'s red-faced wrath.

Chapter 11

Powering Mill

In her freshman year, a therapist helped Mill "find her power" among the wreckage of the day she was assaulted.

To begin, Mill heard clearly from the therapist that the younger Milly couldn't be responsible in any way for her assault.

Mill didn't agree; somehow she had to be responsible. But, the therapist helped her sort through the day and re-consider her self-doubt and guilt.

Then, reluctantly, Mill finally came to agree: young Milly had done nothing to cause herself harm.

Bill Moon bound and betrayed her.

The unknown man kidnapped and raped her.

Milly had done nothing to provoke these acts. She had been, was now, always would be, innocence betrayed and then raped.

Yes, she got unwanted pleasure from his violation. Thanks to the therapist, she could now understand her orgasms as simple physics and biology.

Her pleasure was not something worthy of guilt. She had invited none of it. She could let go of at least this source of self-hate.

With some of her shame relieved and guilt absolved, Mill began to work through her experience, searching for her power. After many discussions, Mill began to see that, as bound and helpless as she had been, she had been powerful in many ways, too.

Mill and the therapist made lists.

Young Milly lived when she might have died. Even in light of the rapist's overwhelming power, and in the face of the threat of death or disfigurement, she had objected to mistreatment throughout the assault. She had asked that he not make her pregnant and he had pulled out of her.

Milly had broken loose from her bonds unassisted. Whether they had been weakened by her rapist or not, her strength had gained her freedom.

She had gathered her wits and clothes, washed and calmed herself, and traveled home safely.

Her strong body had recovered quickly without another healer's touch.

Milly had kept her assault secret, but she rejected any role as a victim.

Instead of falling into depression, she thirsted for revenge.

The therapist pointed out that, for months after the assault, young Milly had searched the faces of woods workers in town, waiting for a flicker of recognition. If she had seen a leer or wink, she would have turned the man in to the police or...something worse, she didn't know what. She searched vigilantly but never saw a hint of any recognition, never heard a rumor, or caught a teasing remark.

And true to her resolve, Milly never spoke to her former gang again. Her exception was her childhood friend, Philip. She kept him a part of her life, although she never discussed the assault with Philip either.

He seemed to know intuitively that Milly had been wounded. Seeing how pained she was, he simply supported her without questioning. With the help of her therapist, Mill eventually understood that Philip had remained strong for her partly because of her strength, not just his own.

Mill and the therapist wrote a script and Mill rehearsed it.

Then Mill acted out strengthening things--the words, sounds, and physical movement that contributed to Mill's emotional and spiritual healing. Mill moved and yelled. She thudded fists and feet into pillows.

Eventually, as she worked through the script over and over, she felt power, control shift from Moon and the rapist to her. And she smeared feelings of loss all over them.

In a couple of months, she found she'd moved beyond the searing, disabling memories. The memories were still a part of her, but Mill soul was mostly free from their oppression.

Still, some things didn't change. After the assault, smiles mostly left young Milly's face, replaced by the slight frown and determined gaze that defined older Mill's face. Anxiety shook her and misted her vision from time to time. And then there were the dreams...the horrible dreams....

Chapter 12

Bull Flies

Sunset spreads east-to-west over flatiron clouds thousands of feet beneath a well-used Northwest 737-200. Grey skies above and orange-blue clouds below, the jet gently descends along the I-66 approach to DC's Ronald Reagan National Airport, getting ready to take a thirty-degree right turn over the Pentagon's South Parking Lot and land in Alexandria, Virginia.

The 737 flies through highly restricted airspace. In the aftermath of the World Trade Center and Pentagon attacks on September 11, 2001, "hot" missile defenses are ready to fire on all aircraft in the DC area, 24/7 with no excuses.

Today's passengers do not know this, and neither do the air crews... officially. Yet, the air crews had heard the rumors about missile defense and they believed them. Thus, the pilots and first officers fly with impressive caution on their way into Reagan National. Their taut communications with controllers and hyper-precise flying makes them only a little less nervous.

Taking in the scattering of people, trash, and business detritus around the cabin, California Regional Forester W. A. "Bull" Meacham mutters under his breath, "God, what a cattle car." Bull is a Westerner by birth and preference. He is big himself and given to seeking big spaces.

The eight hours of enforced confinement in an airliner with 150 other people had oppressed and discouraged him. His bigness spills over the arms of his aisle seat, leg and elbow prey for service carts...the tight seat numbs his ass and he imagines its squeeze means he won't shit again for a week. The stale plane air seems to be sucking the juice out of his lungs.

Bull Meacham is on his way to Washington DC to fight for the position of the Chief of the United States Forest Service. The most recent Chief had stepped down after the last Presidential election. Bull knows that the new crowd is eagerly searching for a satisfactory successor.

Bull feels a passion for taking the throne of the Forest Service that he never felt for any other job, or any woman for that matter. His emotions shift between hot blood lust to hold that much power and cold fury that anyone might deny him.

He is Regional Forester in California. That makes him head honcho over millions of acres of public lands and thousands of Forest Service employees. But Bull finds little satisfaction from that convergence of power and influence. He sees it as a mere stepping stone to his rightful greatness as Chief.

Like his peers across the U.S., Bull had fought his way into the Regional Forester job. He would fight that much harder for the Chief's job. People who got in his way would feel his heat.

Bull knows practically nothing about Darwin or evolutionary biology, but he sure understands survival of the fittest, red fang and claw. To get here today, he had broken many other men and women, souring their dreams and crushing their ambitions. "Screw them before they screw me" had been his motto.

But in DC, career evolution follows different rules, played out with home advantage on the field of politics. Because other people hold the power and influence here, the ruthless tactics Bull had used before do not apply. Here he possesses no special power to coerce, sour, or crush others.

Bull knows in the twisted reality of Washington that an agency bureaucrat like himself can't campaign for the Chief's position. Even though it is a political appointment in everything but name, under DC rules, Bull can't announce his candidacy publicly. He can't show his qualifications through debate and charisma like politicians do because no forum exists for such a thing to happen. In fact, for Bull to campaign openly would give his rivals and enemies the chance to attack him and bring him down like a lame jackrabbit running into cunning coyote jaws.

Instead, Bull has to work through mid-level agency contacts, grasping Hill staffers, self-righteous retirees, and moneyed lobbyists with access to key congressmen and the Secretary of Agriculture. They have to serve as the intermediaries that would place his name before congressional committee members and the Secretary when a decision on who is to be Chief is at hand, delivering necessary political support and spin.

When the time was right, the only things that will carry Bull into office will be well-timed, gilt-edged half-truths about the value and meaning of his experience and a carefully spun reputation as a guy politically loyal and useful to the party in power at the White House.

And worse, once his patrons secure the position for him, they will expect endless favors and fixes down the road. They will want control over his most sensitive decisions. They will want to select his most important employees, here and in remote locations. They will insist on sending money to their pet projects, and want him to scoff at appropriations law and spend public money on their friends.

Having to trade with these jackals means nothing less than putting on a corset and letting them pull the strings tighter and tighter until his head, heart, and balls explode. As he thought about the political straightjacket he would endure, his blood pressure rises and the latent hangover from last evening's fleshy, drunken hours begins to tap, tap, tap again inside his right temple.

The strangle-hold they will have on him would be maddening and emasculating. Yet, he has to accept their conniving and meddling, at least until he improves and expands his own DC connections and power base.

And, there's another challenge. He knows only one other candidate for Chief who can truly oppose him, a PhD woman named Esperanza Pizzaro. She's a relative newcomer around the Forest Service, an immigrant from the U.S. Fish and Wildlife Service, with academic credentials and D.C. Beltway visibility far above his. She's been on leave from the government for the last year doing post-doctoral work at Duke University and earning a big media following on cable TV.

Yet, for all of her big-deal credentials, she lacks Bull's field background and reputation. In the words of agency people, she's never "gotten out the timber cut." Although she holds an international reputation as a field scientist, she's never held a boots-on-the-ground job as a Forest Service line-officer at a field location. She's never eaten smoke on a fire line or been a part of a search and rescue team looking for lost hunters.

So Bull knows her credentials are suspect to employees, retirees, and conservative Hill staffers. He plans to play on their suspicions.

Still, she has plenty going for her that Bull can't touch. Pizzaro personifies the "sexy librarian" when she testifies before Congress or works with the media at a field location in tight-fitting jeans and a bush jacket. She is a favorite "expert source" on Animal Planet and Discovery channels. She turns heads anywhere she goes, a potent mixture of well-tailored expert, curvy sex object, deserving minority woman, and knowledgeable ecologist and conservationist.

As a man, Bull thinks Pizzaro is a "five-alarm chili pepper" of a woman and has idly dreamed of banging her silly during their few past meetings. But as a rival, he sees her as very dangerous.

As attracted as Bull is to her clean good looks, forthright delivery, and depth, in reality, he greatly fears those abilities and her Beltway connections, intellect, and clout.

Driven by subtle passion and fear, he leans forward slightly in his seat. Fingers twining and hands gripping, sexually aroused, he fantasizes about seducing her, bedding her into submission. Or if she resists, he dreams more darkly of invading her home, then sexually abusing and perhaps torturing her to death. Either way, he will slake his lust for her and prevent her candidacy for Chief from being successful.

He mutters, "Greaser cunt" under his breath.

The woman in the seat next to him straightens up, glances at him, and then leans away. He turns towards her trying to dim the angry glare of his eyes by lowering the lids and his head.

She turns further away, flustered and a little afraid. He murmurs, "Sorry" in a low voice.

This can't go on. He lets the seductive vision of Pizzaro's humiliation slip from his mind.

Then, for perhaps the thousandth time in the last few weeks, Bull sourly recalls his father. The man had given him the first and middle names of "Wolfgang Amadeus" after the famous composer, Mozart.

What a flake his old man had been. Naming a Forest Service brat "Wolfgang Amadeus" had been like hanging a sign around his neck saying, "Punch Me." And punch the young Bull they did back in the Forest Service compounds and small towns of his youth.

After he got older and went to work for the Forest Service, to blunt the wussy "Wolfgang Amadeus" business, Bull asked his coworkers and subordinates to call him "W. A." Most complied out of respect or a desire to placate him. As his reputation as a bruising boss grew, they did it to avoid his anger, too.

He had first gotten the nickname "Bull" by being a "bull of the woods" during his early career with the timber industry. He became well known for using his loud voice, and fists if necessary, to push tough logging crews to maximum effort.

When he joined the Forest Service, he re-entered the close-knit, competitive community of "Legacies," children of agency employees. Here, he got to be known as Bull as much for his use of women and the storied size of his male member as for his ability to get work done.

He hadn't liked the nickname because it hinted at things he did not want revealed, things that mocked him, things that could knock his career off track. But he was largely powerless to halt its spread.

Free spirits called him "Bull" behind his back.

Fools used the term to his face.

He kept a list of them all, the ones he guessed at and the ones he knew, the smirking bastards. He took grim pleasure in making them pay for their disrespect with punishing practical jokes and difficult, even dangerous work assignments.

Bull had good reason to guard his dignity and reputation carefully. Bull's great-grandfather, Nelson Meacham, had been a Pinchot "Firster." Firsters were those men chosen by Gifford Pinchot, the agency's founder, to establish National Forests newly created by Congress in the early 20th century.

The Firsters are agency icons, appreciated as men who accepted endless toil and hardship to create natural resource treasure houses. Later arriving employees dropped Firster names to increase their prestige within the agency, trying to gain credibility through the supposed hand off of wisdom from the Firsters.

The Firsters worked hard but they were hardly saints. Like the rough characters they lived around along the last tattered and unravelling edges of the American frontier, many had worked hard in the woods all day and drank hard all night. Some had been brawlers or womanizers and some had been church deacons. Some had been all three.

Bull admires the courage and craftiness of many Firsters. He also considers many of his great-grandfather's friends as gutless opportunists who had cheated destitute pioneer families out of their land. They had done this by arm-twisting families when foreclosure loomed. And they waited until the tax man had seized homesteads, and then bought the property for pennies on the dollar. Misery and government money seemed to go together in those days.

Still, Bull has to have the support of the children and grandchildren of Firsters, and other Legacies, to claim his rightful position as Chief. So, he had kept his opinions on the behavior of some Firsters and their offspring to himself over the course of his career.

The Firsters had also founded the Green Creed. Every Forest Service employee since was required to adhere to it. That is, they followed it if they wanted to get ahead and hold positions of power and respect within the agency.

The Green Creed is the Forest Service employees' view of themselves as the only "true" conservationists, the wiser and wisest protectors of natural resources--those resources to be doled out by agency experts to the common people for the common good.

In this self-serving agency theology, Forest Service employees alone know what's best for the land and the people who depend on it. They alone know to what "wise uses" public lands should be put. They proclaim that they were put on earth to educate the masses and guide other natural resource professionals in their choices.

They reward loyalty to the Green Creed and agency leaders, placing loyalty above public service or adherence to more mundane relationships like those defined in the Constitution or federal law.

The Green Creed can be stated as a simple slogan, "We are right and they are wrong." The Creed also had many chapters and verses, all self-serving, self-empowering, and self-righteous.

Bull is an outspoken but insincere acolyte of the Green Creed. He knows that he could never get the support necessary to rise to the position of Chief unless he spouts Creed dogma. So, he goes through the ritual speak and motions. He does this without giving a shit whether the Green Creed still has any real-world validity or public support.

As a Regional Forester, Bull stands in a Green Creed pulpit. He's a Firster's great-grandson, the grandson of a "forty-year man," and the son of a father who'd seen long years of service with the agency.

Bull is as close to a Forest Service aristocrat as you can find. He knows he is a prominent Legacy. He has traded on his status for his entire 28-year career. So good is his pedigree, he has risen swiftly through the ranks under the patronage of his father's and grandfather's agency colleagues and political friends.

He knows his father would be impressed by Bull's imminent ascent to the Chief's Desk, perhaps the only event that might bring a grudging smile and nod out of the old bastard. Bull had not mourned his father's death several years ago. Now he feels a slight regret that he can't call his father to flaunt his soon-to-be Chief-of-the-whole-fucking-Forest-Circus status.

His father had been a slightly effeminate man, with airy hand gestures, soft-spoken as a general rule. But when crossed, he exploded into red-faced, hands-clenched rages. On those occasions, he waved his fists and thrust sudden-poking, sharp-nailed fingers into Bull's body.

Bull's home had been haunted by his mother's wan face and tight lips--its evenings filled by his father's mumbled, drunken threats and dark secrets.

In addition to being the grandson of a Firster, his father was an unpunished pedophile with a taste for pre-teen boys and girls. Bull learned early that, although he could not always escape, the woods could be a safe haven from his father's spite, lust, and spittle. That is, if he could run quickly and hide before clutching hands approached.

His father's power as a District Ranger and then later as a Forest Supervisor allowed him to practice his lust secretly. He prospered in the seclusion of Forest Service compounds, remote little government villages really, and small timber towns.

There, he used his line-officer power to wrap himself around employees and their children, have his way, and then erase any whispers. Any angry man who confronted him, or allowed his wife to do so, was crushed, discredited, and transferred, his career all but over. And Bull's father was ever so careful to never be seen, never be caught, with any of his victims.

In the old man's day, America had not yet awakened to the wide-spread abuse of children that existed. And, the backwoods enclaves of the Forest Service were not the places where such revelations would surface, or even be talked about, until much later than the rest of American society.

Still, rumors about Bull's father spread...the rumors...spread. No place for Bull to hide from the rumors.

Looking back, Bull thinks wryly that, "At least ruthlessness is something I share with the old man. No one stopped him then. No one is going to stop me now. Be damned what anybody thinks"

The engines on the 737 begin to surge as the pilot carefully jockeys the aircraft for a landing at Reagan-National. Bull cinches his seat belt tighter, no fan of takeoffs and landings.

He again begins to think about how he will deal with Esperanza Pizzaro, by fair means or foul.

Chapter 13

Mist Rising

In the early 21st century, the FBI effectively destroyed Earth First! and the Earth Liberation Front. And they sent the Animal Liberation Front people scurrying for cover. For the FBI, these organizations were the low-hanging fruit, stubborn on the tree but easily plucked.

The FBI did not know that another organization, far more sinister and effective, went unnoticed and untouched as they brought the more public eco-liberationists to justice.

Long before, in the 1970s, more cautious eco-liberators saw they were on a potentially deadly collision course with law enforcement. While respecting the dedication and energy of their more public and flamboyant co-liberators, the cautious ones felt they should go underground to remain intact. Anonymous, they would be more effective in protecting Mother Earth from human destroyers.

True to their intentions, six cautious ones dropped out of sight and never gained a place in public thought again. Over a period of years, the tough, young, like-minded green founders formed an eco-liberation organization called "Mist."

They chose the name to represent their hope for a pervasive yet nearly imperceptible enterprise. Mist would be everywhere and yet nowhere, here and then gone, a powerful invisible force protecting wild nature.

For all of the arty quality of its name, Mist's founders were pragmatic, determined men and women. They quietly and anonymously sought the help of liberation movements around the world—movements that had suffered oppression by reactionary governments, a fate the Founders wanted to avoid.

The Mist Founders eventually set up a clandestine system based loosely on the Irish Republican Army's system of tight-knit cells, intense loyalty, and secret communications. But they were small-time, weak....

Then came a breakthrough. One of them had been part of the Weather Left, radical and close to American anarchists. And the anarchists had been close to the KGB, the chief intelligence and terror organization of the USSR.

Connections got made, trust built, and the six were spirited to a training facility in the Ural Mountains, one designed to build insurgents of the first order.

A year later, the six slipped back into the U.S. through Mexico, well-trained and bankrolled, home from a "working vacation." They were ready to "bring American capitalism to its knees," as their controller, Ivan Kraznin, proclaimed at their graduation.

Kraznin remained their controller until the fall of the USSR in 1989. In the last days, he saw that the counter-revolution promoted by Vladimir Putin of the KGB against the detente-mongers was failing. No matter. He was on the wrong side.

Before they came for him, he barricaded himself in his office, burned his papers, and committed suicide.

He left no trace of Mist at all.

The six Soviet-trained Founders became Mist's first Clan Chiefs, each in charge of one of its liberation functions: Listening, Movement, Money, Friends, Enemies, and War. Together, they worked as the Mist Chiefs' Council and made all critical decisions together, including the choice to use violence.

They called this choice, a "Strike."

Other Mist members were called "warriors" in keeping with their status as champions for earth rights. A few warriors with the right talents and skills were chosen to be assassins. Assassins carried out most of the Strikes.

The Mist Council wanted no warriors with apparent personality disorders or strong anti-social tendencies as full members. So, every Mist warrior-candidate had to pass a rigorous series of psychological tests. Even assassins had to conform although they also had to be edgier and more comfortable with the use of lethal force than most warriors.

As Mist developed over the years, the Chiefs followed Kraznin's advice to use the IRA's political methods rather than heavy-handed Soviet tactics. So persuasion and influence through established Green organizations were the tools the Chiefs commonly used to achieve their ends. Other organizations spoke for Mist, so rarely were any Mist warriors seen in public. And when they went public, Mist spokesfolk were only identified as representing other organizations or offering "person-on-the-street" opinions. Once done talking, they quickly dropped out of the media spotlight.

For security reasons, the six Chiefs were known only to each other and rarely met as a group. They had a suicide pact and carried the means to die at all times.

From the beginning, all communications among Mist members were encrypted and sent through secure channels. The organization was among the first to recognize the value of the Internet and modified cell phones for secret, encrypted communications.

No Mist warrior knew more than three other Mist members. Many knew only two. Mist assassins had only one warrior contact, a Clan Leader who gave them their orders and support. The clan leader in turn communicated with Arrow, the War Clan Chief who had secure access to the whole Chiefs' Council at all times.

Warriors all had legitimate jobs with little public visibility. Assassins worked only for Mist and were rarely out in public.

Raven, the Mist Listening Chief, mainly avoided what the professionals called "signals intelligence" or gathering information by electronic means because the devices doing the eavesdropping could themselves be detected, potentially revealing a clandestine organization as clearly as turning on a neon sign. In addition, hostile intelligence agencies frequently planted false information using "siglint" methods, and set traps to capture or kill their enemies.

Instead, Mist Listening Clan warriors called "Eyes and Ears" used conventional information from "dry" sources such as government reports and correspondence. They also used oral information from many "wet" or human sources from inside government agencies, even law enforcement.

Outside government, Mist's network of informers provided excellent intel on a regular basis, routed to Mist through supportive green groups, media contacts, and academics, most of whom had never heard of Mist or its programs.

The work went slowly but the information was reliable, steadily building their knowledge, and greatly supported the Chiefs' decisions.

No matter how deeply the heavily tech-dependent FBI and other law enforcement agencies might look, Mist was effectively invisible.

To further avoid attention from law enforcement, Mist avoided robbery, drug sales, or anything illegal to generate cash. And, although the Money Chief had to engage in painstaking work to develop secure money sources in the beginning, vast funds eventually flowed in laundered by outwardly legitimate foundations and other donors. These donors were recruited or established specifically for Mist or, if they existed already, secretly refocused to support Mist. Several years before the Soviet Union fell, the Mist Chiefs no longer needed any rubles to fuel their steadily expanding organization.

Mist's Money Chief, Golden Eagle, also made sure generous but targeted grants and donations came from Mist supporters to legitimate Green non-profits. These donations made subtle but important shifts in policy emphasis and behavior by the Green groups.

The Chiefs viewed the corruption of individuals and organizations as legitimate means to attain their goals. In fact, over the years, corruption became the cornerstone of their program.

In doing this, the Chiefs saw their actions as having an ecological imperative. To eliminate threats to nature, the Chiefs chose methods that mixed influence and attrition; their slogan was to "prune the best and leave the rest."

Under this doctrine, they patiently pared the ranks of developer grubs and agency slugs, people who were good at their jobs. Mist left businesses and governments staffed with the weak, the ineffective, the bought off, the intellectually immature, and the emotionally contrary.

The Chiefs' methods were flexible and creative. Here, using prostitutes and video cameras, here they ruined the reputation of an effective forest planner told to increase timber harvest. There, they funded Green groups to campaign for a Congressional Wilderness designation that could place a million acres of commercial timberland into protected status while silencing developer opposition with bribes delivered through lobbyists and development businesses fronting for Mist.

They quietly changed public policies and pruned businesses and agencies of their best leaders. Development opportunities vanished. The people and opportunities left behind made easy prey for Mist-sponsored lawyers and their unwitting judge allies.

The Chiefs rarely used violence but considered it essential. They only used force when grubs or slugs could not be influenced politically, or disabled and destroyed by scandal or corruption.

Decisions to use violence came slowly and reluctantly. And Mist warriors and assassins only carried them out after careful plans were made.

The Clan Chiefs never issued a Strike order to sway political decisions or terrorize the public. As with everything else they did, Mist wanted its violence invisible to law enforcement and the American people.

An automobile accident. A gas explosion. A fall off a cliff. A street robbery gone bad. Murder-suicide. These Strikes were simple to arrange and below almost anyone's radar.

The Chiefs' Council made Strike decisions together. After the Strike decision, consistent with Council security principles, Arrow, the War Chief, reviewed and approved the tactical plans independently.

As they tested their ideas and rules, the Mist Chiefs came to understand that tactical blunders and unanticipated situations could reveal their organization. So, Mist warriors and assassins had the final say on whether Strike plans went forward, right up to the moment of execution. No questions were asked if an operation aborted except to ask how it might be done better when the next opportunity appeared.

The Mist Chiefs' system worked slowly and steadily, its impacts dispassionate and long-term, a seeming force of nature.

The Chiefs culled the talent pool. The best people were chopped down.

The Chiefs delayed or defeated one development proposal after another. Developers gave up.

The Mist Chiefs stymied or eliminated the enemies of nature, one by one.

And no one outside Mist and a few trusted donors knew they existed. No one at all.

Chapter 14

Ekos

As Bull's plane jockeys gingerly on its approach into DC, Mist assassin, Ekos, sits under a small spotlight at a rough wood table topped by a smooth stone slab, honing the slightly curved blade of a dark-colored dagger.

The blade moves rhythmically back and forth, making raspy sighs as it slides. Ekos sets the hone along the blade precisely, a quiet perfectionist, removing barely perceptible nicks, creating perfect bevel.

In the nearly dark room, metal gleams under the spot like a wolf's wet fang in summer sunlight. Incredibly tough and sharp, the dagger is long enough to pierce a human heart.

The dagger had been a gift from Ekos' controller, Badger, a Mist War Clan Leader after Ekos' first kill. An iron meteorite had given strength and a journey-story to the dagger. Badger had known Ekos would treasure the dagger for its symbolism: sky-falling fire turned to vengeance on nature's murderers.

Badger also knew Ekos would find quiet joy in drawing it across the neck of some development grub or plunging it into the heart of an agency slug or thug.

The cellar room Ekos sits in is large, its corners lost in shadows. There are no windows. The walls, floor, ceiling, doors, and the numerous cupboards are covered with cork, making the room anechoic. A listening device pointed at its walls from outside would detect not even a whisper. To make sure no whispers left any other way, Ekos sweeps the room for electronic eavesdroppers at least once a week.

Workshop and workout room, Ekos spends most of the day here. Otherwise, Ekos lives quietly in the small house that sits above a portion of the room, a house with an immaculate yard, a house always in good repair.

The underground lair had been created under the guise of a swimming pool installation. No one knowing about the pool-construction work ever wonders why the site yielded so much excavated dirt and required so much more concrete than a routine pool. Inspectors only saw what Mist paid them to see.

Neighbors are convinced that Ekos works as a day-trader in stocks and commodities. They occasionally ask Ekos for tips when they meet at the mailbox or bump into each other while walking on a nice evening. Ekos appears to be the clean-cut, quiet neighbor everyone wants to live next to. That affluent person that a child or cousin really ought to meet and perhaps marry.

The neighbors would have been frightened if they had known Ekos' true profession. Instead of trading commodities and stocks, Ekos specializes in hands-on assassination using the gifts of nature. Ekos is adept at such things as fashioning garrotes from cured and woven animal gut and extracting plant poisons to season foods. On assignment, Ekos never uses the same tool twice and takes pride in inventing new methods on the spot.

Before each Strike, Ekos spends pleasurable hours researching the simplest, quickest, and least detectable of deadly means and building them into Strike plans for Badger's review and Arrow's approval.

To deal with unforeseeable contacts with people during a Strike, Ekos has the dagger, Skyfire. Also in the assassin's tool chest are sprays and dusts that leave opponents blind or gasping for air, and easily folded and hidden silk fabrics used for concealment.

The sprays and dusts come from dried bloods, molds, pollens, minerals, and spices. Thrown in someone's face or left along a trail to disable a dog's nose, the potent powders immobilize pursuers and help ensure successful escapes.

Mist's custom fabrics are woven of matte silk, usually in dark brown-gray or green-gray. They are similar in weave and texture to those favored by stage magicians who use them for quick disappearances. Such fabrics pull from a small pouch and wrap loosely around. They quickly transform Ekos into a shadow under a downed log or a mossy stump. Dark gray or green-blue fabrics work similarly along city streets or in buildings.

Ekos' basic Strike plan is simple. In the wild, isolate the Strike target, distract or confuse them, then deliver a deadly blow. In human environments, trick human and electronic eyes, strike the target quickly, and depart without being detected. Everywhere, leave no trace. Nature offers a cornucopia of deadly possibilities to build onto the basic plan and the basic plan can always be abandoned if the situation warrants.

In case of human encounters, besides Skyfire the dagger, Ekos had studied several forms of martial arts, eventually settling on aikido as the right form for Mist work. Aikido is sometimes called the most peaceful form of martial art, a form that uses one's opponent's power to bring about his own defeat.

Aikido fits very well with Ekos' view of the cycles and seasons of life. Ekos enjoys using aikido's natural, minimalist, circling motions to defeat nature's enemies. Sometimes at a dojo and more frequently in the cellar room, Ekos practices aikido, alternating *tori* and *uke*, attacker and defender, for several hours a week. Even though in Ekos' Strike plans every human contact other than the target is to be avoided, as a precaution, the aikido training tempo increases when an assignment looms.

Instead of the mythical MBA that neighbors thought Ekos had earned, Ekos held a PhD in Eastern Philosophy and a Master's Degree in Human Ecology. And, to add to the neighbors' distress had they known, Ekos had killed eleven times before Bull Meacham's plane touched down at Reagan National.

_____//_____

Badger enters Ekos' workshop noisily. Badger had no choice but to make noise because the only obvious door into the room leads visitors to walk across a Japanese-style "talking floor," a deliberately creaky and clattery surface built to betray intruders.

In addition to the obvious "noisy" entrance, a cupboard on the opposite wall conceals an escape hatch that leads to a nearby storm sewer and then to a maze of pipes, culverts, and channels beyond. That route is tested only once a year, allowing Ekos the opportunity to swiftly run the maze and escape to simulated freedom. The test is yearly because more frequent ones might run Ekos into public works employees conducting routine inspections or maintenance on the storm-sewer system.

Badger had learned from Arrow that Ekos had been an Army Ranger who spent time with the Defense Intelligence Agency. Using skills gained from these organizations, the intelligent Ekos had guessed at Mist's existence many years before and sought out the organization. At first highly suspicious, the Clan Chiefs had eventually allowed Ekos to join, first enlisted as a warrior then developed into an assassin. No one knew Ekos' motives for joining or, if they did, ever talked about them.

As Badger approaches, Ekos looks up from sharpening the dagger. The look invites Badger to speak, "Ekos, the Chief sends his greeting and thanks for your last kill. It was flawless and undetected as far as we know." Badger smiles. Ekos' cool grey eyes and long face smiles in return for the praise.

Badger asks, "Do you have everything you need for your next Strike?" Ekos picks up a short list of items and hands it to Badger, "Just these. I have everything else." A few insect pheromones and attractants make up the list. Badger nods, "I will have them for you by next week.

Does that suit your time line?"

Ekos nods in return and adds, "Make sure the chemicals are undiluted, perhaps from a government or university research facility." Badger nods agreement, pleased at the suggestion because inventories at such locations are never as tightly controlled as they are at commercial locations.

"Are you concerned that the Strike is on a federal law enforcement officer this time?" Badger asks.

Ekos replies, "Not really. Ears and Eyes reports that O'Reilly's field experience has been minimal. He's gotten ahead by sucking up to his superiors and accepting glamour assignments like serving as a bodyguard for Senators and Congressmen. With all the ass-kissing, he really hasn't kept his training and weapons proficiency up." This kind of professional sloppiness is anathema to Ekos and the scorn is clear.

"Please don't misunderstand me," Ekos goes on, "I don't underrate the danger O'Reilly represents to me and to Mist, the potential for discovery. I will only Strike him if conditions are right."

The O'Reilly Strike had been called because he had stumbled on a small piece of information that, processed by a brighter mind, might reveal Mist's existence. Encryption had failed on a secretary's e-mail message and O'Reilly had seen it. The message was innocuous enough but referenced the name "Mist" and some subtle but important plans. A sophisticated reader could potentially guess Mist's existence and likely resources...investigate further.

The Eyes and Ears dossier on O'Reilly concluded that he had the information but, not understanding its significance, had apparently not reported it. Still, without hacking O'Reilly's computer, the extent of the sharing could not be fully known. And hacking it could potentially reveal even more about Mist than the message did.

So the decision had been made to Strike O'Reilly before he woke up to the significance of what he had seen. That made this Strike quite different than Ekos' other assignments. Rather than eliminating an otherwise incorruptible or proficient leader, the O'Reilly Strike was intended to clean up a possible information leak.

Badger asks, "Once the chemicals are in your hands, will you be ready to move?" Ekos replies, "Yes, please tell the warriors in Movement, I will be ready to go to the Strike zone in about two weeks, a few days ahead of the scheduled drug raid. Start the countdown once you know the chemicals have reached me." Ekos knew that Badger will send the countdown and Movement schedule through encrypted e-mail as soon as things were ready.

Badger stands and Ekos follows. Badger extends a hand but then, acting on impulse, reaches forward and warmly embraces the slightly startled Ekos.

"Ekos, be very careful with this Strike," Badger murmurs, "This is our most visible Strike ever, high risk because it came up quickly, keeping Eyes and Ears from doing their normally complete job. And, most importantly, it involves a law enforcement thug. If they discover what you've done, they will be relentless in trying to avenge their own."

Badger looks Ekos in the eyes, "You will be in great danger from the time you reach California until you are back here, safe."

Badger releases Ekos, turns, and walks back over the noisy floor and out the heavy steel door that guards Ekos' lair. Ekos turns back to the work table and continues honing Skyfire.

As the hone sighs, Ekos reflects on the Strike ahead. The Eyes and Ears warriors who worked on the case were clearly rushed. The dossier is slim compared to any Ekos had reviewed before. Still, some of O'Reilly's traits and tendencies were carefully outlined. From that knowledge, Ekos has built a simple, direct Strike plan. The plan had been quickly approved by the War Chief with few modifications.

The note the War Chief wrote on the plan holds a warning, "The O'Reilly Strike plan looks good. Unknown is the potential for your escape. The area is likely to have many law enforcement and K9 units in the area, carrying several kinds of detection equipment in addition to dogs. Ekos, you must truly act as Mist on this Strike to get away undetected. I am confident you will overcome all obstacles and return, but I also remind you to carry your suicide injector. Hunt well. Strike hard!"

Ekos begins again to mentally rehearse each step in the Strike plan, a discipline that would continue until the Strike is successful. The hone sighs. Skyfire gleams, hungry.

Chapter 15

Bull in D China Closet

In his suite at the Alexandria Ritz-Carlton Hotel, Bull Meacham's stands red-faced. He balls his big, scarred fists and spits as he yells, "You tell that fucker Simon Ball that he better join up right now."

Bull roars his words at Associate Deputy Chief Hammond Hogget, his favorite DC toady and "not-really-campaigning-for-Chief" handler.

But Ham isn't the problem and Ham knows it. So the blast mostly just flies right by him in a cloud of onion and chorizo stink left over from Bull's breakfast, belched up from his boiling stomach.

A small, pudgy man, Ham has a small grey face and small clutching hands. Like Bull, Ham staunchly and rigidly defends the Green Creed. But, unlike Bull, Ham's wed to the status quo. He cloaks himself in righteous indignation whenever others propose change.

Ham's love for the status quo is just pretense. He cares little whether change happens or not. Really, he loves control and personal power more than anything. So, Ham finds a thousand ways to say, "no" to protect his personal fiefdoms and only one good reason to say "yes"—to expand their boundaries.

A sneak by nature, Ham gains power by poisoning the reputations of others or withholding promised support at crucial moments. Bull and Ham are hammer and blade when working together. Bull pounds an opponent down while Ham stabs her in the back.

Considering their differences, Ham and Bull make an odd couple. But together, their mean-spirited cooperation over many years has paid them both big dividends in bureaucratic power and position.

Bull and Ham had just spent two days on the phone, lining up support for Bull's candidacy with the six field Directors for Forest Service Research and Development.

The Research folks had been easy. Bull simply offered to increase their budgets by fifty percent or so. Chronically starved for funding, they agreed quickly and began calling their Ag Department, Congressional, and interest group contacts for him.

Bull knows he will renege on his promises to them later. He just has to plead Administration or Congressional interference in his budgets as an excuse. No one will care if the research Johnnies and Jillies whine about such betrayal.

Besides, Bull thinks of them as a bunch of academic dons with big egos and no accountability. They're always publishing crap that made real forest management harder. So, Bull and Ham figure they have the R&D folks bought and sold, paid off and lied to.

But, Bull's peers, the other eight Regional Foresters, had been a much tougher sell. Led by Simon Ball from Georgia, they had resisted Bull's call for support, telling him he already had all the support he needed from within California.

True, Bull had spent copious time ingratiating himself with the powerful California Congressional Delegation, the timber industry, and key County Commissioners and State officials there. The other Regional Foresters knew it and said that the support he has should be enough.

But Bull knows this Green Creed truth: the Regional Foresters have to support him if he's to get the Chief's job.

Four or even three of them from key Congressional Districts outside California might work to make him Chief. But Bull has bigger interests. The Green Creed calls for the Chief to be a hero leader, with charisma and vision that inspire every employee.

For his reign as Chief, Bull wants to have a clear mandate, even adoration, from within the agency. He wants the full loyalty of Forest Service leaders and the rank and file, too.

Bull knows that Simon Ball and his allies can deny him the support that should be his by right of heritage and privilege. They can turn his years as Chief into one internal blowup after another and make him look a lot less than a hero--more like an ineffective, pathetic putz.

But more importantly, Green Creed Chief-hero bullshit aside, he will need high levels of support to get his long-term personal agenda accomplished. Bull's plan is to hold the Chief position for six years, retire, and take a really high paying job with the timber, minerals, or land-development industries--and to Hell with his crappy federal pension.

To get Bull his big payday, he wanted the other Regional Foresters to get on board and support him at every turn in the road. Otherwise, Bull's plans would be burnt toast. So the others could either join up or die the bureaucratic death of a thousand paper cuts.

To date, Bull had used charm, threats, and promises of better positions in his administration to gain commitment from two of the weaker Regional Foresters. Like the researchers, he could always play King Stork with them later, deciding whether to reward them or beak-skewer them as his whims led him.

But so far, Simon Ball had denied Bull his due. Ball kept the holdout regional foresters working as a group. On the surface they were neutral and not committed to any candidate. Ham and Bull are convinced that they are plotting and scheming against Bull behind the scenes.

And Bull thinks maybe Ball himself is considering taking a shot at the Chief's job. Bull hears that Ball and crew are 'poisoning wells' with retirees and interest groups, laying down a rationale to hire Ball. If Bull doesn't claim the prize soon, he's sure Ball will come prancing in and steal it for himself.

Furious at this, Bull knows Ball's personal life and conduct can't stand much scrutiny. Despite being married, Ball's a career-long philanderer. Plenty of female employees and contractors have complained about his advances.

With one whiff of that scandal, conservative Congressmen would bounce Ball right out of contention. Bull is tempted to make the scandal-mongering calls himself, but the Green Creed rule of public silence over private scandal prevents him.

In his shower this morning, Bull swore to himself that he would rip Ball's scrotum off and feed it to some South Georgia swamp gator if Simon and his crew didn't come into the fold today.

He turns to Ham, "Okay. No more kid gloves, Ham. You tell Simon that his gang has to get on board today. Or, the day after I get in office, I'll play Midnight Massacre with the bunch of them. The ones I like will have a hunert and twenty days to report to their new assignments in Bum Fuck, Alaska, or wherever. And the ones I don't like will get busted down to GS-15s. For all I care, they can start shining shoes for Congressional pages or giving blow jobs at the DC Greyhound Station."

Ham blinks and looks quickly at Bull's face to see if he's bluffing or not.

Bull often scares Ham. In Ham's view, threats like this represent awful risks. If Bull bluffs, gets confronted by an influential retiree or politician and has to back down, he could kiss the Chief's job goodbye. Having tried and failed to twist arms, he'd be a laughingstock within the agency and on the Hill.

If Bull isn't bluffing, the situation's almost as bad. Ham knows people coerced into providing support this way could never be fully trusted later on. So, each would have to be sidetracked, derailed, or destroyed professionally after due time. The job of ending their credibility, influence, and careers would be tedious and professionally dangerous.

Ham knows that a lot of that work would be his. He dreads the task and possible fallout. Ham prefers subtle blackmail to the use of force.

Ham studies Bull's face.

Bull isn't bluffing.

Wincing inside, Ham asks tentatively, "But W. A., do you really think they're gonna cave by being threatened like that?"

Bull responds, "Hell yes they will, Ham! They must know by now that Willy and Christine have joined my team. And they have to know that a bunch of Research people are already working the Hill for me. So, they must know I'm going to be Chief of the fucking Forest Circus with them or without them. And they also know that I can spread them out like ripe manure on a big field. And they know that I've got a big enough shit spreader to do it."

Knowing he risks Bull's full rage, Ham hesitates before replying. "But W. A.," he offers, "Maybe they're supporting Pizzaro for Chief, or at least waiting to see if it looks like she is going to get in. They're cagey enough to wait you both out so they can jump on the side of the winning team at the right moment."

Bull's eyes bug out of his flat, red face as he glares at his sycophant. "Pizzaro! Fucking Esperanza Pizzaro!" he roars at the now visibly stoic Ham, "Nobody in their right mind would support that cunt! I tell you that bitch won't hunt in this field!"

Bull gets a grip and visibly calms himself, "You get to Simon and give him the news. Make sure he knows I really mean it. Give him two hours to decide."

He lowers his voice further, "Don't worry, Ham. I will deal with Esperanza Piss-Me-Off-Aro myself and soon."

Bull walks to the door and puts on his hat and trench coat. Turning back for a moment, he says, "I'm headed up to the Hill for my Senate visits. I'll try to get more information about Ball and his bunch and about Pizzaro while I'm there. Work the phones while I'm gone and call me with any news, like the moment when the fuckers fold. I could start using the news about them giving me their support on the Hill as soon as you get it."

Ham nods, reaches for the house phone, and waves with his free hand. Ham dials the phone and begins his call to Simon Ball. Better he should not use his government-issued cell phone and leave a call record, particularly not for this kind of work.

Observing his toady start to work, Bull smiles grimly and closes the door sharply. He moves down the lushly carpeted hallway to the elevator.

Bull arrives at the fifth floor of the marbled, modernist Hart Senate Office Building for his meeting with Senate staffers. The building's bright marble sharply contrasts with the limestone construction of the other Senate office buildings.

The building had been named after Senator Gary Hart, an able and personable Senator from Colorado, once a candidate for President. In response to Hart's taunts, the media had exposed his notorious philandery. Once revealed, his secrets had likely cost him the Presidency.

For Gary Hart, the building stands as a memorial to his leadership and a mausoleum for his dreams.

From the balcony by the elevators, Bull peers skeptically at the hanging Calder sculpture twisting slowly around in the six-story atrium. He muses to himself, "Where else in America would people build a huge indoor space like this and fill it with a giant piece of junk metal? Looks like two coal cars collided and some idiot hung them here." He shakes his head as he moves to the meeting room.

He's a little early. To his surprise, Esperanza Pizzaro backs out of the room just as Bull arrives. He hears her saying pleasant good-byes to the staffers huddled within. He glowers inside with the thought that she likely got a warm reception from the bastards.

He asks himself, "Why the Hell is fucking Pizzaro here now? Did they overlap us so we'd have a fight in the hallway?"

Overcoming his anger, Bull figures out that the staffers are simply optimizing their time by interviewing Pizzaro and Bull back-to-back.

He knows he should be on his best behavior here. So, instead of sneering at her or ignoring her, he smiles a flat smile and nods to Pizzaro as he moves towards the small conference room door.

Bull starts to brush past Pizzaro but she gently takes his arm, dimples up at him, and says confidentially, "W. A., we need to talk. I hope you have a few minutes after your interview here to meet with me. If it's okay with you, I'll wait in the Senate Dining Room. You can join me when you're done."

Startled by her warmth and her message, Bull hesitates for a moment. Maybe he should decline. One tenet of the Green Creed is "never meet with people who disagree with you."

Is this some sort of trap? He almost says, "no" before realizing that by meeting with her he might get an idea about how her non-campaign for Chief was going.

Instead he answers, "Okay, Esperanza, but because you're a Hollywood star, you have to buy!"

Her eyes crinkle with amusement at this challenge. She smiles broadly up at him, "Okay, W. A. I'm the big spender today. See you there."

Then ducking her head, Esperanza Pizzaro turns and heads down the hall towards the elevators and the tunnels under the Senate buildings that will take her to the Senate Dining Room.

Bull watches her small, lovely figure sway down the hall. She disappears around the corner into the bank of elevators. All in all, he is amazed that she wants to meet with him. What can she want?

Putting Pizzaro out of his mind, Bull enters the small Senate conference room.

An elaborate bronze light fixture hanging from the ceiling greets his eyes. A beautifully textured oak and walnut table dominates the room. Blue silk wall paper and matching blue leather chairs finish the room. Several elegantly framed scenes of 19th century DC adorn the walls.

The colors, textures, furnishings give the room a sense of wealth and gravity. Even this small conference room gives mute testimony to the Senate's power.

The staffers are another matter altogether. Four are under thirty, smart and crafty, thirsty for position and influence.

The other two are over forty, seasoned and cynical, senior and careless with their words and opinions, often aping the senators they serve.

Together, they emit a miasma of menace and disrespect which drifts towards Bull as he takes his seat. No wealth and gravity in this bunch, just sly threats to Bull's plans to be Chief.

The senior staffer present, Mike Reinard, Chief of Staff for Senator Castwell's Agriculture, Nutrition, and Forestry Committee, kicks off the meeting by welcoming Bull. Bull and Reinard are the same height, about six feet two.

But, where Bull weighs well over 250 pounds, Reinard is reed slender and sports a weedy goatee. Reinard uses airy hand gestures and poking fingers to make his point. These mannerisms has always reminded Bull of his father, a fact which makes Bull wary of Reinard and increases tension between the two men.

As he counts red and blue noses around the table, Bull realizes that Reinard had invited equal numbers of Democrats and Republicans. This sign convinces Bull that this meeting would probably determine Senate staff support for him as Chief.

Two separate partisan meetings would have signaled uncertainty about him and any other candidates. Or worse, separate meetings could mean that his candidacy is about to become a political football and Bull himself fodder for partisan cannons.

Holding a bi-partisan meeting serves as a sign to Bull that he is a credible candidate and subject to serious consideration. Then Bull remembers that Pizzaro has just met with the same group.

His stomach sours further.

After finishing hasty staff introductions and greetings, the staffers start in on Bull.

The staffers' views and questions run the political gamut from arch-conservative-whack-it-all-down to arch-druid-protect-everything. Viciously polite, they bat Bull back and forth across the middle ground of environmental and forest issues like a shuttlecock in a badminton tournament.

Bull can't land an idea before someone gives him a whack on his ass and he and the subject take flight again.

To the staffers, the political middle ground smells like a stinking swamp—a place not to be entered--a dry land devoid of lobbyist money and influence. It's a vile, weakling place of compromise and consensus that they visit only when ordered to by their political masters after months or years of political brawling.

Swatting Bull back and forth over this bleak territory, the staffers grill him on his views about forest policy, public-private land exchanges, wildfire management, and fiscal accountability.

They talk about initiatives they will expect if he was hired as Chief--polar opposites that no one can simultaneously attain--one group pushing ecological restoration on every acre and the other timber development.

They ask about his budget priorities and who he plans to appoint as his Deputies and field representatives.

And when they're done with forest policy issues, they begin to ask questions about his career and personal life. Bull's past decisions are ruthlessly torn apart. Small details are held up as indicators of his inherent biases. They throw casual comments he had made in public meetings in his face.

Although these barbs lack the energy of earlier remarks, his divorce from Rebecca and her disappearance is mentioned with suggestions that Bull was to blame for both. To keep them all on track, Reinard reluctantly intervenes in that line of questions and prevents any further attacks based on Bull's failed marriage. It is a juicy tidbit but not worth gnawing now.

Still, near the end of the hour, Reinard grins like a shark and asks Bull, "W. A., you have a reputation as quite a ladies man within the Forest Service ranks. Are there any skeletons in your closet that we need to worry about?"

Bull smiles disingenuously, "Not at all, Mike. I've been alone for years, raising my daughter Milly by myself for many of them. Of course, I've dated around, including Forest Service women, but only if the woman didn't work for me and wanted to go out. I've never heard of a single complaint from any of them. Have you?"

Reinard knows personally of two or three women who would have complained about Bull's treatment if they thought their voices would have been heard and action taken.

As one had put it, "I thought we were going out for a nice dinner. I wound up being banged silly in the back seat of his rental car. All I had for dinner were two drinks at a cheap bar and then lots of his salami. I had way more of the meat course than I wanted!"

But, in reply to Bull's question, Reinard has to say, "No, I haven't heard of anything officially. But, W. A., you should know that if you become Chief, I'll be watching your moves closely."

Bull smiles wickedly in return, "Mike, I'm shocked. I didn't know you liked to look over other guys' shoulders when they're making love."

The group laughs.

But under his laughter, Mike looks more sharply at Bull. Their eyes lock.

Mike is sure that Bull means that careless cries of scandal could touch them both.

Ham and Bull have heard that Reinard lives as a married bi-sexual who dallies with summer interns, mostly male. Bull's hint about "other guys' shoulders" is clear; Reinard's gay flings can easily be made public. Bull's message: each of them has much to lose if their sexual conduct gets revealed.

They hold each other's gaze for a moment and silently seal a mutual non-disclosure pact, a pact that would hold, at least until a third party might reveal their indiscretions.

That's how the politics of sexual secrets works in the Nation's Capitol.

At the end of a long hour, the group parts with handshakes. Bull had endured an intense time with the staffers. His pre-meeting briefing with Ham and the heads of Forest Service Legislative Affairs and Communications, plus his knowledge of western forestry issues, had served him well.

As he always did after Hill visits, he will call back to each Senate staffer over the next day or two to clear up any soft spots in their understanding and cement his relationship with them. All and all, Bull knows he has done well.

Tomorrow, he will repeat the interview process with House staffers. There would be a larger group of them but they would be less prepared.

Senators and their staffers had always been the ones to watch out for on the Hill, way back to the days of Saint Gifford Pinchot of Milford, first Pope of the Green Creed. The Western Senators in whose jurisdictions existed most of America's public lands had always posed the greatest risk.

Bull knows the Senate Republicans try to give public lands and resources for free to their developer friends to turn into money. The Democratic Senators try to set aside vast acreages as playgrounds for their Hollywood and environmentalist buddies under the guise of environmental protection.

The whole thing's a farce, he knows, driven by special-interest lobbyists and campaign funds, staged and paid for by the American people, the poor snookered saps.

At some point in the next week, he will contact Reinard and get a visit scheduled with Senator Castwell himself. But this would only happen after Bull's supporters had made their Hill contacts and the feedback from staffers showed a green light.

Damn that Simon Ball and Twat Pizzaro, too! They could muck up Bull's plans if they don't get out of the way soon!

With that thought, he remembers the imminent meeting with Pizzaro and his feet change course. Just on his way out of the Hart Building, he now turns back.

"I wonder what the sexy little twist has on her mind?" he says to himself, heading down into the tunnels that would lead him to the Senate Dining Room.

Bull journeys through the guts of the Senate Office buildings to the Senate Dining Room. As he gets close to that dignified eating place, legendary for its navy bean soup, Bull isn't thinking about food or drink. His long walk and curiosity had given him enough time to feel a resurgent lust for Pizzaro and to wonder what might come next.

Is she going to ask him to step back so she can have his job as Chief? No, that would be too goofy. She would never invite him to coffee for that.

Maybe she has some trick up her sleeve or some bribe to offer. Well, tricks and bribes wouldn't work either.

Or maybe she is going to admit defeat and congratulate him? A laugh burst out of him, startling a passing tourist.

"Yeah sure," he says to himself, "That's it, she's going to just hand me the job. Sure she is!"

But, to his astonishment, ten minutes later, that's pretty much what Esperanza Pizzaro did.

Wondering if Pizzaro has stayed for their meeting, Bull walks into the red room with its walnut and gilt woodwork and white table cloths. He half expects her to be gone, a snub by the DC sophisticate for the crude Westerner. But, in the corner, Pizzaro sits, pert and pretty, with a wide smile for him as he crosses to her.

He glances around the nearly deserted dining room and sees no one he knows. She had chosen their meeting spot well. She had picked a table close to the entrance where the few other diners and idling wait staff are too far away to eavesdrop. And, no one pays them any attention except for an ancient, slow-moving waiter who takes their coffee orders and leaves.

Once the coffee's delivered, a trifle slopped into each saucer, Bull and Esperanza begin to talk, at first cautiously and then with greater confidence.

Bull begins by saying lightly, "So, are you really going to buy me coffee, Esperanza? Do I have to report it as a bribe?"

Smiling at his ham-handed humor, Pizzaro replies, "No, W. A., no bribe, just a cup of coffee to hear me out. Or, maybe I could actually bribe you with a sweet roll?" She laughs.

Bull has little patience for social niceties like this. So, he cuts to the chase.

"What would you want to talk to me about, Esperanza?" Bull asks, "I'm not in a position to do you much good--that is if you are after what I hear you are."

She responds, "You mean being vetted for the Chief's position, right, W. A.? Well, if that's what you mean, I've decided I really don't want the job."

Bull's mind jerks even if he keeps his face poker-stiff. Is this some trick? People all over the Forest Service and all over DC have told him Pizzaro's in the hunt. Her supporters are everywhere, vocal and connected. The feminist tribe had kept up a steady drumbeat for her. She's known to be making the rounds and charming the powerful at every meeting.

When he does not reply, Pizzaro buys more thinking time for him by saying, "W. A., please call me 'Angie', its short for my middle name 'Angelica'. I think 'Esperanza' is a mouthful for anyone. All my friends call me Angie. 'W. A.' is easy to say and I feel I have you at a disadvantage if I let you keep using my given name. Please? Will you?"

She smiles an engaging smile. Bull can't see how asking him to use her nickname is a trap, so he solemnly agrees, still shaken by her startling admission that she does not want the Chief's job.

What does she take him for, a fool? Is this her dodge to get him to reveal his plans or throw his agenda off track?

Seeming to read his mind, Angie speaks again, "W. A., I know this may seem like I'm trying to divert you from your goal, but I'm really not. And I know this is not what you expected to hear from me today, but I truly have no personal interest in the job. I did. But I dropped the idea when I heard you were coming in to see if you could get it."

Seeing his eyebrows rise in doubt, she continues, somewhat hotly, "I really mean it, W. A. The circumstances certainly warrant skepticism on your part."

She pauses, looking him in the eyes, then says earnestly, "And, besides telling you I don't want the Chief's job, I also have a proposal for you that I hope you will consider."

She looks at her watch, "But, W. A., I have an appointment at Ag in twenty minutes, so I have to go soon. We won't have time now to talk over what I have in mind."

She looks into his face and smiles, bright eyes questioning, "So, could we meet for dinner tonight? I know its late notice but how does your schedule look? Would you join me? Your treat this time."

She laughs but her eyes look serious, intense--her convictions, whatever they are, strong.

Bull pretends to think about his schedule. He had planned to go drinking with Ham and Marjorie Carroll tonight.

Marjorie is his DC "work wife," a Forest Service staffer who supports him as an assistant when he's in DC, makes sure he has all the latest gossip, and sleeps with him when he wants her. He figured he could get a quick hump with Marj tonight. She put out as steady as a milk cow in bed and had the teats to match, but maybe he could see Marj after dinner with Pizzaro.

He says casually, "Okay, Angie, I think I can get dinner to work. Have to be done early though. How about we meet at six o'clock at Union Station, at Carbone's, garden seating?"

Angie knows Carbone's is a toney place at Union Station, not far from where they sat. Tables out in the huge atrium near the Station's Capitol-side entrance constitute the "garden seating" at Carbone's. Noise and reverberations from people and trains fill the big open space. Lovely classical statuary and carvings look down on the diners who eat under soft evening light.

Garden seating at Carbone's made a perfect place for confidential discussions.

"Sounds good to me," she says, "I'll try to be there at six sharp. If I'm a few minutes late, have a double vodka Gibson waiting for me, okay?"

She stands up, puts three dollars on the table for the coffee. She smiles at Bull, "Here's the bribe, fella."

With a smile, she turns and walks away. He watches her trim figure moving towards the door. As she reaches the doorway, she looks back at him, waves a small hand discretely, and then disappears.

Once outside, Bull calls Ham and fills him in on Pizzaro's remarkable turn around. Like Bull, Ham is dubious, saying "W. A., I think she might be trying to throw us off our game while she lines up support with Simon Ball and his crowd or some of the lobbyists we haven't gotten to yet. She can definitely move ahead of us if we slack off while we're waiting for her proposal or support or whatever."

Bull thinks for a moment, "You may be right and we'll know after this evening. So, did you talk to Ball, Ham? If so, what did the bastard say?"

Ham replies cautiously, "Well, W. A., he seemed to understand that you were prepared to get pretty tough if he didn't line up with us. But he laughed at the two-hour deadline you gave him. He said he'd get back to me today. No call yet."

He pauses and then says, a little mockingly, "Maybe Ball's waiting to hear from Esperanza."

As Ham finishes his sentence, Bull hears Ham's cell phone ring in the background. Ham says hurriedly, "Hold on, W. A., here's a call from Simon. Want me to call you back?"

Instead of replying, Bull just breaks the connection. No point in slowing Ham-bone down when he's handling an important call.

In a few minutes, Ham calls back, exultant.

"We did it, W. A.," he crows, "Simon and his gang are backing you. Because you threatened them pretty good, I wouldn't expect them to be enthusiastic, at least not at first. But, they'll make some calls for you to their local delegations."

Bull smiles into the phone. "So, what do you think Ball and Company will want if we ask them to get behind us whole-hog, Ham? I won't accept half measures out of that bunch. They need to get out to the lobbyists and interest groups and work their contacts in the Secretary's office."

Ham pauses before replying, "I'm not sure, W. A., but I'll start sounding them out, starting with George Simmons in Phoenix. I've got plenty of evidence that he's steering government contracts to friends. A few hints in that direction and he may give us their whole game plan. And really, now that they've come around, it should be easy to get him to line up solidly with us. But, I think we need to let all of them lick their wounds for a day or so, or they may start to crawfish on us."

Bull grimaces a little at the idea of blackmailing Simmons with rumors about a contracting scandal. It was one thing to realistically threaten to move people around and give them crappy assignments. It was quite another thing all together to use rumors to bring investigators down on someone and wreck their professional lives.

In Bull's view, if you threaten people's comfort, they became compliant. Blackmail them professionally and you make them dangerous, snaky.

Yes, Bull preferred a direct approach, but he also knows Ham will initially go easy in pressuring Simmons. So, he says, "Okay, Ham, do what you must. But try not to have George feel he's really being blackmailed. If he does feel forced, he's the kind of subtle and stubborn bastard that'll make us pay later, big time."

He continues, "Let me know as soon as you hear anything. And, start working the Hill staffers to let them know that Ball and his bunch have come on board. I assume its okay with Ball if we start sharing, right?"

Ham agrees that they can go ahead. He asks that Bull get back to him after his early evening talk with Pizzaro.

After he hangs up, Bull calls Marj Carroll and makes a date for around nine that night at her place in Crystal City. She sounds pleased, saying "Sure, W. A., for you, I'll have my night light on and my naughty nighty off!"

Bull laughs, "And I'll have your ankles around my neck five minutes after I get there, darlin'!"

Marj gurgles her smoke-throaty laugh, "All right, cowboy, I'll be ready. Wear your boots and spurs."

They hang up.

Bull turns back into the Senate office buildings to buttonhole a few of his California contacts. He wants to share the news about Ball and company coming on board.

Chapter 16

A Dinner to Remember

Bull arrives a little early at Union Station. He takes a few turns around the building and up-scale shops before heading towards Carbone's. He's impressed with the goods in the shops although he'd never part with his hard-earned cash for the stuff they offered.

Hell, they have hundred-dollar silk ties and thirty-dollar socks in those places.

What are those city-slickers thinking?

Bull picks out his work clothes at Sears or Penney's, at a quarter of these DC prices. Just as nice. Wal-Mart or the ranchers' co-op do well for the rest of his wardrobe.

"City!" he snorts to himself, turning away from the bright colors and lights.

Pizzaro and he are dining early by DC standards, so there are plenty of tables sitting empty. Bull gets a nice one well out in the atrium.

The space is so large it actually feels like eating outdoors. Every time one of the big outer doors opens, or trains come and go from the working train area, drafts and breezes flirt with the table cloths.

At six sharp, Bull orders a beer for himself and a double vodka Gibson for Angie.

Pizzaro arrives a few minutes after her frosty Gibson and Bull's beer have been dropped on the table by a waitress in a ruffled mini-dress and fish-net stockings.

Soon after the waitress stalks away with a fifty-cent tip, a young waiter approaches their table. He snaps open Carbone's menus and hands first one to Pizzaro and then another to Bull.

Bull notices every item on the menu is individually priced, including salads and mashed potatoes. God Almighty, how those numbers would add up!

Bull muses again that DC is a different world. Institutions ape the powerful. So, like Congress, Carbone's uses a complicated budget process to trick you into deficit spending.

What would be next in DC, newsboys charging by the page, hookers by the pump and wiggle?

The faux-obsequious waiter announces the specials, portions of his words lost in the Station's susurrations.

He departs to let them study.

After a minute or so, Bull leans across the table and asks, "So, what are you thinking of having, Angie?"

Pizzaro lowers her menu to peer at him over her half-glasses and takes a deep draw on her Gibson, "W. A., I really haven't the foggiest idea. What would you suggest?"

Pleased that a woman of her sophistication would ask his opinion about dinner, he replies a little gruffly, "Well, Angie, I hear the seafood is pretty good. The waiter mentioned the sole in white sauce and I bet that's done well at Carbone's."

Angie nods her head, "I can see you are a man of taste W. A. That sole sounds good. If you know what you want, why don't you order for both of us."

A little flush comes to his cheeks at this deference. Bull nods to signal he'll be glad to order for both.

When the waiter returns, Bull feels a little adrift in the fancy menu, trying to perform in front of a beautiful woman who knew her way around. Bull asks himself, "What have I got myself into here? What the hell do I know about whether soup comes before salad or what side dishes go with which entrees? Christ on a crutch!"

Uneasy and embarrassed, Bull orders with fumbling condescension, patronizing the waiter and stumbling over dishes and the order of service.

But with a little deferential assistance from the young man, Bull finally orders soups and salads, beef for him and sole for her, sides to match, and wines for each course. The waiter smiles and bows slightly to the flustered Bull. Then he moves away quickly to get his order in before the increasing crowd at Carbone's slows down his service.

The waiter smells a big tip. He doesn't yet know about tightfisted Forest Service leadership. He'll soon learn.

Bull watches the waiter smoothly working through the tables like an All-American running back headed for a touchdown. The man's movements seem remarkably energetic for an easterner. What's his hurry?

Bull turns back to Angie, "That double Gibson's a lot of drink for a little lady. How is it?"

She raises her glass to him, "Perfect, W. A. Would you like to try a sip?"

He shakes his head, "I'm not much of a hard liquor guy, Angie. Plus, I want to keep a clear head while I hear your idea from earlier today."

She grins impishly at him, "So, W. A., what's it gonna be? If my idea pleases you, will you buy my dinner?"

He grins back at her and replies teasingly, "Shoot, Angie, I'll need to hear it first. But if it's a great idea, I'll not only buy your dinner, I'll marry you."

She laughs, reaches across the table, and lightly slaps his forearm, "No need to give me the chills, W. A., you can have what I've got with less effort than marriage."

W. A. immediately wonders if she's flirting with him. Ridiculous. She's just heightening the suspense.

Pizzaro considers him through narrowed eyes, "So, here's my idea. It's a simple one. You take the position of Chief and I become your Associate Chief, your second banana."

She sits back and lets the idea sink in. Surprised, Bull drops his eyes to study the plate and silverware in front of him.

Bull's mind races. Of course, once stated, Angie's proposal makes perfect sense. No one put the idea forward before because of the apparent animosity between them. Bull's trash talk about Pizzaro alone would have been enough to keep Ham from mentioning it.

But the two of them would be a smart fit. Together, they could get almost anything done and done well.

But, wait, alarms sound in his head. Is she trying to con him into something? Why hadn't she offered this idea through some go-betweens instead of risking everything by talking directly to him?

She must know he could use this offer against her. What would she want for this concession?

He looks up and sees the waiter moving swiftly towards them with their soup. He holds off answering Angie while the soup is served, croutons applied, and the first few spoonfuls blown on and mouthed.

Finally a slightly impatient Angie asks him, "Well, W. A., did I blow out all your circuits? Is my idea worth a free dinner or not?"

Bull looks at her solemnly for a moment and then grins, "Well, it might be worth going Dutch, I guess."

She laughs and unexpectedly flicks a crouton at him, hitting him on his tie.

"Ouch," he groans, "I'm shot. Gunned down by a tiny piece of toast."

She laughs again, "You better take me seriously, W. A. or I'll beat you to death with this bread stick."

To prove her point, she smacks the back of his hand with the roll. Then, winking at him, she slides the hard bread into her mouth and bites the end off it.

Again, W. A. wonders if she's flirting with him but nothing else in her demeanor suggests that. She simply seems to be having fun, some of it at his expense.

He scowls at her with mock severity, "Okay, Angie, I'll tell you what I think about your idea."

Her face drops. She looks a little scared.

Then he smiles, "First, I think it's a great idea. I'm surprised no one tried to engineer it before now. Second, speaking honestly about my concerns, I'm not sure of your motives in offering this up. I think you could be first banana of the Forest Service yourself...leave me behind with the rest of the fruits. You've got the contacts and credentials. Why do this?"

He looks at her, the question clear in his eyes.

Angie reaches across and touches his bread-smacked hand for emphasis. "W. A., you have to believe me when I say this. Once I heard you wanted the job, I immediately thought that you were the natural fit for Chief. You have the trust of the field staff. They barely know me. You have worked all over the agency. Your roots go back to the beginning. I have no such track record or pedigree."

"So, after I heard you were making a run for Chief, I took a look in the mirror and said to myself, 'Drop the idea of becoming Chief, Angie. Figure out what's really best for you.' So, I did."

"I think I would be a perfect Associate Chief for you. I can bring the academics and the media into the fold. I can get the women to support us. Let's just figure out how to best make that happen."

She smiles warmly at him, squeezes his hand, and lets go.

He fiddles with his spoon as if weighing it and her statement. "Okay, what you say makes sense to me, Angie. I think it will make sense to other people, too. But, what will you want if you give up trying for Chief and come in as Associate? You must want something."

"Well, now that you mention it," she replies, deadpan, "I'd like to have a national forest named after me."

Taken aback, Bull's mind recoils. Was she serious? Could she be that flaky? Only Congress could name or rename a national forest.

He has no idea about the amount of work it would take to get one of them renamed after Pizzaro. Bull peers at her and sees a gleam in her eyes. Laugh lines build around her mouth and eyes.

The joke's on him! Bull gives a great guffaw so startling to the other diners near them that one slops wine over his companion.

Bull bellows above the fuss, "You had me going good there, Angie, well done!" He slaps his hand down on the table, jiggling the silverware and glasses, and roars again, "Damn straight. I was trying to figure out how we'd get Congress to rename the Gifford Pinchot National Forest to the Angie Pizzaro National Monument. Maybe they could carve your head into Mount Saint Helens like the presidents' faces on Mount Rushmore. Serve you right to carve your face into a volcano for blowing such hot air."

They both laugh again and sit back to receive the salads just arriving in the hands of the swift-footed waiter. The waiter also delivers their second bottle of wine, a mellow Chardonnay, to go with the Carbone's Cobb dinner salad.

Bull realizes he is not aware of having drunk the first bottle. Looking back, he figures Angie and he had poured for each other, each receiving about the same amounts.

Where did the little woman put all that alcohol? Does she have a hollow leg she's pouring all the booze into? She's matching him glass for glass of wine after starting with a double Gibson with far more punch than his single beer. He begins to think that if they continue drinking at this rate, she might get pretty sloshed by the time dinner is over.

Bull begins to wonder if, with a head full of liquor and wine, she'd be open to a roll in the hay later. He would definitely make excuses to Marj Carroll if he got a chance with Angie.

But, although he's feeling the effects of the beer and wine, she doesn't appear to be affected at all! Maybe it'll hit her all of a sudden. He'll have to wait and see.

About fifteen minutes later, the waiter serves the main course along with another bottle of wine.

Bull gets Angie to tell some stories about her field work with Discovery, Animal Planet, and NatGeo channels. At first reluctant, she talks about the hard work of wildlife and ecology programming--camera crews and electronics getting in the way or trying to shoot according to some producer's sense of schedule and nature not cooperating.

"The film crews do everything they can to stay out of the way. But they do have to get close enough to get the story on tape. So, the smaller the critter, even with a big lens, the closer they get. And, many of the small critters are really dangerous and don't like to be crowded."

She frowns a little, "I almost got nailed by a Fer de Lance in

Belize during a night taping two years ago because the cameraman kept repositioning himself to get a better shot."

"We were taping using low-light video equipment. I couldn't see too well. I could see the snake on a broad leaf but it's hard to judge distances close up with so little light. So, I got too close to the snake. The cameraman repositioned and tripped, falling to his knees in the direction of the snake. He was behind a small plastic protective shield. I was out in the open, there to handle the snake and describe it for the audience."

She smiles grimly, "I had one of those snake-capture wands in my hand, that thing with the fork at the end and the little retractable loop to put around the snake. I couldn't use the fork to pin the snake because it was on a leaf. When I got closer, I meant to put the loop around the snake's neck. I had almost made it when that cameraman tripped."

Angie shakes her head for emphasis, a look of fear remembered on her slim face, "The cameraman fell towards the snake and the snake went for my warm body." Her voice shudders a little.

She continues, "Fortunately, when the Fer de Lance struck, its head bounced off the wand. Its fangs hit my sleeve rather than my forearm."

She illustrates with her fingers on the sleeve of her blouse. "It missed nailing me by maybe an inch—big snake for a Fer de Lance, too"

Remembering her panic in the damp night, she shudders again, "I jumped back and fell down, yelling. The snake could have struck me again, maybe killing me or sending me to the hospital for a month. But the poor critter let go of my beautifully tailored Abercrombie and Fitch safari shirt and zipped into the swamp out of sight. Thank God!"

Angie laughs a little ironically, "The producer wanted me to find another snake and try it again, the idiot. I swear I walked on water across that swamp to dry ground and went right back to the hotel, the producer cussing me all the way. I had nightmares for a week—of the producer, not the snake."

She laughs again, shakes her head, and vows, hand up, "No more night-filming deadly snakes for me except maybe at a zoo where the critters are all behind bars or under glass."

Her eyes flash anger, "And, I'll never work with that idiot producer again. I sent him a real-looking rubber snake in a box about a month later. I heard he almost had a heart attack when he opened it. Okay by me if he had!'"

Bull smiles at her admiringly. He says, "Angie, that's scary stuff. To think we could have lost you forever that night. What a terrible thing that would have been! Then I would never have had the best Associate Chief ever."

She grins back at him over her sole. "So, we're agreed then? I'll be your Associate if the Secretary agrees?" she asks.

"Sure works for me," says Bull. "First off, I have some regional foresters I want you to use that magic snake wand on."

They both laugh and Bull goes on, "But you still haven't answered my question about what you might want to work on as Associate. I'm sure you have some direction you'd like to go, some passion that drives you."

Bull knows that if Pizzaro declares her true interest, he will be able to use it to control her down the road. An old Green Creed insight shared forever among Legacies states, "Find out what someone wants. Then, make them pay a high price to get it or, if they won't pay, make sure they never get it."

Bull had used this knowledge many times to force people to support him or do his dirty work. In a few cases, it'd brought women he desired to his bed.

No fool, Pizzaro knows she shouldn't tip her hand. So, she replies, "Well, W. A., I have several ideas but what's really important to me is that they mesh well with what you want to accomplish. We probably don't have time tonight to get them all talked through. Maybe we could teleconference sometime in the next few days and get some things thrashed out."

Bull nods and lies, "Well, I'm free tonight and tomorrow night, then booked the rest of the week. In addition to what you want to do as Associate, I could listen to your stories all night about snakes and polar bears and such."

He pauses and smiles inquiringly at her, trying to look innocent, "When we're done with dinner, would you like to go back to my place and talk more? I have a suite at the Alexandria Ritz-Carlton with a nice view of DC. We could sit and sip with our feet up, admire the view, and set some plans together."

Pizzaro smiles back and shakes her head. "That sounds great, W. A. but I have people to meet this evening. In fact, I'm almost late now and have to go soon."

She smiles apologetically, "But, how about dinner and drinks tomorrow night, then get together afterwards? I have tomorrow night open. What do you think?"

A little disappointed that she isn't going to fall into his bed tonight, Bull pretends to think for a moment. Looking for an edge, he replies, "Okay, but I really want to talk this Associate focus business all the way through, so plan on a late evening."

She nods and Bull continues, "I figure we ought to start with drinks and dinner at the Monocle. We can invite some of the Hill staffers to belly up to the bar with us and quietly talk to them about our agreement."

The Monocle is a favorite watering hole near the Senate office buildings. The place and the land under it had been purchased many years before to make way for vitally needed Senate parking. But the Monocle's clientele was so influential and their thirsts so great, the building had never been razed. Staffers still watered there day and night.

Pizzaro had never been there. However, she enthusiastically approves Bull's plan, saying, "Perfect, W. A. Just the right visibility. We can't be too public or the Secretary's people may balk but we also need to get the staffers solidly behind us. Buying them drinks will be good business." She laughs delightedly.

"But now I have to go," she smiles, "See you tomorrow at the Monocle. What time, say an early start at 5? If that's okay, I'll be glad to help with arrangements."

Bull rises from his seat. He takes her hand, saying, "Okay, please make the reservations for tomorrow at 5. I'll leave the arrangements up to you."

He goes on mock roguishly, "But, remember Angie, you're spending the rest of tomorrow night with me."

She dimples up at him. Freeing her hand, she lightly slaps his arm, "Why, W. A., I never said any such thing. All I've agreed to is drinks, dinner, and a good discussion. As far as anything else is concerned, we'll see what tomorrow night brings."

Turning, she works her way through the other tables and diners. She looks back and waves to Bull and then heads out the big doors of Union Station, angling towards the taxi stand.

Bull waits until Angie disappears and pays the $200 bill. He tips the hovering waiter five dollars.

Oblivious to the waiter's laser-like glare, Bull cruises out of the building by the main entrance. He walks to the cab stand, admiring the lights on the Capitol Building a few blocks away. From this perspective, the Capitol stands braced about by office buildings and statuary, boxy old on the bottom and round-topped, a squat antique in a modern world, suffused with history and glossed with power.

Letting go of the image, Bull shakes his head and jumps into his waiting cab, telling the cabbie, "Crystal City, Building Four."

106

Marj meets him at the door with her nighty off as promised, breasts, belly, and pubic patch bold in the bright hallway light.

Bull laughs, kisses her, and steps into her apartment. The door closes on its spring.

Bull's arms snake around her. His hands grab up under her bottom. He lifts her hefty weight up until her face comes level with his.

Marj starts to speak but Bull simply kisses her again. He drops her feet back on the floor.

Mouth busy on hers, he kicks off his shoes. He loosens his belt and lets his pants fall.

She giggles against his lips as he walks her over to the couch, bends her face down over the couch's back, and enters her with a groan of relief.

"I thought you said my ankles were going to be up around your ears, W. A.," she laughs, her joyful, aroused voice muffled by cushions.

He replies, "Later, you horny 'lil heifer, you."

"Moo," says Marj

Chapter 17

A Night to Regret

Bull wakes with a foul taste in his mouth and mood to match. Marj and he had screwed until midnight and then settled into deep sleep.

Marj is gone. She works as the executive assistant to one of the Forest Service Deputy Chiefs. She has to get up at 6 am to make it into the Jamie Witten Building by 8, riding the tide of bureaucrats that rises each morning and falls each night, DC's daily flesh tsunami.

Under the guise of a fictional marriage to a rural-living husband, Marj had birthed three children. They were actually planted in her by a former Deputy Chief whose wealth came from renting out his rich, inherited Wisconsin farms. Her nearly grown kids live with her mother in western Maryland, well supported financially by the now-retired Deputy and Marj's federal salary and benefits.

Bull had never met the children but knew her former plowboy quite well.

Now Bull stretches out in her bed, alone except for a sweet note Marj left on her pillow. Bull glances at it.

Her note strikes him as stupidly insipid. He mainly thinks of her as a farm animal useful for breeding or a crow that squawks gossip into his ear.

Once out of bed, Bull finds Marj had perked coffee and set out breakfast makings for him. Bull has some fruit and cereal with his coffee, wondering if Marj really thought their relationship would ever lead to something permanent. She hinted as much to him several times, including last night.

Bull mutters into his juice glass, "I'd sooner marry a monkey than a bred-out flunkey." He laughs at his poetry.

Bull hurries into his clothes. Outside, he takes a cab back to the nearby Ritz-Carlton to clean up and change. He has to meet the House staffers and make numerous connections today with lobbyists and contacts at the Secretary's Office.

Ham has the lead on many of Bull's appointments, so Ham is first on his call list. Bull also needs to coordinate his Monocle-invitation calls to Hill staffers with Angie. Bull's day will be busy.

Things are definitely looking up.

Bull steps into the Monocle at 5.

The large dining room with its shabby but tasteful cream-and-black décor is already softly and warmly lit for the evening. Some of the staffers are already here, including Mike Reinard and others who had interrogated Bull the day before.

Bull greets them all with bullshit and backslaps. He calls to the bartender for a round of drinks for everyone.

Angie had arranged for the Monocle's small, private dining room to be used for their impromptu reception. With the air of a drum major leading a ravenous brass band, Bull leads the early drinkers into the room and its table of hors d'ourves.

His feet falter at the doorway when he sees the elaborate platters of meats, cheeses, vegetables, and smoked salmon on the sideboard. What could Angie have been thinking? He would rather give these arrogant assholes spam and crackers than salmon and pumpernickel squares.

Bull can hear faint screams from his wallet as the poorly paid younger staffers fall on the food like wolverines on a deer carcass. Even worse, out of force of habit the senior staffers join the gobbling horde.

As Bull watches palely, Mike Reinard serves himself a huge chunk of smoked salmon. He smiles at Bull appreciatively across the crowd struggling to fill plates and simultaneously hold drinks upright, elbows and feet jostling.

Bull cusses under his breath but then decides if Angie and he can buy favor with the staffers tonight, it will have been a cheap investment. In a moment of insight, he realizes again that Angie knows the Washington scene and this crowd far better than he does. He can rely on her judgment in these things.

Still, he looks on, bemused and slightly pained, as Monocle waiters begin to replace savaged platters with new ones. This reception is not something Bull can put on his government expense account.

His wallet whimpers plaintively.

Cost aside, the idea of Angie as his Associate looks better and better.

He glances at his watch. 5:30. Where's Angie?

Bull is anxious that she arrive so that they can test of the waters with the staffers.

After ten more minutes, an even more anxious Bull stops wondering about her whereabouts. He begins to have some doubts about her intentions.

110

Had Angie set him up, he wondered?

Is she going to leave him high and dry here, stuck with the check for a bunch of free-drinking, salmon and summer-sausage-sucking Hill staffers?

His blood pressure begins to rise.

And then at 5:45 Angie stands in the door, looking lovely.

Glancing around the room until she sees Bull then comes right over. "Sorry, W. A." she says in a low voice, "Traffic was impossible and I got a late start."

"You could have called to let me know, Angie. I was beginning to wonder if you were planning to come," he replies tightly, showing a little of the spite and irritation he had been feeling.

Angie grips his forearm, "W. A., we have a deal and I won't break it. You can count on me."

She looks up into his eyes, "I'm looking forward to our time together later. I've made some plans for us after this breaks up at 8 or so. I hope you'll go along with them. I guess we can do something else, too. But, for now, let's get to work on pirating this merry band of pillagers."

Bull wonders briefly about Angie's later "plans" for them.

But he knows she's right about the need to work this crowd quickly. Some of the faster-eating gluttons are showing signs of leaving. A few well-fed, wine-bright faces are turning towards the door.

Angie and he move around the room, buttonholing key staffers and forming small discussion groups.

Angie and Bull had agreed to broach the subject of their partnership in theoretical terms, as if they are testing the waters with a concept neither one is completely sure about. Fanning out, they get their conversational balls rolling.

Ever curious and ambitious, the departing staffers turn back and slip into the groups.

Bull finds total support among his backers. He also encounters a few grudging smiles of concession from people like Reinard--people who have doubts about Bull or want more control over Bull's future choices.

But these folks now quickly realize that events have moved beyond their ability to manipulate. It's clear to them that a deal's been struck between Angie and Bull, a deal that would be almost impossible to deflect or derail.

Drawing Bull aside, Reinard quietly congratulates him, "Welcome to Washington, Chief."

Then, smiling wickedly, he murmurs, "Remember our previous discussion. Yes?"

Bull nods, also thinking back to the silent compact they had made about closeted skeletons. He answers, "I do."

With a nod to each other, they drift apart.

Angie encounters a different reception.

Many of her supporters sense an important feminist victory slipping away. So, they initially resist. But Angie convinces them that her reasoning about experience and field support is sound.

She also tells them with a wink, "So, who do you think will be in line for the Chief's job in a few years, when W. A. moves on? With your help, I will have the inside track and the track record to back it up. We'll all get what we want then."

After a few final feminist protests rise like bubbles and burst above the hubbub in the room, Angie's supporters embrace her vision.

But one supporter, after an angry glance in Bull's direction, says bitterly, "We're still waiting for the day when a woman sits *behind* the Pinchot Desk and runs the Forest Service, rather than *lying on top of it* being screwed by some male in a cheap suit."

At 8, the reception at the Monocle ends, a resounding success. Bull only chokes once at paying the nearly $800 bill.

He remembers that Angie and he are going Dutch on this one and the thought soothes his shy, wizened wallet.

As the party ends, Bull and Angie agree that they need some air to compare impressions and conclusions. They walk out of the Monocle and stroll down Constitution Avenue to the Mall, their path bounded in by silent office buildings, museums, and monuments.

`Walking alone along the Mall's crunchy gravel walkways, Angie speaks with a nervous note in her voice, "W. A., I'm still a little rattled. At first, I didn't think some of them would come around. Matty Jackson was especially tough because she felt like I had the appointment sewed up. I think she had been listening to Simon Ball—he's close to Matty's boss, Senator Counts."

Bull wonders briefly if Ball had truly come into the fold. But then he realizes that any conversations between Matty Jackson and Ball would likely have happened many days ago, before Ball folded and before Angie and he had put their agreement together. "No, we're probably okay there, Angie," he replies,

He asks, "So, you think you won them over?"

"Yes," she answers, "They're all on board, at least for now."

Concerned, Bull asks, "Do you think there's any chance of them backing out?"

Angie replies with a twinkle, "No, with a few days to get accustomed to the idea, they'll accept it as a done deal and move on to fry bigger fish. That is as long as no one tries to clothesline us with rumors or bring up some scandal from our pasts."

Bull smiles at her, eyebrows raised, "You have scandals in your past Angie? My goodness, how could this be?"

They both laugh, Bull a little tightly, thinking of the many skeletons buried in his life's graveyard.

Chatting, they firm up further contact plans. They stroll in the direction of the Lincoln Memorial, lit for the night, jewel-bright off in the distance.

Bull asks, "Where should we go next, Angie? You said earlier that you had some plans. And I'm beginning to think it's time for us to sit down, relax, and discuss what you hope to accomplish as Associate Chief."

Angie's smile brightens at his question but then takes on a slightly anxious expression. "I'm not sure if you are ready for this, W. A.."

She looks up into his eyes, "But I was hoping you'd agree to get together privately. I'm just concerned about being seen together in public before we have our appointments sewed up. So, I hope you don't mind, but I reserved another suite at the Ritz-Carlton under your name where I thought we could go and huddle for a while."

Her face becomes more anxious. She frowns a little, "I hope I didn't overreach. I can easily call and cancel the reservation."

He looks at her for a moment, wondering if this offer is somehow a set up. Is she trying to get something on him? To gain some sort of concession from him to do something he wouldn't support? Is she setting him up for a sexual harassment complaint?

But nothing really seems off kilter. Bull figures there's only one way to find out what Pizzaro's up to. So he nods, "Sounds great to me, Angie. But, why did you get the second suite at the Ritz?"

Angie replies, "Well, going forward, both of us have our reputations to protect, particularly now that word of our agreement will start to spread. I thought we could use some privacy but neither one of us should be seen walking to the room of the other—rooms that people who know us may stop by. So, if you'll go get the new suite at the Ritz, give me a call to let me know when you're there, and I'll come and join you from the lobby."

Once again, Bull appreciates her insight and caution about appearances in DC. Angie was going to be a great help to him. She's clearly on his team.

"Okay," he answers, "Let's grab separate cabs. I'll see you there."

They walk northwest across the Mall to the cab stand at the Marriott. Timing their departures so their arrivals would be twenty minutes or so apart, they take separate cabs across to northern Virginia and the Ritz-Carlton.

Jumping out of his cab, Bull walks up to the front desk. He tells the service associate that he's renting another suite for the evening in order to hold a business meeting. He mentions that his secretary had made the reservation earlier.

The bored clerk makes no response. He completes the paperwork in a perfunctory manner.

Bull makes sure the new room is several floors from his first one. He uses his personal credit card to pay for it rather than his government-issued one.

If the yawning clerk thinks there's anything peculiar about the transaction, he says nothing to Bull. He limply hands Bull two electronic keys for the door and a small, metal one for the mini-bar.

Bull walks casually to the elevators.

———————————————————— // ————————————————————

Bull peers around the vacant suite as he enters, wondering again if Angie would show up.

The room is identical to his other suite right down to the mahogany trim and grey-green walls. As he had before, he snorts at the telephone and bidet in the bathroom.

What a weird place DC is, a place where you can make a phone call while washing your balls in half a toilet.

He pulls his cell phone out of his pocket and calls Angie's number. She answers instantly.

In a warm, merry tone, she asks, "This is Angie in room service. How may I help you?"

Bull laughs, "I'm opening the mini-bar in Room 1114. I need someone to serve as sommelier." He ventures the French term carefully, having just heard it pronounced correctly at Carbone's the night before.

Angie laughs in reply, "I'll send someone right up to help you, sir." She hangs up.

He has removed his suit coat and kneels looking at the contents of the mini-bar when Angie knocks at the door. Angie stands outside, grinning, a bottle filled with an intense green liquid lifted up in her left hand. A soft-sided briefcase hangs over her shoulder.

Lifting the bottle high, she marches in like a drum major, right arm pumping the bottle up and down.

"What's that you're so proud of, Angie?" Bull asks.

She replies, "Well, W. A. it's a special treat I like to have for special occasions. Its called 'Chartreuse Verte' and it's a liqueur made by French monks using a secret herbal recipe. I got some as a gift when I left the university years ago and I've loved it ever since."

She also shows him that in her other hand she holds two small glasses shaped like tiny beer pilsners, engraved with roses. She holds them up to him now and instructs, "You sip the Chartreuse out of these."

She waggles an index finger at him. "No glugging it down, no matter how good it tastes," she warns.

He smiles and walks with her over to the couch and chairs by the big picture window. They take in a great view of downtown DC, the street and building lights patterned and steady—their orderliness challenged by a flow of lights from passing traffic. Occasionally, fast-moving red and blue emergency strobes punctuate the moving white ribbon.

Angie hands the bottle to Bull. He breaks its seal with his pocket knife and twists the top off with a flourish.

She laughs and holds out the two glasses, nodding as he fills them. "Be careful, W. A.," she directs, "We don't want to waste any. It's a lot more expensive than when I left graduate school."

Because he has come to trust her good sense and taste, Bull doesn't ask how much the bottle had cost her. He guesses plenty. Feeling more relaxed, he appreciates how she's trying to put him at ease.

Bull takes a sip of the liqueur. It's like nothing he's ever tasted before, a little sweet and subtly flavorful.

He drains his tiny glass, fills it again, then takes another short, smooth pull.

Angie smiles at him with delight. "You like it, then?" she asks.

He feels the liqueur burn down his belly where it builds a certain warmth. "Very much," he answers, "This beats my regular, 'Ol Forester

Stump Blower,' any day."

For a time, they sit and pour Chartreuse for each other, talking about careers and family. They cover people they know in the Forest Service and other natural resource agencies. They find that they have many people in common and gossip about them quite openly.

Bull takes the opportunity to cuss Simon Ball, calling him a "prick and a bastard."

Angie agrees, saying, "I wouldn't trust the guy as far as I could swing a hippy by his toke." They laugh at her play on words.

After a few more minutes and feeling warmly relaxed, Bull excuses himself to go to the bathroom. He rises slowly to his feet.

He can feel the effects of the liqueur. Picking up the bottle, he eyes it, now half full. Squinting, he asks Angie, "What proof is that stuff, girl?"

She peers at the label, too, "Looks like 110 proof, W. A."

"Holy smoke," he thinks, "Fifty percent alcohol and I've been drinkin' it right down."

"Okay," he says to Angie, "I'll be right back…if I don't fall in!" He weaves his way into the bathroom.

As Bull urinates into the bidet, he recalls he still has not talked with Angie about her desires for the Associate job. He knows he has to find out that missing piece if he is going to be able to handle her down the road. He zips up and washes his hands, willing his half-drunken mind to get down to brass tacks when he joins Angie again in the living area.

But his determination disappears instantly when he walks into the room.

Angie sits perched on the couch, feet tucked under her bottom, wearing a little cat smile. She's dressed in a grey peignoir, the curves of her breasts and hips faintly showing through the translucent fabric.

Bull stops at the end of the couch, stunned. Nothing has prepared him for this.

Angie, smiles shyly up at him, slight worry lines between her eyebrows. She asks, "W. A., have I done something wrong, assumed too much?"

Bull replies, "No, no, of course not, Angie. It's just that you took me by surprise. I never thought….you and I, you know," he trails off.

"Well," she replies, blushing, "I hoped…" Then offering a silly pun to deflect her embarrassment, "I hoped we could seal our deal man to woman, 'mano a femmo.' Would that be okay with you?"

Bull gulps and, speechless, nods.

Angie continues, now more at ease, "Then drink up, W. A. We'll move into the comfort of your big king-sized bed in the next room."

She grins wickedly and throws her head back to empty her glass. Bull downs his drink wondering, as it slides down, which is hotter, the Chartreuse or the thumping lust he feels for Pizzaro.

She gives him a hand up and supports his arm as he sways a little on the way into the bedroom. She leaves him at the foot of the bed and crosses the room, turning off all but one small lamp in the corner of the room.

Returning to his side, she reaches up on tiptoes and kisses him long and passionately. Turning to the bed, she tugs the bedspread off, drops it in the corner of the room. Then she pulls the sheets down into a neat triple fold at the bottom of the mattress.

Turning to him, her small, quick hands strip him naked. She places his clothes neatly on the wing back chair in the corner. Stacking six pillows into a pile, she leads Bull to the bed. She settles him onto the pillows and mattress, his back well supported and his head at waist height.

Bull reaches for her but she takes his hand and folds it and his arm across his stomach. "No," she murmurs, bending to his ear, "Let me start, please."

She kisses him passionately on his mouth again and then reaches down to take his penis in her hand. "I've heard they call you 'Bull' sometimes, my love," she whispers, "now I see why."

Her hand moves quickly and firmly up and down. He groans and quickly stands tall and hard. She moves her mouth down to take him in, then she stops.

"Before we really get going, W. A., I probably should use the bathroom. Keep this hard for me, will you please?" She gives his penis a squeeze.

As she moves towards the bathroom, she sheds the peignoir, giving him a long look at her shapely bottom and strong back.

"She is definitely a...five-alarm...chili pepper," Bull thinks drunkenly to himself.

Angie reaches the bathroom door. She turns to show him her small breasts. She cups them in her hands and gives a little wiggle and dance, raising a delighted snort from Bull. She disappears inside.

Bull's head is starting to spin. He knows that he had quite a bit of the liqueur but figures his rampant passion for Angie will help burn off some of the effects.

He shakes his head. It spins even more.

He clings to consciousness but dark clouds are invading the edges of his vision. Desperately, as he waits for Angie's return, he holds on to tonight's lustful promise. But fulfillment seems to be slipping away.

Bull's eyes close with regret his last feeling. He drops into darkness.

It seems only moments later when he wakes briefly. His mind is hazy.

Angie's mouth burns hot on his penis, a perfect blend of motion and suction. He can barely see her in the dimly lit room but he knows her small head, dark, close-cropped hair, and slender-strong shoulders.

The exquisite pleasure of her mouth stops just before his orgasm and he grumbles his animal displeasure, not able to express himself in words.

Angie quickly pulls the pillows out from under his head and shoulders, leaving one under the small of his back. He dozes a little through this change then rouses a little when she mounts him, sliding his penis fully into her.

She sighs her contentment and begins riding him with her back to his face.

He watches from the edge of sleep. She moves her trim bottom smoothly up and down, occasionally bending towards his feet to change his penetration angle and bring them both extra pleasure.

For a time, Bull struggles groggily, senses trapped by intoxication. What's wrong with him, he wonders? He should have rallied by now.

Just as he begins to doubt that he can ever reach an orgasm in his condition, Angie bends forward and increases her tempo.

Bull groans and mumbles.

After a moment, he releases his semen into her.

Then he feels himself sliding down a long wall with no floor beneath into deep sleep.

Oblivion.

Chapter 18

A Morning for Mourning

Bull wakes up. His head pounds and his distorted thoughts come sluggishly.

Thoughts come and then, almost instantly, slip away.

He can't keep himself awake.

He dozes for several minutes and then rouses. Then he repeats this pattern several more times.

"Damn that woman and her Chartreuse," he grumbles to himself as he finally fights back to consciousness.

He sees his suitcase in the corner and glimpses his shirts and pants in the closet.

Now that's a surprise. They had been in a different suite but somehow she had gotten him back to his own room to sleep off the booze and sex.

He feels better towards her with that thought. So quick to keep him free of scandal. He warms a little at the fleeting thought of seeing her again.

Slowly feeling a little less dim, Bull takes a quick, startled glance at the clock: 8:30 am.

He has no idea how late Angie and he had gone the night before. He doesn't have appointments until 10 this morning, so everything's okay from a schedule standpoint.

He sees a note on the bed stand next to him near the clock. It simply states, "Call me, please. Angie" and gives a number.

His lust for her begins to build a little again. He sags back on his pillow.

Now his head is clearing rapidly. Bull realizes he desperately needs a shower. He smells strongly of lubricant, sex, and sweat.

"Damn, that girl screwed my lights out…I bet I stretched her snapper for her, too."

Maybe he'd wait to call her. Maybe he wouldn't call her at all. Let her call him. She could beg for more Bull cock he thinks with smug, male satisfaction!

Remembering the hour and his appointments, Bull climbs out of bed and walks unsteadily into the bath for his shower. He promises himself strong coffee when he's done cleaning up.

He inhales the steam and luxuriates in the soap and shampoo.

His hangover disappears with unusual speed but most memories of the night before elude him. Tricky booze.

Stepping out of the shower, he shaves and brushes his teeth, purging the imagined taste of Angie's body from his mouth.

Out into the bedroom, Bull hears a faint noise that sounds like his television turned on low. Maybe he had left it on last night after he and Angie had gotten back to his room.

He remembers nothing of that. He hasn't a clue why he would have wanted to watch TV. At least he hadn't left it blaring, a delayed booby-trap for his usual hangover.

Dressed, Bull walks into the kitchen. He makes strong coffee, regretting that he has to use the poisonous crappy coffee grounds even good hotels like the Ritz provided.

While the coffee perks, he gets breakfast from the refrigerator. He had stocked it with fruit, yogurt, and rolls when he arrived.

Because fat Ham Hogget had been left alone and anxious in Bull's suite over the last couple of days, he had made serious dents in Bull's supplies. Fortunately, plenty remains.

Bull leans against the counter and chews a bagel while he watches the coffee drip down into the cup he had placed on the burner. When the cup fills fully, Bull slides the pot into its rightful place as he pulls the coffee cup out.

The coffee maker makes bubbling and hissing noises. The acrid stink of burnt coffee rises into Bull's nostrils.

Blowing on the hot coffee, Bull walks to the couch across from the quietly murmuring TV. He sits down and takes a tentative sip, part of the bagel in his mouth. About to swallow, he glances at the TV.

At the sight of what's playing, Bull's eyes bulge. He spews the mash in his mouth across the coffee table.

"Holy jumping Jesus," Bull yells, "What the fuck is this? My God, how the HELL did this get on cable TV?"

Although Bull doesn't see it, the unbelievable signal actually comes from a cheap DVD player sitting on top of the TV. But the source really doesn't matter.

Before his unbelieving eyes, he and Angie hump and screw.

But wait, he looks closer. That's him...but that's not Angie.

It's someone who looks like Angie.

Not a woman, no breasts....but, my God, a guy. Holy crap, a guy!

120

On the DVD, a miniature Bull lies under a miniature *guy*.

The man rises and falls on Bull's dong—a guy who looks like Angie!! Similar build. Same hair cut.

But, astride Bull's body, filmed with the lens aimed straight in his grinning face, definitely a guy! His male equipment is not only visible; the guy's also turned on, hard, enjoying it!

For twenty minutes Bull watches with fatal fascination as the DVD plays through and then repeats itself.

He turns up the sound. Then, repulsed by the groans and wet noises, mutes it.

Bull watches as the DVD starts yet again. He and the young man walk up to the door of his suite, the number clearly visible. The young man grins back at the camera as they enter.

Bull wobbles drunkenly, his arm over the guy's shoulders. Somehow, apparently reacting to a command from the camera operator, Bull manages to turn at the entrance and wave at the lens.

Inside the suite, Bull and the guy exchange a long kiss.

The young man leads him to the bedroom, strips him, and puts him on the bed. The guy drops his clothes, sucks Bull stiff, and then mounts him.

The lens captures the scandalous all.

Later scenes show Bull with his knees on the floor and his torso on the bed. The two men face the camera.

After positioning himself behind Bull, the young man humps him strongly. He moves his hips extravagantly and grimaces through an orgasm.

A scene later, Bull appears on the edge of the bed, lying on his side with his big butt to the camera. The guy seems to thrust his penis into Bull's mouth. Again, the young man shows every sign of lusty penetration and a big orgasm.

Bull has never felt more horrified and disgusted in his life. His heart sinks low, lower, lowest.

Bull watches the DVD for the third time. He realizes that, unlike the earlier shots where he'd actually been inside the young man, the camera angle makes it unsure whether the guy had actually penetrated Bull or not. A meager crumb, but a tiny amount of Bull's dignity might be preserved, at least in his own mind.

Everyone seeing this would believe what they saw, staged or not... My God, what a debacle! Low, lower, lowest.

Bull slumps down on the couch.

Now he'll have to withdraw from his run for Chief, maybe even leave the Forest Service.

There goes his plans to be famous...get rich.

Pizzaro has won.

He gets a sponge and cleans up the worst of the mess on the coffee table. Then he sits back on the couch...defeated, deflated, and depressed.

After a blank time, he rouses himself. He figures he might as well concede defeat and be done with the whole sorry mess.

Picking up the phone, he dials the number Angie left for him. The phone rings three times before someone picks it up. A man answers, "Esperanza's phone."

Simon Ball. Without speaking, Bull gently places the handset back in the cradle.

Bull settles into a funk. He misses his ten o'clock meeting with lobbyists. He misses his eleven o'clock, too. He ignores repeated calls from Ham Hogget. Bull stays slumped on the couch, coffee untouched and cold in its cup.

At noon, he's startled out of his depression by a knock on the door. Thinking that the knocker is here to clean the room, Bull opens the door only to find Esperanza Pizzaro, Simon Ball, and Mike Reinard standing in the hall.

Bull's face goes ashen. He stares at them for a long moment, considering whether to slam the door in their faces.

Then, silent and smiling grimly, he waves them in. They enter, their faces, too, are sober and grim.

As they pass, Bull exchanges hostile glances with Simon and Mike. He refuses to look at Pizzaro.

Bull returns to the couch and drops into his seat with a thump. Ball and Reinard sit across from Bull in the cushioned chairs.

Pizzaro walks to the window and stares out at the now cloudy and colorless DC skyline.

Ball outlines the situation. Bull has his copy of the gay-sex DVD. The three of them each have a copy, too. Another one will soon be in the hands of Reinard's attorney who has orders to send it to Fox News if anything ever happens to any of them.

Weakly rallying his defenses, Bull tells them he isn't interested in being Chief any longer so they can "stick their DVDs up their asses."

Ball and Reinard smile wolfishly. They tell Bull that they will use the DVD against him if he refuses to be Chief, ending his Forest Service career and heaping dishonor on his head.

They will make him and his Legacy family a laughingstock

throughout the agency's rank and file and all of DC.

He really has no choice but to take the job.

And once he's Chief, they'll use the DVD against him if he fails to follow their orders.

"Don't worry, Bull," Reinard mocks, "We'll make screwing you as painless as possible."

Reinard waits a moment and then asks, "You will do what we want when we ask, won't you?"

Bull glares at him, ready to slam his fist into Reinard's mouth.

Then seeing no way out, Bull agrees.

The straight-jacket he had imagined when he'd flown into DC a few days earlier was turning out to be far tighter. Now they also have his straightjacketed balls in a vice. They can clamp down on his balls any time they like.

He can do nothing about it. He can make no noise no matter how much it hurts.

He'll never get out of the straightjacket or the vice.

Bull turns from Mike to Simon Ball and asks, "So, what do you get out of this cesspool, you bastard?"

Simon smiles with mock innocence, "Why, W. A., you are looking at your new Deputy Chief for International Forestry. You'll recreate the position with unlimited authorized travel and no need to report back, at least not to you. You'll put me in it and keep me there until I retire."

Bull knows Ball has no interest in forest management in other countries. He barely cares about U.S. forests. Ball just likes the power and pussy that comes with position and prestige.

Then, Bull realizes that Ball has cooked up this idea so he can travel on official business and nail women all over the world. But, as Bull thinks further, he realizes letting Simon take this new assignment means that he will also be out of Bull's way...gone to other countries.

So, Bull's bottom line: meeting Ball's demand is an easy concession.

Faking resentment, Bull snarls, "Okay, Simon. You win."

After Ball's deal's struck, Reinard stands up, "Well, it's all settled then. You'll be Chief. Congratulations. We'll work out the details of our relationship as we go along. You can be sure I'll be in touch, Bull!"

Reinard draws Bull's nick name out, mockingly making the word into a low bull's bellow.

Then, nodding towards Pizzaro by the window, Reinard sneers, "I think you two love birds have some things to work out."

Laughing harshly, he leads Ball to the door. They go out without looking back.

Silence falls.

Bull sits on the couch, unmoving, staring at Pizzaro's back.

Pizzaro stands at the window looking out for several minutes. She finally turns and walks over to Bull. She sits down opposite him and looks at him, her mouth a tight line.

He still refuses to meet her eyes.

"Okay, W. A.," she says in a firm tone, "If you won't look at me, then I'll talk and you will listen."

She pauses, "I needed an edge to keep myself out of trouble with you. I knew you could dump me at any time and mess up my plans to be U.N. Secretary of the Environment some day. So, I used that 'date rape' drug on you last night. I put a small dose in that last ounce of Chartreuse you slugged down. It made you easy to work with. I'm sorry if you had a big head this morning."

As she said these words, she doesn't look sorry, just determined.

Then Pizzaro drops a bigger bomb, "I directed and taped your love match with Raoul. Don't worry; he's my black-sheep cousin and a gigolo by trade. He's not from around here. He won't talk, at least as long as I'm okay."

She looks even more seriously at Bull, "The camera tells a different story, but, even though Raoul wanted to, I wouldn't let him screw you. I figured letting him have you might send you over the edge."

When he doesn't respond, she asks him sharply, "Was I right?"

Strangely grateful for what she'd spared him, Bull only nods, still stunned at her malignant plan and appalled at how easily he had fallen into it.

Pizzaro continues, "So, that's what happened. I say that now we are on an equal footing. Do you agree?"

She waits for a response from Bull. Hearing none, she continues, "Don't worry, I'm not going to hold this over your head at every turn. I simply want you to give me the latitude to lead my part of things, free from the worry of being betrayed or overruled by you."

"Think of the DVD as an insurance policy that guarantees our relationship goes smoothly. It also means that down the road, when the three of us tell you to step down, you'll do it and support me strongly for the Chief's position."

He sits unmoving, at first unwilling to give support to her plan. Then, accepting the inevitable, Bull nods glumly.

Bull will still not meet her eyes.

Pizzaro reaches across the coffee table and grabs his arm, saying tersely, "We have a deal, right, Bull? Say it!"

He meets her eyes. At bay, he snarls, "Yes, Angie, God damn you, we have a deal."

She sits back with prim, smiling self-satisfaction.

"Great," she grins, "And I have one other thing to get straight with you."

He glares at her, waiting for the next humiliating shoe to drop on his balls.

But as he looks at her, Pizzaro's face transforms itself into a muscled mask, eyes slightly slitted, boring into his.

Transfixed by the startling change, Bull immediately thinks of a big hunting cat, a jaguar or a tiger.

Pizzaro now speaks quietly but fiercely, "I liked how you responded to me sexually last night. I liked even more what I saw through the camera. W. A., you're built like a man ought to be built, a regular bull. So, from now on, when I want your mouth on me or that bull cock of yours in me, you'll make sure I get what I want and quickly. Do you understand?"

Astounded, Bull shrugs dumbly.

She's neatly reversed the roles he had fantasized about on the flight into DC. On the plane, he had been the hunter, pursuing, ready to take her or destroy her. Now he knows that he had been the prey all along.

She'd shaken her tits at him and trapped him like a mindless, hungry bear slobbering for salmon in a culvert-trap.

He glances at Angie with new-found respect, once again unwilling to meet her eyes. But now, his reluctance stems not from resentment but from a rising tide of fear, an intense shyness in the face of her ruthlessness.

Instinctively, Bull knows that, among the three conspirators, she'd been the mastermind. She'd held the role of "high stalker" in his capture. Bull wonders if she will stop at simply dominating him to retain her independence or destroy him just because she could.

Then, he grasps at a slightly more reassuring straw. Maybe his capture is more than just an ambitious ploy to get Angie ahead. Nothing shows she's a sadist. Instead, her whole life had been about observing and collecting specimens. He isn't prey to be slaughtered when she grows tired of him. No, to her, Bull probably represents a useful animal live-caught, a valued prize bound for her personal collection, a captive in her wall-less zoo.

And in a more personal and human way, she's clearly the sort of woman who wants to dominate powerful men. She'd used the same skills on him that she had with that dangerous snake or when she'd neck-snared a plunging rhino for TV. She would relish bending him to her will far into the future.

What would Angie do next? Whatever it could be, now that he's corralled, Bull knows she'll soon set the bit in his teeth like a wrangler bridling a green gelding before breaking him to ride.

So, he's not greatly surprised when Pizzaro leans back in her chair, reaches under her short skirt, pulls black nylon panties slowly down over her thigh-high stockings, and slides them over her shoes. Throwing them into his lap, Pizzaro slips out of her chair.

She walks slowly around the coffee table until she stands directly in front of Bull. She pulls up her skirt up to her waist, sits on the edge of the table, and leans back on her elbows.

Propping her feet against the front edge of the couch, one foot on each side of him, Pizzaro opens her legs widely. Her gleaming black pubic patch and pink labia inexorably draw and hold Bull's eyes.

"On your knees in front of me. Now," she whispers hoarsely, eyes gleaming. Light from the window reflects from her grinning white teeth.

Then Pizzaro lies back, prone.

Humiliated and yet aroused, Bull hesitates and then says, "Okay, Angie."

As Bull slips to his knees in front of her, she says flatly, "No one calls me 'Angie,' you idiot. You will call me 'Esperanza' from now on."

Only a little surprised at her deception and scorn, Bull bends to his duty.

Bull puts his tongue in her, reluctantly tasting what he lusted for only a day ago.

She loops her right leg across his shoulder blades and uses her hands to pull his head more tightly into her. She begins to move with the rush of pleasure from his touch.

Now fully caught in her pink trap, he realizes that she might allow him to pleasure himself with her someday. But then, as now, her pleasure would always come first.

Silently acknowledging this, Bull works his tongue and lips. Guided by her moans and movements, he eventually helps Pizzaro to a crowing orgasm.

She releases him and pushes his head back. Her fingers work busily on her clit and she frees the last of her passion in front of his eyes.

She rests for a time, ignoring him.

Satisfied with her performance, Pizzaro stands and makes Bull hold her panties out so she can step into them.

She tells him to pull them up, saying, "You'll do this every time I ask, won't you W. A.?"

After Pizzaro leaves, Bull sits for a long time, taking stock of his situation. He would have the job he came to get, Chief of the United States Forest Service. But, of the power he'd thought would come with it, he would effectively have none.

His "victory," if you could call it that, stands hollow like one of those bronze statues you see all over DC. Pigeons shit on them. Bums piss on them. Ordinary people walk past them without the slightest glance.

Tough and heroic on the outside…empty shells within. Pizzaro and her crew have cast Bull into the hollow-hero role even before he starts work as Chief.

Over time, he might battle back against them and gather some measure of power back to himself, but that meant years of toil for little gain. They would always have the DVD. That fact would serve as the ace-high card in any political or bureaucratic poker match.

And to make matters worse, Bull'd helped them.

The Romans made sure that their victorious generals knew that "all glory is fleeting." But Bull would never even taste glory, fleeting or otherwise.

No, today's taste would be the best of what he would ever get--a taste of loss, grey-grainy, like campfire ashes, flavored by Pizzaro's tangy-sour snatch.

Bull feels tears in his eyes. He swallows a lump in his throat.

Then, suddenly sick, he runs into the bathroom and vomits.

After a time, he rinses his mouth with mouthwash.

He returns to the couch, tired and dispirited. His face sags. He lies back on the couch and rests his head. After closing his eyes, he nods off.

He sleeps for hours, as if he were dead, his body in sick sync with his ambitions.

When Bull wakes, his mind calls him to act. He has calls to make—Hogget and other supporters, for example—to let them know he will get the Chief's job.

Still, he moves slowly. He can't seem to get his hands and fingers to cooperate, to dial the phone. He feels bruised and stiff as if he's been in a bar fight—a losing fight made worse by not even landing a punch.

He decides the telephoning will have to wait, for at least a little while. He wearily raises himself from the couch and twists his neck around several times to get out the kinks.

Bull takes a quick, hot shower to help him relax further and drive off more of his lethargy. Recent days have been exhausting. As he showers, Bull realizes he's ready for some relaxation, not more work or more battles. In a couple of days, he'll go home to California and unwind, maybe hole up at home and not answer the phone.

While in the shower he also realizes that since his authority as Chief had been co-opted by Pizzaro and her crew, he will soon find himself appearing to run the Forest Service but not having to make any decisions. In most respects, he'd have no responsibilities. Those would belong to Pizzaro, Reinard, and Ball.

Bull begins to muse that being a simple figurehead, while galling to his spirit, might not necessarily be a bad thing. He would be able to leave the huge forestry problems of the nation alone from the beginning, along with DC's punishing power struggles.

While he'd show up at the office from time to time, he'd essentially be on paid vacation until he retired, drawing about $250,000 per year pay and benefits from the federal government.

He'd be forced to have fun at the taxpayers' expense, lolling about, useless as milk tits on a Black Angus steer.

He'd always liked to work, pleasured in the sense of control that work had given him. These things fed his ego and helped him realize his giant ambitions.

Yet, even as he finds being forced to do nothing irksome, Bull feels satisfaction in the idea of revenge based on being paid to do nothing at all.

Then his thoughts darken again. Bull wonders if, his ambitions foiled, he will truly be an empty statue, a hollow man. Scared by this possibility, he takes comfort in recalling some successes from his past, from back when he had heat and others felt it.

128

Bull now understands better the Green Creed adage that "the best job in the Forest Service is District Ranger." He recalls back to those days of his youth, when he drove his District employees with arrogant energy, not to improve their performance as public servants but to further his ambition, to get ahead and achieve his Legacy destiny.

It felt good...back then.

He hadn't minded putting his foot up their asses. He doesn't much regret his treatment of them now.

After all, the Green Creed said those sad bastards had been put there by the hiring system for his use, not his care.

Still, today he'd learned personally what sharp hobnails up his rectum felt like.

He yearns back to the time when he could be the "kicker" rather than the "kicked."

And to when he had bent his blue-blood wife, Rebecca, to his will.

Chapter 19

Rebecca, Long Ago

Rebecca Theophile was a graceful woman back in 1973, blond and slender, born to city life...yet somehow a lover of all things green and wild.

Why they had been attracted to each other in college, Bull never knew. They seemed polar opposites, he born to little Forest Service compounds near timber towns and she to big, wealthy suburbs of Chicago.

He was a Forest Service brat. She was a once-moneyed Brahmin.

But they had joined somehow, passion carrying them to the altar and beyond.

In her arms and presence, Bull knew love and tenderness for the first time in his life.

Their life together went well while they'd lived in the bigger mill towns, Bull at work within the timber industry. They had a little money for adventure. They roamed western America on occasional vacations, sampling white city lights and black star-painted skies.

But once Bull began his Forest Service career, things changed.

After two stints in tiny Forest Service towns, Rebecca's desire for city life and its pleasures became stronger. She didn't want to live in the city; she loved the outdoors. But, she did want some of the city amenities from time to time--shopping and the arts, an occasional nice dinner out.

And, frankly, she had been a little spoiled by her moneyed upbringing. She expected some of the finer things in life--deference to her beauty and background, little expensive gifts.

When it came to privilege, Rebecca was her own kind of Legacy... different certainly, but her pedigree defined her as strongly as Bull's did him.

But, Bull would have none of her fancy living.

He earned a lot less with the government than he had with private industry. There was no surplus for high-cost "city slickin.'" Rebecca's modest monthly trust fund check notwithstanding, money was always too short for frivolous things.

Their money conflict grew into a small, festering sore between them, sometimes more hurtful than other times. Tenderness and trust were reduced in proportion to the soreness.

After five years together, Bull received promotion to District Ranger on the Far Mountain District of the Wasatch-Cache National Forest in Utah, a place hours from even a supermarket.

Bull's advancement had been quick and a surprise to many. But, his father's influence and Bull's Legacy status propelled him ahead of many other more seasoned candidates. And, once Ranger, Bull charged along, headstrong, determined to make his time on the district a success so he could move up to Forest Supervisor as soon as his father and his Legacy friends could manage his promotion.

Within the isolated Far Mountain District compound, Rebecca tried to make things work. She joined clubs and socialized with the other women. But, unlike them, she had an advanced degree and came from money.

Through the lens of her privileged youth and education, she saw the Forest Service people as small-minded and very conservative--highly supportive of friends but cliquish and condemning of people like her.

No matter how she reached out to them in her youthful clubwomanly way, they seemed to retreat, sometimes benignly and sometimes with spite.

After a time, she gave up thoughts of being accepted and simply climbed the nearby green mountains and swam in the bright rivers. She took what nurturance she could from the land and waters.

In every corner of the vast Utah landscape, Rebecca found beauty and value, a sharp contrast to the social desert back at the compound.

Bull noticed her absences from home and avoidance of Forest Service events like the District's monthly potlucks. Bull knew that the Green Creed declared District staff a "family." Under that dogma, the family eats and socializes together regularly.

In their roles as District "Dad" and "Mom," the Ranger and his spouse were supposed to preside at the "family meal." So, Bull expected Rebecca to not only be at his side for these functions, but also to play a major role in organizing and managing them, complete to table decorations.

Bull would acidly ask the returning Rebecca where she had gone. She'd answer honestly that she didn't care to attend, incurring his wrath with her indifferent attitude.

"Damn it, Rebecca," he would say, "You're the District Ranger's wife. You have to show up for these things, be involved with the other women and their families. This is important. I can't get ahead if people see you being unsupportive. You can't wander around the countryside doing your own thing! People are already talking and it's not good."

At this, Rebecca would smile, concerned, but not knowing what to do. She thought to herself many times that the Far Mountain District "family" showed the same sort of pain and conflicts she had felt as a child-

-isolation punctuated by harsh treatment, embarrassing ridicule from her ambitious parents, experiences she'd learned to meet with a frozen smile.

Bull thought that her smile meant she was indifferent to his feelings...or worse, that his words were worthy of her contempt. He would get madder, more forceful.

Stung into action by his words, she would try again to build relationships with people at the compound. But the results were always the same. She would find herself disappointed and alone again, take out her map, put on her boots, pick up her pack and walking stick, and head for the hills. In the winter, telemark ski boots replaced the hiking ones, skis and poles replaced the walking stick.

As she wandered the hills in the spring of their second year on Far Mountain District, Rebecca saw road building in many locations. She knew the mission of the Forest Service included timber harvest and access roads had to be built. Still, she saw a lot more construction than she had at other Forest Service locations.

When she questioned Bull about the work at dinner one night, he answered proudly, pointing his thumb at his chest, "That's my leadership in action. Dad helped me get a ton of money from the Ogden Regional Office to build roads and bridges. I plan to build a road up every drainage on the Far Mountain District so that every suitable timber acre gets harvested over the next ten years."

He smiled, "Even better, I've got a handshake agreement with Green Creek Timber to get them 100 million board feet per year. If I can get the roads built over the next two seasons, they will open a new mill in town. People'll get jobs. I'll get promoted to Forest Supervisor. Not a bad deal, huh?"

Rebecca sat back in her chair, a little amazed at his words and the implications for the rivers and mountains she knew well. She frowned.

Now angry, Bull looked at her, "Well, Becka, I thought you wanted to move, get out of this awful Forest Service compound. This is our way out. If I pull this off, we'll get to move to a bigger town where a Supervisor's office is located. Isn't that what you wanted?"

She looked first at the table to gather her thoughts, and then into his eyes. "W. A.," she said, "If this is the only way, I think the cost is too high. So much logging will tear these hills apart and damage the streams."

She looked at him with compassion, "I know you want to move up. And, sure, I'd like to get out of here. But couldn't we just do that another way and leave the land mostly alone?"

Bull stared at her intently. "What are you, Becka, some kind of fuckin' environmentalist?" he roared, "Don't you get it? The Forest Service doesn't do pansy-assed environmental stuff. Around here, we push timber and cattle. On the Wasatch-Cache, you either get the timber out and the cattle on or you fail!"

He pounded his fist on the table, "And I won't fail!"

From then on, they fought regularly over possible impacts of his actions on the waters and mountains.

Gradually, Bull stopped sharing news, trying to starve out Rebecca's interest.

In turn, to get the news about what was going on, Rebecca joined Friends of the Far Mountains, a small local environmental group. Through the Friend's meetings, she began receiving highly biased interpretations of Bull's actions.

When she confronted him with these, their conflict grew. He would accuse her of bias and misinformation. She would accuse him of secret destruction of nature. Neither could convince the other that their facts or arguments should prevail.

Constantly in stalemate, their positions only got more fixed as Far Mountain District contractors built more roads. Eventually, he simply refused to speak to her at all about his actions, staring angrily at her while she confronted and accused him.

One night, Bull felt so provoked that he jumped up from the dinner table and grabbed her, tearing her blouse, fist back for a punch.

For the first time, Rebecca saw the well of violence within him and feared it. She cringed away.

Instantly apologetic, a deeply confused and disturbed Bull felt his rage vanish to be replaced by his own fear.

He could not grasp that, little by little, in fulfilling his aching desire for advancement, he had lost his wife's trust and with it their direction as a couple. And now, frustrated at levels he also could not comprehend, the violence in Bull's soul erupted towards Rebecca, a woman he once loved but now felt he barely knew.

This rage against her...well, most of all, he feared he couldn't control it.

All along, their arguments had been noisy and easily heard in the nearby houses. Tonight was no different.

Word spread around the compound that Rebecca had become "an environmentalist" and some people now refused to even speak to her.

134

Bull began to avoid her more and more, afraid of his own rage, angry at her concerns. She was left alone.

After a month or so of nearly complete isolation from Bull and his employees, Rebecca sat him down in their tiny kitchen. She told him she would be spending two weeks a month in town, working on her doctorate. She told him that he could use her interest in more education as the reason why she wasn't around the compound. She was going regardless. He really didn't need to create excuses for her choices but he could make up some if he wanted to.

Bull expressed his outrage in some careless words but Rebecca was ready for them.

She repeated her intentions more firmly, saying "I'm leaving because I want more in my life than a silent husband who resorts to violence to get his way and hard looks from everyone on the District. The land matters to me but not as much as our relationship. So, to save our marriage, I want to go and get some perspective, a fresh start, and take pressure off of you as District Ranger."

She looked at him earnestly and with care in her eyes, "Can't you see we are coming apart at the seams? I don't want that. So, as long as you stay here, I'll be back often but not to stay. When you get promoted, maybe we can be together again."

When he calmed down, she took him in her arms and then to bed. She made love to him all night.

The next morning she drove southeast to Denver University.

Her move shocked everyone, including Bull, even though she had warned and reassured him. He had thought that the security of the compound and her meager funds would keep her at Far Mountain.

But she had moved beyond the cloistered forest service life and would find ways to stretch her money with grants and work-study into a PhD.

Many locals believed she had left for good. Women who had scorned Rebecca now either pitied or blamed Bull behind his back, depending on the trajectory of any day's gossip. Still, the overwhelming consensus was that Rebecca had left for good…and good riddance to her.

True to her word though, Rebecca came back in a month and stayed for two weeks, then left again. And over the next many months, she repeated and varied this pattern in sync with her school schedule.

That she would do such a thing at first upset the district women. But after a time, they began to look forward to Rebecca's return, maybe even more than Bull did.

They loved it when Rebecca would bring the latest newspapers and magazines, tell crazy stories about town and gown life, and comment on her progress at the university.

Ironically, now that Rebecca was frequently gone, she was better liked; women who had once pushed her away or ignored her now sought her out. But, Rebecca put little energy into those relationships--ones that she had once craved and worked hard to secure.

Her relationship with Bull changed, too. Rebecca tried to build her way back to him, but their interests had diverged along two very different paths. Dismissing Rebecca's choices and Hell bent on furthering his Forest Service career, Bull focused on advancement more and more.

And, Rebecca cared less and less whether he advanced or not or, eventually, whether she would be a part of his everyday life.

Time away made her more objective about Bull, life in the Forest Service compound, and the impacts of Bull's leadership on the land.

She saw Bull treating his employees and the land in about the same way. Bull's chose to drive both people and land relentlessly and remorselessly to their limits. Their only value to him lay in their contribution to his advancement.

She began to think of the compound more as a concentration camp, a place where Bull dominated relationships with acts of censorship and control. Quite a "family" indeed.

In contrast, she found the bustling university life far homier. On campus, she entered a raging debate about environmental policies and the impacts of development. Listening to the intellectuals' debate philosophy, she silently added her personal on-the-ground experiences on Far Mountain District and the other places she had lived with Bull.

While her convictions about the importance of protecting nature increased, her understanding of how to create protection got more obscure. Rebecca found the range of choices bewildering. Her real world experiences caused her to reject many of the simple solutions advanced by intellectual proponents of development or self-appointed Luddite protectors of the environment. Active management like logging and brush clearing had its place to be sure, but so did protection and letting nature take her own course.

Oddly, in the midst of academic hash-making, she began to see Bull's actions as more moderate than she previously thought. She still thought he was going too far but she realized that he wasn't out to destroy nature. If he had been driven by a love of humanity or nature, rather than personal ambition, she might have approved even more of his actions.

136

Rebecca had begun to recognize that, in important ways, intentions were equally important, maybe more important, than actions when judging the value of a land manager's work. Intentions carried built-in limits, ethics, and values—things important to know.

But, intentions could be a whole lot harder to discern clearly than actions, particularly when managers refused to share them. So, if you wanted to care for nature, getting to know land managers and coming to understand their values might be the most important task of all.

Rebecca saw that many environmentalists did not understand this fundamental truth. Many developers did not understand it either. And developers and environmentalists alike would often not admit their own intentions.

All in all, Rebecca found the resulting confusion a poisonous brew that sickened society around her, no more clearly than back on the Far Mountain District where labels like "environmentalist" got carelessly thrown and meant loss for everyone.

Bull was oblivious to the changes in his wife's attitude or her slight softening towards him. Even when she tried to explain, he brushed her off. He had less and less time for her when she returned to the Far Mountain District.

Rebecca eventually recognized that his isolation was connected to his ambition.

If she was present, she could further his career.

If gone, she couldn't—that simple.

She had become just another resource put on the Far Mountain District for Bull's use.

To add to the stress on their relationship, he increasingly insisted that she become pregnant, an event she wanted to delay, perhaps indefinitely. Bull knew that having a child or several would further cement his Legacy status and gain support from his father's friends. The Green Creed dictated that Forest Service Legacy men were to be family men.

Bull was determined that, although Rebecca might be off on her own a great part of her time, she could at least carry his child as she roamed. In addition, Bull hoped that the demands of child rearing would finally make her come home and stay.

Because she was gone half the time, their disagreements and detachment from one another did not boil over as before, just simmered and bubbled

.

Then, one May day, close to semester's end, Rebecca returned, ready for a dose of high-mountain spring.

She dropped her stuff at the Ranger's Quarters and walked over to the rec hall to put out the magazines and newspapers she'd brought back with her. As she passed the screened windows of one of the government houses, she heard two women talking. Their voices sounded familiar, but Rebecca couldn't place them immediately.

One woman spoke clearly. "Connie," she said, "No wonder they call him 'Bull'. I thought he was going to split me in half with that dong of his. And he stayed at me all night. Look at the circles under my eyes!"

She laughed with mock regret.

Rebecca imagined a rueful head shake.

Rebecca now realized she was listening to Betty Mixx and Connie Waring, two close friends. They were two of the women who had spent some congenial times with Rebecca since she returned to the university.

Connie replied in a hushed voice, "Aren't you afraid Buster will find out, Betty? I mean that would just wreck his life and blow this little Peyton Place up."

"No, W. A. makes sure Buster is gone to the field over night before he comes visiting. And he always comes to the back door. I just leave the lights off and the door unlocked. He let's himself in. We try to keep the noise down." Betty giggled.

Rebecca wanted to keep listening but she knew that anyone could come along and catch her eavesdropping. And, really, she had heard enough.

Cold anger inside, she calmly finished her errand and then returned to the Ranger's Quarters.

She waited until Bull came home to quietly confront him about banging Betty.

Bull denied everything, saying, "That's crazy, Becka. I don't even like her, let alone want to sleep with her. I would never jeopardize my career for a quick roll in the hay with someone else's wife."

But Rebecca saw his school-boy red face and knew Bull lied. The cold spread in her chest and smothered her few remaining feelings for Bull. She said nothing in reply, prepared to drop the whole business.

In this moment, she had no frozen smile, nothing. She had become that indifferent.

But as she started to turn away, Bull roared, "Besides, if anything did happen, it would be YOUR fault. You're the one who left me for who knows who. I figure you're putting out for some college professor. Do you sleep

138

with me here and pork him there? Is your bed too cold when you don't have a man in it?"

His taunting drove her to anger. "You slimy bastard," she yelled, "You can hump the whole neighborhood for all I care. But one thing for sure, you'll never get me in your bed again."

Of course, when their fight ended, they did indeed sleep together. Still, the wide cracks in their relationship had now developed into deep fissures.

Back on campus, Rebecca was taking a seminar on ecosystem management. It'd turned out to be mainly a theory course about an infant science. The university brought in several distinguished scholars to explain the concepts and early attempts at implementing them.

One of the lecturers was Dr. Jack Ward Thomas, senior research scientist at the Starkey Experimental Forest in Oregon, an expert field biologist with world-wide experience. Dr. Thomas' lecture brought the theoretical into sync with the practical. He explained how the concepts of ecosystem management could be applied to resources at different geographic scales, a "concept in search of a context."

Close to the end of Dr. Thomas' lecture, Rebecca's eyes opened wide. Protection and active management worked together. They were not opposites; they worked together.

She got it!

Dr. Thomas offered numerous examples of how his concepts had worked when applied at local and watershed levels. Still, he warned, people were doing too little, too late. Ecosystem integrity was slipping away worldwide. The pace of loss was accelerating. People kept fighting over ideas when the health of the world was approaching the precipice of total collapse. Laws and management ideas had to change and quickly.

As she thought about these ideas, Rebecca recognized that the pace of destructive development held the edge. Ecosystem management concepts had to be put in place quickly. Once natural conditions were gone they couldn't easily be recovered, if they ever could. And, no one really looked out for natural conditions beyond national boundaries.

People who should love their planet's life were killing it, developers and environmentalists alike, wrapped in conflict, consuming and protecting Mother Earth to death. They were fighting one another when they should be helping nature to heal and evolve.

She began to get angry, very angry.

Another student in the seminar showed some of the same emotions. Although he had never spoken to her before, turning to Rebecca, he said, "Do you believe this guy, do you think he's legit?"

Rebecca looked at him and replied, "Sure seemed to click with everything I've seen. But, thinking about the implications, I'm really upset, 'outraged' might be a better word, I guess."

He answered, "Look, I'm just boiling over with ideas and feelings. Would you like to get coffee? I really want to talk to someone about this right now!"

Rebecca smiled her willingness. They gathered their books to head off to the Student Commons.

On the way, Jacob Mountainspring introduced himself, mentioning he was attending the university on a scholarship for Native American students.

Rebecca asked about his tribe. He said, "It's a little complicated. I've got a lot of white and brown faces peering out of my family tree, but I'm an enrolled member of the Shoshone." He smiled a brilliant white smile in an intelligent face, his pride in stating his connection with his people obvious.

Rebecca mentioned her background and that she was married to a Forest Service District Ranger. Their backgrounds propelled their conversation for the next hour. Rebecca shared many insights into land management from an agency perspective with Jacob. And Jacob informed her about Native American thinking and preferences.

Both of them felt a rush of feelings and thoughts. They talked and laughed as if they had known each other forever.

As hours passed, Rebecca realized that she felt attracted to Jacob's bright eyes and intellect, to his muscular shoulders, wide mouth, dark hair. A little flustered by her growing attraction for him, she checked the time with him and then ended the conversation, promising to get coffee after the next seminar lecture, two days later.

For the mildly infatuated Rebecca, the time to the next lecture passed slowly. Feelings of attraction notwithstanding, she wanted to make sure that she kept perspective on her life.

Jacob would represent a major complication to her if anything developed between them. Yet, he was so damned smart and cute.

The two days passed slowly. When she thought of him, Rebecca's pulse would jump.

After the next lecture, they walked towards the Commons, coffee the plan.

But at the big glass door, Rebecca took Jacob's hand. She led him silently away, back to her apartment. The door barely closed behind them before they hurried out of their clothes.

Their passion dragged them to the floor before they reached the bed-- urgent, groaning love on the rug. They spent that first night together and then many more, finding richness in each other that they had never found with others.

Neither spoke of love but both felt it.

Their affair of mind and body lasted the summer months and into the fall, all kept private and behind doors.

And then, papers written, grades final, Jacob was done with his undergraduate degree. He had to head back to the Wind River Reservation in Wyoming for tribal service, a condition of his scholarship.

Although neither of them had ever mentioned another love interest, Rebecca somehow knew that Jacob had a girl waiting there for him. And Rebecca, too, had other plans and obligations, including finishing her doctoral dissertation and figuring out what kind of life to have with Bull.

So, knowing they could never share their lives, Rebecca let go of Jacob's care with deep regret.

She and Jacob spent their last night together. They made love with all the passion they had known that first time many months ago.

The next morning, she helped Jacob load his old pickup. Although they vowed to keep the departure cheerful, they both wept when the final box went in and the tailgate clanged closed.

Then, quite without intending to, Rebecca kissed him and held him close, her love now public.

Just as her lips touched his, she half heard a loud horn blast. About a block away, the horn went...ahhn...ahhn...ahhn...for a long time, someone obviously irate at stalled traffic or a slow walker.

Rebecca refused to let the noise distract her. Her mouth stayed firm against his. Pulling her mouth away reluctantly, she whispered in his ear, "I love you. Anytime you want to be with me again, just get in touch. You have all my love, no strings attached."

Jacob nodded, unable to speak, then cried again.

They released each other.

He climbed into the pickup. He started it, put it in gear, and drove away, flashing his white smile at her through his tears.

She never heard from him again.

When she lay awake at night in later years, she remembered his laugh and his touch. Sometimes she could hear his voice, sense his warmth, and smell his body.

She thought this to be signs of a soul bond. She imagined him lying awake at the same moment, dreaming of her, bonded in the same way. And perhaps she was right.

Two weeks after Jacob left, Rebecca returned to Far Mountain District and Bull. Her classroom work was done. She wanted to complete her research and write her dissertation. She would only have to return to defend her dissertation when it was done.

School was out for Rebecca, perhaps for good.

A week after Rebecca returned, she missed her period.

A month later, she knew she was pregnant.

Bull was delighted, believing they had started his child on her last visit home. He jumped around like a boy with a new B-B gun.

But, concealed behind her frozen, smiling face, Rebecca reflected on his delight with a sense of great irony, sauced with a certain pleasurable feeling of revenge. After all, her discovery of Bull's infidelity had opened her eyes fully to his nature. And this knowledge, in turn, had opened her body to Jacob.

She mused darkly, "One cheating fuck deserves another!"

But an even more delicious thought warmed her patrician soul. She had not only cuckolded her philandering husband, but she would also deliver him a bastard child.

What an elegant practical joke.

The May birth was easy. Labor took only four hours.

Millicent Meacham arrived in the world, red faced and squalling, born with dark blue-brown eyes.

Knowing both parents had blue eyes, the doctor said nothing to either one. She merely gave Rebecca a long look.

Then, seeing the joy and love Rebecca showed when she first held Milly, the doctor kept her genetic suspicions to herself. She signed the birth certificate which showed "Wolfgang A. Meacham" as the father and congratulated him on a perfect daughter.

Seven years passed.

In 1985, the family moved away from Utah. Bull became District Ranger at the Summit District on the Targhee National Forest in Idaho.

His earlier ambition to rise quickly to Forest Supervisor stalled when

142

several lawsuits stopped his aggressive plan to put roads up every drainage of his previous district. The Legacy leaders of the Forest Service had decided Bull "needed more development" as a ranger before he could advance to the next level.

He fumed about it endlessly but knew he could do nothing about their decision. He blamed most of his problems on the unflattering impact of Rebecca's absences and on her "environmentalist" leanings.

Rebecca's dissertation took five years to complete. It was titled "Plant Preservation in High Mountain Eastern Utah Ecosystems." Her work rapidly became the reference standard for ecological field restoration in that region.

Bull did not appear to realize that she had used her research and analysis to support the environmental groups that sued and stopped his building program. Court cases were handled much higher up in the Forest Service so he never had an opportunity to compare her bibliography to the one supporting the Sierra Club suit. The two lists were not an exact match but they were so close, the connection could not have been missed. The arguments made by the environmental groups sounded very much like those Rebecca used in defending her dissertation against her academic interrogators at the university.

But, to Rebecca's relief, no one checked the bibliographies. Bull, of course, did not attend her dissertation defense or read federal case transcripts.

Over the years, their marriage became one of nervous accommodation. Each one was afraid of the anger that would come from secrets revealed. The fear had grown because their fights easily turned violent.

Minor spats could result in a gut punch. But when fights got vicious, Bull's violence got extreme.

Over the seven years since Milly's birth, Bull assaulted Rebecca more than a dozen times, punching the resistance out of her and forcing himself on her sexually.

Two of the blows knocked her unconscious. One required a hospital visit to treat a dislocated jaw.

A fearful Rebecca always accepted his stumbling apologies after the attacks. She even covered for him at the hospital when Bull described her jaw injury as the result of a flag football game.

Rebecca would have left Bull but she wondered what would become of her and Milly if they tried to run and hide. Rebecca would angrily condemn herself saying, "What the Hell am I staying here for? I have an excellent education. People support me. I have a reliable set of parents. Milly and I can just go and never look back."

Then she would think of the shame she would feel having to admit that her life was a well of fear, a daily shambles.

And then would come the certainty that Bull would hunt her down. She was sure he would hurt her worse then ever for stealing his little Legacy and further upsetting his career.

When her parents died in an automobile accident, what was left of the once-storeyed family fortune got parcelled out to various relatives and foundations. A small packet came her way, quickly disappearing into the family budget.

Her options seemed to disappear with the cash. So she stayed...and stayed...ducking Bull's anger...holding on...holding on.

Sometimes she would think of Jacob and his gentleness. She would wonder what his response would be when he met his shy, pretty daughter for the first time.

She daydreamed about calling him. She would explain her circumstances to him. He would be glad to hear from her and urge her to leave and come to him. He would keep her safe.

She would pack the car and leave while Bull was at work. She would drive to central Wyoming, not too many hours away.

When she got close, she would call. They'd meet at a diner. He would rush to her and lift Milly up to admire. They would drink tea and catch up...make plans.

She knew if she saw him again she could not take her eyes or hands off him...unless, of course, he had married, had children, had another life...and she somehow knew he did. As often as the daydream came, she let it fade...did not make the call...holding on.

Her life with Bull teetered along, balanced on egg shells and pretense, smothered by fear.

Rebecca and Milly grew closer and closer. They adored one another, souls intertwined.

Milly was Rebecca's ever-loving, loving-forever companion.

Chapter 20

Hail to the Chief

Senator Castwell looks skeptically into Mike Reinard's eyes, trying to judge his slippery sincerity. "So, you've checked everything...from pedigree to pussy...on Meacham? You've called every contact we have in California about this guy?"

At each question, Reinard nods, "Yes, boss, I have. W.A. checks out."

The Senator frowns, "Something doesn't smell right to me about this guy...too 'wild and woolly' or something. I guess my main concerns about him are two. Will the bastard do what we want when he's Chief? And will he embarrass us down the road with some crazy outburst of the truth or an original idea, or some damn thing that stops one of our good works in the water?"

Reinard smiles foxily, "Senator, Bull Meacham will do exactly what we ask, nothing more and nothing less. You can trust me on that." Reinard winks and looks up to the expensive crown moldings decorating the Senator's huge office.

Castwell smiles back, taking the hint. Mike's got some big bag of dirt on Meacham and will use it if Castwell asks.

Good enough.

"What's the Ag Secretary's number, Mike?" As Reinard checks his contact numbers, the Senator picks up the phone. He looks at Reinard and beams, waiting to dial.

As the phones connect, Castwell leans across the desk, "Mike, make sure Chief Meacham is here in my office before noon tomorrow. I want to hear him say, 'I'll do whatever you ask.' Make it happen."

Reinard jumps to his feet and leaves Castwell's office to call Bull.

The call connects, "Mr. Secretary, this is Castwell. Yeah, thanks. Listen, I think we should move on this guy Meacham for Chief of the Forest Service...yeah...please me to no end...you know what I mean...Ag Bill's coming up and, well, I know you need all the help I can give you...sure... sure...thanks...just let me know what you need...."

Chapter 21

Rebecca's Firestorm

One long night in August 1986, Rebecca waited at home for Bull.

Wildfire gripped the Targhee. Fire chewed through the lodgepole pine forests, sending embers across a wide front.

Animals scurried for safety in smoky havens.

The fire had consumed thousands of acres and grew bigger every day, nasty and dangerous, eating up resources.

Interagency fire teams battled the flames like the true professionals they had honed themselves to be.

They gave up ground reluctantly...fighting, fighting...waiting for saving weather.

Bull came home furious from a meeting with the firefighters. He felt they weren't aggressive enough, that they were jeopardizing young tree plantations and improvements on his district.

He had harangued the firefighters for an hour. He ranted at what he felt were their weak and timid attack plans and tactics. The fire boss finally escorted Bull out of the meeting room and ordered him to stay out of their way. Bull was livid at this rejection, dripping with rancid ire.

Bull told Rebecca he'd stopped at a roadhouse for several drinks on the way home. He had several more sitting at the kitchen table.

Rebecca eyed him warily, her back against the counter. She positioned herself as far from Bull as she could be and still remain in the kitchen.

She knew this mood. He had been this way before some of his assaults, insulted by the world outside and burning for revenge at home.

She also knew she had to remain there in the kitchen. If she left, her departure would trigger his rage. He would hunt her down, beat her, and drag her back.

Once she had gone to bed while he glowered in the kitchen, pouring down whiskey. He dragged her out of bed by her hair and down the stairs to the living room where he assaulted her.

Even as he hurt and bruised her, she tried not to make a noise for fear of waking baby Milly. Who knew what Bull would do to Milly in such a mood?

After he passed out on the couch, she crept back up to bed. Under the covers, she hugged her knees and wept for hours.

This August night, seven-year-old Milly slept upstairs, a good, sound sleeper.

Bull glowered up at the terrified yet stoic Rebecca. "You're such a cunt, Becka, with your degrees and your crap ideas about logging. You fucking environmentalist. Do you know how much damage you've done to my career, you bitch? I'm stuck here because of your big bullshit ideas and big mouth."

His words covered familiar territory. Rebecca knew what would lie ahead if he felt further provoked. She also knew if she gave him no provocation he might pass out before attacking her.

But tonight, she just couldn't seem to stand still. Something compelled her to shrink from any more violence. Every time he looked somewhere else, her body reacted involuntarily. She edged slightly away, slowly approaching the back door. Over twenty minutes or so of his sour ramblings, she got within a foot of the door knob and freedom.

She glanced at the knob....

Bull unexpectedly moved with rattlesnake speed. His right hand caught her by the throat. His left hand cocked back for a punch.

Rebecca lowered her head and cringed away from his flying fist. Unh! The punch hit her above her right ear. She dropped dazed to the floor.

He put his hands on her. She expected him to tear off her clothes. But unlike the other times, Bull grabbed the back of her belt and picked her up. Her arms dangled and her legs dragged as Bull hauled her out the kitchen door towards the detached garage and workshop.

Grabbing at the door frame, she feebly tried to stop him from pulling her through the door of the work shop.

He reached down and punched her again.

She lost consciousness.

When she awoke, Rebecca hung upside down--naked, gagged with a bandana, her hands tied behind her.

Her head thumped and ached abominably from the punches and from being suspended.

Shock made her nauseated. She worried briefly if she would choke if she vomited into the gag.

Her feet were caught in the noose that Bull used to hang game animals for butchery. Her ankles hurt from the grip of the noose and her feet were numb.

As she hung there, she turned slightly one way and then the other, the movement adding to her nausea.

She looked up hopelessly at her feet. She noticed that her breasts drooped oddly down towards her.

She looked around for Bull and found him at the edge of her vision. A small light over the work bench along one wall shone on Bull seated on a stool.

He glared at her with hatred, a filleting knife in his hand. The thin blade flashed dully.

"I'll gut you, you bitch whore," he whispered hoarsely, waving the knife at her mid-section. "You think I didn't know about that Siwash bastard you were fucking back in Denver? I knew. I saw you two together. You kissed him before he left in his pickup, you cocksucker."

He stopped, closing his eyes, and then said bitterly, "Do you remember hearing a horn blow when you kissed him, you cunt? Well, that was me, damn you, me, your husband."

Rebecca opened her eyes wider, half remembering the irritating noise. She closed her eyes, expecting to feel the knife bite into her next. But Bull had more to say, "I had come to town to surprise you and have a weekend together. There you two were, practically fucking on the street corner. Just so you know, he never made it home. I caught him at a rest stop, and I finished him there."

Could it be true? Surely Bull would never take the chance of getting caught, but could she be sure…?

"Oh Jacob, no, my love, not because of me…!" Rebecca thought wildly, distracted from her peril.

Bull moved towards her. He made a shallow, burning cut across Rebecca's belly. She opened her eyes wide and grunted pain behind her gag. Blood began to run down her chest towards her neck and face.

"I should cut off your tits first before I gut you," Bull continued, making two small cuts on the undersides of her breasts for emphasis.

Rebecca grunted again, tears starting to flow. Pain and panic caused her to move and sway.

Bull steadied her with a hand behind her knee. He drew the knife back for a thrust into her stomach.

He stared into her eyes, his face an evil mask.

He held the knife back for a while and then, twisting his eyes away from hers, let go.

For a moment, Rebecca's spun away. She could not see what Bull was doing. She waited for another burning cut across her back or a thrust into her body from behind.

Now she would almost welcome death if it meant this nightmare would end.

But if she died, she thought with a sob, what would W. A. do to Milly? Did he suspect that Milly was Jacob's child? What would he do to her if he found out?

Momentum slowly turned her back to where Bull sat again on the stool, his face a still mask of hatred.

She cried, making no noise, blood seeping from her three wounds and running with her tears across her face.

"So here's how it's going to be," he said thickly, "I'm going to cut you down in a few minutes. Then you leave. You never come back. Milly will stay with me. If I ever see or hear of you again, I'll kill you both. I'll start with her. I'll make it last a long time with you watching. Nod if you understand."

At his command, Rebecca nodded strongly, wanting him to see her clear signal.

Bull came forward with the knife. He cut the rope holding her feet, partially supporting her falling body. Thumping down on her shoulder, she lay sprawled on the concrete floor, hands and feet still bound.

He rolled her onto her belly, lifted her hips.

After a moment, he plunged himself into her, adding rape to Rebecca's humiliation. As he thrust against her, she tried to keep her face away from the rough floor.

But the muscles in her back grew tired. She drooped down. His powerful shoves rubbed her face, shoulder, and knees across the surface, grating her flesh.

When he was done, he pressed her fully down to the cold concrete again. He rolled her onto her left side.

Then, he laughed with pleased surprise as if a new idea had struck him. Holding the knife like a pen, Bull carved his initials into her right forearm, cutting away small slivers of flesh to make sure the scars would be deep and permanent. He moved to her right buttock and cut his initials in again.

At the cuts, Rebecca wailed behind the gag, the sound of a dying animal in a leg-hold trap.

Finally free of his touch, Rebecca lay bloodied and curled on the floor for a time. Bull sat on the stool and admired the ruin he had brought to his wife.

Finally, he stepped down and cut her hands and feet free.

Rebecca lay there flexing her hands and feet to get feeling back, shuddering with shock, anxiety, and pain.

When she could, without looking at Bull, she lifted herself up. She dragged on her clothes, walked stiffly to her car, and climbed in. Finding the keys in the ignition and her backpack on the backseat, she grasped remotely that Bull's actions had not been the spontaneous drunken attack they seemed.

It didn't matter. She had to leave. If she didn't, she would die now... and Milly with her.

Rebecca started the car. She reached up to remove the gag. Then she saw Bull's face inches from hers, glowering at her through the driver's door window. She dropped her hands and left the gag in place.

Rebecca drove away, stunned, yet glad to be alive.

Like the initials cut into her body, this night's violence was carved into her mind.

She understood the lesson:

Bull's threats towards Milly and her were real.

Unless his death intervened on her side, if he ever saw her again, Bull would not be stopped in killing them both.

She drove on, blood soaking through her shirt and jeans into the seat. She felt trapped into flight by her profound love for Milly far more than by her real fear of Bull.

She left the gag in place until she had driven almost fifty miles, its tight grip muffling her grief screams.

She drove all night, stopping only for gas, looking for an end to her flooding anguish...on a path to her nowhere.

With each mile, her anger built.

———————————//———————————

On the couch at the Ritz-Carlton, Bull nods his satisfaction.

Becka had felt his heat back then.

The Bull of the Woods might have had beat down from Esperanza and her crew, but he still has the heat.

Angie...Ball...Reinard, watch out!

Chapter 22

O'Reilly Down

An hour before daybreak, John O'Reilly hurries up a path on the Mendocino National Forest in California north of Sacramento. He's heading towards the 50,000-plant marijuana "grow" that a multi-agency drug task force had been watching for months.

Just after dawn, federal, state, and local cops were going to descend on the campesinos tending the grow for a Tijuana drug cartel. Today, O'Reilly's on the trail early because he plans to be the hero of the operation.

Drug cartels in Mexico long ago moved their marijuana production into the U.S. to place it closer to markets. Their U.S. grows were less prone to confiscation and, with reduced transportation costs, more profitable.

The drug lords found many remote areas of national forests and other public lands ideal for cultivating marijuana. They cared not at all if fisheries were destroyed by their water diversions or if hikers were blown up by booby-traps set to protect the marijuana.

Yet, far from Mexico and direct cartel control, the plantations were also subject to police raids and attacks by drug-rustlers. So, security at U.S. locations was always on the drug lords' minds.

To improve security, the drug lords armed the campesinos with automatic weapons. They set up grenade and claymore booby-traps along approaches. They told the campesinos that they would have to fight to the death to defend the marijuana, particularly if they expected their families back in Mexico to live.

Knowing the conditions the campesinos labored under, the drug task force leaders expected a fire fight. So, they plan to come in with overwhelming force, including a National Guard Apache gunship and two heli-assault Blackhawks.

Although the feds know they will not rope in the cartel's leaders in this bust, they will likely grab the local guards and gardeners. In nearby cities and towns, other cartel employees would be picked up, too. These are the people who supply the campesinos with such things as food and fertilizer, haul away the plants, dry them, process them into bags, and then distribute the pot across America into barrooms and schoolyards.

Law enforcement agencies had video taped, wiretapped, and followed some of the suspects coming and going from the grow site for months. They had identified more through surveillance at the locations where the suspects lived.

The task force expected to net as many as 200 people, although, if past experience was any guide, a more likely figure would be fewer than 50.

Moving in ahead of everyone else, O'Reilly is not officially assigned to the drug task force. He knows his boss, Sam Priest, the Assistant Special Agent in Charge, or "ASAC," would be livid if he knew John was in these woods on this morning.

John has not been briefed any further than reviewing the task force action plan. He's studied the accompanying maps and high-altitude photos as carefully as their small scale would allow.

But this is O'Reilly's big chance to show that he can "go tactical" with the best of them.

He had done the political part of his job and is well regarded in the right places. Now, he needs to show his courage and ability, try to do something heroic. This recognition should launch him high into the Forest Service law enforcement ranks, maybe even into the Director job in Washington after a few more productive field years.

Who knows? Maybe the DEA might invite him to move over and take up a top role with their organization. His ambitions glow with the possibilities.

Today he plans to single-handedly capture a bunch of campesinos while they breakfast at their central camp along Rocky Creek. He will get the drop on them, cuff them, and be smoking a cigar when the rest of the task force guys arrive.

Clint Eastwood!

The camp is clearly marked on the maps and photos. Probable sites for booby-traps and alarms are displayed on the maps, too. He doesn't need help to get there any more than his man, Clint, would.

Once he had the greasers down and in restraints, O'Reilly would light up his radio and call in the cavalry.

He's heavily armed with flash-bangs, concussion grenades, his .40 caliber Glock Model 22, and an M-4 tactical automatic weapon from the weapons locker at the regional office.

The green-black M-4 looks bad ass, like an M-16 with a flat top and collapsible stock...an assault rifle for Navy SEALS. He also carries numerous nylon restraints for the bad guys, a small first aid kit, water, and his Epi-pen, an epinephrine injector he would use in case of bee or scorpion stings.

154

He's put a basic night-vision scope on his M-4 to use for travel in the dark. But, after entering the forested area near the grow, he's been unable to get it to work.

O'Reilly knows that he's barely trained on most of his weapons, but he reassures himself that they're simple to operate. He hadn't thrown a flash-bang in years but it's just like throwing a rock anyway...right? He had not qualified with the Glock for some time, the weapon that he knew fairly well, but it's well regarded for it simplicity. He's kept it clean and ready to fire.

Besides the handgun's big bore should have those greasers pissing their pants as soon as he drew down on them. He'd cover them Dirty Harry style with the Glock in one hand and the M-4 in the other.

Without the night scope, his walk through the forest has been slow-going and noisy. Thus he hurries now as the edges of daylight begin filtering through gaps in the forest canopy. He's late but not too late to jump the campesinos at their breakfast.

He nears the area marked as "camp" on the maps.

He smiles with the thought of getting the drop on the bad guys, maybe popping a cap in a couple of them if they force his hand.

———————————//———————————

With fully functioning sixth-generation night-vision goggles, Ekos has no trouble keeping up with O'Reilly's fumbling walk through the darkened forest. Ekos is simply waiting for O'Reilly to pause before implementing the Strike plan.

Just ahead of Ekos, O'Reilly stops to study his map. As he closes in, he's now wary of booby-traps and noise-makers that might alert the camp. He opens his canteen and takes a sip of water. He peers around at the low brush and dense forest and the dark trail ahead.

Ekos is dressed in camouflage designed to fit the sugar pine and noble fir ecotype that spreads across this part of the Mendocino National Forest. Silent in soft boots with a wide sole and pebbled tread that leave a natural imprint like no commercial boot or shoe, Ekos slips to within thirty feet of O'Reilly.

Concealed behind a broad sugar pine, Ekos quickly takes two tightly woven, slightly buzzing twig baskets from a light pack and sets them on the ground.

Then Ekos slides a compressed-air-powered paint-ball gun out of its thin, back-slung scabbard. Ekos shoulders and aims it, dark green nitrile-gloved hands contrasting with the dark brown wooden barrel.

With the intention of making the gun invisible to metal detectors, Ekos had carefully machined the barrel from straight-grained ironwood, the internal surface of the barrel alternately charred and bored to achieve remarkable hardness and precision.

The air canister is a blown-glass ball. It holds enough pressure for about ten shots.

Only the plastic magazine and metal firing mechanism have come from a commercial paint-ball source. The actual amount of ferrous metal in the gun is less than three ounces.

Propping the gun on a tree knot, Ekos fires a pellet at the top of O'Reilly's back, hitting him just below the neck line of his jacket and ballistic vest. The splat spreads across his shoulders and up his neck sending spray onto his hat.

Shocked and surprised, O'Reilly spins, trying to pull the Glock from his holster.

Ekos fires again and O'Reilly takes a Splat! to his face. He's blinded by the fluid and holsters his weapon to reach for his eyes.

Thwap! Thwap! Thwap! Three more paint balls hit his groin and both legs.

"My God," thinks O'Reilly, bent over and clutching his groin in pain, "Some shit shot me in the nuts! What IS this stuff? It STINKS and it BURNS!"

"Who the hell is shooting at me?" He shouts, "You fucking bastards. You pussies."

One hand on his testicles and blinded, he turns to stagger up the trail out of the firing line, trips, and falls heavily.

Before O'Reilly can stumble back to his feet, Ekos steps out from behind the tree with a twig basket in each hand. Thrown high in the air, each twig basket lands next to O'Reilly's squirming figure and bursts open.

More than 200 yellow jackets explode out of the broken baskets. They dive onto O'Reilly's pheromone-soaked clothes and body, the musty, attractive smell driving them into frenzy.

The carnivorous insects sting and bite him viciously, easily avoiding his flailing hands and arms. They rapidly fill his nose and mouth.

O'Reilly makes a noise between a gagging cough and a scream.

His tormented senses keep him from reaching for his Epi-pen. Even if he had been able to find it and inject himself, the bee venom pouring into his system would have overwhelmed his body before the medicine could

156

work.

O'Reilly convulses with shock and pain. Within fifteen seconds, his tongue closes his airway and his consciousness fades. He gradually stops moving. After a few more moments, even his post-mortem twitching stops.

Ekos moves towards O'Reilly's body, stopping to find and pick up the five florescent-green paint-ball casings. Ekos quickly rolls the gels into the nitrile gloves as they, too, came rolling off fingers into a ball.

The small bundle of gloves and gels goes into an air-tight plastic container to prevent the yellow jackets from attacking the pheromones now smeared on the gloves. The container goes into the light pack.

Ekos puts on some light camouflage gloves for the work ahead.

Closer to the body, Ekos moves slowly to minimize defensive attacks from the yellow jackets. Ignoring O'Reilly's body and the buzzing insects coating it, Ekos locates the remnants of the twig baskets and crushes them gently under the soft boots.

Taking a small canister from a pocket, Ekos pours a putrescent smelling attractant over the body. The smell will bring carrion-loving flies and beetles from far and wide. They will follow the flesh-tearing yellow jackets into O'Reilly's body.

The day is warming. The site will soon be alive with the carrion-eaters. They would make O'Reilly's body that much harder to identify and confuse forensic technicians by obscuring evidence of the yellow jackets' attack.

Ekos quickly checks the back-trail, removes a few disturbed items and scuffs over any slight tracks. The tall figure scans the horizon for movement and sets off, heading east, away from the likely direction of the nearest incoming drug task force teams--a camouflaged figure slipping from tree to tree, footsteps guided by caution and hastened by urgency.

Manuel Herrera steps off the trail to piss. He's guarding the trail and arroyo to the east of the main growers' camp.

Manuel's hoping for breakfast soon.

He misses his family in Ciudad Juarez but knows he cannot return home until the marijuana is harvested, maybe in a few weeks. The work at the grow is hard, covering a lot of ground with planting and irrigation, but the crop has come along well.

He had been tricked into coming along on this job in Northern

California.

Manuel had been working for the Tijuana cartel as a mule, bringing bundles of drugs across the border into Texas and New Mexico. The work was hard and dangerous, skulking through the arid landscape trying to avoid the *migra* border patrol and local red necks who would kill him to get his drugs.

But it paid well. And, most times, he had been gone for only a few days and then back home with his *familia*.

Then his *capitan* had sent him on this trip, now months long. Manuel began to worry if his *esposa* thought he was dead or run away. Still, she would be glad if he returned with lots of dollars.

He rocks back on his heels as his stream disappeared into the sandy soils, leaving a wet spot, thinking of his wife's firm body. He lifts his shoulders to try to prevent his AK-47 from slipping to the ground.

"*Donde desayuno?*" he wonders aloud, one urgent hunger replacing another, for-now, impossible one.

Manuel never hears or senses Ekos behind him until Skyfire slits his throat. Ekos holds Herrera tightly by the hair on back of his head until his weakening body can be pushed forward off the trail, air gurgling through his cut, bloody esophagus.

Dying, Herrera falls face down into a puddle of his own blood and piss, hungry no more.

Hoping to obscure the kill time, Ekos pours more of the putrescent attractant on Herrera's body. Moving east again, Ekos pauses to wash the man's blood from gloves and sleeves in the small stream that trickled through the bottom of the arroyo.

Ekos had watched Herrera for five minutes before acting, regretting the need to kill him. But, Ekos can't afford to be pinned down near a drug grower for any length of time, particularly one who's likely to get into a fire-fight with the drug task force at any minute.

So, Ekos acted and now moves on.

Herrera turns out to be the last person Ekos sees on the trail eastward towards the small town of Paskenta, California.

But Ekos is not unseen.

Chapter 23

Tech High, Boots Below

The Drug Enforcement Administration Blackhawk surveillance helicopter hovers at 2,000 feet over the southeast slopes of Ball Mountain. It's positioned at the center of the cordon that five law enforcement agencies have thrown around the marijuana grow. Over 200 personnel are present on the ground.

In the helicopter, the Deputy Regional Director for the DEA and the Forest Service ASACs for California and the Pacific Northwest sit uncomfortably in the vibrating helo, excited and alert, wearing helmets and flight suits like the rest of the crew.

On the ground far below the "suits," Bill Zumo and his green LEO, Mill Meacham, have been brought in for the effort.

Bill had been surprised when he got the order to join the California task force but he also realized it was a great chance to get Mill some field experience with marijuana-eradication operations, a common field operation in Oregon, too.

Today, he wryly thinks that Mill having a daddy who's California Regional Forester might explain why Mill got brought in. And that he's likely the one along for the ride, not Mill.

Bill's quietly amused.

Far above Bill and Mill, the Blackhawk hovers in the dark sky. It's a variant model developed to support covert operations by the military. It's been modified by the DEA specifically for dealing with the War on Drugs, as politicians liked to call it.

The helo has advanced sound suppression for its engines and blades. It carries extra tankage for extended flight and hover time. To carry the extra jet fuel and a big electronics load, the helo had been stripped of its armor except for fuselage plating right under the pilots.

The two pilots wear state-of-the-art night-vision equipment. They also monitor advanced avionics on helmet-mounted face screens, similar to those found in jet fighters, radar and laser equipment that allow them to monitor other aircraft as far as 100 miles away. Because today's flight is blacked out with ultra-dim instruments in the cockpit, no radio transmissions, and no aircraft warning lights, the pilots' ability to sense other aircraft is critical to mission safety.

The pilots also control the few defensive weapons on the aircraft including a small .30 caliber chain gun and three air-to-air missiles. If fired on by missiles or anti-aircraft artillery, they could also deploy defenses such as flares, chaff, parachutes, and radar and thermal decoys.

The Blackhawk's cargo and passenger areas are loaded with electronics under the control of the senior intelligence officers, one assigned to Communications and the others to electronic intelligence, or 'E-lint'.

During radio blackouts like this morning's, the Communications Officer uses a gimbel-mounted satellite dish nestled in a small dome on the upper side of the fuselage behind the rotors. A small computer chip and servo motors maintain alignment of the gimbel-mounted dish to a Homeland Security satellite in geosynchronous orbit over California.

This precise transmission system allows the Comm Officer to otherwise maintain radio silence while communicating two-way with headquarters.

Later, once the task force moves in and everyone's using their radios, the officer can use a small forest of antennae placed around the skin of the helo to switch among many common and tactical radio channels and support ground activity. She also monitors any radio transmissions coming from non-task force elements and has a fix on each government ground-pounder through transponders located in their radios or on their gear.

Seated beside the Comm Officer, almost elbow to elbow, are two E-lint Officers. One officer monitors the presence of ferrous materials as well as transmissions from noise, vibration, and movement sensors previously covertly placed around the grow by law enforcement staff.

Under some circumstances this Mag Officer would parachute ground sensors into remote locations but this had not been necessary on this mission. The available sensors are currently in standby as a result of radio silence.

The second E-lint Officer monitors infrared data, "seeing" people, animals, and other non-living "hot spots" such as warm springs or operating automobile engines. Although the IR sensors work best when a least two degrees Celsius separates the target from its surroundings, the equipment is precise enough to sense differences down to one-half degree.

The computers can hold a trace even if IR tracking becomes intermittent. If air temperatures rise to above blood temperatures, the equipment could "flip" and follow the now cooler living targets, although this method doesn't penetrate hot, roiled air as well.

Similarly, cloud cover is not usually much of an issue for the system but forest canopies are. The greater the closure of the tree canopies and the more their leaves warm under the sun and reflect heat, the less clear the infrared signal is from targets on the ground below the canopy.

When the infrared system struggles to penetrate the forest canopy, the IR Officer might also lock on the target using "lidar," a form of laser-radar. But even carefully tuned lidar is limited; it performs better on hard objects and tends to "ghost through" softer ones like animals and people.

With an array of e-lint sensors mounted in an instrument bulge under the belly of the helo, the two officers monitor several square miles. The information plots on screens displaying maps, including ground contours, water bodies, and roads or trails. The officers can transmit much of the information to ground commanders who read it on hand-held units.

The DEA Deputy asks the intelligence officers for status.

Following protocol, the Comm Officer reports first, "NHQ contact pinged and active. All frequencies clear. Two bad guys are using low-frequency hand-helds, no alarms. Two telephone linemen talking on business freqs about five klics south."

The Mag Officer reports next, "No heavy weapons located. I see vehicles and possible small arms at the camp. Some ferrous hits scattered across the area, some likely debris and others possible weapons. I see correlation when weapons are cross-matched with infrared locations. So, I declare all bad guys are armed. All ground sensors on standby."

The IR Officer then says, "I confirm sixteen bad guys at the camp location. Some movement. Cooking fire is lit. Possible five more bad guys about 100 meters from camp spaced like perimeter guards on high ground. What look like ATVs are cold. I see two bad guys inside the perimeter, moving towards the camp from the north. They are moving slowly about one mile out, one armed, one not. I show our assets one to five miles back from camp and almost in pre-op position."

The Deputy Director looks at the two Forest Service ASACs and asks, "Ready to go?"

They nod, faces stoic, stomachs churning.

The air and ground operation is officially the DEA's. But the law enforcement troops on the ground are under the command of an experienced BLM Incident Commander chosen by all the participating agencies, federal, state, and local.

Once the Incident Commander got the "go" sign, the helo crew would be strictly there for support to the ground and as a communication link to the higher-ups at state and federal levels.

The Deputy turns to the IR Officer, "When all assets are in position, tell the IC to execute."

The Comm Officer flips on the command channel transmitter.

A moment later, after rechecking the location of the last ground elements moving into position, the IR Officer calls crisply, "Mendocino Six IC, this is Sky One, you may execute. I say again, IC, you may execute."

The IC acknowledges Sky One's orders and then uses the command channel to notify her four sector supervisors whose divisions had by now completely surrounded the camp and the general grow area.

In turn, they tune their radios to their common channels and order the waiting personnel to move in. Radios and transponders go active all around the perimeter. The drug task force moves out smoothly and warily starts to close in.

———————————————//———————————————

With the "go" order, Mill surges forward excitedly, starting down the north trail ahead of Bill and the rest of her squad. Then, feeling incredibly green and more than a little embarrassed, she steps to the side of the trail and waits for the seven more experienced law enforcement officers to pass.

She takes up her place at the rear.

Bill smiles as he passes her, saying quietly, "Take it easy, Hot Shot. Let the old folks lead the way, at least for today."

Her cheeks burn a little at the comment. She knows he's reminding her that, as woods-wise as she is, she has no experience with the possible booby traps and fire fights that might lie ahead. She might blunder into something that would jeopardize the whole team and the whole operation.

Mill nods and bites her lip.

The first two members of her team are former "Force Recon" Marines, now California State Police SWAT officers, dressed in field camo and armed with light machine guns. They have given up their sharpshooter rifles for the day, feeling that the machine guns give them the right tactical advantage.

The team doesn't need night-vision equipment because day break was chosen for the "go" time. But, as they move forward, night still dominates the forest floor with deep shadows under the forest canopy.

So, the point man moves slowly at first, the narrow beam of his gun-mounted flashlight pointing a few feet ahead on the trail, probing dark pockets for trip wires, his shrouded light invisible to any anyone ahead or on their flanks.

162

Mill's pleased a little while later when the daylight strengthens and the pace picks up. She chilled standing around, waiting for the team to move out. Now, she feels welcome warmth build under her new ballistic vest and radiate out to her cold hands and feet.

She grips her matte-black, seven-round, Remington tactical semi-automatic shotgun tightly. She handles it carefully so its metal barrel doesn't scrape against branches or brush, safety on.

At the rear of the team, Mill thinks they're making plenty of noise with boot scuffs and thumps, rub and squeak of gear, and muffled breathing. She tries to hold the noise of her own breathing down but soon finds that she feels light-headed.

Smiling at herself, she breathes deeply and concentrates on not tripping as she swings along.

She smiles even more when she thinks of the green and brown paint Bill had smeared on her face before they left the Expedition that morning.

"I hope it matches my uniform," she grins to herself, remembering past thoughts on Forest Service fashion.

Little does she know that Bill had first painted her face dark brown-green and then painted a yellow "smiley face" over the darker pigment.

He can hardly wait until the rest of the team sees her in full daylight. It's what you did to rookies, particularly when you like them.

Ahead of Mill, Bill struggles to keep the smile of anticipation off his face.

Bill has never heard Mill's opinions about the uniform and fashion train wrecks. By day's end, he would know her opinion of what it meant to be a green jack o' lantern instead of just a green pumpkin.

Boy would he.

_____//_____

As Mill's team moves along, a half-mile ahead on the trail, Ekos' Strike on O'Reilly is over.

The IR Officer in the helo has seen it but doesn't know what's happened on the ground. As far as he can tell, the two men had simply met for a short time. Then one moved off east; the other stayed put.

He keys his radio on the Tac channel for Mill's team, "Team Leader 16, this is Sky One. You have two bad guys one-half mile ahead. One is in position along the trail. The other has left position and is heading due east at about 3 klics. Mover is almost out of your sector."

Mill's team has been maintaining voice silence as they move through the brushy forest floor. The team leader, in position behind his point, keys his radio's "clicker" button twice in response to Sky One. His acknowledgement is clearly heard by the IR Officer above.

The team leader decides the team will focus on the apparent trail guard ahead and not worry too much abut the bad guy moving east out of their sector. They would make too much noise and have to go too far to catch that bad guy.

Let Team 12 reel him in.

After getting Team 16's response, Sky One turns to other urgent matters.

IR doesn't note that the body temperature has started to drop on the "bad guy." And, if he had been watching closely about ten minutes later, he would have seen a similar cooling "bad guy" to the east where Manuel Herrera's body lies beside his guard post.

But, by then, the alarm has been given in the camp. Marijuana growers are scattering to the winds, pursued by drug task force teams.

Sky One has too much to do to worry about one or two immobile bad guys. Free from the need for stealth, the helicopter begins to orbit the operations area at lower altitude, guiding the task force and getting video and photos for transmission to headquarters.

The political appointees in the federal and state agencies want to milk this for all its media value. A successful operation would give them political credit when it came time to argue for next year's appropriations as well as some swagger value among their friends.

After killing Herrera, Ekos moves out towards the advancing drug task force teams coming in from the east.

Everyone is moving through broken and difficult country. Even with help from Sky One and canine units, the drug teams are slowed by the need to search carefully for escaping bad guys.

Ironically, Ekos moves east far faster at first than the drug teams come west.

Although Ekos has studied and practiced small-unit evasion tactics in both urban and wild settings, the techniques are not something that Mist assassins got to practice very often, especially against a large, well-prepared force. So, more cautious for the lack of experience, Ekos stays in deep cover within the forest believing that surveillance aircraft are likely to be used in the raid but not knowing the sophistication of what hovers above.

Mist training also emphasizes that even dog units, as dangerous as they are, can be evaded by careful use of cover and concealment. Assassins have been trained to allow searchers to pass, move to a well-concealed location, and hide, after spreading false scent or scent-suppressants around the area. Then the assassin waits out any searchers that continue to cover the area, moving several times more if necessary, until the searchers give up.

They are told the keys to successful evasion are skilled concealment, stealth movement, and patience, patience, patience.

Ekos would have been alarmed to know that the IR Officer in Sky One above is tracking each step and radioing and downloading geo-marked location information to the advancing teams, some of which are K-9 units.

But, Ekos assumes units are in the area. When the drug teams get to within a mile, Ekos can hear dogs occasionally yipping and barking and so is warned.

Above, due to the warming forest canopy, the IR officer loses Ekos' position. He tries for a lidar fix but gets nothing.

Noting the target's last known position and the direction and the probable rate of movement, Sky One speaks to Team Leader 12 and reports what he knows.

The IR Officer keeps Ekos' last reported position designated in his computer. The target can't be seen visually or tracked by the Mag Officer. The sound and movement sensors are overwhelmed by the presence of the drug teams. So, IR can't be sure that he will be able to reacquire the "bad guy" until the cool of the evening, if the target can be reacquired at all.

IR knows the operation has been a success with more than a dozen campesinos captured so far.

Losing one wouldn't be a big deal.

Still, the suits want to get them all. Sky One will keep hunting until stood down.

Soon, no longer tracking well and low on fuel, the helo is ordered back to base. It will fly again later in the cooler afternoon and evening.

As they fly off, the crew hopes they can dump the suits and be more comfortable when they return for another six-hour shift.

On the ground, dog-wary Ekos looks for a good hiding place. A few Giant Sequoias dot the area, massive, old, fire-scarred.

The ecotype containing the Sequoias is at its northern range limits so few of the giant trees are present. The massive Sequoias dwarf the other trees in the area.

Sensing the people and dogs moving in, Ekos explores a few of the Sequoias to see if they can be climbed, thinking that a perch on a massive branch more than a hundred feet in the air might do nicely to avoid capture.

Unbeknownst to Ekos, Sky One's IR sensors would have made such an airy perch high in the forest canopy fatal. Later in the evening, the assassin's body heat would easily reveal a "bad guy" location high up in the tree.

But, after some quick measurement and thought, Ekos finds that the girth of the trees make climbing them impossible without special gear and so drops that concealment plan.

The fire scars look more promising.

One of the Sequoias has a fire scar burned half way into its interior. The opening rises tall enough for a person to stand up within it. Ekos enters cautiously. Looking upwards in the dim light within the scar, Ekos can see lots of rot and dangling fungi and webs above.

Then, reaching up, quick-working hands drag down arm loads of smelly, rotten wood. Insects and mealy sawdust cascade down with the material.

Ekos ducks to keep the worst of the material off head and torso and out of eyes and mouth.

Cautiously, Ekos keeps probing and bringing down material by hand, and eventually uses the gun stock as a poker, until at least semi-solid material surrounds a high opening big enough to crouch in.

Standing precariously on some knobby, crumbling outcrops along the wall of the scar, Ekos sets a climbing screw into the top of the opening, tests it to see if it will support enough weight, and rigs a simple harness to the screw as a dangling seat.

Dropping down and stepping outside the scar, Ekos takes out a container of concentrated deer urine and spreads it in a long line past the base of the tree, one end of the line towards the oncoming dogs and the other leading back towards the growers' camp.

Slipping back into the scar and up to the perch, Ekos pours a mixture of CS tear gas powder, dried blood, and cayenne pepper down onto the debris pile beneath. Then, feet perched on two woody knobs and seated in the harness, Ekos pulls out a mottled brown-black piece of matte silk and forms a loose fabric "floor" beneath the hollowed-out chamber by tucking fabric corners and edges into rotten holes and crevasses.

Ekos waits.

166

Teams 12 and 13 sweep into the area. Their GPS hand-helds clearly show Ekos' last probable position as well as their own. But the IR officer has Ekos' last position plotted where the signal was lost several hundred yards to the west.

The dogs become excited by the fresh deer urine. They lunge forward in their harnesses pursuing the scent towards the GPS marker on the handler's hand-helds.

The handlers let them move ahead, believing they're on target. As they sweep past Ekos' Sequoia, the teams simply give the giant tree a quick security check, intent on covering one another in a hostile situation and catching a bad guy.

As the faint but musky urine trail runs out, the handlers quickly realize the scent isn't human. They quickly figure that the target has moved on from the position marked by their GPS. Reacting to the handlers' shouted Czech commands, the dogs begin searching for the bad guy again, working back eastward along his last reported path.

The Team Leaders confer by radio and order the team members to fan out, work a search grid.

Team Leader 12 radios for more backup.

Team 14, advancing from the east, shifts northwestward to help join the search.

One K-9 team searches Ekos' Sequoia, the dog instantly losing her ability to smell when she sniffs the CS, blood, and cayenne combination. She snorts and paws her nose briefly.

Observing her behavior, her handler thinks her distress is simply from the pungent rotted and moldy material lying in heaps within the scar. God knows his nose's nearly overwhelmed by the stink, too.

He flashes a light around and up into the scar. He pokes the debris pile with his foot, but nothing moves. He sees nothing other than rotted wood and a few ferns. The damp interior and moldy stink are so oppressive, the searcher backs out and moves on.

The dog continues to act and sniff normally, though with her tracking abilities impaired, her handler notices she's not holding steady on any scent trail. When the third team arrives, the area is swept again and the dog participates.

This time, she refuses to stick her head into the scar.

The teams move out.

As temperatures cool in the afternoon, Sky One returns.

IR re-acquires the area where Ekos hides but senses nothing. The heat from Ekos' body is fully shielded by the massive, bark-warm Sequoia. After two more hours spent orbiting the area, the DEA Blackhawk returns to base.

At dark, Ekos slips to the floor of the scar, takes up a position as far from the entrance as possible, and spreads the brown-black silk as a sleeping and concealment cover. Ekos pulls debris over the silk for further camouflage.

Night-vision goggles in place and suicide injector in hand, Ekos sleeps lightly until dawn.

Another day in concealment and Ekos will head to Paskenta and meet the wise warriors of Movement, homeward bound.

About an hour before Ekos begins looking for a good place to hide, Mill and Team 16 find O'Reilly's body. Inspected cautiously from 30 feet away, the prone figure is clearly dead and infested with yellow jackets and other insects.

The team's operational orders require teams to guard death sites until a crime-scene and mortuary team can arrive and process the site and the body. Or, if that isn't possible because of enemy fire or other circumstances, the bodies are to be noted on a map for a return visit when threats end.

The Team Leader assigns two team members to secure the area and cut off this potential escape route while the other six finish the sweep into camp.

Because of their inexperience, Mill is assigned to the corpse site with Buddy Macomb of the Mendocino County Sheriff's Office. At the Team Leader's direction, they conceal themselves well away from the body at locations where they can capture bad guys trying to leave.

Mill hates the idea of being dropped from the action this way but is delighted to be far back from the buzzing insects and odor of decay.

Hunkered down between two large dead-fall trees, she has a good view over a wide area. She takes a few sips of water from her canteen and waits for developments. She fingers the shotgun a little nervously and clicks the safety on and off a few times to make sure it works smoothly.

The Team Leader said he would radio them with orders once the camp surrendered.

But, as minutes slip into an hour, Mill begins to get restless. She has heard a few single shots off in the distance, probably warning shots commanding bad guys to surrender.

She also heard far off a brief rattle of gunfire that went on for thirty seconds or so, followed by a few dropping shots, likely meaning that a firefight broke out and then quickly ended.

The sound of gunfire was unnerving. Mill is not religious in any particular way. Even so, she prays briefly for Bill and her team members and then for everyone in the area today--even the bad guys.

No reason in her mind for anyone to be killed over a bunch of ganja. She wants good busts and long jail times for cartel members, but no one hurt if possible.

She ends her reverie abruptly when she hears a twig snap in the direction of the camp. She sharpens her observation. Moments later, a small mule deer doe runs past her about 100 feet away, tail up in alarm. Behind the doe come three more does and a small buck, moving along at a good pace but not running full out.

Mill knows from her years in the field that deer are skittery critters, running off at any threat, real or imaginary. Still, on this day, Mill wonders what spooked the deer.

Clearly, a lot had been going on over at the camp. So many people thrashing around or the gunfire may have sent the deer into flight. They could run for miles at the pace she had observed so whatever startled them could be miles away. Still, she wonders "why now after the firing has ended?"

Shifting position and putting the shotgun across the log in front of her, she looks intently out along the deer's back trail. Her attention is about to shift after a few minutes when she sees a flash of movement through the brush.

Something or someone is coming almost directly towards her.

Wild thoughts race through her mind. Is it a bad guy trying to escape...a gang of them? Maybe the team leaders sent one of the team sweeping back to join her and Buddy? Maybe it's another deer; could it be a larger buck trailing the others?

As each possibility enters her mind, she thinks of how she'd handle the encounter.

The deer could pass.

The team member would be greeted, first by radio to prevent startling him since guns were in hand, then face-to-face.

A gang of bad guys...unh!

Then she sees more movement and…it isn't a deer and…and…it isn't a team member!

Far off, a small man heads her way through light brush, the distinctive shape of an AK-47 gripped in both hands, a campesino clearly trying to escape.

Above the brush, she can just see his blue baseball cap, gray tee shirt, and the barrel and forestock of the AK.

His face is not yet visible.

She jumps when she hears a voice in her earpiece, "Team 16, Meacham, this is Sky One. You have a bad guy 200 meters south moving your way at 4 klics. He just appeared on IR. Vector shows he may have been hiding in the pond between you and camp."

She grabs her mike and responds to Sky One with two clicks.

Then she hears Team Leader 16 say on their Tac channel, "Meacham…Team Leader 16, we are on his six headed your way. Stop him. Drop him if you must. Take no unreasonable risks. Mill, I *know* you can do this; you are ready! Macomb move north and east to back Meacham. Buddy stay out of sight!"

Mill again keys her clicker to acknowledge Team Leader 16. But, with her mind now totally focused on the guy moving towards her, she misses Buddy's clicks.

As she watches the man approach, Mill first gulps nervously. Her vision begins to blur at the edges.

She steadies down as the Team Leader's words sink home.

Team 16 is on the way to help.

Macomb would have her back.

But, more than anything, more than *everything else*, Team Leader 16, a man of incredible experience in combat command, had said she's up to the task of stopping the heavily armed man coming her way!

Mill feels her anxiety fade.

A warm determination fills her body. She smiles grimly behind her war paint.

The man continues to come forward, growing larger in her view until she can see his face. He's young, browned by the sun, medium height, and strongly built. He moves quietly through the brush, darting glances left and right.

He moves purposefully, as if he knows where he's going and is wasting no time getting out of the area. His path will take him a few yards to Mill's left and down an inviting arroyo that might lead to freedom if he gets past Mill.

She stays low behind the log and shifts the barrel towards him slightly.

He holds the AK across his chest, right hand at the trigger assembly, barrel pointing upward and in her general direction. She knows he can move the automatic rifle into firing position in a split second. If it's set on full auto, he can "spray and pray" her position in a heartbeat, almost certainly hitting her. He has a lot more firepower than Mill does with her shotgun.

Still, Mill's autoloader shotgun is a formidable weapon, too. Seven rounds of alternating double-aught and "four buck" make for a lot of mayhem even if the rounds are more slowly delivered than the torrent of 7.62 millimeter bullets from the AK. And she lies in wait...concealed...ready with lethal surprise.

She grips the shotgun tightly and slips the safety off. The man steps within 10 yards of her and looks towards the arroyo. Then, he moves even closer. As his gaze turns elsewhere, Mill sees her chance.

Staying low behind the log, Mill points the shotgun squarely at the man.

Slipping off the safety, she screams, "Alto, Hombre! Alto! Drop the weapon! Drop the weapon and manos arriba!"

The man jerks violently. He turns towards her, searching for her location. His gun barrel begins to drop towards her position behind the log.

She screams, "No!" and centers the shotgun on his chest, sure to hit him at this range.

As he peers to see who has confronted him, he finds he can't see her camouflaged image very well. But he instantly sees the round "o" of the shotgun barrel pointed right at him from a few meters away.

He hesitates for a long moment, a brave man who wants freedom and his family, a man also unwilling to die for a drug cartel.

He drops the AK and begins to run towards the arroyo.

Mill stands and yells "Alto!" again.

She has only a few seconds to prevent his escape down the slope of the arroyo. She swings the shotgun and fires a round directly in front of his head, leading him, cutting it close.

The blast shakes the man. He hears the whizzing bee sound of pellets and feels them fly by his face. One pellet hits the brim of his ball cap, spinning it madly off his head into the brush.

Unnerved at last, he skids to a stop with his hands up.

Keeping the shotgun pointed on his torso, Mill eases over the log and moves carefully to within ten feet of him.

She holds that position shouting, "On your knees, hands behind your back" a couple of times until she realizes he understands no English, at least not these words.

About the time she begins to wonder if she should kick the man's knees from behind, Macomb comes up, shoves the man to the ground, cuffs him, and secures his ankles with a nylon leg restraint.

Grinning, Mill and Buddy "high five" each other over the good collar. He seems especially amused when he looks at her.

Arriving ten minutes later, the rest of Team 16 does the same...high fives, back slaps, and laughter.

"What's funny about all of this?" Mill wonders. Nobody got hurt and the bad guy is secure.

Zumo hugs Mill, lifting her slender body off the ground, spinning her around, shotgun dangling.

He still feels the ebbing wash of panic that had come over him when he'd heard a bad guy was headed her way. He hadn't been there to cover her.

Grateful she had come through her first armed encounter safely, Bill knows for sure now that Mill has the guts to be a cop. She would keep a cool head in future confrontations.

Zumo knows this day couldn't have turned out better.

By now, displayed in full light, Mill's war paint is fully exposed. Mill wonders to herself, "What in Hell are these monkeys grinning about? Am I crazy?"

Finally the Team Leader comes over and offers her the small, metal hand mirror he uses to see around corners and to signal aircraft in a pinch.

Smiling kindly, he says softly, "You might want to check your makeup, Ma'am."

And there...there are her brown eyes in a hideous greeny-browny gargoyle face. Then Mill sees the rest, a slightly smeared yellow SMILEY FACE staring back at her from the mirror!

She yells, "Zumo, you bastard! What have you done? Does this shit wash off? Wait 'til I tell your wife, you bastard."

She glares at Bill.

She looks back at the mirror and yells again, "No wonder that guy dropped his AK. I'd scare the crap out of anyone with this face!"

Looking a little sheepish, Bill says, "Or they'd die from laughing, Mill."

His words cover a little internal qualm. By making her look

so absurd, he might have actually endangered her, undermining her effectiveness in a dangerous tactical situation. She came through unharmed, thankfully, but he realizes he's gone a little too far.

Seeing that the upset look has not left her face, he steps close and murmurs, "Sorry Mill. Just a LEO initiation rite. Won't happen again."

He pauses and, stepping well out of her reach, says, "But I wonder what that poor bastard thought when he saw your beautiful face," and then breaks out laughing again.

Mill responds, "Damn it, Bill. You better watch out. I'm pretty good at practical jokes myself."

With that, she grins ruefully and walks away, still a little hurt at the joke but willing to give up her resentment and get on with the day.

She has passed this initiation with only a little dignity lost.

Most importantly, her instincts tell her she's now fully accepted into the ranks of Forest Service law enforcement.

Mill knows this day could not have turned out better.

Chapter 24

Mop Up and Wonder

Team Leader 16 sends Macomb and another team member with Mill's collar to the prisoner-processing van and transport vehicles. They are parked in a Forest Service campground a few miles away.

To get there, they would hoof it to a parked vehicle and then drive over to the drop off. They would grab some late lunch at the Red Cross canteen there.

They grin their good byes and take off, their sullen prisoner in tow.

The rest of Team 16 fans out for more search and seizure work, sweeping north and then east.

For all of her success in making the capture, Mill's still assigned guard detail back at the corpse. She's to wait for the forensics and mortuary team now headed her way.

The team leader reassures her that headquarters viewed deaths on a drug raid as really important business. She shouldn't feel disrespected by having to guard one.

Still, Mill can't rid her mind of the nagging thought that she stands guard here because they weren't ready to trust her somewhere else. Either way, she had shown her value today.

That knowledge allows her to relax into a quiet vigil near O'Reilly.

The crime scene and mortuary team walks up a few minutes after Mill gets back to the corpse. The area still buzzes with quite a few yellow jackets, working their way from the body to distant sites. The decay smell hangs strongly in the area.

"Man oh man," says the team leader Chip Minor, "This is the second smelly one we've worked today. There was another body east of here that smelled the same way. That one was dead this morning but smelled dead a week. I figured the smell came from something some animal did on him after he was killed. Now I figure maybe not."

He takes out a little well-used tin and reapplies some Vick's Vaporub near his nostrils. He moves carefully towards the corpse, his eyes on the yellow jackets.

Two busy yellow jackets buzz him.

Chip sees how many there are, darting around and working for lunch on the body. He tersely tells one of the team members, "Let's get some more bug dope on everyone. Bill, get the broadcast bug sprayer out of the bag and do the whole area. Avoid spraying directly on the corpse or in a five foot circle around it."

Pretty soon, flying insects start clearing the area, including the yellow jackets and their many eager allies particularly the obvious and noisy big green and black flies. The team photographer starts documentation shots from every angle around the body.

The photos of the undisturbed site done, Chip kneels down beside the body. He peers in closely, hesitates.

Calling to his forensics tech, he says, "George, help me roll this guy over. Be quick."

Together, disturbing the site as little as possible, they roll the corpse until he lies face up. Ravaged by the yellow-jackets, the body's features can't be made out.

But his gear tells the story—here lies a heavily armed federal employee...dead.

Chip shakes his head, "This looks like one of our guys. Look at his weapons and gear." George nods.

Chip stands and yells, "Everyone back the Hell off. Get tape around a perimeter about 100 by 100. This is bigger than we can handle."

He calls out to Mill, "Tell Sky One to call in the FBI. Right now, dammit."

Things had been bad with three bad-guy deaths on this operation. Now, with a fed down, things were worse, much worse.

The team pulls back carefully, creating as little disturbance as possible, and sets tape around the enlarged boundaries. Mill calls Sky One and shocks the Communications Officer with the news. She then reports the turn of events to headquarters and then to Team Leader 16 who says, "Holy shit, it's really hit the fan!"

Within a minute, watch officers at DEA's, Forest Service', and FBI's national headquarters receive notice that the death of a "friendly" has occurred on the operation.

Five minutes later, Mill receives a radio call directly from the Watch Operations Officer at the FBI Headquarters in DC. Mill gives a brief situation report.

Before she finishes, the FBI Watch Officer cuts the communications without comment. She hurries to brief the FBI Deputy Director for Operations.

Mill wonders if they will call back. She's still listening for the call

176

when the IC arrives on the site along with Team Leader 16.

Things really get busy.

Within an hour, investigators from the California State Police Crime Lab arrive at along with a couple of FBI crime scene investigators from Sacramento.

The case is transferred to their control. They go to work immediately.

The FBI agents question Mill and Team 16 at length at the staging area. Towards midnight, the agents allow them to head home.

The operation is over for them, just beginning for the agents. They find out that three bad guys are dead and fourteen captured.

One apparent task force member is dead. But according to the IC, it's no one under her command.

No one can account for the dead fed.

Mill and Bill drop their weary butts into the Expedition and drive north. They take turns driving, drinking bad coffee loaded with non-dairy creamer and sugar.

At first, they talk about the operation and the death of a "friendly."

Later, Bill's not enough of a gentleman to stay awake to hear all of Mill's comments on Forest Service fashion and face paint. But, then again, it isn't hard to catch her drift.

Married a long time, Bill knows better than to argue with a woman over fashion.

———————————————//———————————————

Two days later, Bill gets off the phone and swivels his chair in Mill's direction and starts to speak.

But ear phones and music on, she has been drowning out his conversation with the Forest Service Assistant Special Agent in Charge or ASAC in Vancouver, Washington, a man named Sam Priest. Working from her field notes, she's struggling to finish her report on the drug operation. Bill's conversation was animated, head bobbing and hand waving from time to time, but she'd tuned him out.

Now, she cuts the music off and pulls out her ear buds.

Bill smiles grimly, "So, guess who the dead guy is."

Rumors had been swirling, but Mill ignored them while finishing her report.

She raises her eyebrows, "I haven't got a clue. Enlighten me, oh master."

Their relationship had improved a lot since the operation. Mill can tell Bill is more confident in her abilities and now willing to banter.

Bill shakes his head, "Okay, young LEO. The victim was John O'Reilly, the ASAC's deputy in Vancouver, one of those ambitious guys who seem to be in every picture, shaking hands with politicians and dignitaries, gun-bulge under his coat. The poo-bahs are in an uproar all the way to the Secretary's Office, maybe the White House."

He continues, "O'Reilly's death is going to be fully investigated. But, I think the canons of the Green Creed have been invoked. I predict that why he was there will not be looked at, at least not seriously."

"From what I hear elsewhere, I'm pretty sure he was never officially assigned to the drug bust. But now the ASAC's saying that he sent him as his personal special observer on the ground. Smells like Greed Creed whitewash."

He pauses to think, "From what you and I saw, O'Reilly was certainly equipped for field work but no one working the operation knew he was going to be there. The IC's operations staff says privately that the Sky One observers classified him as a bad guy on their screens because he was way inside the perimeter before we got the "go" call and he had no transponder in his gear. Very strange."

Mill's normal frown deepens, "I wonder if that means he missed meeting us at our start point and just went ahead? Maybe he thought we had already gone in."

Bill shakes his head, "No way. He must have known the operations plan and slipped in ahead of us."

Then a thought strikes him and he guesses O'Reilly's motive, "I bet he was hot-dogging, trying to be a hero. Holy smokes! Then he goes and gets himself waxed by a bunch of yellow jackets."

"No wonder Priest is claiming John as his man on the ground. Otherwise, O'Reilly would look like a complete idiot and the ASAC would be jumped for having a rogue special agent that slipped his collar and then died, a real career buster for Priest. Not a complete cover-up from Sam's standpoint but definitely a spin. Helps out John's family, too, since he will be considered on duty when he died."

Bill stops talking and looks thoughtful.

Mill feels uncomfortable and asks, "So what do we do with this information? Seems like someone ought to know." Bill looks at her, "Let's table this part for now. A lot of what I've heard is from reliable sources but nothing's confirmed. People are still guessing. We should let the

178

investigation run its course. We'll know more after a couple of weeks."

She nods, saying, "Okay. But, what else? I sense we're not really through with this."

Bill agrees. "Yeah what's bugging me is that the ops staff says Sky One saw someone in the area where O'Reilly was found, no ID on that person either. FBI calls this kind of mystery suspect an "unsub" for "unknown subject." That's what you'll see in their reports."

"Anyway, Mr. Unsub appeared to approach him from the *rear*, meaning he came from the direction of our perimeter, also before the "go" signal came in. After he met O'Reilly, Mr. Unsub turned and headed east. Could be that one of our LEOs was tailing him and covering his flank or something. But we don't know who that person was and he is otherwise unaccounted for. After moving east, he was never seen again as far as the ops guy knows. Also very strange."

Mill thinks for a moment, "Remember Chip Minor, the forensics team guy, said O'Reilly smelled way too bad for a fresh corpse and that another body had been discovered to the east smelling just as bad. That guy was a marijuana grower. He had been knifed or something similar. Does the fact that they both smelled like they had been dead for a week mean anything?"

Bill's face shows his confusion, "Beat's me. Still, the stink does connect the two deaths and Mr. Unsub headed east. So, there could be a connection. I'll figure out a way to get a copy of the crime scene report as soon as it gets to Vancouver."

They chew over what they know and what they suspect for a while longer. Then they go back to writing their reports.

Zumo gets a few more calls with information and gossip to share but nothing new surfaces. Later, he heads out to the Dunes to cover yet another accident.

Mill thinks a little more about the strange events during the operation and her confrontation with the marijuana grower. Thank God she had not had to shoot him.

Then she thinks, "I wonder who Mr. Unsub is and why he was heading east. Maybe he killed O'Reilly but there's nothing to show he did. And, if he did, how did he do it? We sure couldn't tell out at the site. No one reported hearing a gunshot before we got the 'go' sign. Knife maybe? You couldn't tell from the messed-up body."

The questions linger in her mind but she has no immediate answers.

She does not know she had missed meeting Ekos by about a half an hour.

Or that Sky One operators were among the first law enforcement people to observe a Mist assassin at work.

Mill picks up her phone and dials Manny Suemez' desk number in Washington DC. Her mentor, Manny's recently been promoted to Deputy Director for Investigations for the Forest Service, a big job.

His phone rings several times and then goes to a blah, blah, blah recording.

Mill leaves voice mail at the beep, "Manny, this is Mill. You probably heard about John O'Reilly's death. Well, I was on the team that found him. I had a couple of thoughts and questions to check out with you. So, give me a call when you can...and we probably have some other catching up to do, too. Thanks."

As she's packing her gear to head home, Mill's phone rings. Hoping it's Manny, she picks it up and hears a booming voice say, "Milly, this is your dad!" She mentally flinches and holds her emotions tightly to herself.

"Yes, Dad, what's up?" she responds in a measured tone. Bull answers, "I just wanted to tell you how proud I am of your work on the drug bust. Damned good show, girl."

As always, he continues to bellow his comments into the phone. She holds the receiver back a little ways from her ear to keep from being deafened.

She answers, "Thanks, Dad. Nice to be appreciated."

He bellows, "And you are. Keep up the good work. Here's a damned crazy thing you should know. I'm going to be named the new Chief in the next few days. A good opportunity will be coming your way soon. Take it."

With that, Bull hangs up. No affection. No connection. Just a barrage of words and then orders. Par for the course of their lives together.

Her Dad as Chief? Crappy idea!

What's that about?

What could those people in DC be thinking?

Mill shakes her head in amazement, a little proud of him in spite of her doubts about what kind of leader he'd be for a big, diverse agency like the Forest Service.

Mill had tried hard to keep her career out of her father's influence. She'd made her opportunities on her own. But she knows that keeping her Dad out of her work life was impossible, at least to some degree.

180

She's a Legacy, after all, and the great, great granddaughter of a Firster. Still, she's tried to ignore her family connections as much as possible, and has always avoided asking for Dad's help in her life, personal and professional.

Now he's called her as the future Chief...head of the agency, el Caso Grande...telling her to take a forthcoming "opportunity."

She has very mixed feelings about that order. Well, she would just have to see about that if and when the opportunity ever appeared.

She grimaces and shoulders her backpack, headed home.

Chapter 25

Badger Checks On Ekos

Badger sits in Ekos's underground lair, looking at the triumphant assassin. They perch on stools as they sort through the O'Reilly Strike details.

As the KGB had trained them, Mist uses an extensive check list for Strike debriefings. So, in exacting detail, the two cover plans, logistics and movement, then equipment, and finally tactics and actions.

Overall, they agree that for a high-risk, high-exposure operation, the Strike had gone well.

They review Ekos' logistical support and equipment and find a few ways to improve future operations. Ekos will stop using temporary debit cards, for example, and replace them with gift credit cards paid for in advance with cash.

In addition, Movement warriors would be better trained in coded recognition. Some of the newer warriors thought they didn't have to memorize a recognition sign and counter-sign.

Ekos had almost killed one of the Movement warriors in Paskenta because he didn't counter-sign properly to Ekos' sign, "The Mendocino Mountains are green this time of year."

After several hours, they come to the place on their list that concerns tactics and actions. Badger first congratulates Ekos, "Your escape was masterful. Your evasion of the K-9 teams was text-book perfect."

Ekos glows with Badger's praise and replies smugly, "Those drug teams were pathetic. They scrambled around for hours looking for me and never looked in the most obvious place."

Ekos laughs disdainfully. "So much for the fucking DEA's finest."

Badger frowns. Is Ekos getting arrogant, careless?

If that's true, Ekos might begin to take risks, to improvise more than Strike plans and good sense allow. Carelessness could not be tolerated in the Mist organization, especially among assassins whose rash actions or capture and death could reveal so much about the organization.

Badger tests this idea, "Why did you kill the guard? It seems to me that the kill was unnecessary. It left a possible connection to O'Reilly's Strike."

Ekos replies, "The guard stood on high ground. He could see a wide area. I thought I wouldn't be able to get past him without risking him seeing me. He had the AK-47 and I had the blow gun, not a good match up. So, I took him out with Skyfire."

Badger nods, "I understand that part and I would never second-guess a field decision like that. Compared to O'Reilly, your use of a different weapon and method to kill the guard would normally not have established a connection. I wasn't clear in my question. Why did you put the decay attractant on the guard? That would be the connection I'm concerned about."

Ekos hesitates for a moment and hen replies, "I'm not sure I thought about it. I was charged up...worried about getting out of the area. Using the decay scent was in the plan. I just followed the plan. Besides, it's no big deal."

Badger smiles slightly, "Okay, Ekos, it's something we'll have to work on in future training. This Strike was very different than nearly every Strike we've done in the past. You had to deal with a really dangerous tactical environment, drug teams and dogs coming in from every direction and drug cartel members all around, armed and primed to shoot."

"Usually, the tactical environment is highly controlled. An assassin would abort the Strike if police and criminals were crawling all over the area. Don't worry about it. We'll use this learning to get better."

After discussing a few more details, Badger hugs Ekos and leaves.

An hour later, Badger calls the War Chief on an encrypted land line and delivers a synopsis of the close-out with Ekos.

Badger ends with the observation, "I'm concerned that Ekos is getting cocky and careless, indifferent to security risks. I will work on those things in future orientation and training but the situation will bear watching." The War Chief agrees.

A worried Badger hangs up.

Chapter 26

The Marvelous Matilda

Tilly left early that day to lead an inter-agency team looking at wetlands issues. She organized and fielded the team to try to break an impasse over protection for the purple-tufted moonwort, a small, fragile plant found in several small pockets across Southwest Oregon.

If Tilly couldn't get the regulatory agencies to agree with the BLM's protection plan, too much of the next ten years of timber harvest would be tied up in large buffer zones around the plant's core habitat.

To make Tilly's present work life tougher, the Deputy State Director had included himself on the team. Worse, he turned out for this field trip, too.

Tilly had been at sixes and sevens trying to make the tour arrangements; make sure everyone actually showed up, and then conduct the tour--all while handling arguments and watching out that the Deputy didn't mess things up with a "premature ejaculation of his decision," as she liked to think of this point in settling disputes.

To make matters even more complicated, the Deputy had shown a personal interest in Tilly, hinting that he wanted more than a professional relationship.

She thought that he had included himself on the field trip because of this attraction to her. Otherwise his involvement seemed too early in the decision-making process.

Tilly knew men desired her blond beauty and lively personality. In public, she chose to appear as a single straight woman pursuing a successful professional career. A very private lesbian, she knew her public demeanor and style could confuse male suitors.

She has no interest in men sexually. But unlike some other lesbians, men do not repulse her either. She enjoys warm relationships with them at work and around town. She doesn't mind when they compliment her figure or tease her with sexual suggestions.

She just doesn't feel any more for them sexually than a duck might feel for a giraffe.

Always hampered by the incongruity between her public persona and her intimate, personal life, Tilly became adept at handling misunderstandings about her love interests. She learned to gently dissuade guys bent on seducing her.

In the early years of her career, she would just make it clear that she had no interest in them, citing the need to keep work relationships within ethical bounds. Her cheerful and kind words took most of the sting out of the rejections she delivered.

She would say things like, "You're gorgeous, darlin', but I just can't let myself...." and the disappointed guy would back away. Three rejections and they never asked again

But a few years before meeting Mill, Tilly watched how other women used flirting and unsolicited propositions to buttress their workplace careers. Tilly realized she might be missing important opportunities.

After a lot of reflection, she decided that she would consider sex with men if the act could help her get ahead. She would not seduce them....but, well, if they wanted her, then she would consider the possibility.

Because she knew she'd never have romantic interest in men, Tilly found herself very objective about the whole straight-sex business. She was quite impartial and almost indifferent.

She considered any passion that men might feel for her as just one more advantage in her favor. As long as their lust remained firm, Tilly could build the men up or swat them down, just like anyone else.

She came to understand the agreement to have sex with men as sort of a binding handshake contract.

He would have his passion slaked.

She would have her future secured.

Each man, his lust satisfied, would drop behind her as she moved up. The concepts worked together seamlessly like a space shuttle launch with the men in the role of rocket boosters and Tilly as shuttle commander.

She decided to call this agreement a "love contract." She framed it as a business deal with performance requirements and a termination clause, just like the government contracts she dealt with at work.

Since love contract terms would never be written down, and even discussing them in advance would be unlikely, Tilly knew that she would have to have her own clear set of expectations and rules that she could enforce firmly and unilaterally as needed.

Based on what she saw in the workplace, Tilly worried that men might refuse to end the love contract when she decided it was over. She didn't want a complicated ending. She wanted a clean break--to move up and leave them behind, love contract cancelled and intimate contact terminated--Tilly orbiting at a new high.

So, she decided that one rule would be that she would only form a love contract with married men. From what she could see around her, she would be better able to control them, and eventually cleanly end the contract, than she could with single men.

Another rule would be that she would only contract with men higher up in government...and never with her own boss. This way, she could lubricate her promotions but not at the expense of damaging everyday office performance and relationships. She would avoid gossip and scandal.

At work, contractors were often given nicknames—the BLM was often called "the Bureau" in contract language for example. She began to imagine a love contractor nickname for herself. So, she tried out a few names. She decided on "The Marvelous Matilda" or "TMM" for short.

When it first came to her, Tilly had laughed at The Marvelous Matilda idea. She realized TMM might be her way of mocking her impersonal approach to something as deeply personal and physically invasive as sex.

But then the idea gradually took hold. Why not have a "nom de sexe" for herself as a love contractor? The nickname would help her keep her private life and her work life separate.

TMM would be lesbian Tilly's straight alter-ego. TMM would be each man's expert, intimate love partner--sexy and sexual, friendly and attentive, caring and creative, flexible and fun.

TMM would work the contracts.

Tilly would reap the benefits.

Without really thinking anymore about it, Tilly's mind simply embraced The Marvelous Matilda and assigned TMM to the role of love contractor.

Then Tilly waited for her first opportunity.

Having prepared herself, she unconsciously began to signal her availability. So she did not wait long.

Her first lover showed up within a few months -- a BLM Manager from a nearby District, an older fellow, kind and ardent, sadly caring for a wife slowly dying of cancer.

At first, Tilly could not read Mitch's understated intentions. And then, she got it—he wanted to make love to her.

Not one to fluster or delay, Tilly took a deep breath and began to hint to Mitch that she had an interest similar to his. Like flirting with other women, the preliminaries seemed simple enough.

And Mitch responded, his interest clear. He mentioned sexual and companionable things they might do together.

At this point, Tilly almost panicked.

After all, Tilly and The Marvelous Matilda had no sexual experience with men. Everything had been ideas up until now. With Mitch, she would have to perform.

Tilly realized, too, that even as she took on her TMM persona, she would not be able to admit her inexperience to Mitch. TMM presumably had the experience to be an expert love partner, "sexy and sexual"...and all that.

Facing the real potential to consummate a love contract, Tilly began to wonder if she could pull her first one off.

She had taken stock of her situation. Mitch seemed very respectful and willing to let TMM set the pace. She had time.

She put Mitch off for several weeks, telling him kindly that she wanted to be certain intimacy with him was the right thing before beginning. Tilly had used the time to research straight sex in manuals and begun taking birth-control pills. She watched sex-instruction DVDs, a little straight porn.

Tilly found some things clear, others weird, and some a little threatening.

She compared learning about straight sex with learning a foreign language similar to one's native tongue. The lesbian and straight "languages" were sufficiently similar to make much of the learning easy.

Yet they were also dissimilar enough that TMM might easily get into a situation fraught with misunderstanding, frustration, or even danger. She had likened its potential to that of a sort of sexual Cuban missile crisis--one where frustrated sexual expectations took the place of cold war tensions and Soviet missiles.

Tilly wanted détente, not mutually assured destruction. She wanted to raise her career orbit, not get blown up on her first launch pad.

What if the Mitch wanted some form of sex that TMM did not want? Would she offer another choice or skedaddle for the bathroom?

Would TMM scream with laughter if Mitch turned out to be hairy like an ape?

Or what if he behaved badly and tried to hurt her? Would TMM laugh at him or twist his balls?

Or, more specifically threatening, what about oral sex—sucking on a penis looked simple enough but would TMM actually be able to do it. Could she tolerate such a foreign touch and taste; could TMM suck and swallow as the women on video had done?

The whole business was intimidating but...it had to be done.

She worried more and more as their first time together approached. Thankfully, their first night together went well, quite well.

For all of Tilly's fears, it had all come down to Mitch and his behavior. Another man might have scared her with rough, muscular urgency. But Mitch's kindness and respectful touch eased her fears.

Although her heart pounded and she stiffened at his first touch, she gradually opened her legs and then herself to him.

Quite unaware that he was serving as TMM's first lover and Tilly's sexual tutor, Mitch unwittingly taught them a great deal that first night, gently taking the lead in slow and respectful sex.

Their early nights together had been filled with insights for TMM along the lines of, "oh, this fits this way" and "that works better in this position." Awash in learning from movement and sensation, Tilly had struggled to find any emotion that could make their mutual experiences genuine and caring, or help her to an orgasm, something Mitch wanted.

Mitch just didn't turn her on...no way he could.

She had almost despaired for a time. But then, in the midst of a sweaty embrace among twisted sheets, she had found inspiration and a pathway to meeting Mitch's request and pleasuring them both.

It turned out TMM could have an orgasm quite easily. And with that physical release came genuinely warm feelings towards Mitch.

On that splendid night, stretched out across pillows with Mitch's mouth on her clit, TMM had found she could muster a fantasy lesbian lover.

Up a lovely orgasm bubbled. Then another.

All along, she had not lacked for physical stimulation. She just lacked the right partner or, rather, an imaginary threesome.

Later, while Mitch smoothly banged her belly-down across the same pillows, TMM conjured another orgasm. Tilly rejoiced.

Eventually, the relationship started to unravel.

Tilly began to think about contract termination.

Mitch had begun to think about a long-term relationship. He fancied he would marry TMM after his wife's imminent death and an appropriate mourning period.

But, Tilly, of course, had no interest in marriage with Mitch or any other man. And, she had known that in the future other men would want to mount TMM's belly and buttocks.

Tilly would want to let some of them to further her career. So, she had sweetly fended off Mitch's hints about a future together.

She let TMM pleasure Mitch and herself for almost three months more. She'd gotten her promotion, partially because of Mitch's enthusiastic endorsement.

At the end of the three months, Tilly calculated that her love contract had ended and she gently broke up with him.

Mitch had been a convincing test. After his love contract, Tilly knew she and TMM were skilled and capable.

Tilly waited for more contracts to come her way. Over months and years, several did.

The pesky Deputy State Director was the latest and the best opportunity for a successful love contract so far.

As far as her relationship with Mill was concerned, well, TMM just didn't figure in that. Tilly shared real love with Mill, not a TMM love contract.

As the field trip ends, Tilly is well prepared when the Deputy asks if she would like to stop for dinner before returning home. Under the guise of continuing their business discussion, Tilly agrees.

They go to one of the better Thai restaurants in Medford, a small, quiet location in a strip mall located on the east side of town. Inside, the quaint red and gold oriental décor gleams under kind lights. The delicious smells of Thai spices fill the dining room.

Over drinks in the congenial atmosphere of the restaurant, the Deputy propositions Tilly gently.

After teasing and flirting with him a little, Tilly agrees to a one-night stand with a wide smile, saying "I thought you'd never ask."

They linger over dinner for only a little while longer before returning to his room at the Red Lion Inn in downtown Medford.

TMM guides the government vehicle carefully, steering with her left hand, while the Deputy holds her right hand from the passenger seat. He kisses her fingers and palm occasionally.

When she feels his lips, she turns to him and smiles. She says sweet things to him like "I'm glad you like me" and "You're my dessert tonight, darlin'," as she'd rehearsed.

The Deputy appears to be quite smitten with TMM.

When they get to his room, TMM undresses quickly, making a demure show of her body. She places her clothes on a chair near the bed and her purse on top of them.

190

Bending away to cover her movements, she triggers a small digital voice recorder built into the purse's bottom. She places the purse to aim the hidden microphone at the bed.

Tilly had added the recorder to TMM's tool box after a previous lover refused her the support TMM had earned when she asked for it. That betrayal taught Tilly that having a little more contract-compliance muscle might be a good choice.

Today's recording will go into her small collection, to be used only if absolutely needed someday.

TMM speaks casually but distinctly for the microphone. She calls the Deputy by his full name under the pretext of telling him about her two rules of love-making. He can't leave bite marks or hickeys and he can't suck painfully on her nipples.

She smiles wickedly, "Be a bad boy, Ben, and I'll spank...hard!"

Goggling at TMM's slender beauty and small breasts with tight pink areola, the desperate Ben quickly agrees and folds TMM into his arms.

An hour later, the Deputy musters a last orgasm with TMM astride him, smoothly sliding him in and out of her trim, tight self. Knowing Tilly would be late getting home, TMM has not tried for an orgasm for herself.

As the Deputy wilts, TMM dismounts and stretches out next to him, hands touching. Spent and peaceful, the Deputy falls asleep immediately.

Figuring he's out for the night, TMM gets up and gathers her things to leave. She dresses and speaks quietly to the Deputy's unhearing body. She deliberately says his name and hers. She works the day's date into her monologue for the recorder.

TMM tells his comatose body how well he had satisfied her and that she looked forward achingly to their next tryst. Then she turns the tiny machine off.

The Deputy begins to snore raucously.

TMM sits down at the desk in his room.

Tilly writes him a sweet little note of thanks, leaves quietly through the door, and walks down the dusty, carpeted hall to her government car. She hums happily as she drives away across the sun-cracked parking lot and then out on city streets to I-5 North.

Tilly likes contract administration. She always feels a sense of progress after TMM starts a new one, of moving along her trajectory to success.

Chapter 27

Bye, Bye, Tilly, Goodbye

About two days after her father's call, Mill's cell phone rings. "Is this Millicent Meacham?" a sharp, rushed woman's voice asks.

"Yes, this is Mill Meacham," Mill answers in her calmest LEO voice.

The woman continues quickly, "Please stay on the line for Dr. Priest."

Before Mill can answer, the line clicks. She's on hold.

Dr. Samuel Priest is the Assistant Special Agent in Charge for the Pacific Northwest and John O'Reilly's boss.

"Now former boss," Mill corrects herself.

Mill barely knows Sam Priest. She met him once in person but she has heard him speak at LE conferences. She found him a little pompous and theatrical for a senior federal cop, but he seemed to know his trade craft and had a reputation as a real bulldog on cases.

On the down side, LEO gossip said he would throw a subordinate under any passing bus to protect his career or his friends.

Her Dad mentioned that he considered Sam a friend. Because Priest stood high up in her chain of command, Mill has tried to ignore Priest's connection with her Dad until now.

Mill wonders what Sam Priest would want with a lowly green LEO, Legacy daughter or not. She figures he's probably following up on her Dad's call maybe to add his congratulations or, less likely, to offer her "an opportunity."

If Priest was the opportunity knocking, maybe it will be time for Mill to say "No" diplomatically.

The phone clicks a few times. Mill wonders if the connection might have been lost.

But then, Sam Priest's measured voice comes out of the cell phone. "This is Sam Priest. How may I help you?"

Mill replies, a little smile on her face, "Dr. Priest, this is Mill Meacham. You actually called me. So, I would ask the same thing of you. How may I help you?"

Sam laughs, "Sorry, Milly. So many calls, so little time. I'm afraid I got my brain twisted around." They both laugh.

Sam continues, "Milly, you did a great job on Mendocino Six."

Mill thinks, "So that's what they called the drug bust!" Like some of the other grunts, she had never heard and mostly doesn't care what the DEA, Forest Service, and BLM called their joint operation.

Sam goes on, "You had a great arrest – armed bad guy and no causalities. Nice work!"

Mill thinks she can detect false bonhomie in Priest's voice. Clearly, Sam has delivered "puff" praise before. He's pumping out his best snake oil to a Legacy and soon-to-be Chief's daughter.

Mill murmurs, "Thanks" into the phone several times. Her mind going into standby as Priest rolls on with more congratulations, laced with statistics about the number of arrests and marijuana plants destroyed.

Laboring under the verbiage load, Mill wonders to herself, "What the Hell does this guy want?" But she also knows she has to wait him out until he can reach some sort of punch line. Just as he seems to be winding down, she begins to detect an undercurrent of anxiety in Priest's voice.

Mill remembers Bill Zumo's comment about the ASAC having to cover for O'Reilly because John may have been at Mendocino Six without authorization. The anxiety Mill hears behind Priest's words could well be coming from his need to cover for both his dead subordinate and himself, just as Bill had surmised. Mill listens more intently as Priest concludes his blather.

"So, Milly, you may think you played a small role in a big operation. But, I would say you made significant contributions. I'm very proud of you."

"Many thanks, Dr. Priest," she replies, "I really appreciate it that you took the time to call me with your support."

Mill gives herself a small mental pat for diplomacy.

If she worked at it, maybe she could spread the manure as well as Priest someday. Well, maybe not, she concludes, too much energy leading to nothing worth having.

Hoping to move on, Mill asks, "Dr. Priest, is there some way I can help you or the investigation out? Do we know yet how John died?"

Never having met O'Reilly, Mill feels a little uncomfortable using his first name in a conversation with someone who had been close to him. Still, she doesn't want to seem stuffy.

Priest replies, "Now, Milly, I want you to call me 'Sam.' I feel like we already know one another after all my years of working with W. A. So, will you do that—call me 'Sam?'"

Mill hesitates. Not wanting to be ungracious, she answers, "Sure, Dr. Priest, I'll call you 'Sam.' And you should know that I go by 'Mill' rather than 'Milly.' Milly is what my Dad used to yell out the window when I'd done something wrong!"

Priest laughs, "Yes, I know the feeling. When I heard 'Samuel' as a boy, I knew I was in trouble."

They both laugh. Mill's chuckle on automatic.

Mill wonders yet again where all this convivial bullshit would be taking them. Would Priest ever get to the point?

So she tries again. "Sam, even though I'm enjoying this call, I should probably be letting a busy guy like you go. I really mean it though. Is there something this district LEO can do for you?"

Priest's voice takes on a serious note as he answers, "Well, Milly, I mean Mill, I really *could* use your help. With John dead and the investigation into his death on-going, along with all the other activities throughout the Region, I could really use some help here in Vancouver."

"Would you be willing to come in for a detail of about 90 days? You'd work for me as a special assistant. You'd focus on rounding up all the information, reports, and everything for our part of Mendocino Six. And, because you were there on the ground, I'd let you work with the task force investigating John's death. I'd love to have your on-the-ground knowledge there at the table. You'd get a real good lesson in the serious way we deal with the death of one of our own on the job.

"So, what do you say, Officer Meacham? May I count on you?"

Mill doubts that she can really help out at the level Priest mentioned. Still, she knows this is a great opportunity and nothing like she had figured would happen when her Dad called.

This isn't the usual spotlighted, make-work, coached assignment that Legacies often got to build a baseless reputation for performance. No, Priest has offered her real work in areas where she wants to grow.

Nice.

"Okay, Sam,' Mill replies seriously, "If I can clear it with my supervisor, when do you want me there?"

Once off the phone with Priest, Mill calls Bill Zumo to give him a heads up. Zumo has been around long enough to agree immediately to her Vancouver detail, even while grumbling a little inside.

"Okay, Mill, "he says, "You've got my blessing on one condition. You have to keep me up to date on what you're doing and what you're finding out. I don't mean you have to give me any secret-squirrel stuff. If they tell you to zipper your lip, do it. But if you can share in confidence with trusted colleagues, then make me the first trustee, okay?"

195

Zumo laughs ruefully, "Fifteen years in law enforcement, and they've never given me a call like the one you just got. So, go and enjoy it. Learn lots. Try to cut the whole business down to 60 days."

He pauses, calculating, "And, another condition--bring me back a six pack from one of those pricey micro breweries in Portland."

Mill laughs back at him, replying in mock awe, "Oh Master, you are letting your humble assistant off lightly and she is grateful."

Zumo snorts, "Okay, smart ass, make it a whole case of big-town brew, then."

They promise each other that they will catch up on current cases before Mill leaves. Then they sign off.

Mill arrives back home at about 6 pm and begins to pack for her extended trip to Vancouver, about a three-hour drive from Florence. She plans to leave the next day after finishing up with Bill at the office.

Priest's secretary had arranged for Mill to stay in a Marriott Residence Inn at Lake Oswego, a nice spot for a long stay.

From that close-in location, Mill looks forward to seeing some of Portland's night life. She also plans to call a few friends in the area to get together. She predicts that the work for Priest might take a lot more than a LEO's normal fifty-hour work week, so she has decided not to build a big social calendar, just a nice little one with a few friends.

After packing, Mill waits a little impatiently for Tilly to get home so that they can rethink their calendars for the next three months. They have little planned with each other but enough items to cause complications if they can't get them reconciled.

At 7 pm, Mill makes a sandwich in lieu of dinner. She opens a bottle of wine.

––––––––––––––––––– // –––––––––––––––––––

Tilly heads home along I-5. She will take the Sutherlin cut-off to Elkton, Reedsport, and Florence where she and Mill live.

Rolling hills and mountain passes lie ahead. Tilly hopes that traffic stays light and the big trucks stay in the slow lanes.

Her wishes come true.

The miles roll by with beautiful scenery and small towns around every curve. Because she had made this trip many times before, Tilly pays little attention as she motors past vineyards and timbered mountains.

She begins to wonder what could be going wrong between Mill and her. Things had been so tough, even harsh at home lately. She frowns,

196

squinting through her dark glasses into the hot, soon-setting sun.

Why did Mill have to act so distant and demanding all of a sudden? Was it something Tilly had done?

She could think of nothing it might be. Everything seemed so right about their quiet, cloistered home life—enough money, good food, cute pet-- the clamoring outside world at bay, she and Mill safe within.

Whatever it was, they'd probably not get a chance to talk about it tonight because Tilly wouldn't reach Florence until after midnight. She hopes that Mill will have gone to bed and that they would not argue about her late arrival.

But, when Tilly gets home hours later, Mill sits awake in the living room. Mill pretends to read with most of her bottle of wine on board.

Tilly stops in the doorway to the living room. Her arms are full of luggage, her purse, and her briefcase. Popcorn dances around her feet, begging for attention.

She asks, tentatively, "Mill, love, you awake?"

Mill simply sits, unmoving, mute.

Tilly tries again. "Mill, dear, are you okay?"

Tilly picks up the chill from Mill's posture. She thinks uneasily that this homecoming is not the quiet trip to her room and restful sleep she had hoped for during her long drive home.

When Tilly first came in, Mill had been simply angry about Tilly's late arrival. She was irked at Tilly's failure to consider Mill's schedule and call.

But as Mill savors Tilly's entrance, she detects a certain indefinable air to Tilly, a patina of self-satisfaction on her, a glow of fulfillment, a lilt to her voice--all of which cries out to Mill that Tilly had been unfaithful again.

Mill seethes at this insight. Whatever this is, it's enough...a tipping point.

Tilly drops her gear in the doorway and picks up Popcorn. Holding the dog protectively in her arms, Tilly walks to the couch and sits down across from Mill in one of easy chairs.

She looks at Mill's angry face, "Are you mad because I'm getting home so late. I guess I should have called but things got so crazy, I just didn't."

She moves uneasily, hugging the little dog defensively.

Mill glares at her.

Tilly speaks in a quiet voice, "I guess I should apologize...but I don't know...things have been so cold between us lately..."

She trails off. Tilly just sits and looks sadly at Mill's hot face. Mill stares back. She says nothing. Tears start in Tilly's eyes and begin to slide down her face.

After several minutes of heated silence, Tilly stands and walks to the doorway. She picks up her suitcase with her free hand and cuddles the dog in her other.

As Tilly's foot touches the carpet runner in the hallway, Mill speaks, "I'm leaving early for a 90-day detail in Portland tomorrow. When I get back, I want you to be gone."

At Mill's words, Tilly's shoulders droop a little and then straighten. She saves her first sobs until she reaches her room on hurried feet.

Tilly knows she has done nothing to deserve this. Clearly something had happened to kill the love she and Mill had once shared.

Tilly sits on her bed, arms tight around her legs, rocking. She mourns her broken life, so secure and so under control only a few months ago.

What had happened…what?

She shrugs and lowers her head.

Tears again.

Well, she has her career...and TMM.

Chapter 28

Portland, Badland

Sam Priest almost leaps out from around his desk to welcome Mill when she appears in his doorway. At his request, she'd walked straight to his office when she arrived to check in, get her desk assignment, and find out more about what work he'd planned for her.

After the handshake, she stands awkwardly, acutely aware of having worn her "city clothes" and carried a briefcase shoulder-bag to an unfamiliar place, likely filled with strange rituals she would not understand.

Even more, her clothes fit her. They show off her figure well.

She feels a little embarrassed at how chic and "girly" she looks.

These aren't things she worries about when dressed in her ballistic vest and uniform--strange to now miss the comfort of the ugly uniform and bulky LEO equipment.

If Priest picks up on her discomfort, he does not acknowledge it or halt the gush of greetings he sends Mill's way.

As she smiles her best diplomatic smile at Priest, Mill wonders to herself if the man ever really draws a breath or simply sucks air in some hidden orifice so he could keep on gabbling without pause.

Her smile grows bigger as she thinks how much she would like him to bend over so she could see the top of his head. After all, he might have an air-sucking blow hole, sort of like the kind you'd find on a warty humpback whale.

Priest takes her widening smile to mean appreciation for his words. He continues to gush with great enthusiasm.

After several minutes, Priest senses that time has passed. He winds his words down.

Preliminary to getting down to the work at hand, he asks Mill, "So, I bet you'd be glad to find your spot and get started, huh?"

Mill agrees instantly, hoping to get free from Priest. She yearns to scurry away to hide her awkwardness in some obscure cubicle where she could lose some of her city clothes and get set up.

"Okay, Mill," Priest says, "My secretary will show you where you'll be working once we're done here. But before I ask Carrie to step in, I want to go over what you'll be doing. And, I'd like to hear if you have any ideas, too."

Priest pauses, "Is that okay?" he asks. Not waiting for her answer, Priest waves her towards one of the leather chairs that sit next to the little round table he uses for small meetings.

Mill is used to ranger district offices with their dusty vinyl-tile floors, bad carpeting, and thirty-plus-year-old furniture. In comparison, Sam's office looks quite luxurious.

The walls and furniture are finished in mahogany. Her eyes travel across dark blue carpeting to a nice view of the treed campus surrounding the forest headquarters where the ASAC's office is located.

Mill muses to herself, "I could get used to this." Then she remembers the serious reasons why she had been detailed into Priest's organization and tries to focus on her host and his comments.

Priest sits down opposite her. He stretches his arms out along the top of the table, elbows together, hands clasped, with index fingers pointed at Mill's chest.

Mill is struck with the impression that Priest holds a gun pointed at her. She wonders what this mannerism could mean. Has she offended him somehow? Does he resent her father asking him for a favor? Is he warning or threatening her?

Perhaps the gesture is simply unconscious on his part but still she can't shake the odd feeling of threat that Priest's "pistol" fingers give her.

Because Priest's odd behavior distracted her, Mill misses his first comments. She forces herself to focus and catch the thread of his remarks. They seem to concern his continuing guilt for having sent O'Reilly to the drug bust as a lone ranger.

From everything Mill had learned from Zumo, she figures that Priest is laying down a smoke screen. Her "bullshit-o-meter," as one of her FLETC trainers had called a cop's intuition about liars, starts spiking and flashing red.

Sam talks on, offering an elaborate scenario about his discussions with and orders to O'Reilly. Mill thinks to herself, "I bet none of this took place. I really don't give a shit if it did or not. I wish he'd just move on."

Priest speaks on for another minute or two, expiating his non-existent guilt and finally stops for a moment.

Mill prods him innocently, "So, Sam, I heard you say you never put anything in writing to John. I mean it's not my place to judge anything either of you decided to do. But I figured you'd have given him some kind of orders or travel authorization or something. I guess I'm too green to know how these things work."

200

Sam lowers his head and shakes it. He looks at Mill. One hand moves to his chest and he feigns heart break. "I tell you the truth Mill, I wish I'd never sent him. He had a blanket travel authorization for anywhere in the U.S., so we really didn't need an authorization for him to go there. I told him to just go and observe. But he showed up loaded for bear."

"Knowing him as I did, I'm sure he just wanted to be there to back you field troops up if you needed him. He was a generous and brave man. What a loss."

Priest shakes his head again, trying to look convincingly sad. His hand drops back to the table, once again forming the finger-pistol aimed at Mill.

With sudden insight, Mill realizes Priest has already told this story to investigators and his superiors in DC. Priest is putting the jive on her so she will pass it on to her father, the new Forest Service Chief. He's scamming her so she would help him build his case with the Legacies.

She doesn't know whether to laugh out loud or get angry at the presumptuous fool, so she just sits quietly. Priest talks a little more and then looks at her expectantly.

Measuring her words carefully, Mill says, "Sam, you've been through a really rough patch. Although I didn't know John, it's clear to me that you and the Forest Service lost a lot when he died. I'll remember what you've told me and mention it when people ask me about the case. You've given me a real education today."

She looks at him in a way she hopes is sympathetic, and then continues, "Sam, please tell me what I can do for you while I'm here."

Her words work. Sam Priest relaxes his arms. He puts his hands flat on the table, in effect "holstering the pistols" he had been aiming at Mill. He sits back in his chair and seems to ponder her question for a moment.

Surprised, Mill wonders, "Surely this geek has already figured out what he wants me to do. Why is he pretending to formulate his thoughts now?"

But Mill's suspicions about Priest's preparations are wrong. Priest has been so anxious to make his points about the propriety of his conduct, that his thoughts about her program of work were only half-formed when Mill walked in.

Right or wrong, Priest figures he could lose his job or at least his influence over the O'Reilly debacle. So, he had adopted a "let no stone go unturned" communications approach to cover his tracks and protect his backside.

If Mill had been as savvy about Forest Service politics as Priest was, she would have understood his motives better. She could have used them to her advantage from the start of her detail for that matter.

But she is not that sophisticated, or corrupted by the Green Creed, which strongly promotes the tenet to "*cover your ass at all times*" and its corollary, "*deny, deny, deny...then lie, lie, lie.*"

Priest ends his reflection, "Mill, first and foremost, I want you to help the investigative team looking into John's accidental death in any way you can. For example, they'll need someone to take notes at all meetings and assist with drafting reports. They have a secretary assigned to them for that but your knowledge of law enforcement and the O'Reilly field situation could contribute a lot. So, help her out when you can. You may also be asked to help them organize their records and evidence."

"As I mentioned before on the phone, the team will want to visit the field site at least once. You'll be in charge of that trip, working under the Investigative Team Leader, Jake Burns. Carrie'll take you down to meet him and the team as soon as we are done here. I know you are the best qualified person in the Pacific Northwest to help the investigative team...."

And, again, Priest launches into a speech about how wonderful Mill is and how much she will contribute to the team.

Mill's mind takes a time out from the frothy praise. She has definitely gotten marching orders about the team. She finds that valuable because Priest could obscure most anything in his baffle of words.

When he winds down, Mill waits until he takes a breath, "Sam, I really appreciate your kind words. Let me see if can restate what I think you want me to do for the team."

She runs down the list Priest had mentioned. Sam nods agreement. Then Mill says, "Okay, good. I'm glad I heard you correctly."

She waits for another torrent of words but none comes.

Changing to a different subject, Mill asks him, "I know you mentioned a desk and everything but it sounds like I'll need keys or codes or whatever for computer access and some way to get into evidence storage. What will we do about those things?"

Priest frowns for a moment, "Jake Burns has control of all access. It's up to him to decide what access you can have. He runs a tight ship. I'll give him my recommendation that you have full access. Just don't be disappointed if you have to work through someone else or have someone present for those parts of your job. It's not personal. It's about security."

Mill nods, "Okay. I understand."

Mill decides she can safely change subjects again. She asks Priest, "When we talked the other day, you mentioned that you'd also like me to help get all the files and records together for our part of Mendocino Six. Is that still part of what you want me to do?"

Sam nods again, "Yes, it sure is. Each of the Forest Service Team Leaders and Team Members has the responsibility to pull their records together and submit their reports. They were due last Friday. About half of them are in."

Mill thinks to herself, "Thank God Bill and I got ours done and in here, or I'd look pretty stupid right now!"

As if reading her thoughts, Priest states pompously, "And your report was among the best, Mill, complete in every detail." He beams at her, "With such a great start on your part, I know you'll understand the need for us to get all the reports in and review them to make sure they're complete. I expect only the highest quality work to come out of Law Enforcement in the Pacific Northwest Region…"

Priest launches off on another avalanche of words about his record of high attainment in report writing and timely submittal. Mill grabs a chance to think again, tuning him down to half volume. She began to see an advantage to Priest's verbosity—while he tried to suck the oxygen out of the room, Mill had time to think.

After Priest's barrage of statistics covering the last three calendar years of reportage ends, Mill asks him, "Sam, when do I need to have the records compiled and on your desk? I want to make sure I'm meeting your needs. And, will I have some help in putting things together? A writer-editor would be a good choice now that I think of it."

Priest answers, "I'd like to have the compiled reports here on my desk by a week from Friday. I review them. Then they go to the Incident Commander at BLM. She puts everything together from all the agencies. Then the big package goes to the DEA. As far as someone to help you, I'll get Regional Public Affairs to assign you a writer-editor or at least someone with those skills. Will that work for you?"

Mill smiles her thanks, dimples showing, "You couldn't be more supportive. Thanks, Sam!"

As a deacon of the Green Creed speaking to any acolyte, Priest feels he has to add a few more tidbits to Mill's situational knowledge. So he continues, "The FBI sent a liaison to work with Burns' team, named Gregory Stillman. Only because John's death occurred on a joint operation and John was a federal employee at the time of his death, the Fibbies sent Stillman over to watch us do our work."

The Green Creed held that Forest Service employees, particularly Legacies, could do anything and do it better than anyone else.

Mill remembers watching the coolly professional FBI investigators roll up at the Mendocino Six staging area; they had been ultra focused, every inch and action professional.

She returns from her memory to listen to Sam some more, "…we know our people and how best to work this kind of case in the woods. The day that Forest Service Law Enforcement can't handle its own investigation is the day we should all quit."

Priest rambles on for awhile and then finishes with, "You let Burns handle Stillman. Stay away from him and, if he approaches you, be friendly but send him back to Burns or Burns' Deputy, Chip Minor."

Mill's interest jumps at the sound of Chip Minor's name. He had been head of the Crime Scene and Mortuary Team that first arrived at O'Reilly's body. Mill appreciated Chip's professionalism and how quickly he'd assessed the facts around O'Reilly's body and death. Chip's quick thinking played a key role in securing O'Reilly's death site, preserving it for the FBI and California Crime Lab folks from Sacramento.

If O'Reilly's death turned out to be something other than a bee-sting accident, Mill feels that Minor will be a big asset for the team.

With this thought, an unformed idea that had been budding somewhere in her mind grows a small branch and a leaf or two, then slips away. When it comes to insights, Mill hates the way she can sometimes almost get the full thought and then lose it.

Damn, if only Priest would shut up for a second, it might come back.

But Priest has gone on talking about the "Fibbies" for awhile, leveling some kind of half-respectful criticism at them and their methods. Within LEO ranks at FLETC, she had always heard them referred to as "the F.B.I." or "the Bureau," never as "Fibbies."

She has to wonder now why Priest would use the term with some derision in a conversation with her. Is Priest treating her as a Legacy insider, now privy to his mean comments about others? Or, maybe he wants her to see how salty and independent he can be?

Well, she can't understand how his comments could help her work with Stillman and his agency. She motions to Priest, "Sam, work with the FBI sounds pretty complicated. I'll just follow your direction and stay out of Stillman's way."

Priest smiles, "I think that would be best, Mill."

He looks at the large government-issued clock on the wall, "Well, look how the time has flown. Somehow that always seems to happen to me, particularly when I'm working on an important case like John's. Let's get you down to Burns' unit."

With that, they stand up and shake hands. Priest's enthusiastic hand pumping makes Mill's breasts shake conspicuously inside her scoop-neck blouse, increasing her awkwardness. She pulls her hand free and heads for the door.

Although she clearly does not need the help, Priest takes hold of her arm and steers her to his secretary's Spartan work area. He gives Mill a little pat on her shoulder as he turns her over to Carrie Soames.

With a nod to Mill, Soames springs up from behind her desk. She whisks Mill down to Jake Burns' secure office area on the first floor.

Mill has never walked faster in her life. The slender Carrie has long legs. She moves like a big bird, elbows several inches out from her sides and slightly lifted.

Mill lags her by four or five feet all the way until Carrie practically skids to a stop before a metal door displaying only a room number and an electronic lock. The lock is massive and can accept a typed code, encrypted ID card, or thumbprint to gain access.

Carrie raps on the door like a woodpecker drilling for beetles. The staccato noise carries for at least a hundred feet down the carpeted hallway

"Doesn't that hurt her knuckles?" Mill wonders, "Note to self: never let Carrie rap on me that way."

As the peremptory knocks fade, the door opens and a long, dour face fills the gap. "Yes?" Jake Burns says politely.

Carrie snaps, "This is Millicent Meacham."

And with that, Carrie spins around and launches herself back towards her cubicle, elbows out. She's out of sight in seconds.

Mill watches Carrie's amazingly speedy departure. Mill imagines a sonic shock wave spreading before her, quiet settling behind.

Checking the direction of Mill's gaze, Jake laughs, "That Carrie. She's a tri-athlete and race walker. And, she never lets any of us forget it. Some of the younger guys can beat her in a sprint wearing track shoes. No one in bureaucrat shoes has ever been able to keep up."

He laughs again and ends his thought with, "Least of all me. Come on in, Meacham. I've got work for you to do." He opens the door wide and ushers her in, gazing appreciatively at her rear as she walks past.

"I call you 'Mill', right?" Burns asks.

Mill nods, "Of course. Bill Zumo said he'd give you a call. Did he get that done?"

Burns replies, "Yeah. He called this morning before breakfast, the bastard, right when I had my mouth full of Wheaties, sitting at the breakfast table in my tighty whities. Ruined my breakfast."

"Called to tell me he was headed to the Dunes for some damn boondoggle. He rubbed my nose it. Told me I was a desk-pounding pussy and that I should get a real job. Then he told me about you and that I could rely on you as if you were my sister, which is a crock because my sister is a whore in San Diego. Not really, my sister. She's not a whore; she's a defense attorney which is about the same thing. And she's good at it which makes real whores look bad."

Mill starts to laugh half way through Jake's careening speech and can't stop.

Zumo had not prepared Mill for Jake. Zumo preferred to let her experience Burns without any warning.

"Please, Jake, have some mercy on me. Too much information!" Mill gasps between laughs.

How totally unexpected Jake Burns turns out to be. She wonders how Jake and Sam Priest could work together; they came across so differently.

They chat for a few more minutes about Mill's work experience. Then Jake brings her next door to a medium-sized conference room. His team is about to start their daily morning check-in. Jake thinks the meeting is the perfect place to introduce Mill and let her both make and get first impressions.

As they enter, team members head for their seats around an oval oak conference table. A side table holds coffee, sweet rolls, fruit, and a donation cup partially full of change and dollar bills.

Most of the team members have helped themselves to the goodies and filled large mugs with coffee or tea.

Mill notices right away that everyone is dressed in civilian clothes. The women present are wearing business clothes similar in cut and style to Mill's. She will fit in, a fact which reassures her.

Everyone appears armed, guns in belt holsters. Most carry .40 caliber Glocks. A few old timers carry 9mm Berettas, proud of their weapon's worn grips, a sign of long service.

Mill had locked her weapon in a portable gun safe in her vehicle before coming in. Mill would ask Jake if she should carry it while on duty, figuring that the answer will be "Yes."

The conference table is crowded. Team members sit elbow to elbow, some with stacks of files and paperwork around them. Everyone has a laptop computer.

A digital projector sends a standby image to a large pull-down screen at one end of the room.

Because the table seems crowded, Mill decides to sit in one of the spare chairs ranged along the wall. But Jake stops her, "Meacham, get your butt up to the table and raise the intelligence of this crowd by a factor of four."

Mill blushes immediately, anxiety spiking.

The faces she has begun to focus on immediately blur. Through misty tunnel vision, she sees people looking at her, some approvingly and some annoyed.

She recognizes Chip Minor. He grins at her down the table. Mill feels relieved at seeing his friendly face.

Her vision clears.

Chip holds up his hand to quiet the hubbub, "Mill, you look a lot better than the last time I saw you."

Chip goes on to explain Mill's bravery in capturing the fleeing drug cartel member. And then Chip announces, "Of course you were more cheerful then!" He punches a button on his laptop.

My God!

Mill's yellow smiley-face lights up the screen! Chip shot a picture of her at the O'Reilly site, the scoundrel!

The group roars! Jake laughs more than anyone else and almost tips his chair over.

Cheeks burning, Mill sends a telepathic message to Bill, "Fear me, Zumo, this is the work of your hands—revenge will be mine!"

The laughter dies down. Mill recalls that almost everyone on the team had nodded or smiled approvingly at her during Chip's story. So, although the vision of "warrior Mill" with a yellow smiley face had been embarrassing, it served to make her acceptable to the team.

Only one woman appeared to scowl. Mill questions herself, "Do I know her? She seems angry at me for some reason."

Mill makes a mental note to approach the woman on break and check this out..

Jake directs the team to make introductions. Each gives their name, rank, home unit, and a short synopsis of their duties with the team.

Most hold the rank of Special Agent. Two are from other federal agencies. One is from the California State Police's Special Investigations Unit.

FBI Agent Stillman is not there.

Mill tries to keep up with the names and organizations. But she finds it impossible to maintain eye contact with people and also make anything more than a few scrawled notes. She'd have to nail down names and duties later.

Introductions over, the team begins their daily situation reports. Each gives a short overview and emphasizes any new facts that had come to light since the last meeting. When appropriate, team members project information up on the screen and use laser pointers to highlight things. The whole business goes smoothly.

Mill quickly realizes she's several days behind in her understanding of what the team's put together. So, she'll be studying notes and documents a plenty.

A lanky woman named Talbot Robertson gives the longest presentation. Her report concerns the latest forensics information that's come in from the California State Police Crime Lab. The autopsy had been performed within a day of O'Reilly's death. That was some of the old news that Mill would have to read soon.

Today's briefing concerns the chemical screening that had been done on O'Reilly's blood and tissues and on his clothing and equipment. "Tal," as she is called, starts with the initial finding that O'Reilly died of apparent natural causes induced by toxic yellow-jacket stings. Sting venom and resulting histamine levels in his blood were several times higher than would have been lethal for a man with his medical history.

Tal mentions that although the number of stings had been calculated at over 300, and the number was unusually high, even higher numbers had been reported in other cases. She states that, although such calls were hard to make, anaphylactic shock probably killed O'Reilly in less than five minutes.

Tal summarizes by saying, "John died hard but likely went fast." Several people shake their heads, faces neutral, eyes pained.

They could be stoic about the death of someone they did not know. But one of their own had died horribly. Even these professionals couldn't shrug that off easily.

Tal notes that O'Reilly's death had occurred away from the sunny, dry habitats where yellow jackets usually nested, although such habitats were less than a mile away.

She says, "The CSP's consulting etymologist thought it was quite unusual for so many yellow jackets to attack O'Reilly so far from any nest. It's an anomaly that he can't explain. But, we have other information that might tell us what happened."

Tal begins to look more animated, like she's ready to share a secret.

Jake holds up his hand to pause Tal's report, "Let's take a look at that situation on the field trip. Mill, make a note to have the etymologist there if we can corral him. Thanks."

Mill sees several heads look in her direction. They nod, her role with the team becoming clearer to them.

Tal continues with her report. Her face now shows real excitement. "The most interesting part of the chemical analysis is that O'Reilly's clothes were saturated with several insect attractants."

At this comment, several heads snap up and two agents look at each other as if to say, "We were right."

Tal goes on, "I won't give you the chemical names. They're about three inches long. But, there are two kinds of insect attractants. One is a sexual attractant called a pheromone. All species, including humans, have these and they are intended by nature to induce mating. Another kind of attractant is called a feeding lure or bait scent."

Tal points to the screen, "As you can see from this photo and visual overlay, O'Reilly's clothes were saturated with a pair of yellow jacket attractants, one a pheromone and one a bait scent, at neck level front and back and also at his abdomen and lower legs. The back of his ball cap and the underside of the bill also showed attractant in high concentrations, suggesting he had attractant on his head and face, a fact born out by the sting and bite patterns noted in the autopsy."

Excited hands begin to go up from the group and small side-conversations break out. Jake waves them down, "Let Tal finish and then we'll get questions."

Tal says reassuringly, "I really don't have much more. In addition to the yellow-jacket attractant at several locations around his gear, O'Reilly had a different chemical, a decay-emulating bait scent, in a line along his back from neck to belt line."

"This stuff's chemically complex and hard to analyze because it oxidized and broke down so quickly the lab people did not have much to work with. Let's just say it was highly concentrated and had no more reason to be on O'Reilly's clothes than the yellow-jacket stuff. Oh, one last thing, the same decay scent was found on another DOA, a Mexican national...ah, Herrera... found to the east of the O'Reilly site with his throat cut, a clear homicide."

Tal stops speaking. The room explodes with comments and hands.

Jake again shushes the group, "Okay, don't all of you bust a gasket. It'd be a hell of a mess for newbie Mill to clean up." He looks around to emphasize his "shush" and the hubbub stops.

"Okay, let's agree that what looked like an accident now looks like a homicide, by a person or persons unknown, and likely connected to another homicide on the same day."

The hubbub starts again, so Jake says louder, "Okay, okay, hold it down. We're going to sweep around the table starting with Chip. You get one question and a follow up on the same subject. Then pass to the person on your left."

Mill immediately sees the wisdom of Jake's approach. The sweep means everyone will get their turn. People will ask their highest priority question after listening to previous answers. She begins to realize why Jake had been chosen to lead the team even with his wild and crazy guy stuff.

Chip Minor turns to the screen and gestures, "Tal, did the lab have any intel or ideas on how the attractants were delivered? I mean, could they tell if the stuff was already on his clothes before going into the site or if some perp shot him with a sprayer or squirt gun or anything there?"

Tal shakes her head, "No clear picture on that, Chip. But, no attractants were found in or around O'Reilly's vehicle. Oxidation rates of the attractants suggest they were delivered in the field. The perp could have used anything that delivered the stuff to a small area for the yellow-jacket attractant. Hits patterned in a circle more or less. Decay stuff was in a line so probably got sprayed or poured. Anything else, Chip?"

Chip shakes his head. Tal shifts her attention to the agent on Chip's left.

The agent looks at his notes, "I thought I heard from the DEA that their aerial intel guys saw the likely perp and O'Reilly together and then tracked the perp to the east after the meet with O'Reilly. Anybody else remember that, too?" Several people nod in answer to his question.

He continues, "So, if they met, how come the perp didn't get all messed up with the yellow jackets? I mean, I've been around those bastards when they're out to get you. They will attack anything moving. Those traps you put around your house are a hassle. If you get any off that stuff in the traps on you the yellow jackets come right at you."

Tal nods and answers, "I'd guess that the perp knew what he was doing around yellow jackets and he may well have worn insect repellent."

The agent nods, "That's what I figured too. And that would mean he'd come thoroughly prepared to deal with O'Reilly but maybe not with the other guy, uh, Manuel Herrera."

There are nods around the table at this line of reasoning.

Jake says, "Let's move on. Phil, another question, please."

Special Agent Phil Gammon turns to Tal, "So, if the perp used attractants, how could he be sure that the yellow jackets would come all the way to the site? I mean a mile is a long way and in such concentrations."

Tal answers, "Again I'd be guessing, but maybe they'd been planted there prior to the raid or brought there that morning somehow. I don't know how you could do that but the etymologist might know."

Mill has been keeping copious notes. She now realizes that the secretary had been pounding away on her laptop the whole time. Mill stops writing things down verbatim and simply takes a few notes as she listens to the questions and answers that follow.

The sweep goes around the table twice before it peters out. Jake hands out a few more team assignments. Then the meeting breaks up.

Jake motions for Mill to stay with him. After a few comments to individuals, he leads her away from the conference room to a small, locked first-floor room that has hastily been set up as an office.

"This is your home, Mill; only the finest accommodations for our field visitors."

Burns smiles.

Mill smiles back and thinks, "If only Jake knew about the broom closet Bill and I call an office…" "But, then again," she muses, "maybe he does."

At least this office has a window even though it overlooks the area where the refuse company park the garbage bins. A few discouraged shrubs and mildewed grass edge the stained concrete.

Jake smiles when he sees the direction of her gaze, "Sorry, grasshopper Mill, this is a high-security operation. You're on the first floor, so you'll have to paper over the windows to keep prying eyes out. No grand view for you."

Mill feigns exasperation, "Just when I thought I had moved up to the big show! You take away my view of the garbage trucks and now, see, my hopes are ruined." They both laugh.

Jake starts to leave. Mill stops him with a gesture, "Jake, how secret is our investigation? What I really mean to ask is, may I share information and discuss what we are working on with Zumo? He worked on Mendocino Six. He asked me to check with you if I could keep him up to date with what we're doing. But we've just gone from an accident to homicide. That's big stuff...bigger then we thought before."

Burns thinks for a moment, "With an ordinary guy, I'd worry about leaks. But, Zumo's dumb as a bag of hammers. No, he's not as smart as hammers, make that rocks. He's barely smart enough to roll down hill in a landslide. So, he's not smart enough to leak anything."

They both laugh at his craziness. Then Jake continues, "More to your point, you can share anything with Zumo unless I tell you otherwise, okay?"

Mill replies with a mock salute, "You got it, boss!" and Jake departs, whistling "Bridge over the River Kwai." He's on his way to share the news about O'Reilly's probable homicide with Priest.

Mill spends the next two hours setting up the empty little office, including papering over the windows. Taking several colors of highlighters, she draws a scene of a garbage truck and garbage cans on the paper. With her "landscape" painted, she thoughtfully adds a pony-sized rat named "Unsub" hiding behind the truck.

That night, she calls Zumo on his encrypted cell and fills him in on the forensics report that had shaken up the investigation so much.

When she finishes her brief, Zumo remains uncharacteristically quiet for a long time. Finally he speaks in a low voice--one that carries concern clearly to Mill, "This case has become capital murder of a federal agent while on duty. On a DEA drug operation, no less. So, get ready for gobs of FBI agents and a federal task force to show up and take over. I'm not sure Jake's team will get to continue even in a support role. There's sure to be some turf issues. But if you get to stay on, watch and learn--you'll get a real education out of this."

Then his voice gets even more concerned, "Mill, I hope you won't walk into a bear trap. There's sure to be security issues, and some leaks. They'll be gunning for some grunts to take the blame for any leaks. That'd be you, young Millicent. So, get your work done and on time. Be respectful and sincere. And, stay low in your foxhole or you may take a round."

He remains silent again for a long time.

Mill waits, wondering about how to be "respectful *and* sincere" with someone like Sam Priest.

Then Bill speaks again, "Mill, everything we know suggests O'Reilly's killer is a very sophisticated operator. We have no idea of motive. I mean, who would kill that stupid putz John O'Reilly? He was just an ambitious Green Creed doofus. But whoever did it and why, the means used by the unsub are like something out of a spy novel or covert CIA ops. The whole business is creepy."

Hearing his words, Mill feels a chill on her neck. The sensation evokes the same feeling she's had when she found the scrap of cloth down the trail from Bud Miller's accident site.

Had she told Zumo about that yet? She couldn't remember.

The feeling runs its course. Oddly, it lifts the nagging, unformed thought she'd had in Priest's office a little higher in her consciousness.

The thought grows another branch and a few more leaves. But then the seedling eludes her again and slips back down into her unconscious.

Damn!

Zumo finishes his remarks, "Mill, Justice will tighten up security a bunch after today. So, as of tomorrow, you may not have official approval to contact me. But, unless you get explicit orders otherwise, Jake has approved you to keep me briefed and I'll expect to be able to call you for updates. Once you hear what the security requirements are, you can let me know if calling you works for you down the road. I'll understand if you feel you can't keep me in the loop. Just say so. You can fill me in after the whole business goes down."

Mill knows how Zumo loves to be in the middle of every investigation and every gossip network. He is showing a lot of sensitivity to Mill's situation by his willingness to accept security limits without bugging Mill for updates.

Mill replies, "Bill, thanks for everything, for all your good thoughts. I'll let you know what's up with security tomorrow first thing. If I can't talk to you, maybe Jake can. Besides, you two boys need to have a long talk about your relationship."

They both laugh. Zumo says "He's a real kick in the pants, isn't he? He's the biggest bullshitter I know in law enforcement and that's saying a lot. He looks like a mortician. He acts like a stand up comic. But he's also one of the best cops I've ever known. If he's got your six, your six is secure. Trust him. He won't let you down."

They chat a little more and then hang up.

That night, young Milly Meacham fights through that fearful, shameful, suffocating dream again.

This time, she lies bound in her new little office, caught in black and yellow crime scene tape that holds her firmly. She would get a hand or arm loose from the sticky tape but then some other part of her would stick to it.

She writhes against the sticky mess--struggling to get free--knowing she has done something wrong...very wrong.

Outside, something dreadful lurches along the hallway, moving towards the opening door. It comes to punish her black, black sins. Milly sobs her shame.

She hears a scratching noise just outside the unlocked door.

It opens.

Carrie Soames appears in the door wearing a devilish grin, prancing in on taloned bird feet red with blood.

Soames waves a twisted gold cross at Milly; the cross hangs around Soames' neck on a rope.

She holds it out in bloody feathered fingers.

Milly opens her mouth wide and screams

...and screams.

Chapter 29

Dream in Daylight

Mill wakes up to the sounds of her own whimpers and pleadings. She's bathed in sweat, hands covering her breasts.

As she had done many times before, she works her way through her "Mill has power" scenario. Under its calming effects, even though the dream lingers in her mind, she relaxes quickly.

She processes her dream fears, looking for ideas about what's bothering her sleeping mind. She finds none and, after five minutes or so, she gets up, leaving the cold dream squatting on her bed.

Mill takes a shower, dresses, fixes a quick breakfast, and sits eating it at the little table in her room at the Residence Inn.

On her second cup of bad, motel-perc coffee, Mill suddenly realizes that, as she struggled through her suffocating dream, her unconscious had grown the illusive idea from a seedling into a sapling.

Her breath catches in her throat.

Mill thumps her cup down, coffee slopping onto the plastic table top.

Could Bud Miller's death connect somehow to the O'Reilly murder? What could ever make her think that?

The chill along her neck comes back, more intense now. She chides herself that she has no evidence of any connection. The weird gold coin and the little piece of cloth she had found down the trail at the Miller site counts as nothing, nothing at all, when it comes to the O'Reilly case.

Then, she shudders again, remembering the twisted gold cross that the bird-demon Carrie had waved at Milly. Maybe bird-Carrie was driving home an idea that seemed too weird—that two federal employees died of causes that seemed "accidental" at first blush and then turned out to be murder in one case and oddly suspicious in the other.

Still, no evidence connects the two.

And the ME had ruled Miller's death an accident.

Even though she knows he might laugh at her, Mill picks up her phone and dials Zumo's secure number. She shyly tells him her hunch. She keeps her dream to herself.

He does not laugh.

When her call with Zumo ends, she calls Manny Suemez and catches him at his desk in DC.

He does not laugh either.

Chapter 30

Meeting Moeller

When Mill arrives at the conference room for the morning check-in, near chaos reigns. Twenty minutes earlier, Burns had been called to Priest's office to meet with the FBI and Justice Department representatives, including Special Agent Stillman and his boss, Regional Special Agent in Charge Frieda Tomlin. The team has heard scuttlebutt that the FBI's Deputy Director had teleconferenced in to talk with Burns and the group in Priest's office.

Out from under Burns' control, agents sit around the table talking loudly about yesterday's briefings and what they'd learned since.

Cell phones go off regularly. The agents hurriedly answer. They huddle in corners with their phones or with hands on the shoulders of other agents, talking earnestly.

The team has ravaged the snack table. The coffee pot shakes empty when Mill tries to pour a mug.

Not surprised, she takes her mug to the canteen on the second floor and has the coffee barrista fill it with an americano, triple shot with a bean.

After a tough night, Mill wants her eyes wide open all day.

As she leaves the canteen, she almost runs into the woman who had scowled at her the day before during team introductions, the team's secretary. Mill smiles at her and asks her name, mentioning that Mill had not been able to keep up with her notes during introductions the day before.

The small, slender woman smiles shyly and says primly, "Agent Meacham, I'm Arianne Moeller. You may call me Arianne."

Mill waits for more, but when nothing more comes, Mill answers, "Thanks, Arianne. Please call me Mill. And, you should know I'm not an investigator--just a grunt like you, a ranger district LEO, sent in to help out the team. I served in Mendocino Six, actually on the team that found John's body. That's why I'm here."

As Mill mentions O'Reilly's death, Arianne's eyes glitter and fill with tears. Mill senses that the woman had been deeply moved by the event.

"Did you know John?" Mill asks Arianne kindly.

Struggling now, Arianne nods. A tear runs down her cheek. She sighs before answering in a strained, tight voice, "John was my supervisor. He was so nice, so brave. I miss him every day. I can hardly stand to hear about all the bad things that happened to him. I just want to get up from that conference table and run away, run anywhere at all."

Arianne's words are filled with regard for O'Reilly but Mill detects something slightly off, a bitter sing-song core, which darkens the admiring tone.

Before Mill can ask more, Arianne sobs, head down.

Mill puts her free arm around Arianne's shoulders.

Turning, Arianne buries her face in Mill's blouse. She cries a long wail.

People passing the two women in the hall try not to stare but their sidelong glances cause Mill to be acutely self-conscious. But what would those passersby have Mill do with coffee in one hand and an arm around the little sobbing woman, push her away, tell her to pull herself together?

Under the curious gaze of strangers, Mill squirms a little inside. Yet she holds Arianne closely and gently, letting her cry out her grief.

After Arianne's anguish quiets a little, Mill asks her, "Arianne, do you need to take some time for yourself, maybe talk to someone? I can't imagine how terrible this assignment must be for you. I'm surprised you're on the team. Does Sam know how you feel?"

Arianne quickly replies, "No, please, Mill, I *asked* to be on the team because, well, I had *feelings* for John."

Mill thinks to herself, "She 'had feelings for John!' Is this some kind of Victorian romance novel? What the hell is this woman doing involved with this investigation?"

Still, Mill has no reason to betray Arianne's confidence or order her to recuse herself.

Arianne seems to realize she said too much. She searches Mill's face with teary eyes. "You won't tell anyone, will you, Mill?" she asks plaintively.

"No, Arianne, I won't," Mill replies, "But please tell me you will go speak to a counselor or someone about your feelings. John's death obviously matters to you but it shouldn't ruin your life. Please tell me you'll do that."

Arianne looks relieved at Mill's words. Then she bows her head and nods agreement that she would seek help. Her tears start again.

Arianne turns abruptly and scurries into the nearby women's room. As the door closes, Mill hears Arianne wail as her soul frees more of her pain and...somehow...rage.

Mill wonders if Arianne wants revenge for John's death. Is that her motive for joining the task force?

Mill shrugs. No way to tell now.

When Mill gets back to the conference room, people have settled back in their chairs.

Tal catches Mill at the door. She tells her that Jake will be in to brief the team in about ten minutes and, with a look at Mill's coffee mug, that she should not stray from the area.

Mill smiles at Tal. Raising the mug, she says with a wink, "Three shots and a bean—I'm not going anywhere except the ladies room and that will be after a while!"

Tal laughs, "I bet I can make it to the canteen and back before Jake gets here." With that, Tal disappears, moving like Carrie Soames.

Mill finds a seat at the table. She begins sorting through the handouts that had been dropped on the table that morning. Several reports catch her attention. One of them summarizes all the weather data for the Mendocino Six operations area, covering two days before, the day of the operation, and two days after.

Mill appreciates how carefully the writer had prepared the one-page brief. Looking at the bottom of the page, she sees that Chip Minor authored it.

She looks up and smiles at him, waving the report, as he talks on his cell phone. She mouths, "Nice." He smiles, bowing a little to her compliment.

Another report covers the vegetation in the O'Reilly murder area, listing each species by its common and scientific names. The author included sample photos for each species, obviously taken from a text book or field guide, as well as some actual images from the site.

Mill finds this report a much tougher read. The author used scientific names and listed every plants found within a grid laid out in one-meter squares.

"This is like wading through molasses in February," she fusses, "What the hell was this guy thinking? I have good scientific training, in botany even, and I can barely get through this crap!"

Determined to mine anything valuable out of the report, Mill plods through. She finds her one nugget in a footnote on page five. It reads, "The survey found several examples of 1-3 centimeter small stems from an eastern willow species. They were located within two meters of O'Reilly's corpse. The stems appear to have originated from the same source and were broken into small pieces. That species is not found on that site and we have no explanation for its presence."

Mill thinks, "Here's another anomaly. But, what can it mean? Did some hiker just have these twigs in their pack and dump them out sometime ago? Do they have anything to do with O'Reilly's death at all?"

She gives up on the thoughts, again seeing no real connection to either O'Reilly or, after her nocturnal, haunted brainstorm, to Bud Miller.

As Mill picks up another report, Arianne slides inconspicuously into the room. She reaches past Mill's shoulder and drops a small, handwritten note on Mill's "already read" pile.

As Mill picks it up, Arianne moves up to her note-taker place at the mid-section of the table. Arianne looks back at Mill. She smiles a sad but thankful smile at her.

Mill opens the note, "Dear, Dear Mill, thanks for taking time with me. I apologize for being so sad and by burdening you with my troubles. You were wonderful. I thank you from the bottom of my heart. Yours very truly, Arianne."

Mill is struck again by the sense she had blundered into a Victorian drama. Yet, Arianne's gesture touches Mill's heart. She turns to smile warmly at the still distraught woman.

At that moment, the conference room door opens. Jake Burns comes in, followed by two people dressed in suits and wearing FBI credentials. Jake steps to the front of the room. He motions for the pair to join him.

All business now, Burns turns to the waiting team, "Some of you already know this gentleman, Special Agent Gregory Stillman. With him is Regional Special Agent in Charge Frieda Tomlin. I have several announcements first and then I'll ask for comments from our FBI colleagues."

Burns pauses and looks around the room, meeting everyone's eyes. He begins, "You've all done a terrific job of getting on top of John's death and you've done it quickly. Three days from now, on Friday at Noon, we will pass the investigation off to a joint task force led by Special Agent Stillman. At that time, I expect each of you to have all your records and notes up to date and on the Forest Service ASAC web site, ready for access by Greg's team."

At these words, several of the team members frown. Clearly they do not want to give up control of the investigation, particularly now that they know it's a homicide and one of their own had been murdered.

Several hands go up. Jake handles a few questions about records and evidence.

Mill notices that Stillman frowned when Jake called him "Greg."

She wonders if he doesn't like hearing his nick name used in this important setting or maybe having a nick name at all.

Stillman stands over six feet seven inches in his size 15 shoes, a strong-looking African American, measured but quick in his movements. A little awestruck by his imposing presence, Mill realizes he looks remarkably like a stern Sidney Poitier--handsome and intelligent--writ large.

Mill suspects he probably gets asked about a past basketball career more often than he might have liked. Although she could not know it, Stillman would reply to those questions by saying, "In my day, I was too tall for football and too clumsy for basketball. So, I became a cop, then a lawyer, and now an FBI agent. Now, I shoot hoops with high schoolers and tell 'em how I'm gonna bust them if they get out of line."

Burns goes on, "So you will know before you hear it in the hallways, Sam Priest has been placed on administrative leave for the duration of the investigation. The Law Enforcement Director in DC took this action at the request of the FBI to assure that Sam isn't put in a bad position, trying to oversee and support the investigation while having been close to John and having had a part in sending John out to the operation."

The group immediately knows what Burns left unstated. Priest was somehow under suspicion or in the way.

Even Mill knows things look bad for Priest. She believes Jake is putting the best light on Sam's circumstances.

A hand shoots up and Jake points to the person raising it. "Who will be taking Sam's place?" a special agent from the Wallowa-Whitman National Forest asks.

"I will be acting for the duration of the investigation," Jake replies, his undertaker's face poker straight.

Several team members smile at this news. Mill agrees the choice of Jake makes sense, given the FBI involvement and the importance of the case to the Forest Service.

Jake continues, "Most of you will be heading back to your home units with my sincere thanks. You will each be subject to immediate recall for anything concerning the case. Three of you will transition to the FBI team, at least for several weeks, maybe longer."

"Arianne Moeller will assist the FBI joint task force with records and computer access. Special Agent Minor will serve as the Forest Service liaison to the team. Officer Mill Meacham will assist the task force with evidence, coordinate field trips, and conduct field liaison with Forest Service units."

Several members of the team glare at Mill when Jake mentions her role. They obviously wish that they had received the assignment.

But a couple of them smile at her and bob their heads in congratulations. The rest simply remain focused on Jake.

Burns asks for more questions. Several hands come up. He answers each in turn and then gestures for Tomlin to come forward.

The stylishly and impeccably dressed Tomlin's demeanor speaks volumes. Tomlin is the *woman in charge*.

A head taller than Mill, Tomlin sets her jaw. She eyes each team member like a wolf intimidating woolly sheep.

She sternly thanks the group. Then she bluntly tells them that if there are "any leaks on this case to anyone, anytime, anywhere—even if it's your fuckin' mother on Mother's Day" she would see the leakers in federal prison, after escorting them there personally.

Then Tomlin walks back to her position, standing against the conference room wall. No one dares to look her way.

"Wow," thinks the impressionable Mill, "RSAC Tomlin is one tough, hard bitch." Mill visualizes Tomlin smiling happily as she uses a steel fist in a tungsten-carbide glove to thump team members' heads.

Mill would try to make sure Tomlin wouldn't be thumping any Meacham heads.

Gregory Stillman steps forward. Looking at a thick wad of notes, he fills the team in on schedules and locations for the transition. He has a smooth, no-nonsense style that settles the team back down after Tomlin's comments.

Mill realizes she has seen a fine example of the FBI's best working the time-honored "good cop, bad cop" approach on bureaucrats.

The meeting breaks up. Jake asks Mill, Arianne, and Chip to stay behind.

Once everyone else clears out, he sits them down, close together, knees almost touching. He takes out a purple I-Pod and attaches it to a small amplifier-speaker set. He selects some wildly chaotic music and turns the volume up high. Jake leans forward in his chair and gestures for the three to lean in to speak to him.

Baffled, Mill leans in until her face almost touches Chip's and Jake's who are seated on either side of her. Mill strains to hear as Jake speaks quietly but distinctly. "Look at us. Here we are looking like convent girls talking about sex." He laughs.

"I'm playing the music and we're in this huddle because I have my suspicions this room may be bugged. Just a gut feeling...no evidence. I'm going to have it swept today when we're done here."

Mill and Arianne smile at his comments. Both are a little excited at the "spy" implications.

Jake goes on, "Forget about my precautions for our little tête-à-tête. Tomlin and Stillman have agreed that you will represent the Forest Service and me personally on the joint task force. You will be expected to share with me anything and everything you hear or do there, no exceptions. Do you understand?"

The three nod.

Jake continues, "You'll see lots of other agencies there, including DEA and some other folks who may not be willing to tell you who they work for. Do not push them to find out because it's none of your business. You could wind up in a secret prison in Butt Fuck, Bosnia, for all I know. I would miss you, but not very much. So wipe your noses and asses and be respectful."

Arianne blushes a little at his salty words but looks excited and more positive than she had earlier with Mill in the hallway. Jake looks around the group and they all nod again to show that they understand his direction.

Jake finishes up with, "Okay. You'll also see me over there at Justice from time to time. Just pretend you don't know me 'cause from now on, to everyone on the task force, you work for them, not me. Just play Secret Squirrel and you'll do fine. And, stay focused, stay safe, or I'll show you what "being Burned" really means."

With that, Jake Burns turns off the I-Pod. They stand and leave the room silently.

Mill goes back to her little office. She begins boxing up her paper records. She makes sure to store all of her electronic information on her laptop's hard drive. According to Stillman, at the FBI task force hub her laptop would be security scanned and enabled. The machine would remain inside the security perimeter at all times. Nothing could leave the secure electronics environment. Stillman had emphasized that no thumb drives, portable hard drives, or wi-fi cards were allowed.

And, depending on how the case came out, Mill's laptop might have to be abandoned to the FBI evidence locker for a long time, maybe forever. That would chap the ass of the admin people back on the Mapleton District because they'd have to buy her a new one with no expectation of ever getting money from somewhere else to cover the purchase.

She opens her cell phone and calls Manny Suemez on the secure line.

He's at his desk and apologizes for not getting back to her sooner, "Way crazy back here, chica."

She rapidly fills him in on developments. He listens quietly and then tells her, "Mill, with the kind of resources being put on this case, things will probably move quickly. Make sure you keep your head down. Pull your weight; otherwise, you'll be on the street in a heartbeat. I've been making a few calls and the O'Reilly case is getting big attention, even up to the White House and the Senate Select Committee on Terrorism."

Shocked, Mill asks, "Terrorism? What the hell would some Senate Committee on Terrorism want with this murder?"

Suemez replies in his serious tone, "I have no idea, no fuckin' idea at all, but that's what I'm hearing. It's fuckin' weird because there seems to be no connection to anything international, no big splashy murder, and no threats about more to come. Isn't that what terrorists do? Don't they do a bunch of bad shit to spread fear and screw up peoples' lives? It doesn't fit for me."

They kick around a few ideas but come up with nothing. Talking off the top of his head, Suemez can make no direct or indirect connection between Miller and O'Reilly, other than they both worked for the Forest Service and both of them died on duty within 300 miles of each other.

Manny promises to call and e-mail around and to let Mill know what he hears.

After the call, Mill finishes filling her boxes.

"My goodness," Mill says to herself as she packs the last of her stuff, "What kind of mess has this country girl gotten herself into?"

She will find out soon enough how big a country-girl's mess can be.

Chapter 31

Mist Circles

The Mist Clan Chiefs have come from every point of the compass to meet in dry karstic limestone caverns under private land in northwestern Missouri. The dozens of rooms have walls and roofs of limestone--worn, sculpted, and etched by water over millions of years. A safe, solid meeting place for leaders facing an uncertain future.

The caves were discovered by farm boys over a hundred years before. First used to stable animals and store hay, they were later developed into a spa for wealthy people seeking nature cures. As the developers built the spa, expert craftsmen leveled and ground the floors smooth.

Stone masons used a big rift in the limestone as a chimney for a huge brick-lined, field-stone fireplace. Its opening gaped large enough for a tall man to stand within, turn with arms outstretched, and touch nothing.

A Mist-friendly millionaire now owns the place now and keeps it as a Spartan get-away and hunting lodge. Modern lighting and plumbing and a functional kitchen will make the Clan Chiefs' stay easier.

For all the modern touches, the caverns still evoke a strong primitive response. A big central cave serves as meeting and eating room. Rugged but well-made log furniture blend well with the cave setting. Finely knotted hemp rugs or woven rush mats cover the floors in many places. Native American statuary, bowls, and artifacts stand in corners, perch in natural stone niches, and dangle in shadowy ceiling coves, sometimes giving a visitor delighted or shocked surprise. Windows set into natural-appearing breaks in the rock produce odd patterns of light and shadow.

As the Mist Chiefs and Badger trek towards the camp, they focus on one grim certainty. They all know that, for the first time in their history, they are on the brink of being exposed--if not in name, then in substance--as a shadowy, domestic eco-liberation organization.

They had worked so long and so hard to avoid being known. But now, for all their efforts, law enforcement may be sniffing on their trail.

As they arrive, the Mist Chiefs admire the hidden stony clutch of their lodging, the green hills and mountains all around, and the two warm springs close by.

They learn bats inhabit many of the other caves in the area; several species are present, including the Thompson's Big-Eared Bat, an endangered species. While the old spa is screened off from the bats, they can be seen pouring out of other cave entrances and rifts every night at dusk. A good omen for the servants of the Earth Mother.

So cautious are they, the Clan Council has not met face-to-face for years. And even now, the members all hike in at staggered times and from different directions.

The original six Mist warriors are getting old. For some the trails were a challenge. Yet urgency added vigor to their strides and all had made the trek safely.

With the consent of the rest of the Council, Arrow, the War Chief, has invited Badger to help them sort out their situation and its implications.

Badger's attendance violates Mist security principles to a degree. A Mist warrior, even a Clan Leader like Badger, generally does not know more than one or two other Mist members, let alone the Chiefs.

But in this case, the urgency is too strong to exclude Badger. And, of course, in this remote location, Badger can't learn the Clan Chiefs' cover names or home bases.

For their first full day together, they simply move about the property, taking in their natural surroundings, enjoying the geothermal waters. They meditate or pray as they choose. They calm and focus their minds.

If they meet someone else, they often simply sit and catch up with one another's lives and interests. By mute agreement, they avoid the topic that brought them together until the whole Chief's Council meets the next day.

If the Mist Clan Chiefs found some personal peace the day before, their first Council meeting proves unsettling.

The six sit in a circle of chairs in front of the magnificent fireplace. The high cavern arches above them. Natural light streams in textured by the room's only window, a large roughly hexagonal piece of isinglass set above the massive front door.

When together, the Council uses a "talking stick" to aide discussions, passing a highly decorated Native American totem stick around the circle. In turn, each holds the stick to speak and then passes it. The stick passes until everyone has said all they want to say on a subject.

When a discussion of one subject ends, the talking stick passes around the group until someone raises the next subject. If no one raises another subject, the meeting ends.

That first morning, Arrow takes the talking stick from its holder. His parents had named him Brixton Bragg, a big name for a tiny boy, one he had grown into slowly.

Bragg personally chose "Arrow" as his Mist name. And now, holding the talking stick, he stands straight as his Mist name implies, tall and thin in the meeting cave's shadowy gloom.

He gets right to the point, "Brothers and Sisters, we meet at a time when Mist is at a crossroads. The decisions we make here and the directions we go after we leave will either keep us safe from public view or thrust us into the public spotlight and perhaps our doom."

Arrow looks around the Council, noting the grim faces," "For over thirty years we have done our noble work out of sight of the world. Kraznin would be proud. We have done *well*."

At his words, a couple of the Chiefs mutter their agreement and snap their fingers in support, causing whispery reverberations in the cavern--rat feet scampering across a wooden floor.

The War Chief continues, "We alone acted to save Our Divine Mother Earth when no others would or could. We alone stand against the Greed Machine that drives our nation, the machine that would destroy the natural things that we love and that love us back. Yes, we have done *well*!"

Again, the Clan Chiefs voice their praise for his words and the cave echos with rats-in-shadows sounds.

Arrow speaks again, "Yes, we have done well but now things have happened that could potentially reveal Mist to the world and, more importantly, to police and intelligence agencies. Some things you've heard about. I have more to share with you today. Before I begin, with your permission, I'd like to pass the talking stick to Badger so that you may hear the story of how we've arrived at this crossroads."

The other Chiefs nod their consent.

Badger moves forward from the corner of the room and stands before the great fireplace. Badger looks gravely at the Council and then gives them a detailed account of the O'Reilly Strike from the time the Strike plan had been approved to the de-briefing with Ekos.

Badger finishes by saying, "With each successful Strike, Ekos has become more confident. Unfortunately, that well-deserved confidence now borders on arrogance. I'm beginning to believe that Ekos is starting to feel that no one can stop one of our Strikes. Although not reckless, I perceive Ekos feels nearly invincible and is prepared to act as if it were true."

Badger gives the talking stick back to Arrow. He says, "Thank you, Badger, for your very capable leadership and your report. I now call upon Raven, the Listening Chief, to give us the latest information."

Raven takes the talking stick and stands at her chair. Small in stature, slightly bent, her dignified presence and energy make her seem larger than life size. Anytime she stands in front of the Council, Raven always seems immovable, rock solid.

Yet, unlike her avian namesake, Raven always speaks the absolute fewest words of any on the Council. Though few, her words often have the greatest impact on Council decisions.

She stands for long moments before starting to speak in her measured way, "We have a Mist warrior on the Forest Service law enforcement staff...a secretary...who serves the thugs investigating the O'Reilly Strike. She has given us excellent information about...the focus of the Forest Service investigation. We rarely use listening devices...but we have used them in this case."

"Our warrior has planted and removed them several times, putting them in different meeting rooms and offices and then removing them after short periods of time. She controls them remotely...sometimes she records while she's in the room and sometimes in her absence, when she knows...critical meetings are taking place. This minimizes the chance that someone...will detect our ears and...us."

Several of the Chiefs nod approvingly. They all know Raven maintains the utmost security as Kraznin's people had taught her.

Raven goes on, "Mist also has other federal...informants. They tell us that the DEA believes our Ekos to be...a killer for hire...perhaps from a drug cartel...perhaps an assailant from one of O'Reilly's past cases...a skillful revenge killer."

"The FBI believes that the DEA has...a plausible theory but they... also conjecture that Ekos could be an escaped criminal, drug hijacker, or foreign terrorist...a killer who came haphazardly through the area at the time of the raid...panicked...and killed two men who got in his way."

She pauses to let her words sink in, "So, the DEA...and the FBI... offer no threat to Mist that I can foresee...for now."

Two of the other Chiefs show visible relief as her words sink in, smiling and leaning back into the thick cushions on their wide Adirondack-styled chairs.

Raven pauses for at least 30 seconds looking upwards into the shadowy arch of the cave before continuing, "Forest Service investigators represent...a bigger threat. Eyes and Ears warriors from several locations have seen...or heard of...messages from William Zumo...a respected Patrol Captain on the Oregon Coast. In the last two days...he has begun to

228

ask questions…to promote theories…that connect the deaths of Clarence Miller…John O'Reilly…Manuel Herrera."

"The warriors believe that these theories may also be held by… perhaps come from…acting Assistant Regional Special Agent in Charge, Jacob Burns."

Head turning and darting almost like her totem bird, Raven searches the eyes of the others until she sees they understand what she had shared. Then she continues, smiling a little at her next remark, "Our brave warrior… the secretary…has not been able to put an ear in Burns' office or meeting rooms because…he is using covering noise…loud discordant music…when discussing sensitive information…and also randomly sweeping office spaces for bugs. Our warrior has…wisely…stopped using the bugs in the Forest Service offices…for now."

Raven stops speaking for almost a minute, then begins again, "I believe…strongly…that the greatest present threat to Mist comes from the two Forest Service thugs. We may have little time to prevent them from…learning more…reasoning more…ferreting out our existence…and convincing the FBI and DEA to act against us."

Raven stops speaking for a long moment. Her face creases with pain, "And then...as Kraznin taught us and our experience has shown...we would be revealed."

"Our supporters...their money...their influence...would...disappear at even a whisper of our existence. Without resources, some...perhaps many... of our warriors...would desert us...reveal more to the thugs...make deals with them."

"Mist would first...implode...then explode...like a super nova. All lost…. Nothing must be revealed...not even our name...especially our name... wonderful, obscuring, secret Mist."

Raven stands for almost a minute more, silent. She listens to her inner thoughts and impressions, searching for any more words that should be heard. Then she nods absently to herself, turns to the War Chief, and hands him the talking stick.

Struck by the gravity of Raven's words and her demeanor, Arrow, too, stands quiet for a moment. He looks at the faces of his Mist brothers and sisters, gauging the shock and concern he sees there.

He says simply, "Thank you, Raven."

Then Arrow draws himself to his full height. He lifts the talking stick higher, "Now, brothers and sisters, fellow Clan Chiefs of Mist, search your hearts and minds for wisdom. Remember our great love for Mother

Earth. Now we pass the talking stick. The Council begins!"

With those words, the War Chief passes the talking stick to his left into the hand of the Money Chief, Golden Eagle. The Money Chief holds advanced degrees in finance and economics from Wharton and Cambridge. He fancies himself a supreme strategist. And, indeed, his strategic approach had been invaluable in guiding Mist's secret programs over many years.

Compared to Arrow though, Golden Eagle is also more inherently violent and bold, at times excessively fierce and wildly impetuous. So, in times past, Golden Eagle had pushed for simple, violent ways to advance Mist's cause, to Strike hard and be gone.

In turn, Arrow had found himself arguing for more deliberate, careful action.

The two men disagreed loudly at times but both had always worked to find an effective middle ground.

Today, Golden Eagle takes the talking stick and waves it passionately, almost threateningly, at the War Chief. He says in a loud voice, "We must cauterize this wound now, before the infection spreads. Fire and blackened, broken flesh are the only things that will work. I say we give the War Chief the direction to eliminate anyone who threatens us, especially the two agency thugs, Zumo and Burns. We must Strike now, damn it, now!"

Emphasizing his words, the Money Chief slams his fist down on the arm of his chair. The wood makes a loud crack like a pistol shot, although the arm does not break.

Two Chiefs look alarmed at Golden Eagle's vehemence and the sharp sound. They relax but remain solemn.

The talking stick begins to pass and words flow.

Several days come and go.

The talking stick passes around the circle uncountable times.

As the Council sits, Badger no longer speaks but simply serves the group's needs—water, food, or neck massage. When the Council takes a break, Badger strolls or sits with the Chiefs, encouraging them and providing answers to tactical questions.

Somehow, although sunlight touches and moves through the caves, meeting underground makes the passage of days and nights less perceptible, less tangible.

The Chiefs have bound themselves to the threats that confront Mist.

So, although they go outside and drink in the scenery and fresh air, the sunshine and moonlight, they quickly return to the dark caves to map Mist's destiny.

The Clan Chiefs of Movement and Enemies speak long about the need for Mist to disappear from public view, avoid Strikes for many years, and spread rumors and false information to confuse the federal authorities.

The Listening, Money, and Friends Chiefs respond forcefully about the need to Strike the two Forest Service thugs. They tie their deaths to the goals of making Mist less visible and spreading confusion.

Throughout, Arrow speaks rarely. He's deeply troubled by the risks of following any of those paths.

After a time, the Clan Chiefs get close to agreement. At that point, Arrow sends Badger home to await orders.

His action keeps knowledge isolated to only those warriors who needed to know it. Badger leaves, satisfied that the Chiefs are working on the right issues yet worried that events radically outside Mist's control might still overwhelm them all.

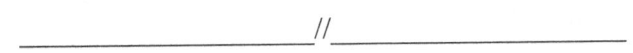

Badger walks briskly along the 20-mile route to the bus station in Moody, Missouri. The trail skirts the bases of Rocky River bluffs. It winds through rural tracks and dirt roads.

Walking at a brisk pace, drinking in warm nature all around, Badger's worries drop away. Badger's soul rests on Earth Mother's bosom.

Two days later, the War Chief walks the same route.

But Arrow has no peace in his heart.

The Mist Clan Chiefs have decided to Strike both Zumo and Burns, each to be killed by different assassins and each death to be cloaked in deception.

The War Chief worries that these Strikes, coming on the heels of the Miller and O'Reilly Strikes, will provide more hard evidence for investigators.

He suspects, no, he knows intuitively that Mist assassins have made unreported mistakes in the past, small ones perhaps but nonetheless revealing hints about Mist's existence. Things clever police work could reveal.

The sharp cat eyes of law enforcement may already be looking for Mist, watching for flickers of movement, ready to pounce with ripping claws.

Still, Arrow knows that Mist warriors and assassins can be very clever and effective in making sure the Strikes appear completely accidental or unrelated to any others.

He smiles grimly, knowing that Strike plans would have to be drawn up quickly. Eyes and Ears warriors would have little time, once again, to gather enough information to make the Strikes work smoothly and invisibly.

No time to plan "accidents." Maybe just enough time to plan Strikes clever enough to keep Mist invisible.

But those concerns are minor compared to the War Chief's growing perception that the Clan Council has begun to make decisions under pressure --decisions that might be fundamentally flawed.

Only a year ago, they would have taken months, sometimes years, to plan a Strike. Now they are going to hurtle forward and complete two Strikes in less than a month.

Because Mist has long operated as a slow-moving, secret organization, the Council might not be able to judge operations in a fast-moving, more exposed threat environment.

Another, bigger issue looms in Arrow's mind. As War Chief, Arrow had been the principal architect of the War Clan, had built it painstakingly with his own intellect and craft.

His War Clan operates as a small, elite, clandestine force of self-reliant assassins and warriors, most unknown to each other. Only the War Chief and a few Clan Leaders like Badger have routine contact with them. They are not trained as a group in team work or in small unit, force-on-force tactics.

The bigger threat lies in the Council's back-up plan should the Zumo and Burns Strikes fail to sidetrack Mist's pursuers. It is that plan that causes Arrow's face to pale when he thinks about that desperate mission. He hopes he will never be asked to lead it.

Because, in that direction, Arrow knows lies the War Clan's sure death.

"*All lost....*" as Raven had said.

Chapter 32

Underbelly of the FBeastl

Mill, Chip, and Arianne enter the Justice Building together and pass through security on their way to their entry briefings.

They figure strength in numbers will make their transition easier. They figure wrong.

Instead of three small targets, together they make a large one.

They receive temporary security badges and are escorted to a small briefing room.

There they wait, and then wait some more--for two hours all told. They sit uncomfortably on metal office chairs. Each time they move, a red light on a small video camera in one corner of the ceiling blinks on and off. The camera serves as the only recognition that the FBI knows they exist.

The door suddenly opens, loudly banging against a chair. Special Agent Gregory Stillman and RSAC Frieda Tomlin stride in. They walk to the head of the conference table.

The three Forest Service folks had been chatting quietly, grumbling at the delay. The sharp sound of the metal door striking the metal chair makes them jump.

The stern looks on Stillman's and Tomlin's faces quiet any complaints the three might have about the hasty entrance.

Dressed today in a severely tailored blue pants suit, Tomlin addresses the group first. "Okay, you cherries," she spits, "Do any one of you remember my promise from yesterday—the one about leaks and federal prison?"

They nod, impressed again by her directness.

"Well," she grits, "My promise goes double for you cow cops. I know *you'll* screw up. The minute you do, you're gone. Screw up big enough and I'll haul you to prison in my very own FBI sedan. It's the big black one with the pretty flashing lights, so the rest of the cons will know you weak-shit bastards are coming."

Tomlin glowers at the group, "As far as I know, the only thing you Forest Service cops are good for is chasing rustlers and arresting campers smoking pot. Frankly, I don't want you amateurs here but you know some things and have contacts the FBI needs to get our job done. You understand me?"

The three nod again.

"So, do your damn job and give me no grief. You may survive that way," Tomlin finishes.

She stares each of them down. Then she walks rapidly out the door, slamming it behind her.

Mill realizes her jaw had dropped open at Tomlin's performance. She quickly closes it.

Goodness! If Mill had been sent here to watch and learn, Tomlin sure plays the teacher with conviction. Can the FBI think this was the way to run a partnership? Yikes!

Gregory Stillman sits at the head of the table. He looks at the group thoughtfully, his face quiet. Enough seconds pass for Mill to wonder if he plans to speak or if he's simply waiting for one of them to ask questions. Just as she opens her mouth to ask a few, Stillman speaks.

"Special Agent Tomlin means what she says. In fact, she's rarely this nice. Let me explain. Soon after she started to work for the Bureau, she was part of a joint operation with a couple of other agencies. A local cop left his post. Agent Tomlin wound up taking two rounds, one to the head and one to the chest."

Stillman looks at each of them in turn, "From her own gun. The perp blind-sided and disarmed her. Her vest stopped one round. The impact broke a rib and collapsed a lung. The other round grazed her skull but didn't enter. Good thing the perp couldn't shoot straight."

"Agent Tomlin was in rehab for months. She doesn't trust anyone, particularly locals. In her mind, you'd be locals. If you work with her through me, everything should go okay."

After sitting through today's "tough cop, buddy cop" routine, Chip figures the time has come to end the posturing. Chip looks Stillman in the eyes.

He answers dryly, "Look, Agent Stillman, we're here to do a job, not get lectures from people who question our professionalism. Frankly, as far as Forest Service Law Enforcement is concerned, you and Tomlin can keep your opinions to yourselves. As I said, we're here to do a job. Why don't you both can the Bureau shit and tell us what you want done?"

Minor leans back from the table, and stares into Stillman's eyes again, one eyebrow raised.

Stillman glares back angrily at Minor for a moment, locking eyes with him. Minor coolly stares back.

Mill remembers boys on the playground acting like this, eyes locked,

234

each waiting for the other to blink.

Finally, Stillman looks away with a slight smile, his handsome dark face graced by a kinder look. Stillman looks up at the camera, "Frieda, come on back in when you're ready. We're going to get started."

Mill keeps her face in "poker" mode. Her mind races over what she just learned. She had no idea that Tomlin and Stillman had been bluffing, trying to get an edge on the Forest Service employees. She had bought their act hook, line, and sinker.

"Mill," she says to herself, "Here's lesson one when working with the FBI: they're going to bluff and when you're ready, call their bluff." Mill looks admiringly at Chip who seems wary but at ease after the mating dance.

Mill then looks at Arianne Moeller who seems to be working through what had happened much as Mill has done. Their eyes meet.

Mill winks and Arianne giggles and looks up at the camera. She then sits up straight on the edge of her chair. She crosses her hands primly on the conference table, ready for work.

Mill looks off into a corner of the room. She laughs to herself. She shakes her head, finally turning to look at Stillman who is gazing thoughtfully at Mill.

"Ready to get going, Meacham?" he asks.

Mill blushes a little, bats her eyes, and says in a schoolgirl's sing-song, "Yes, Agent Stillman."

Stillman laughs out loud, a bellow-laugh from a big man. Stillman roars, "Okay, you cow cops, let's get started."

Stillman spends the next half hour giving them their assignments. Chip would handle all aspects of forensics. Gregory tells him to brief the task force in depth the next day and be ready to answer tough questions.

Once Chip thinks the task force has gotten up to speed, he would fly back to the FBI Crime Lab at Quantico, Virginia to brief them and rework the existing evidence. Then, he would help process new evidence as it came in. Over video link, Chip and a Quantico team would brief the task force daily on forensics and suggest probable lines of investigation.

In a similar way, Arianne would manage all records, written or electronic, that the Forest Service investigative team had put together. Tomorrow, she would provide the joint task force with a summary of the records and answer any of their requests to see them or to interview the Forest Service employees who had written or recorded them. Many of the records would stay over at the Forest Service Regional Office, so Arianne would shuttle back and forth as needed.

Stillman turns to Mill with a thoughtful look. "Meacham," he says, "You're a special case. As I understand it, you're the daughter of W. A. Meacham, the new boss of the Forest Service. True?"

Mill nods.

Stillman looks at her gravely, "Okay. First, I'm not saying you have this expectation, but nobody should expect to get a free ride on this joint task force. That means you, too."

Mill blushes a little but nods again. She could tell by his firm but respectful tone that Gregory is carefully treading sensitive ground. He wants to know Mill's expectations and where her loyalties lie.

Mill looks at Stillman and states distinctly, "Agent Stillman, please forget what my father does for a living. As far as work is concerned, our relationship is an accident of biology. I'm here to make sure an unsub goes to jail for killing O'Reilly and Herrera. That's all. And, I'm ready to do my job."

Gregory nods, appearing satisfied for the moment.

At that moment, Frieda Tomlin walks through the door. She strides over to Mill and sticks out her hand, "Meacham, that's what I needed to hear. Welcome aboard."

Frieda Tomlin smiles down into Mill's eyes, releases her hand, and pats her shoulder in an almost motherly way.

Tomlin then sits down next to Chip. She smacks him lightly on his arm, saying, "Call our bluff will you, Major-Smart-Ass Minor?" Chip snorts at her play on words.

Once again, Mill sits stunned by understandings she'd never had before. Talk about an education!

The mighty FBI was concerned about Mill Meacham and the fact that she's W. A. Meacham's daughter!

Now she understands. The Bureau had been in a tough spot--they could not offend another agency, one they relied on professionally from time to time; or the powerful Congressional committees that dealt with law enforcement policy and appropriations. So, they had to know if Mill was a spy, fluff along for the ride, or a cop ready to dig in and get the job done.

First, they'd tried to run Mill off and she didn't run. That covered the "fluff" part.

Then they'd asked about her loyalty and gotten an answer. That covered the "spy" part.

And commitment? Well, Mill's pretty sure they'll keep a close eye on her, at least for awhile, until they're sure she means it about being committed to the joint task force mission.

A cold thought hits her. She guesses that Frieda kept the camera aimed at her from the time the three Forest Service people entered the conference room. Now that's a little scary.

Mill tries to remember if she had acted unprofessionally or not. Well, Frieda's not shown her the door, so okay.

Stillman looks at her again, "Meacham, we want you to get a field trip scheduled for two days from now. You'll handle all the logistics. Work with security on keeping the trip under wraps. No media. Got it?"

Mill nods.

He goes on, "Once the field trip's over, I'll give you a role with the joint task force, running down leads and doing interviews. Don't expect a big assignment. You just don't have the experience. For a new LEO, just being on the team should feel like an honor. So, don't feel bad. You okay with that?"

Mill nods again, smiling agreement.

Stillman ends with, "And we'll also want you to help Moeller out when she needs it. You two know where things are stored over at the Forest Service. So, you can get them located and over to us faster than we could fumbling around on our own."

They spent the next half hour covering questions and refining assignments. Not wanting to be seen as a crank or an amateur, Mill keeps her theory about a connection between O'Reilly and Miller to herself.

When the discussion ends, Stillman leads the three of them to their work spaces. Chip has a desk with the task force and also one in Quantico. Mill and Arianne get small door-less offices off a conference space.

Four other offices opening into the conference area are staffed with FBI agents. All rooms with doors are code- or fingerprint-secured.

Mill's ten-by-ten office gives her room to spread out. To make work go smoothly, offices and the conference room are fully equipped with electronics, including computers with massive external hard drives, printers, faxes, and video-conferencing gear.

Returning to her previous thoughts about the FBI needing to know about her loyalty, Mill realizes that the web cam on her computer could be watching her full time. Her phone and office could be tapped and recorded. Yes, they could be.

Mill believes that the FBI's intimidating reception was largely aimed at her. So, she promises herself she'd behave professionally at all times. She guesses that she might be a little paranoid but, given her situation, maybe some caution wouldn't hurt anything.

—————————————//—————————————

When Mill gets back to her room at the Residence Inn that night, her caution lamp stays lit.

As she starts in through her door, something tells her that someone, probably the FBI, has searched her room. Whoever had done it had been so good that nothing seems out of place. Still, she sees that a small corner of her personal journal peeks out from under her underwear. She can't remember having left it that way.

And the pencils on the desk are definitely aligned in a precise, non-Mill kind of way. Faint impressions of footprints can be seen in the rug near the window.

Mill's breath catches in her throat. What if someone's still in the room? Is the curtain out from the wall far enough to conceal a small person?

She pulls her Glock. She moves quietly forward with her hand on its grips, peering in corners, listening for intruder sounds, feeling her heart bang away in her chest.

A noise outside!

She stands frozen for a few seconds, her vision starting to blur from anxiety.

Then Mill relaxes, shakes her head, and laughs out loud. My God, she was becoming such a nut. Most of the "clues" she discovered could easily be explained by the maid coming in to clean and straighten up.

Mill laughs at herself again and vows she'll stop being such a ninny.

Still, Mill knows she should be careful. So, from a bug standpoint, she'll be just as cautious here as she planned to be at the FBI offices. And, until the investigation ends, Mill will sleep with the Glock holstered between the mattress and box spring, ready for a midnight-groggy quick draw.

Mill shucks out of her work clothes and takes a quick shower.

Under the caressing spray, drawn by loneliness and the sexy allure of a hotel room, she wonders briefly about calling Tilly and offering a truce--making up. She fanaticizes about Tilly hurrying to Lake Oswego...and a night of passion.

Then the crush of Tilly's betrayal hits Mill again. She shudders with anger and outrage, tears in the corners of her eyes.

Milly and Tilly are over. Tilly better be getting out of Mill's house and life.

238

Mill's thoughts turn to her friend Philip from her childhood days on the Summit District of the Targhee National Forest.

He had seen her through some of the worst days of her life and they had remained in touch. He works and lives near Chehalis, Washington, as a pastor in a mid-sized non-denominational church.

Chehalis is only an hour or so away from Portland. Mill called him before coming up for her detail. They'd agreed to get together while she worked in the area.

Wrapped in a towel, Mill reaches for the house phone to call Philip but then remembers the possibility of bugs. She thinks about opening up the handset of the phone to look for a small, blinking device like in a James Bond movie.

But she knows from her FLETC training that modern bugs are so tiny and so sophisticated that anything she finds would likely be a decoy. Any real, active bug would be well concealed.

Plus, her clumsy efforts would alert the people spying on her. They would know she suspected their presence. She doesn't want to communicate her suspicions or cautions to anyone.

Mill laughs at herself again. Her thinking has become so convoluted and weird, pretty soon she'd be creeping around the motel complex, spying on herself to catch someone spying on her!

She'd be arrested as a Peeping Tomalina for peering through her own windows!

Mill decides again that she should tone the whole paranoia business down.

Then she's struck by a more practical thought.

Mill grabs her backpack and heads out to the nearby mall. She walks in to a Radio Shack and buys a prepaid cell phone with cash.

Her calls from this phone would be essentially untraceable. Yes, if her number became known, a really sophisticated snoop could eavesdrop on her calls. But the likelihood of that seems low.

Stepping into the noisy food court, Mill dials Jake Burns on the prepaid cell phone. She gives him an update on their adventures with the FBI.

He seems preoccupied. After Jake thanks her for her report, he has no questions and they end the call quickly.

Then she calls Manny Suemez and catches him up on the education she had received from Stillman and Tomlin.

Manny laughs out loud at her description of the first days of "inter-agency partnership," saying, "Mill, the Bureau sure knows how to knock a scab off a sore. They do that stuff because they have to protect their backs, so you can get a lot of this crap from them at the start. But, once they have confidence in you, you'll get to see what real high-level police work is all about. Stay cool and watch."

Mill tells Manny, "I wouldn't miss it for anything. I just wish they'd stop using pepper spray on us at the start of every meeting."

Suemez laughs, "Hell, you lightweight, when I work with them they start every meeting with bullets!"

Mill replies tartly, "You are such a bull shitter, Manny."

As they laugh again, Mill realizes she's becoming Manny's friend as well as his protege.

Such a friendship is a common enough thing in the Forest Service, an agency where bonds could last a lifetime and connect people across thousands of miles, different jobs, marriages, divorces, and even death.

The Green Creed states that such friendships should transcend other loyalties, sometimes to be elevated above family and even the law. As a Legacy, Mill respects this new bond with Manny, although she will be cautious not to stray into trouble while honoring it.

Manny has continued talking about what his networks reported about O'Reilly's death. "Rikki Schultz is the ASAC in California. She's an old friend of mine, going way back to the days when we were LEOs on adjacent districts in Colorado. She's been the Forest Service representative on Homeland Security's terrorism and border-security task force for a couple of years...a job I'm just now taking over."

Hearing the warm tone in his voice, Mill wonders if they'd been more than just colleagues. Mill would just have to ask Manny about Rikki later over beers when she could check his expression and tease him about his conquest, real or perhaps merely hoped for.

Suemez goes on, "Rikki says Homeland Security started with some vague intel on terrorism aimed at our employees, coulda been domestic, coulda been international, maybe both...coulda been some kind of weird criminal enterprise. They just didn't know. Nothing much came of it."

Suemez pauses for breath, then continues, "Then, when the fed agencies doing law enforcement started sharing more intel a couple of years ago, things got more interesting. The FBI's Domestic Terrorism and Organized Crime and Racketeering Units have worked together for a few years now looking at certain homicide and assault patterns. Some were in VICAP--the national violent crimes data base--most weren't. No, they were

240

coded as accidental deaths or unknown assailants in state files and never reported to the feds. So, it took them a long time to pull data together."

"No similar MOs but similar victims—all people some way or another in the natural resource business, many of them in leadership positions, and others who were IDed as up-and-comers, headed for big jobs with government or industry in the future."

He stops talking long enough for Mill to ask a few questions.

"Manny, this certainly fits with my harebrained guess about a possible connection between O'Reilly and Miller. But, this sounds like just a theory looking for evidence, rather than the other way around. Couldn't most of these deaths just be what they appear to be, accidents and random attacks?"

Manny laughs ruefully, "Yeah they could, I guess. You and I will never know what all case information the number-crunching geniuses have been looking at. According to Rikki, after September 11th, the FBI got a lot more resources to look at terrorism. They bought a bunch of super computers, surveillance equipment, and math experts."

"Once they had the resources, they reviewed 50 years worth of domestic and international terrorism information and closely studied guys like the Unibomber, Ted Kazinski, and groups like the Weathermen and Earth First! They correlated all that to gang and other organized crime behavior... what they knew...what they suspected. Out of it came some kind of big computer model that sorts data for terrorist and organized crime patterns, using something like 'fuzzy logic' or 'funky logic.'"

"The model generates GIS maps and charts to pinpoint probable bad-guy locations. Rikki's seen some of the maps and charts—pretty impressive, she says. And Rikki says they've found an identifiable pattern with a probability greater than 80 percent that an unsub or an unsub organization is operating in the U.S. No guess on the location or size of the group, if it's even a group."

"Crap," thinks Mill, "Mr. Unsub the Rat might just have a family." Out loud, she asks Suemez, "So where does this leave us, Manny? I mean do they think O'Reilly and Miller and, uh, Herrera, are a part of this pattern?"

Suemez thinks for a long moment before replying, "Mill, it beats the shit out of me. Rikki wasn't that specific, although she wouldn't have brought up the whole FBI number-crunch thing except that at least one of the cases fits the pattern somehow. I'd guess O'Reilly rather than Miller or Herrera, but what the Hell do I know."

"I have a transition meeting with her in a few days and I'll see if I can pump her for more backgound...you know, what's not in official reports."

Mill grins to herself, "Slip of the tongue, Suemez? I bet you'd like to 'pump her' more, you doggy."

Speaking aloud, she asks, "So what do you want me to do, Manny?"

He replies, "Nothin'. Just stay in touch."

After good-byes, he hangs up.

Mill calls Bill Zumo and fills him in on what Manny had found out. Zumo gives a long, low whistle, "Wow. This is way more than we figured. Terrorists, huh? Since there's a supposed connection with natural resources developers and managers, I'm going to run my trap lines with environmental groups. I'll see if I can pick up anything about an organization that uses assault or homicide to take out the opposition. I'll let you know if I hear anything, rumor or fact, and you can pass the intel on to Manny."

They talk some more about things on the Siuslaw National Forest and Mapleton Ranger District.

One of the unmarried bio techs they both know well had gotten pregnant. Although Zumo identified several suspects, most people are betting on the handsome and funny intern that worked for her, a rangy and useful post-doctoral guy from Corvallis. They both marvel how a simple everyday love match can so easily be turned into a scandal by Forest Service employees.

Mill finds herself wishing the couple well even as she laughs with Zumo about his comment, "I figure most of the men wished it was them that had got her. Most of the women wished they'd been got by him -- typical Forest Sex Circus stuff!"

After Mill finishes the call with Zumo, she calls Philip and gets his voice mail. She tells him she's arrived in Portland and looks forward to seeing him when he has time. She mentions a few evenings she might be free and then ends the call.

Philip calls back a few minutes later, explaining he had been talking with a parishioner when she called. After Philip explains that Mondays and Tuesdays are his "official" days off, they quickly settle on meeting Monday night. Though, as he says a little ruefully, "When you get down to it, pastoring is all-day, every-day--keeps me busy, but never too busy to see my friend, Milly."

Hearing him say her youthful name brings Mill a rush of feelings—kid fun, pain, thankfulness, warmth, a profound yearning for her mother and easy childhood times.

Mill swallows a lump in her throat and answers Philip's kind words,

"I really look forward to seeing you, too, Philip. It's been so long."

Mill wants to scream, "And I've made such a mess of my life. I want you to help me sort it out like you did when I was fourteen."

She stifles the impulse. Maybe she could talk a little about Tilly and everything when they met. Maybe not.

They talk a little more about friends and family and then end their call.

_____ // _____

The next morning, Mill arrives early at the Justice Building. She quickly strides to the joint task force offices, leaving coffee for later.

She still has a lot of details to put together for the task force's trip to the Mendocino 6 site. Stillman has not yet given her the names of the participants or even the likely numbers. And the trip's scheduled for the next day! Wild!

She's already nailed down the transportation, though—FBI jet to Sacramento, helicopters to the site, and Forest Service vehicles and support people ready to assist there. Reverse the process to get everyone back to Portland.

She's also tentatively lined up hard hats and hand tools, food and field gear, port-a-potties and pop-up shelters to cover any possible field needs and weather.

As Mill enters the main conference area, Arianne bustles around in her little alcove office. Her hands move confidently as she cranks through records and slides documents into briefing folders and background books. She's a wiz at that sort of task.

Mill's never worked before with a person who has such a genius for organization and shows such crisp self-discipline.

Arianne's professional self-control in the office contrasts sharply with Mill's experience of her during her melt-down over at the Forest Service building. No matter what Arianne's cool and meticulous exterior broadcasts to the world, Mill knows that she can be as vulnerable and emotional as anyone else.

Mill wonders again if Arianne had been in love with John O'Reilly. If so, Mill figures O'Reilly would never have known because nothing of Arianne's feelings would have ever surfaced.

Arianne looks up when Mill enters, "Good morning, Mill. I'm glad you came in early. I know you're real busy, but I could use your help a little later this morning to go over and retrieve some hand-written notes from the

Forest Service records room. There'll be about two boxes full so if you could help me gather them up and haul them back, I'd be most grateful."

Arianne smiles brightly, her normal reserve replaced by the peculiar excitement of harvesting records for the task force.

Mill's habitual frown deepens for a moment. She thinks about Arianne's request and the time away from getting the field trip details nailed down—not much flex, for sure.

"How long do you think we'll be, Arianne?" Mill asks.

"I'd guess an hour," Arianne replies.

An hour! Ouch!

About to decline, Mill considers her orders from Stillman to help Arianne and then agrees, "Okay. Let's hit it hard right after lunch and get back as quickly as we can."

Mill hurries the twenty feet or so to her office. She sits down and fires up her computer. As it boots, she quickly runs through items in her hard-copy inbox.

Good. Stillman had finally come through with the names and numbers of people going on the field trip. "Just in time," Mill smiles to herself, "And maybe still a stretch to get everything covered as it is."

Her biggest concern had been the numbers of helicopters available. Each allowed four passengers. She had found three helos. Stillman's list shows eleven folks making the trip, so Mill has enough transportation resources.

Mill would be the only woman along. She would call the FBI office in Sacramento and the Forest Service folks on the Mendocino National Forest to get everything else dialed in.

"Just barely-fuckin'-in-time, indeed," she thinks.

Thankfully, Arianne is putting together all of the briefing and background packets they will need on the field trip. Mill knows Arianne will have the materials ready.

Mill can hand them out on the plane tomorrow. Everyone could study them along the way.

Mill would be there to answer any questions that she could and have radio communications available to get more answers if needed.

Mill plunges into the details, making phone calls and working her way down her check-lists with the people who answer.

Mill loves working with the Forest Service ground-pounders on the Mendocino. Like their counterparts in most Forest Service units across the nation, they are so quick and competent that they make her job easy. They

244

solve problems even before Mill can think of them.

Agents might show up without boots? District folks would round up ten or twelve pairs in different sizes from employees and have them out at the site where the helos were to land.

And so it goes all morning.

Mill and Arianne eat their lunches together at the conference table. Like most Forest Service people with field experience, both bring the equivalent of a lunch bucket to work.

Their FBI colleagues take off for the Justice Building cafeteria or the many restaurants in the area while Mill and Arianne simply find the nearest table and chow down. For both of them, cooking a little extra dinner the night before means having a nice lunch the next day—no fuss, no bother, self-sufficient--in the office or sitting on a remote log landing in a driving rain.

They finish quickly and head over to the Forest Service building by cab. As they enter, security seems lax by comparison to the Justice Building with its impressive array of guards and metal detectors.

But once they get to the Forest Service law enforcement records room, Mill notices the same solid security lock on the door as she had seen on their FBI-assigned records room over at the Justice Building in Portland. Arianne presses her thumb against the ID pad on the lock. After a click, it opens with a thunk.

They enter. Arianne turns on the bank of overhead lights.

The large room has deep shelving along all four walls. Four long, stand-alone shelves divide up the center area.

A flat-screen glows near the door. A keyboard below it allows them to query the location of boxes and files. Arianne consults the list she'd brought with her and taps away for a long moment. She hits "enter" and a small printer spits out two pages.

She hands one to Mill, "Mill, if you will take the top four on the list, I'll get the bottom five. You find each box by its shelf and space number. See, this shelf is number six and down here is space 30. Shelves are two boxes deep. So, along the wall there is one number for two boxes and down the middle rows, there are numbers on each side. Get it?"

Mill smiles, "Yeah. Clear as mud but I'll get the hang of it."

Arianne smiles in return, "Then when you open the box, the files are numbered and should be in order. When you take a file out, you make a note of the file number, date, time, and your initials and ID number on the card attached to the front of the box. Clear as mud again?"

Mill nods, "Mud."

This procedure closely matches what they do with evidence in the field, although generally each field LEO keeps their personal cases under separate lock. Separate case files means no break in the chain of evidence.

She looks down at her list and then up at the selves looking for numbers. Doing the same, Arianne hurries off with the air of a person on a treasure hunt.

Mill labors along gathering files slowly.

Arianne zips through her task. She hums a little efficient tune. She slaps files against her hand as she removes them and places them in the box to return to the Justice Building.

Listening to Arianne tallying her successes, Milly wryly realizes that little Arianne could be quite competitive—but in such a weird way.

What's next, Paperclip Olympics, the Highland Scotch Tape toss?

Mill eventually finds the last of her boxes in a corner on the bottom shelf, along the wall. She realizes that the box she had sought is the inner one. She moves the outer one to the floor before grabbing her target triumphantly.

She locates the few remaining files on her list, places them in her box, and signs them out on the ledger. She slides the box back into place with a sigh, glad to have this adventure in bureaucracy over with.

Mill turns to put the other box back.

She looks at it closely for the first time and recognizes her signature and Zumo's on the tape that had once held the box closed. This box contains the Miller records and evidence!

Mill sees that someone has cut the tape, perhaps so they could verify the contents against the inventory list she had prepared and sealed inside. Curious, Mill looks at the ledger on the box but finds no date or initials for whoever had done the check-in; those spaces are empty—an oversight maybe.

Impulsively moved to see the gold coin again, Mill opens the box and paws through evidence bags…and then paws through them again more urgently.

The Miller Krugerand is gone!

In its place, bagged and tagged, is a costume-jewelry replica of a Roman coin with a big-nosed emperor on it!

Mill can't believe it.

She looks at the ledger on the box again. The coin is gone and, of course, with a substitute in the box, no one had signed it out!

246

"What the Hell is going on here?" she wonders.

Mill suddenly feels the hair on her neck stand up as it had done before. The chill runs icy-fingered up her spine.

Someone has had sufficient access to steal crucial evidence in the death of a federal employee...from a secure room.

Who could have done it? Who would want to do it and why?

Suddenly struck by the conviction that a nest of unsub rats are behind the coin's disappearance, Mill knows she has to be very careful in sharing this news about evidence tampering.

Who would be safe enough to tell?

Jake...Zumo...Manny?

She quickly runs through the rest of the evidence bags and files, checking the inventory list. She doesn't readily see anything else missing.

Mill mutters, "Shit!"

Waiting impatiently by the door, Arianne hears her. She asks, "Everything alright, Mill?"

Refocusing, Mill answers quickly, "Yeah...I...uh...just saw a spider. Not my favorite things, spiders. I'll be done in a second."

Mill quickly puts the top back on the box. She slides it back in its slot on the shelf, memorizing the space number. Mill stands up, brushes off, picks up her transport box, and moves to the door.

A smiling Arianne says, "Spider, huh? Not my favorites, either. Sometimes I dream about being caught in a web, struggling, spiders headed my way from every direction I look. My dream ends just before they reach me."

"Sounds awful," replies Mill, glad that she doesn't have *that* dream. She wonders if the dream reflects Arianne's experience, just as Mill's recurrent dream reflects hers. Mill would have asked but such a question seems way too personal to ask given their short acquaintance. Besides, she might have to share her dream if she asked.

As they pass through the door, Mill asks Arianne innocently, "How many people do you guess have access to this room?"

Arianne looks thoughtful, "Well, only a few of us trained in evidence management come here regularly. We're on thumb-print access. But even though they usually send us to get records and evidence, most of the Special Agents have key-card access. Some of them use their access pretty often. I guess it depends on the case they are working. Why do you ask?"

Mill answers, "I was just wondering. The security seems tight but I know most police departments have a full time person handling access to evidence and case records."

Arianne replies, "Yes they do. You should see the one over at the FBI. My goodness, they have two clerks to serve visitors and video to record every movement and comment. Still, our Forest Service system is pretty good. You probably didn't notice but we have a movement-activated video in our store room, too."

Mill thinks for a moment and then realizes she had seen at least one dark-glass camera 'bubble" in the ceiling. She answers, "Okay, I remember now. Yeah, that's good. Thanks, Arianne, for explaining."

As they walk down the hall, Mill asks Arianne, "So, isn't it a pain to store all those tapes?"

Arianne replies, "No, not really. People don't go in there that often. Not for sure, but I've been told that the video actually gets recorded on two big disc drives...two in case one goes down."

Mill feigns amazement, "Wow! Big city stuff. Too much for a country girl."

They both laugh and chat about other things on the way back to the Justice Building.

Mill listens absently to Arianne. She wonders if she can get access to the video on those hard drives and whether she could use the video and door-lock records to catch the person who had stolen the Miller coin.

Now that would make her trip to Portland worthwhile!

When they get back to the joint task force room, Mill finds that a bunch of small and large pieces of the field trip have come unglued. She works the phones until quitting time, applying needed glue, and then readies her gear and stuff for the next day.

As she leaves, Arianne hands off the briefing materials to Mill in a small basket on wheels with a telescoping handle. Mill appreciates Arianne's kindness in assembling the bulky load and tells her so.

Arianne waves her hand in the air and replies modestly, "Just doing what I can to help, Mill. Have a great trip. I'll see you when you return."

—————————————————//—————————————————

Once Mill reaches the street, her mind goes back to the violated Miller evidence box. She finds her pre-paid, almost-untraceable cell phone. After she looks around to make sure no one can eavesdrop, she calls Zumo's encrypted number.

Zumo answers on the third ring. Mill fills him on what she's found.

248

Zumo explodes, "Holy Christ, Mill. Somebody tampered with evidence, OUR evidence? Damn it, damn it, damn it! How did that happen?"

Mill goes over the security arrangements for the storage room. She explains that, if the LEOs could get access to the video, they might be able to figure out who had stolen the coin and the inventory sheet.

"But, Bill," she asks, "How do we do that without giving ourselves away, without alerting the unsub rats if they took the coin? I mean, we don't know they took it. Somebody could have stolen it because they thought it was a real Krugerand. We don't know."

Zumo explodes again, "The hell we don't know, Mill. We may not have *proof* but we *know*. Understand me?"

Mill answers that she did understand him. Her intuition agrees with his.

Zumo continues, "As far as who we can trust, that'd be Jake Burns and Jake Burns only. You go tell that crazy sumbitch what you've found out. Then watch him go to work. He's got all the juice it'll take to get the videos reviewed and door-lock records checked. I'll leave it up to you, but he might not like it if he found out you mentioned all this to me first. He'd probably like to think he's in charge of his own organization, you know what I mean?"

Mill does know. The Green Creed holds that somebody's dirty Forest Service laundry belongs to them to clean up, at least until a public scandal breaks or political heat flares. That way, both the person and the Forest Service are protected.

The person has some time to clean up the mess.

If the mess becomes public, the agency can claim that no one had known about it officially; that responsible people would look into it.

Under a smokescreen of denial and a wall of delay, Legacies could cover for their irresponsible buddy. As often as not, they could arrange to punish or destroy the reputation of some largely innocent employee to get the critics and reformers off their backs.

Mill and Zumo talk some more. After they hang up, Mill thinks of something: the scrap of cloth she had found at the Miller site. She calls Bill back and tells him about the scrap and where to find it in her locked evidence files.

At first Zumo is mad because she hadn't told him about it before. But after a few cuss words, he calms down. He agrees that up until now, the scrap held no significance. He promises to make sure it's secure when he gets back to the office.

Mill calls Jake Burns. Jake impresses Mill once again. He uses cuss words far more colorful and heart-felt than Zumo used.

Later she calls Manny.

He says only, "Okay, *chica*, now you got my full attention. I'll be in touch."

Chapter 33

Compliments of the Forest Service

A day later, at the FBI hanger to the west of Portland International Airport, Mill carefully checks in each agent by name, verifying their identities from their official ID cards.

One agent has Madonna's face taped over his picture. Mill makes him remove it and compares the revealed mug shot to the agent's face, "You're prettier than Madonna, Agent Gerard. I really like your eye makeup."

Gerard laughs and ambles towards the jet.

The last agent to arrive drives in quickly, grabs his gear from his car trunk, and runs to Mill's checkpoint at the entry gate.

Puffing a little, Agent Collins tells her he has left his ID behind or misplaced it, but since Mill knows him she could "Cut him some slack."

Mill points him back towards his vehicle, "Adios, Agent Collins. Find it or forget it."

This isn't what the agent wants to hear. He stands about six inches taller than Mill and outweighs her by eighty pounds.

He moves close to Mill so he can tower over her. He begins to bluster and threaten her, talking about how "no Forest Service girl cop" could stop him from coming on this trip.

Mill looks up at him with a tight smile, "Step back, Agent Collins. You need to present your ID before you can get on the plane. Tomlin's orders. No exceptions."

Collins bumps Mill with his chest, forcing her back a step. Mill grabs Collins' left hand in a thumb hold. Twisting quickly, she drops him to his left knee, ready to put him on his back on the tarmac with a further twist.

Mill leans over Collins, her mouth close to his right ear, and whispers, "Bump me again and I'll bust your balls, Agent Collins."

The grimacing Collins looks up at her annoyed face, "Okay, okay, let me go." She gives his hand a little more twist and lets go.

Collins stands up, rubbing his hand. He looks at her ruefully and said, "Cripes, Meacham, you didn't have to break it off. I won't be able to jerk off for a month."

Mill suddenly realizes Collins' aggressive behavior has been an act, yet another FBI test.

She shakes her head.

Would these FBI guys ever stop trying her out?

She looks Collins in the eye, "I guess you're right, Agent Collins! One hand won't fit around your neck! It takes both of them, doesn't it?"

Collins looks at her in astonishment and roars with laughter. He yells, "Meacham, you are a feisty little shit aren't you!" With that he turns towards the jet.

He takes two steps before Mill grabs the back of his belt. "One more step, Agent Collins, and I'll give you an undershorts hoodie. Produce the ID or prepare to be wedged unconscious."

Collins turns with a grin, hands up in surrender. He shows her the ID he'd been palming since coming through the security gate.

At that moment, Stillman walks up to them and says with a slight smile, "Okay, you two, time to get on the plane. Nice work, Meacham, but let's stop beating up on Collins, as much fun as that is, and get to work."

They board the little 18-passenger FBI jet. The two lines of seats divided by a narrow isle remind Mill of the "flying culverts" she had bounced around in during her years in Alaska as a fisheries biologist—and those were the big airplanes up there.

As she enters, Mill's eyes widen when she sees Frieda Tomlin sitting in the co-pilot's chair. She's dressed in a crisp business suit, going down the pre-flight checklist with the pilot.

Frieda turns to Mill as she enters, "Everyone on board? Then we'll get going."

Seeing the look on Mill's face, Tomlin says, "Oh, darn, I bet Agent Stillman didn't tell you that my plans have changed and I'm coming along on the field trip. Isn't it nice that I'm multi-engine jet rated and can help out?"

Tomlin's eyes twinkle as she studies Mill's expression. She watches it change from shock, to wariness, to thoughtful concern and finally to neutral competence, a slight frown around Mill's mouth and eyes.

Mill quickly calculates the implications of Frieda's presence. Frieda can be accommodated easily at almost every turn except for clothes, boots, and personal gear.

Mill looks at Tomlin's polished shoes and close-fitting wool skirt and asks, "Agent Tomlin, did you bring other clothes or boots for today?"

Encumbered with the bulky headphones and microphone, Tomlin shakes her head awkwardly She bats her eyes with mock girlishness and asks innocently, "No, did I need to?"

Mill quickly thinks to herself, "Doesn't this woman read her own memos?"

But then she realizes Frieda's supposed oversight is another test of Mill's ability. This time the FBI is checking on Mill's ability to think on her feet under stress and adapt to changing circumstances.

So, Mill thinks to herself, "Okay, let the wardrobe chase begin." Then she smiles at Frieda, "We'll get you fixed right up, Agent Tomlin. No worries."

Mill walks back to her seat. She pulls out her lists of contact people.

Tomlin and the pilot work the jet out to the runway, rev the engines, and the little vibrating plane shoots swiftly into the sky.

Once they get airborne, Mill goes through the cabin passing out the briefing materials Arianne put together.

When Collins kids her about not offering coffee and "sky nuts," Mill responds that there'd be coffee at their first field stop and that Collins had been appointed to play with his "sky nuts" for the flight.

Mill goes up to the little flight deck and puts on a spare headset. Frieda assigns her a radio channel. Mill begins radioing ahead to line up resources for Frieda.

After a few calls, things come together. Mill quietly arranges a little surprise for Tomlin as part of the helo ride from the Sacramento Airport. She also makes sure field clothes, boots, and a small pack with water and other gear would be waiting for Frieda at the first stop on the Mendocino National Forest – the helicopter landing site or "helispot."

After they touch down in Sacramento, the agents grab their gear and jump in a couple of vans. They speed over to the waiting helicopters near the locked and quiet National Guard hanger.

The agents climb out and walk over to the helos. Each gets handed a fire-resistant Nomex flight suit and a flight helmet with earphones.

Frieda Tomlin looks at the flight suit that Mill got for her. It's at least one size smaller than Mill's estimate of Tomlin's normal size.

Watching the other agents climbing into their flight suits, Agent Tomlin looks a Mill darkly, "You mean I really have to wear this fucking smelly thing? What the Hell for?"

Mill replies evenly, while noting the other agents' grinning faces over Tomlin's shoulder, "Federal regulations, Ma'am. Don't ask me why. Dates back to when helicopters ran on aviation gas and in-flight fire was a big risk. They use jet fuel now. But even though fire's no longer much of a risk, we still wear the Nomex flight suits and over-the-ankle boots."

Tomlin looks closely at Mill to detect any hint of bullshit, but Mill's face betrays nothing. She says to Mill, "How am I supposed to put this on? I'm wearing a skirt."

With her face utterly serious, Mill answers, "Well, Agent Tomlin, I can think of only two ways. You'll have to remove the skirt or roll it up high enough to get your legs in the flight suit. You could do either one in the privacy of the van."

"Well," Tomlin replies, "I'm not stripping in front of these hee-haw jackasses. And I'm not rolling up a three hundred dollar skirt to pack it around my waist like a spare tire. Besides the skirt's too tight to do that. And what am I supposed to do when we land, moon everyone getting out of this monkey-ass suit? So what do you suggest we do?"

Mill looks up at the sky for inspiration, "Okay. With some help, maybe we can stuff the skirt down the pants legs, keeping it as straight as possible kinda like a skort, while you pull the flight suit up."

After some inspired cussing, that's what they do.

Mill stuffs on one side and Stillman on the other, working Frieda and the skirt down into the tight-ish flight suit as Frieda pulls it up by the waist.

Before they start the process, Tomlin warns Gregory, "You touch my ass, Stillman, and I will send you to sexual harassment training for a damn month."

But, of course, there's no other way, except to touch her ass, and other troubling parts, too, as he thrusts and smooths the skirt into the suit's tight legs and seat.

The other agents almost die trying to keep from guffawing,

Stillman piously directs his eyes towards the heavens, pretending nothing much is happening, while his hands are clearly smoothing Tomlin's skirt down her ass and thighs.

After being stuffed in, Tomlin carefully zips her ample bosom into the flight suit's tight top.

She can't bend at all, so Stillman and Mill have to put her borrowed, moldy-looking boots on. Then she walks stiffly to the helo. She has to have Stillman's help to get in, her suit clings so tightly, bound especially tight in the crotch.

Noting the loose fit of the other agents' flight suits, Tomlin gives Mill a baleful gaze, "Meacham, you're sure a fucking bad judge of sizes. This suit must be for a midget. You've got my panties in a jam and I'm not happy about it."

Mill murmurs, "Sorry, Ma'am."

After she sits down, Mill turns her face to the window, biting her lip to keep from smiling.

Fortunately for Frieda, the flight takes less than half an hour. When the helos land, Mill has arranged for a full change of clothes for Frieda and a tent to protect what remains of her dignity.

The field portion of the trip turns up nothing new in terms of evidence but the FBI agents get a much clearer and essential understanding of the field situation--the picture of who died where, of cover and concealment—all things that can be hard to figure out from maps, diagrams, and photos.

The sites have grown over some from the time of the drug raid, obscuring small details. Signs of trampling are mostly gone, even to Mill's knowledgeable eye. Still, Mill walks them from place to place---staging areas to kill sites, campsite to capture site.

She takes them over the route that the mysterious person had traveled from O'Reilly to Herrera and then, presumably, well beyond. They agree it looks exactly like an escape route, pointed east towards roads and freedom.

After the recon, the task force members lunch and talk together until no one has any more questions. They trail out and board the Forest Service vehicles to return to the waiting helos.

Back at the helispot and back in her skirt, Tomlin starts to ask Mill and Stillman to help her put on her flight suit. Then she realizes the suit she has been given was a different, baggier one—no help needed. Frieda's legs go into it easily. She can tuck her skirt in discretely by herself.

As Frieda dons her suit, Mill stands by the end of one of the helos, checking the safety of the tail rotor with an air of innocence around her. Frieda walks up to her.

She says quietly, "If I didn't know better, Meacham, I would think you had set me up for a grab ass. But I *do* know better *don't I, Meacham*? You would *never, never* attempt to play a practical joke on me would you, Meacham?"   "Oh, no, Ma'am," Mill replies, "Just a mix up in sizes back in Sacramento. Thankfully, we had a larger suit here on the forest that we could bring in for you."

Mill points to the stenciled words "Mendocino Flight Operations" over the suit's right breast pocket.

Mill continues, "I will always look out for your welfare, Agent Tomlin."

Frieda looks at Mill with a slight smile, "I know you are a prime bull shitter, Meacham, like every other asshole on this task force. I like that in a woman...unless it causes me real trouble."

"I'm glad you are looking out for me...keep doing that. And I....I will keep an eye on you."

With that, Frieda Tomlin walks away with her usual swift, compact step. Mill smiles broadly, her face once again turned to the rotor.

Mill spends Friday calling in "thank you's" to all the people who had helped with the field trip, making sure equipment wound up back where it belonged, and organizing photos shot of the trip by the other eleven task force members.

She has somehow been placed in charge of the team's photo library. Although the photos will stay in easily-stored electronic form, she has a big job coding all the field notes that went with each photo into the album database.

Mill realizes that electronic cameras have a big flaw. Silly FBI agents could keep blasting away with them like John Dillinger with a tommy gun, producing hundreds of shots where ten or so might do.

"Oh well," she thinks hopefully, "At least they'll have a lot of pictures to choose from when the unsubs go on trial for O'Reilly's and Herrera's murders."

Mill leaves the FBI offices about 7 pm. Outside, she calls first Jake and then Zumo, updating them on the field trip.

Jake speaks tersely to her again, sharing little. Mill had hoped he would give her a progress report on who had likely tampered with the Miller evidence. But because Jake is short with her, she first thinks that she's made him angry by reporting the theft. Then she realizes he's probably still worried about possible bugs in his office or on his phone.

Mill offers to meet him for lunch on Tuesday.

He simply says, "Okay. At Noon by Portlandia," referring to the city's mascot, a huge, plump, gilded statue of a woman.

Jake hangs up without another word.

Zumo has much more to say.

He updates Mill on the young lovers with baby on the way. They've moved in together. Scandal tongues are wagging all across the Siuslaw National Forest.

Then Bill turns more serious. "Mill, at his request, I checked with Manny's contact, Rikki, about that computer model. She let me know that

O'Reilly and, get this, Bud Miller, both come up as high probability targets. Herrera's a 'maybe'. Your gut was right, girl! And, Rikki has heard from her Bureau friends that you're doing a good job for the task force. Nice to hear, huh?"

Mill replies, "Nice to be loved, I guess." She laughs, thinking of Agent Collins and iron-fist Frieda.

Zumo's voice changes and turns more somber, "But there's something else. Remember that scrap of cloth? You sure it's in the second drawer of your locked file cabinet?"

Mill replies that she's sure. In fact, it's in a labeled file, in a sealed evidence bag, tagged and initialed.

"Well," Bill answers, "I don't know what kind of whacky tobaccy you're smokin' but there's no Miller file and no evidence like that in that drawer. In fact, there's nothing like that in the whole file cabinet."

Mill's stunned.

Cold runs through her veins.

It spreads up her neck, lifting her neck hair again.

What the Hell? Had she moved the evidence and forgot about it? No way!

"Bill, I swear it's in that cabinet. At least that's where I left it…" Her voice trails off.

Then the realization hits her—someone's gone through their office in Florence and stolen the evidence.

Struck by the same idea, Bill yells, "Christ, Mill, you don't think someone…."

Interrupting, Mill jumps in, "I sure as Hell do, Bill. Somebody's been through our office. Holy crap! Are these people everywhere? How could they even know to look? How could they get past our security lock... into my locked cabinet? Holy crap!"

Zumo takes a long time to answer. When he finally does, he simply says, "I'll get back to you" and then hangs up.

Looking disgustedly at her silent phone, Mill exclaims, "Shades of Jake Burns! Can't these guys finish a conversation? I'm busy breaking the case and they're busy hanging up on me! The Age of Chivalry is clearly over!"

Then she laughs at her silliness. This is serious stuff. Both Jake and Bill have similar, intensely pressing security issues to deal with.

She dials Jake back to report the new problem. Jake's just gotten off the phone with Zumo.

Throwing phone security aside, he gives Mill a new lesson in creative cussing.

She hadn't known that the "f-word" could be used seven ways in one sentence...but it can.

Chapter 34

Philip, New and Again

Although she can't quite grasp why, on Monday Mill wears a new dress to her dinner with Philip. Acting on an impulse that surprised her, she'd spent Saturday afternoon at Nordstrom's picking the dress out and had it tailored there for Sunday pickup.

The other dresses she owns are for office wear and look it, trim fit and almost severe.

The new dress is, well, about something new and about something familiar, too. Dark blue, the dress has a slightly festive feel—not something she would have bought for the office before but, well, maybe something she might wear there in the future.

Black embroidery traces leaves and vines across the western-styled, button-up bodice. The embroidery flows over her shoulders and across the yoke. A pleated skirt flares a little from the waist and ends just above her knees.

She had bought a dark brown and blue scarf to wear with the dress. The dark brown matches her eyes and the blue matches the dress—touches she never thought to add to any other outfit.

After bringing the dress home, she stands looking as it hangs against the wardrobe door. Although the dress is clearly womanly and not girlish, Mill thinks perhaps its embroidery and wide skirt capture a bit of the carefree feel of her youthful relationship with Philip.

After falling asleep Sunday night, she wakes from time to time. Half asleep, she looks at the dress in the dim light.

The shadowy form is a strange but comforting presence--a dark woman figure poised with skirt slightly askew, somehow ready to dance.

And the next evening, before she walks out of her Residence Inn room with the dress on, touching her, concealing her, Mill thinks fleetingly that its newness might repel past bad things she had endured.

It might somehow screen out the demons of sexual assault and broken relationships.

The new might defend against the old.

She looks in the mirror. She first buttons the dress up to the neck and knots the scarf below the collar.

She half consciously thinks she might be less vulnerable this way and leaves her room. But when she reaches her car, she shakes her head at her silliness. Removing the scarf, she opens the top three buttons of the dress and loops the scarf around her neck, tucking it in like a casual cravat.

Much better. Pleased, she drives away.

Now that dinner with Philip lies directly ahead, she has to confess that the situation scares her. She's meeting the man who probably knows, or could guess, more about her than anyone else in the world.

And to make matters worse, Philip is a pastor--probably a skilled counselor and advisor--someone who might see through her surface façade to her deepest sins. He might look deeply into her hurts, even hear her soul's cry for revenge, for love. Her secrets might be revealed...awful.

She pulls into the restaurant's parking lot. Regardless of her fears and hopes, as she checks her minimal makeup, the rear view mirror reflects the eyes of a more carefree and calm young woman.

Mill's slight frown lifts into a smile. With the smile comes a feeling. Finally, she looks forward to Philip's warm hug.

She walks through the door of the small Greek restaurant.

Philip's first reaction is to gawk, not hug.

"Milly," he gasps, "You look terrific. Wow, being a cop must be good for you." He laughs delightedly and folds her into his arms.

Mill slides her arms around his waist, and puts her head against his chest. She snuggles her face into the collar of his shirt.

She revels in the kindly peace that quickly fills her.

Philip can definitely *hug*, a gently tight embrace that conveys intimacy and care without sexual interest.

Hugged tight, Mill's fear of secrets revealed ebbs away to pool in a deep dark place where rapists and unsubs hide.

They hold each other for almost a minute, rocking slightly. Then, a polite voice intrudes, "Ahem. Would you like to be seated now?"

The question brings them smilingly out of their hug. They follow the respectful waiter to a quiet booth.

The owners keep the restaurant clean and well-polished. Wonderful spice and meat smells come from the kitchen. Light glistens off white-painted sconces and hanging lamps. White tablecloths with bright blue weaving grace each table. Candles cast soft light over heavy, traditional silverware

260

A beautiful mural covers one long wall showing a sun-drenched Greek island in the Mediterranean. In it, fishing boats bob at anchor in a light sea.

Mill looks around, "How did we get so lucky? This place is great."

Philip replies, "I've been here once or twice before. I thought it would be good for us. Everything's cooked from scratch and is completely authentic. And, thinking of authentic, watch out for the ouzo. It tastes like licorice candy but it's got a real punch."

"Paul says in his letter to the Romans, 'take a little wine for your stomach's sake' but Paul never recommends ouzo nor retsina, the wine the Greeks make from tree sap! Wow!"

They both laugh.

The waiter comes back to the table, mentions the specials, and then asks expectantly, "Would you like something from the bar?"

Mill immediately says, "Ouzo, of course!"

Philip smiles broadly and says, "And one for me, too."

The waiter bows slightly, turns, and walks casually over to the small bar in the back of the restaurant. Mill watches the waiter for a moment and then she turns to meet Philip's gaze.

"So how have you been, Milly?" he asks, "It's been what, six, eight years?"

Mill calculates quickly and agrees with his estimate. They'd stayed in touch all this time, writing and calling. But they'd not actually laid eyes on one another for at least six years.

Philip had been in seminary.

Mill had been working on her fish biologist degrees and then working in Alaska.

He'd travelled from congregation to congregation, seeking a "calling" as churches termed a permanent pastor's job.

"Yes, at least that long," she agrees, "But you've only changed for the better, Philip. You look like a proper pastor now."

Philip laughs, "Whatever that look is, Milly! I just look like myself, I guess, something like the face I've seen in the mirror for 28 years."

Mill thinks to herself, "He looks more like an actor than a pastor—grey-green eyes, strong jaw, wide smile, dark hair—kind of like a tall Johnny Depp."

About to mention this to him, she stops herself. She senses he would be embarrassed. Somehow, with Philip...on this night...she wants to avoid her normal teasing and flippancy.

The ouzo arrives. They raise their little glasses to each other and then take small, cautious sips.

As the ouzo slides warmingly into her stomach, Mill smiles at Philip, "You look like a fine and proper pastor and I don't want to hear anything more about it."

"Okay," he replies a little sheepishly, a slight blush rising to his cheeks, "Fine and pastor-ly. Got it."

He gazes at her, "And you look…well…all grown up….beautiful. Somehow when I picture you now, I'm looking out with those eyes from my mirror…my older, more tired eyes."

His voice turns quieter, a little probing edge coming into it, "But…I see you as my friend Milly at fourteen…my friend Milly who suddenly turned into a young woman, a changeling…haunted, helpless, hurting, driven…the same and yet tougher…different."

He leans towards Mill and looks in her eyes, "I know I'm not really making sense. But, all these years…I wonder what happened to you back then...when we were fourteen.... Milly, you changed so quickly and so completely. Now you are a beautiful, accomplished woman, but...back then.... Well, will you tell me what happened?"

Philip has hit Mill's panic button dead center!

Her fears come screaming out of the deep, dark pool.

She knows if she tells him what had happened to her everything will go bad between them.

He would be patronizing or, worse, contemptuous.

He would be repulsed.

He would accuse her…shame her.

Never speak to her again.

She looks at him. Her cheeks burn with shock and shame.

And then she thinks…as a pastor, surely he had heard stories worse than hers…and, as a pastor…then…didn't that mean he would listen?

The urge to tell her story becomes overwhelming, engulfing. He's here. He asked…her best friend. They're separated by years from the bad...the worst.

But still, the danger.... For a moment, torn, she can't speak.

She almost jumps up and runs from the building. Delaying, she downs her ouzo and considers her escape.

The sweet liquor burns deep and the burn clears her head and her intentions.

"Give me a minute, please?" she asks, almost whispering, her hand patting her chest.

He looks at her with compassion and concern. His care for her is so clear in his eyes.

The ouzo relaxes her slightly and she remembers her hard-won power. Eyes begging for a moment's reprieve, Mill quietly says, "Okay. I'll tell you, but...but...let's order first."

Philip keeps his eyes on her while he beckons to the waiter, "Please serve us your house special meal for two and take plenty of time between courses. And, please give us two small glasses of retsina with the main course."

The waiter bows again slightly, "Very good, sir. The first course will come in about 10 minutes. May I get you anything while you wait?"

Philip looked thoughtfully at Mill, "Yes, another ouzo each, and if you have a box of tissues, we may need some."

Mill's face becomes defensive.

Philip quickly says, "For me, not her."

The waiter smiles and walks away.

Mill glares at Philip for a moment. Unable to keep up her fierce look, she allows the laugh lines to grow around her mouth and eyes.

Although apprehension still holds her throat, they both laugh and feel a partial release of tension.

After a deep, ragged breath, Mill begins to tell her story....

Mill tells Philip about her rape.

She explains the events, her thoughts and emotions, and the work she had done with her counselor.

Eyes on the tissues she twists in her hands, she never looks at him except for tiny, quick glances. She's still deeply afraid of his condemnation and rejection. Mill occasionally dabs at her eyes with a tissue while she waits for sobs and hurting gulps to subside.

As she tells her story, the waiter brings three courses of excellent food, which, even in their distracted state, they eat and enjoy. The arrival of each course allows Mill to refocus and relax a little, the new look and taste a welcome distraction.

When the last morsels disappear, the waiter clears the dishes for baklava and demitasse espressos.

For most of her story, Philip sits quietly, face neutral, eyes on her face as her words check and flow, flow and check. His training as a pastor and his friendship with Milly tell him to let her get the whole story out, without coaxing if possible. If she could tell it her way, he hopes she could find peace and rest.

He has often helped others suffering from similar trauma—loss of family, rape, robbery...a rogues gallery of violence and pain. Many of them suffered from what the experts call 'post traumatic stress disorder.'

But Philip has never before supported someone with whom he had such a long-term, close relationship.

He fights to stay neutral, reflective, and compassionate. He struggles with the desire to ask questions, to express his outrage, to cry with frustration. He wants to slam the table or the wall, but he holds himself steady and focuses on Milly for Mill's sake.

Even when she tells him about the rape and sodomy, although the words make his stomach churn and his heart ache for her, he holds steady. But, when she speaks about gaining her freedom and walking injured to the river, he stops her by putting his hand on her arm.

Startled by his touch out of the flow of her words and feelings, Mill looks up at Philip. She sees grief on his face, tears running down his cheeks.

"Oh Milly," he says, "Just give me a second to pull myself together. I feel so bad about what happened to you. I feel worse that I did nothing."

He wipes his eyes with a tissue. After looking away from the table for a moment, he says, "Please go on. I'm sorry I interrupted you." His face smooths, although pain still glows from behind his eyes.

Mill sips her coffee in its tiny cup. She feels stronger for his compassion but puzzles at his words about doing nothing.

After all, he had been there for her that day on the trail home. And, really, although their lives had moved them in different directions since, he had been available to her.

Mill puts the question mark aside. She finishes her story.

For a moment, she thinks about telling him more...about college craziness, wild life in Alaska, and Tilly. But she doesn't have the energy for more.

A tired fog of emotional release has started to envelop her...a peaceful emptiness. She stops talking and looks at Philip directly, holding his eyes with hers.

A little of her impish humor returns. With it, comes a twist of irony. "Well, Philip," she says, "Am I going to Hell for disobeying my father and

264

being lustful?"

As she asks her question, she realizes she's challenging Philip as a pastor to make unknowable evil known. Would he explain the harm done to her in terms of her sins, a tit-for-tat from an angry God, a just punishment she well deserved? Would he try to convince her that others had suffered more and the harm to her had turned out to be trivial?

Philip knows that Mill is not a Christian. He has never tried to push her in that direction. Their relationship dated back well before he'd found his own faith.

He knows that she would find faith in her own time, or not at all, if that's where her life and choices led her.

He also finds himself uncertain about how to discuss religion with friends and family—long-standing issues and boundaries seem to be always in the way when the subject comes up with them.

So, he has rarely spoken of religious things to Milly. When he did speak up, he took care to be simply factual and forthright about what he thought the church would say on a subject, while trying to keep the warmth of their personal relationship out of his remarks.

This time, though, he feels a deep conviction rising in him. His feelings surface in his words.

He looks upward for a moment. Then his eyes drop down, level to hers. "Milly, the horrible things you talked about were done *to* you, not *by* you. Yes, in some tiny things you did, you placed yourself in harm's way. But, Milly, others did the harm to your body and your spirit."

"In the way the church explains things," he says with some force,"*you* have *not* sinned in any of the things that happened. You are not *going to Hell*...you were *forced* into a kind of Hell on Earth. I just thank God you survived."

He drops his eyes to the table, afraid he has offended her with his passion.

When he looks up tentatively again, a young, smiling-silly Milly face looks back at him. For a few moments, her face glows with the peace of youth and the innocence he remembered so well.

Then her adult face slowly returns, one softened by his care.

Philip feels deeply moved by the effect of his words on her.

But in this good moment, pain touches Philip.

He speaks slowly and haltingly, "Milly, I don't quite know where to begin with something I'd like to tell you. I have a confession to make. You can hate me after I tell you if you want to. I will understand if you do."

265

Inspired by Mill's candor and trust in him, he continues, "I did something stupid back then. Without thinking, I gave away your hiding place. I...I never thought it mattered until now...until tonight when I heard what happened to you. But, I bear some of the responsibility for you getting captured, and raped, and, and...all the bad stuff happening. I'm so unbelievably sorry for what I did."

Mill looks at him skeptically. "You mean you led Moon and Jake to my hiding place?" she asks.

Philip shakes his head. "No," he answers, "But I might as well have. A couple of days before the game, one of the Generals cornered me in the boys' bathroom next to the urinals. He was ready to punch me and push me in. He demanded I tell him how you could get away so easily. I told him, not everything, but I now know it was enough so they could hunt you down."

Philip stops to swallow the huge lump in his throat, "I never thought...never thought...that anything worse than you getting captured might happen. I mean, I really didn't give him directions or anything, just what you did to get away..."

His voice trails off, his face working painfully, "And tonight I found out what they did to you."

He chokes up and can't continue, tears in his eyes. He wipes them away, fiercely angry with himself and the weakness of his young self. "I hate what I did...stupid...weak...cowardly...my best friend," he finishes, looking at her face to see how mad she is.

Mill stares at him, frowning.

Philip's eyes move over her face. Her apparent calm encourages him to move to another subject.

"And Milly," he goes on, "I'm pretty sure I saw the man who assaulted you; at least I think it was him."

Her frown deepens into tears.

Seeing her hurt coming back to the surface, he rushes out his next words. "I saw you with Jake and Moon after you crossed Cottonwood Creek. I followed you three back to the camp and hid. I waited, planned to free you, when the two of them headed out straight at me. I ran off a good way so they couldn't catch me and slid into cover until I figured they were gone."

Philip stops to take a long, shuddering breath, "I circled around back to their camp but, when I got there, you were gone. I figured you had gotten away on your own. I thought you'd gone out to try and find someone to tag. So, I went hunting again, too."

Philip stops for a long moment, his memories getting more painful.

"Then I must have heard you wail...when he...when he...you know...oh Dear God, when he did what you said."

"I hurried towards the sound but didn't see anything. I started to circle around. After he...was done...he must have left you and headed my way, turning off towards town just before we met. I saw him through the trees."

"He was tall...big...and, Milly, he...he wore a Forest Service uniform. I saw the green shirt and his hat. It couldn't have been anything else. No one in town would ever wear something that looked like a Forest Service uniform...you know...I mean...they just wouldn't."

Philip stops, now empty of strong emotion and story.

Mill sits, stunned. Her mind whirls.

Philip had betrayed her and left her...and tried to help her...has always helped her...and the rapist wore a Forest Service uniform!

Now furious, she stares at him who, after a few moments under her hot gaze, turns his face away.

Rage boils up in Mill.

Her vision blurs.

Philip's face becomes all she can see at the end of a tunnel.

"Philip," she says with deep venom, "What the Hell were you thinking to tell that shitheel how his soldiers could find me. You asshole. I confided in you...showed you my safe place. You sold me out. They dragged me away to be raped...to be *raped*!"

"Damn you, you total son of a bitch."

Mill stands up from the table.

She walks quickly to the entrance, face working with tears and outrage.

She looks back once at Philip, now sitting stooped over with shock and grief.

She disappears.

Philip sits for a moment.

He speaks quietly to no one, "Yes, I am damned. Now. I love you, Milly. I always have."

Only his God listens to this, the last of Philip's confession.

Chapter 35

Confusion

Mill drives back to the Residence Inn in turmoil.

She can only see the pavement directly in front of her car.

Everywhere else, blurred lights and darkness drift by.

Her mind screams. "How dare he keep secrets from me?" she rages, "What a fucking bastard. He's the reason I got raped! He ratted me out! He sent me into years of living Hell!"

Her mind rolls and roils through hatred, anger, and grief.

The image of Philip jumbles up with Moon and Jake and a tangle of fallen trees and...and...a big man dressed in a green Forest Service uniform, walking away from a ruined Milly.

Mill arrives at the motel at about 10 pm. She parks and steps out of the car.

Cool air touches her face wet with tears. Her vision gradually clears.

Suddenly anxious, she looks around blankly at the pools of light from the street lamps.

She can't remember the trip back from the restaurant.

Shocked, she tries to force memories of the trip but she really doesn't have any.

The trip isn't just a blur...it isn't a memory at all.

She also can't remember what she's wearing.

Looking down, she sees the beautiful blue Nordstrom's dress. Now she remembers her trips to the store, one to buy it and one to pick it up.

She unclenches her fists and takes the sides of the skirt in her hands. Mill spreads the material out, seeing the sheen of the fabric reflect the street lamps, changing from shadow to light and back again.

She smiles a little remembering her pleasure in picking it out and her nervous anticipation of dinner with Philip.

She was beautiful for Philip.

He said so.

Puzzled shock hits her.

Philip! What about Philip?

She remembers arriving at the restaurant and their meal. She told him about her assault.

And now, standing by the car, her cheeks once again color with shame and regret.

But...Philip had been so understanding, so calm and caring.

And then he told her his part of the story and...and...things got so jumbled...she can't remember the rest.

Like a gap in a movie, her memory stops at the point she sat looking at Philip with horror...and then started again here in the parking lot of the Residence Inn.

How had she gotten back here?

And Philip!

My God, what had she said?

What had she done to him?

Where is he?

She takes out her pre-paid cell phone and calls his number. The call goes to voice mail.

Now even more anxious and quite suddenly shy, Mill hangs up without leaving a message.

Chapter 36

Mist Strikes Hard

To the two other Chiefs on a secure three-way web cam connection, the Mist Money Clan Chief, Golden Eagle, looks startled, suspicious.

"What the fuck? Is this for real?" he sputters, "What kind of fool would let himself get in this situation? This has got to be a fake, a setup!"

The Friends Chief smiles at Golden Eagle's skepticism.

"The offer came through one of our contacts at the California Sierra Club and a UCLA campus recruiter for Earth First! A male prostitute was offering to sell a video recording of him and W. A. Meacham having sex, lots of sex. Seems the guy had been caught with a bunch of drugs. He needed to raise a lot of cash to pay for his defense."

A twisted smile on his face, Golden Eagle asks, "So, how much did he want? Did you buy it? Christ, this is worth a ton if it's for real! I'd love to see some sleazy, shit-bag bureaucrat like Meacham under our thumb."

The Friends Chief responds, "He wants a million dollars for the DVD. I gave him a hundred large as a down payment and required that he give us a minute of the DVD to authenticate. I gave that to Raven so that she could have Listening Clan analysts evaluate it. Raven has the results."

Golden Eagle shifts his attention to the window on his screen that holds Raven's image. Raven looks solemnly into the web cam on her laptop, the lens distorts her face making her nose more pronounced, almost like a beak.

The Friends Chief finds this very funny but keeps his face solemn. Excited by this possible coup against the Forest Service, both he and the Money Chief wait impatiently for Raven to speak.

After a moment, Raven speaks in her measured way, "The clip we reviewed is authentic...clear...it is the Forest Service Chief. I suggest we buy the rest...twenty-three minutes we are told...and do a further evaluation of...its authenticity...and of...its blackmail value."

She pauses for ten seconds, "I also require that...you...find out how many more copies...exist...and...who has them. If we have to...we should pay the man more...for this information. Who has any copies...in significant ways, that knowledge is even more valuable than...the images themselves."

Raven stops.

The other Chiefs wait until she finally nods, signaling she has no more to say.

The Friends Chief smiles broadly. He asks the Money Chief, "So how about it, Golden Eagle, should I make the buy?"

Golden Eagle lets out a war whoop, "For fuck's sake, why are you still sitting there? Let's buy that little atom bomb today! And, get that slimy piece of shit who's selling it to throw in the names and information that Raven wants. Then he gets the whole million. Clear?"

The Friends Chief yells, "Shit yes. I'm gone." He breaks the web connection.

Without comment, Raven follows suit.

Golden Eagle leans back in his chair, "What a great day. We just bought ourselves a red-hot poker to go up Chief Meacham's ass! Now how best to use it!"

———————————————//———————————————

Arrow, the War Chief, sits quietly reviewing the Zumo and Burns Strike plans. Badger sits next to him, looking at the intensely textured furnishings of the War Chief's large den and work space.

Security demands minimum contact among Mist leaders. So, this visit is Badger's first and likely last to Arrow's Iowa farmstead.

Badger looks around with interest, taking it all in. The place reveals much about the man. Most of the materials in the room had come from Arrow's farm and land.

The den walls are papered with reeds, bamboo, and tapia fabric. The vegetation's muted grays, greens, and buffs intensify the textures.

A tall stacked-stone waterfall gurgles and chuckles in the corner, water coming in from the stream that runs through Arrow's garden. The water tumbles down rock faces. Then it flows away back across river rocks and vegetation through the foundation to merge back with the stream course and pond below the house.

Arrow channeled the water and stacked the rocks himself as he built his house many years before.

Arrow had also carved dead stumps and tree trunks into book shelves and end tables, into work surfaces and lamps. He polished and oiled the wood until its planes and curves glow golden like a low summer Moon.

He wove reed mats to cover the floor and replaced them every year with more complex colors and patterns until now they impressed visitors as exotic art much like expensive African imports.

His hand-knotted sling chairs and firm pillows give his visitors gentle welcome.

Today, the War Chief has dropped his lean body into one of the sling chairs next to a window, feet crossed on a hemp-pillow-topped burl.

He studies the plans for an hour, asking Badger a few questions. He makes a few notes in plan margins and end pages.

To Badger, Arrow looked leaner and more frail than before, cheeks a little sunken. Maybe the threats to Mist and the strain of making plans are getting to him, driving him harder and faster than his normal hectic pace.

Chronos, an assassin under Badger's leadership, is assigned to the Zumo Strike. Chronos specializes in making Strikes look like hunting or fishing accidents. He uses every sort of hunting weapon—black powder and conventional firearms, crossbows, long bows—to Strike targets.

He also kills with contrived equipment failures—off-road vehicle roll overs, canoe capsizings, firearm explosions due to plugged barrels.

Arrow credits Chronos with 19 successful Strikes so far, a fine record.

The Zumo Strike plan is simple and solid enough. Arrow signs off on the plan.

He hands it to Badger, "This looks good. Take a look at my notes on the last page while I finish up with the Burns Strike."

Badger turns to the last page. The War Chief has scrawled a number of minor changes there, including the requirement that Zumo be completely isolated before the Strike and another that Badger must make sure 'Zumo's body disappears permanently.'

The Strike plan also covers the requirement to create uncertainty about what had happened to Zumo. After the Strike, Mist warriors from the Friends and Enemies Clans would spread false rumors and trails to confuse law enforcement, Forest Service employees, and Zumo's family.

The War Chief has also written that "Badger will accompany Chronos on the Strike as backup" and that "the Zumo Strike will occur in two weeks."

The last comments startle Badger.

Assassins almost always work alone. Badger has rarely seen the order for someone to accompany an assassin.

If the War Chief orders someone along, usually a regular War Clan warrior goes to guard an assassin's retreat or to provide a lookout for police or passersby.

So, for Badger, a Clan Leader, to serve as the assassin's contact...to go along on the Strike...seems unprecedented, risky. Arrow probably wants everything to go ultra smoothly on these two critical Strikes. So, he had ordered Badger into the operation to improve security and ensure success.

Okay.

But the two-week schedule! They can barely be ready in that time.

Given the unusual orders for the Zumo Strike, Badger makes a mental note to ask Arrow for more specifics.

But Badger is even more surprised by Arrow's changes to the Burns Strike plan. Arrow has approved the plan, adding only two comments, "Badger will team with Ekos for this Strike and be present for all elements except movement to and from the Strike site" and "The Burns Strike will occur in three weeks."

These orders truly concern Badger.

Two Strikes in three weeks? Essentially impossible.

Badger turns to the War Chief, "Arrow, I'm not sure it's physically possible to complete preparations, put all the pieces in place at the Strike sites, and then carry out the Strikes in the time you have allowed. One might be done, but two?"

Arrow replies thoughtfully, "Badger, I have the same concerns. When you think of how we usually do things, they are beyond reckless. Still this schedule is what the Chiefs' Council has asked us to follow. The Strike plans build. Coming one atop another, the Strikes should create maximum confusion for law enforcement and speculation among any media who try to cover them. We must divert them away from Mist at all cost!"

Arrow continues, "Under the cover of the confusion, Mist will go deeply underground, with no more Strikes for a long time, maybe years."

The War Chief does not mention the Council's strategy if this approach fails.

Arrow sees no reason to worry Badger on the eve of the War Clan's most difficult operations ever.

Arrow wonders if Badger might refuse to carry out the hastily planned and hurried Strikes. Mist assassins could turn down assignments or abort them in the field.

But as Clan Leader...doesn't Badger know this situation demands action--risky, fast action?

Arrow's anger rises as Badger remains quiet. Minutes tick away as Badger considers what lies ahead.

Arrow's anxiety peaks. His thoughtful, restrained temperament crumbles into fear and quiet rage.

He decides that he will have to kill Badger today, now, if Badger

274

balks.

Badger knows too much.

Out of sight, Arrow takes hold of the cold steel of the antique Cherokee tomahawk looped to his belt. He slips the leather hood off the blade. He begins to slowly slide the handle out of its sheath.

Oblivious to his thinking or the threat, Badger sits still and stares out the window at the far, wooded horizon. He grips the handle firmly.

Finally, Badger asks, "Arrow, why do you have me deeply involved in the operations? I can understand having me serve as back up in such critical missions, but you've asked me to team with Ekos on the Burns Strike. You've never asked me to be that involved before. Please don't misunderstand me. I'm honored to be a part of this Strike against these agency thugs. You know I'll do my best. It just seems so unusual."

Arrow smiles at Badger grimly.

Rationality slowly returns and he slides the tomahawk back into its sheath, "You are there first and foremost to make sure that nothing goes wrong. But if it does go wrong, you must act and then clean up the mess. These Strikes must succeed. Mist must remain hidden. No other outcome is acceptable to the Council, not even if it costs all of us our lives."

Arrow's last words startle Badger again. "You'll be there, too?" Badger asks.

"Yes," Arrow replies, "The plan does not mention it but I will be there as back up for you and Ekos on the Burns Strike."

The War Chief as back up...out in the open...impossible...crazy!

Badger almost yells, "No" but then thinks better of it and simply looks back to the horizon again.

Impressed with the Council's vision and intentions, Badger slowly says, "Okay. I feel stronger knowing you will be there."

The two sit quietly for a long time.

They watch the western horizon until daylight begins to shade into orange-purple dusk.

Their thoughts cover Strike plans. Their emotions cover the range of their hopes, fears, and grim determination.

Arrow gradually returns to full trust in Badger. They are comrades again, warriors bound by the blood and death of Mist's enemies, by Mist's ruthless creed, the soul of Mist.

Finally as the den grows dark, Arrow uses a safety match to light several thick candles that sit squat and strong on top of a large stump.

He had hollowed out the stump many years before, creating a deep pocket to trap wax. But, over time, the hollow filled.

Now, the colors of many candles flow over the mass of wax that fills the hollow. Frozen wax torrents cascade down and form widening puddles on the stump's stone base.

They both look long at the little candle flames. Arrow shifts in his chair and turns, "Badger, I have something else to talk to you about before you go. This is personal."

He looks into Badger's eyes, "Please don't be concerned, but you should know that I'm dying. I have pancreatic cancer. It's a middling kind, not the worst kind. It's treatable, possibly for years, but it's also terminal."

Badger draws a quick breath, shocked and concerned, instantly sad for Arrow and Mist.

Could the doctors be wrong? They must be.

What would Mist do without Arrow's leadership? He had built and molded the War Clan for decades. Badger had learned everything from the man and deeply respects his cunning and murderous craft.

Badger begins to speak, but Arrow holds up his hand, "No reason to talk of illness now. I have many treatments to go, both western and eastern medicine. Just know this, Badger, I'll be around for awhile yet and then, sooner than I expected, I won't."

Badger begins to sputter a reply.

Arrow holds up his hand again, "There's nothing to say now. Let's talk about 'how long' after we make the Strikes a success. I also want you to know my recommendation to the Council will be that you, Badger, take my place as War Chief. I'll surely live long enough to gain their consent. And I'll tell you everything I know before…departing into the mist where no one else can follow."

A thoroughly pragmatic man, Arrow smiles at his poetic whimsy.

Beyond amazement, Badger blurts out, "But, Arrow, I'm not ready for these things…for you to die…for me to take over. I'm not qualified or ready!"

Arrow smiles wanly, "Badger, you are the best suited among all the War Clan leaders to take over. I know. I know them all."

"You alone have the fire in your belly. You have the brains and guts to smash Earth Mother's enemies, pound them to pulp when nature cries for help."

He stops and looks intently into Badger's eyes again, "You will do what I ask and become War Chief, won't you?"

The cold determination in Arrow's voice chills Badger. It was

276

something he must have.

It would not be wise to resist him in this, his death wish.

Badger can only stare back and whisper, "Yes, of course."

Breaking the tension, Arrow gestures out the window, "Its dark and time for you to go. Remember to drive with your lights out until you reach the highway."

Badger has night-vision goggles along for this purpose, "I will. It's good practice. The trick is to remember to take the night vision stuff off and turn the headlights on!"

They both smile. They know how other drivers react when a fully darkened vehicle passes them, flashing lights and honking. Hardly the stealthy way Mist warriors like to travel.

Badger stands up to go, still dizzy with the effects of Arrow's words—life, death, the future. Arrow stands, too.

For the first time ever, he hugs Badger gently, warmly. At his touch, Badger's tears well up and overflow with mixed desires, to placate his anger, to comfort Arrow, to heal him, to thank him.

Without thought, Badger's lips brush Arrow's. Badger's arms tighten.

Lips press firmly.

Their eyes close.

Their breaths intermingle.

Arrow chuckles, deep in his throat.

Passion ignites. Mouths and arms refuse to part.

They stand for a long time, kissing…kissing and only let go to undress one another hastily…breathlessly.

They mate on the rush mat below the candle log.

Arrow sits in Tantric position. Badger mounts him, and then moves slowly and dreamily, feeling him deep inside. Their eager, rhythmic movements make the rushes crackle and sigh.

The flickering, wavy candle lights throw their shadows against the textured walls. One moment, ecstatic human images ripple there. In the next, distorted, demonic shapes dance like flames.

Passion and movement peak. Wax drips from the brimming log onto Badger's arm--digging, scalding.

Badger moans on orgasm's edge.

She's not sure whether the sound forced out of her comes from the burn, Arrow's exquisite penetration, or his looming fate.

Chapter 37

Mill Grinds On

Mill tries repeatedly to reach Philip Tuesday morning. He calls back, reaches voice mail, and leaves messages of his own. They do not talk directly.

Philip sounds tired. His messages are terse, just a "This is Philip. Call me." or "I'll be tied up today. Try me this evening."

Mill is sure his messages are short because he's mad at her.

She can't remember the end to their evening together So, she doesn't know whether to apologize to him, laugh at him, or cuss him out.

Philip is the best and longest friend she's ever had and now…now this…this frightening, confusing memory gap!

What the Hell had happened between them? Until she finds out, she would just keep her phone voice and comments neutral…even while her thoughts and feelings rocket all over everywhere and question marks pick at her mind.

For his part, Philip feels racked with remorse for upsetting Milly so much. He knows that she greatly over reacted to his story. He correctly attributes that to her trauma. That's the easy part—the thinking part.

But, as a man he loves his ideal of Milly, once a girl and now a woman. His role in increasing her pain and confusion deeply distresses him.

He can barely contemplate the newly discovered horror of his involvement in her assault. So, not wanting to make matters worse between them, he, too, keeps his voice and comments neutral.

Each one waits until they can speak in person. They suffer in their silence.

——————————————//——————————————

The giant statue called Portlandia squats on an odd blue portico, partially obscured from the street. Mill meets Jake under it at noon, wondering idly if the portico is strong enough to hold the massive woman figure up.

As Burns approaches her, Mill sees him gesture towards a nearby alley. She follows him, walking casually behind his rapid steps. This creates a gap between them meant to confuse anyone following.

As she enters the alley, she sees him look back and beyond her. He ducks into a door.

Mill, too, looks back quickly to make sure she has not been followed. She walks up to the door and tries the door knob.

The gritty old brass nob is unlocked and rattles loosely. Turning it, Mill steps into a small darkened room. She closes the door behind her. The door lock makes a solid thunk. She realizes that the flimsy knob is just a ruse Jake uses to hide the room's purpose.

As she closes the door, the windowless room goes pitch black.

Now blind, she frees the strap on her holstered Glock and wraps her hand around the grips, ready for a fast draw.

Where the Hell's Jake?

Dry and laconic, Jake's voice sounds from a few feet away, "Okay, cowgirl, you can let go of the shootin' iron. The posse has passed."

Mill jumps about a foot in the air.

She sheepishly lets go of her weapon.

"How the Hell did you know I was holding my Glock?" she asks.

Jake answers, "Because that's what we teach you to do. And that's what I would do. At least you have enough sense to not show a light and make a target out of yourself. I could tell you stories…including ones about that idiot O'Reilly who got us into this cesspool. Fuckin' moron."

He shuffles a couple of steps. A second later, a small, dim light comes on, one weak bulb in an old brass wall sconce.

Small and dusty, the room's wallpaper and lights hint that it once was a dining room or lounge. Now, it stands almost empty.

A few folding chairs are stacked against one wall. The oriental-style carpet is nicked, thread worn, and even bare in places.

Jake walks over, takes two chairs, opens them, and gestures for Mill to sit down. Mill inspects hers skeptically and dusts it with her hand before sitting.

"Think its dirty now?" Burns asks, "You should have seen it when I first started using this place for private meets--cockroaches and rat turds everywhere. Place reminded my of my boyhood bedroom. But you don't want to hear about my boyhood bedroom. I don't want to remember the smell."

Mill can tell Burns is blowing off a little steam before getting down to the purpose of their secret meeting. She smiles tolerantly and encourages him with a lifted eyebrow.

Burns looks at Mill sharply, "This'll be the last time we both take the same route into this rat hole. If we meet here again, I'll be coming in from one direction and you from another. Two alleys intersect just a couple feet from the door, one we came down and another connecting the side streets. We can't take the risk of falling into a pattern."

Burns points towards the door. Rising, he walks to a dusty scrap of cloth hanging to the left of the door frame and pushes it aside. Under it is a faintly glowing screen.

He pushes a button to the side of the screen and a short video of Mill's and his arrival runs on the screen. "Motion-activated camera," he grunts, "useful gimmick. Mounted in that rusty light above the door--the one that doesn't work and looks like it's going to fall on your head at any moment. I can watch this from my office or even my freakin' cell phone if I want to. You may call me 'tech lord' when I allow you to talk from here on out."

Mill and he laugh.

Jake shakes his head, "So, here and at a couple of other meet rooms I have set up, you'll see the same kind of gear. There's also a radio-controlled system on the doors that sends me a silent alarm if anyone breaks in."

He waves a small grey fob on his key ring at her, "this dingus shuts the alarm down when I get within a block or so. I'm so mod-ren." He shakes his hang-dog face and his jowls wobble mournfully at Mill.

Mill laughs and looks at him, wide-eyed, expressing awe and worship for tech-lord Jake. She dimples and bats her eyes.

Seeing her expression, Jake snorts and gestures towards the main door and then to a small door hidden in an alcove. "This building used to be a whorehouse. Now it's a Chinese restaurant, at least on this floor. Go figure, people'd rather eat than get laid. Anyway, in the red-light days, the room had a small bar, a wash basin, and overstuffed furniture including a big couch or chaise lounge. I've seen pictures."

Burns points at less-faded squares on the wall where paintings had once hung, "The carriage trade would come in through the door we entered. Then sporting women, or fancy boys I suppose, would come in one by one until the patron would make his selection."

"The patron could then enjoy his purchase by bouncing it all over the furniture. Or, he could sit in that little alcove and peer through a screen while the professionals put on a fuck show. That little door in the alcove could be used for escape if the police or an angry wife made a raid. Hell of a deal."

He shakes his head and laughs, "I bet the owners and madam made a bunch of money. Too bad it all came to an end in 1956, when the mayor at the time, James Cockburn Smith, got six holes bored through him just outside our alley door. Never found the killer."

"The good-government types and blue bloods made sure the poor little whorehouse got closed. Bad for Mayor Smith. Worse for Portland. I mean the loss of the whorehouse, not Smith."

"People still remember. Took the narrow alley outside to keep the history-buff tour buses away. Even so, a walking tour comes by here looking for blood stains every morning. Good cover for our comings and goings as long as we keep clear of those cotton-topped tourists."

Mill laughs at the thought of dodging hoards of little white-haired old ladies with scandal on their minds. She looks expectantly at Burns.

Jake grins, "Okay, okay. Enough sordid Portland history. We're here to work on sordid, stinking Forest Service crap. So, the big green elephant in the room is the question, 'Who tampered with evidence here and in Florence?'"

Burns grimaces and swallows sourly, narrowing his gaze on Mill.

"Meacham," he says levelly, "The shit I'm about to flush your way is for your consumption only, at least for now. Don't give it to anyone else...no one, okay?"

Mill nods, her typical frown deepening.

Burns goes on, "Here's why. I have names, but not one name. I have possible motives but not one motive that makes sense yet. And I have evidence but no real proof. So until we connect all the dots, or at least most of them, all we got is shit. If we share it widely, the perps could easily just walk away, flippin' us the bird."

Mill responds, "Got it."

"Not even your buddies at the Bureau," he emphasizes.

She puts her hand up as if taking an oath. "Not even my buddies at the Bureau," she pledges, a little flush coming to her cheeks.

She is a little insulted at his insistence and thinks, "What does he want, a contract signed in blood?"

But, with her last reassurance, Jake's ready to move on. "Seventeen people have access to the evidence room, including me," he reports, "And I'm saying I'm not the thief, so that leaves 16. You okay with leaving my sorry ass out of the line-up?"

Squinting at him, Mill answers, "Yes, for now."

Burns gives her a sharp glance followed quickly by an understanding smile, "Good cop. Okay, of the 16, we show no record of 5 ever entering. These are special agents mainly—the ones that have their assistants manage the evidence or that work undercover or other special assignments that mean

282

they don't deal with evidence. So that leaves 11. Okay so far?" Mill nods.

Jake continues, "So, of the 11, two were gone during the Miller and O'Reilly investigations. One is in DC in the Director's office screwing off as an acting muckety-muck--and I emphasize muck—head's swelled as big as Portlandia's ass. The other's a female assistant on maternity leave. So, between the two of them, one's screwing off and one's been screwed and both are happy for their circumstances, I guess. In case you wonder, I'm not happy."

He thinks for a moment, "I was going to list the names of the 9 suspects for you, but most of them wouldn't mean anything to you--bunch 'a nameless, faceless bureaucrats anyway. Kinda scary when you think about the faceless part; you know what I mean—no eyes or nose…just drippy holes and a bare brain poking out…yeech!"

"Anyway, of the group, door-access records cross-matched with the video record give us two possibles: Carrie Soames and your buddy, Arianne Moeller. Both had access during the target time period. Both are shown on tape near the Miller evidence box, handling boxes. Problem is that the video doesn't have enough resolution to pick out lettering on the boxes. And the camera angle doesn't let us pinpoint the exact shelf location of the box being handled."

He stops talking.

Amazement settles over Mill. Carrie or Arianne! Or maybe Carrie *and* Arianne!

Either way, unbelievable!

Both women seem so dedicated and so, well, Forest Service—wear "green undershorts" as the Legacies liked to say—committed and supportive.

Jake had been looking at her face, "I can tell you're skeptical, and so am I. Shoot...these gals, if you cut 'em, they'll bleed Forest Service green. But, they're the only two that fit the evidence closely. No one's tried to jigger the video record that we can tell. And, I've sent the hard drive data over to the FBI lab for enhancement. We may be able to get the words on the boxes clear enough to read. Then we'll out the perp."

Mill nods and asks, "How soon will the lab be done with the enhancement?"

Jake answers, "This Friday. I'll let you know if it comes in sooner."

Mill looks at him intently, "So, what about motive? Why the hell would either of these women do this…jeopardize their careers…blow it all for a fake gold coin?"

The chill climbs back up her neck. Words begin to rush out of her,

"They weren't on Mendocino Six. Both could have known O'Reilly's travel plans, maybe, but Miller? I mean this makes no sense…unless…unless they are helping the murderers. And then, who are the murderers? And so, if Carrie or Arianne stole evidence here, who took the folder out of my cabinet in Florence? Is there any evidence that they traveled there or called there or anything?"

She jumps to her feet, saying, "We need to know this crap. Let's bring them in and sweat them…get the bitches to talk!"

Burns laughs gently at her, "Sit down, trooper. Sweet Jesus, Meacham, if I had all that stuff nailed down, I'd a collared one of them and be poundin' her with rubber hoses. Or better yet, I'd be givin' her an upside down trip on the water slide."

Mill knows that Jake referred to the torture technique called "water-boarding." His exaggerations reminding her that she's a neophyte, a baby investigator. She's out of line in pressuring him with her questions. She smiles ruefully.

A little chastened but still charged up, Mill sits back down on the dusty, bent chair. Burns will begin to question the women as soon as he had sufficient evidence.

To begin earlier could warn the perp. She might disappear or leave the questioning to destroy other evidence at work or home.

Mill pulls her mind back from all the possibilities. Still energized, she asks, "So what do you want me to *do*? I can watch Moeller for you but I don't want to give anything away."

Jake responds evenly, "Yeah, exactly. There's this famous quote from a great UCLA basketball coach, John Wooden, 'be quick but don't hurry.' My word for you is 'sniff around but don't be nosey.'"

"Moeller's a nervous twitch if I ever saw one. If she's guilty and thinks you're on to her, she'll rabbit like a bunny with her cotton tail on fire. So, you just act normal. Pay a little extra attention to what Moeller's doing. Don't search her desk or anything like that. But if she asks you out for drinks or the chance to shove dollar bills in some cowboy's sequin g-string, do it! Get her drunk and let'er talk. Okay?"

Mill laughs at the thought of Arianne drunk at a strip bar for women. She also gets Jake's point. "Okay," she smiles "Get her drunk, soak her in male sweat, and let her spill her guts. Can do."

Jake roars at the absurd vision of a male stripper giving Moeller a lap dance, "Okay. Maybe just a glass of wine or two…if she wants to. Nice and easy…nice and natural. If she pukes up something actionable, like a

284

full confession, arrest her on the spot, cuff her, call me, and bring her in. Otherwise just be her best friend forever and let her talk. Okay?"

Mill nods agreement, "Okay."

They talk a little more.

Mill finds out that Jake has been keeping Zumo up to speed.

Zumo was discreetly working his end of the evidence-tampering case, including coming in to the Mapleton office at 2 am to dust for fingerprints. But whoever had stolen the file there had been careful and professional, leaving no evidence, not even "belly lint" as Jake put it.

Burns warns her to not discuss anything about the investigation unless they're both on secure lines. Then he adds, "And I'm still leery of the phones over at my office. I want you to stick to land lines to avoid any kind of cell-phone snoopers. Use the Bureau's phones if you want to talk to Zumo. The Bureau monitors for snoopers all the time."

Mill agrees readily to the extra security.

Burns tells her to wait five minutes after he goes out the alley door before leaving herself. He tells her that the alarm will re-activate ten minutes after he leaves and she better "skedaddle" before it does.

He rises and folds his chair, re-stacks it against the wall, and turns out the little light. He opens the alley door and steps quickly through it, closing it sharply but quietly behind him.

Mill stands up and turns on her small high-intensity flashlight. She looks around the shabby room, thinking of the old days when it had been a part of a bawdy house.

She imagines men in frock coats with hookers in petticoats perched on their knees, drinking bubbly from crystal glasses.

Mill shakes her head at the Hollywood image. She knows that the reality would have been hookers who were virtually slaves, often beaten, diseased, forced to be sex workers, crooked and criminal.

Their customers might be drugged and robbed, or sometimes, like Mayor James Cockburn Smith, even killed. Rough trade then…even rougher trade now.

She examines the exit doors and frames, admiring how well the installers had concealed alarm-system microchips in them. No sign of them at all.

She briefly opens the two locked doors that lead to the interior of the building. The larger door opens easily into a dusty hallway with cracked marble floors.

She peers out. To the left, heavy bronze doors stand solidly, locked with a chain, windows covered with faded, tattered paper.

To the right, the hallway angles off to a staircase leading upwards. Mill closes the door and locks the dead bolt.

The small door in the alcove opens with effort. Incongruously, it leads into a stuffy closet filled with mops, brooms, and cleaning supplies.

She smells cooking and hears water-washing noises beyond. Raised voices speak both English and Chinese. So, the closet must have once been a short hallway, one that now opens into the kitchen of the Chinese restaurant or at least near it.

She has an impulse to step through and surprise the workers there... yell "moo shoo pork" or something...make them jump.

She smiles at her foolishness and closes the door. She walks back to the alley door and opens it. After making sure the deadbolt will lock from inside, she slips out and closes the door firmly behind her.

When Mill gets back to the FBI task force office, she looks around for Arianne. She's not there.

Mill calls Philip's number and gets his voice mail again. She does not leave a message.

"0 for 2," she calculates and plunges in to organizing and finishing all the notes, photos, and evidence from the Mendocino Six field trip.

At about 3 pm, Arianne comes in with another box of records. She walks to her little office to organize them.

Mill gives her a few minutes to settle in and then walks over to say hello. They chat for a few minutes.

Mill makes a date with Arianne "to catch up," promising tidbits from the field trip. They agree to meet the next night at the wine bar three blocks from the Justice Building.

Talking to the prim little Arianne, Mill's sure any male strippers and lap dances would wait for another outing, maybe one in about a million years.

Chapter 38

Mist Shrouds

After blowing out the candles, Badger and Arrow take their passion from the den floor to his snug, four-poster log bed. They walk naked, clothes in hand, hips touching. Both feel the cold stone beneath their feet. In their bellies, they feel the ache for more sex.

Rejoined under the covers, they move with desperate energy, coming up from beneath his down comforter only for short respites and cool air.

They join again. Their moans and cries cause frightened chickens to flap in Arrow's coop and his horse to stomp his feet in his stall. After two vigorous orgasms each, they sleep for a time, hands and legs touching.

Well before the nearby farmers rise to milk cows or to leave their farms for "town" jobs, Badger reluctantly wakes.

She lights a candle by the bed and dresses in its tiny, soft light. She tip-toes into the hallway and lights a candle there. Then she slips back to nudge Arrow awake and say goodbye.

He jumps out of bed to hold her close, standing naked in her arms, lean warmth pressed against her jeans and T-shirt.

Finally, Arrow pushes her out to arms length. He smiles at her, "Badger, what a wonderful gift you've given me. But, you know, don't you, that we can't repeat this…at least not until Mist is secure again? I mean we have to put this aside to focus on the Strikes and on taking care of… the rest."

Badger looks back at him in the quiet, dim light.

They have something together. This night proves it. But it can't be called love...probably could never become love.

Arrow is married to the War Clan, to killing the enemies of Mist. She's wise enough to know that love and merciless killing can't coexist.

He'd married the decaying flesh of secret death long ago.

Badger could only ever really be his dark-blood mistress, the one he used to give him respite between Strikes...never his wife, his closest one.

And Badger, War Clan Leader, holds a black well of rage in herself, too. She can't love him either, not fully, at least not until her own killing thirst gets slaked.

So, she answers, "Of course, Arrow, after tonight we are back to business. You'll be the War Chief. I'll be your clan leader on a Strike.

That's the way it will be…until it's over."

Arrow smiles knowingly, approvingly at her words.

He appreciates that her passion has fulfilled him even while their future looms so dark. He knows she's left a lot of feelings and womanly plans unsaid in deference to Mist's imperilled future.

They walk out into the hall hand in hand. Badger puts on her black coat. She picks up her dark mask and night-vision goggles. She turns to go.

He takes her hand and pulls her back for a final kiss. Their lips cling, mingled breath hot.

Badger breaks the kiss and kicks off her shoes. She slides her jeans and underwear to the floor. She sits up and back on a hallway table next to the candle, and pulls him to her.

Instantly aroused, he enters her. They cling tight as he rocks against her and thrusts. Badger's legs encircle him. She feels him slide and rub deep inside her, the angle of their contact exquisitely stimulating.

Her locked heels spur him in…in…in.

But even as her pleasure mounts, Badger feels her spirits sinking. Her long-lonely heart tries to take Arrow in, to store her present feelings for the bed-empty nights ahead.

Two tears roll down her cheeks.

She hugs Arrow tighter, senses him, absorbs his smells and textures and movements.

Their orgasms come too quickly for Badger, intense, wave on wave of pleasure that softly fades.

When just a glow remains, they hold each other a little longer and smile into each other's eyes.

Finally, Badger lowers her legs. She gently slips off the table and stands on tiptoes to keep Arrow inside her. S
he squeezes him tightly within her…feels him slowly wilting, withering. Then she lifts herself off.

She pulls him close once again…feels his warm, wet penis against her abdomen. "Goodbye, Arrow," she whispers, "I'll see you again in Portland…three weeks…be well."

Badger turns him and shoves him gently back towards the bedroom. She watches his too slender body move off into the shadows and disappear.

She wearily puts on her scattered clothes and boots, a long drive ahead. She will begin it exhausted, feeling quite hollow yet calmly happy at the same time.

She pulls on the mask and night-vision goggles. She heads out into the dark, dark morning.

————————————————// ————————————————

Badger meets Chronos at a ranch about 20 miles west of Medford, Oregon. Badger had selected the site because the terrain where they've planned the Zumo Strike closely matches the ranch setting.

The ranch spreads across broken fields and timbered areas high in the Coastal Mountains. A battered house stands worn but weather-tight.

Heat comes from a wood stove. Water comes from a pump with a long handle.

Chronos' strong organization and physical skills have impressed Badger before. Discharged from the Army Rangers after the first Iraq War, Chronos simply knows how to put together an ambush better than any other Mist assassin.

In his past Strikes, every step, every move had received his meticulous touch. He'd rehearsed each move dozens of times before going ahead.

But the Strike itself is not the biggest challenge. Zumo can be isolated fairly easily. Chronos' skill at arms virtually guarantees Zumo's death.

No, the difficult part lies with the people who love Zumo and care about him. He has a wife at home and many colleagues in law enforcement and the Forest Service.

They care about him.

They know his honest integrity well.

Zumo's disappearance has to be done in a way that leaves strong doubt about what had actually happened to him, about what he himself has done.

No evidence of Zumo's death can remain at the death site, none.

And plenty of credible evidence about where he'd gone has to be found in distant places.

Those things take a lot of organization, time, and help. Arrow and Badger know that his disappearance would be carefully scrutinized…by experts…the best in the business of crime detection.

When they first arrive at the ranch, Badger still wonders if the Zumo Strike is really necessary. But after two days there, Raven, the Listening Chief, calls Badger and confirms that Jake Burns and Zumo have been sharing information about the Miller and O'Reilly Strikes.

And so, the Zumo Strike moves forward.

Now, Badger makes sure Chronos' rehearsals have surprises built in—what war gamers call "inputs."

A hurried and riskier Strike lies ahead. Badger knows Chronos might have to react quickly to emerging threats and make good decisions on the fly. So, she shapes her inputs to shake up Chronos, challenge his wits, distract him at crucial moments, and force him to think on his feet.

Sudden noises blast him. Human silhouettes suddenly appear where none should be. Things drop on him from trees.

Chronos conquers them all, sometimes not the first time but always in the end.

After three more days of sweat and practice, Badger sends Chronos towards the coast in an old but serviceable RV.

He will travel around for a few days, playing tourist along the Oregon coast. She will contact Chronos by secure cell-phone when she and her helpers have the rest of the Strike plan fully in place.

After Chronos chugs away in the aging Winnebago Warrior, Badger walks the whole area where the rehearsals had taken place. She finds a few small traces of their work, mainly tracks in the dust. She quickly obliterates them with a leafy tree branch.

Her biggest find is a shell casing oddly lodged in the notch of a tree where Chronos' back-up weapon, a semi-automatic hunting rifle, had ejected it.

"What's the chance of that?" she asks herself, "About one in a million, I suppose." She reaches up and plucks it out and slides it into her pocket for later random disposal in some far-away trash can.

All the rest of their trash had gone with Chronos in several thick plastic bags. He will drop the bags in a trash transfer site near Brookings, way west on the coast in Curry County.

Badger takes one last look at the old homestead and then drives out across the cattle guard to the dusty asphalt road beyond.

––––––––––––––––––– // –––––––––––––––––––

Badger drives north along I-5. She follows a different route than Chronos. Her memories of Arrow's quick, hard body and their love making provide her a warm reverie as she rolls along. The miles flow by quickly.

She drives for over an hour and then turns west on Oregon Route 42, a road that rises over the Coastal Range from Winston to Coos Bay.

290

Badger's heart beats quicker.

Her speed seems to slow. A quick glance at the speedometer shows that the cruise control remains locked on her safe, inconspicuous 55 miles an hour pace.

She guesses that her fatigue makes her want to speed up, to reach the end...whatever end there was to be. But she's too tired to speed along twisting, unfamiliar roads.

A dim glimpse of Arrow, caught in the mirror in his bedroom, thrusting into her from behind flashes through her mind.

That memory mingles with the mounting lust she feels for Zumo's death...to reach the end of this.

A week to go until Mist-enemy Zumo would fall before her blood stroke!

Chapter 39

Moeller Pain

Arianne's tight, stiff-backed reserve melts somewhat under the flow of half a carafe of merlot from Oregon's Henry Estate's Winery. Having downed her half, Mill feels the erosion of her wits and coordination, too.

"So, Arianne," Mill ventures a little thickly, "Any men in your life? You're young, have a good job, drop-dead gorgeous…"

Moeller giggles, red-faced. She shows her slightly gap-toothed smile for a moment. "Oh, Mill," she replies, "You know that's not true. I'm just a plain Jane, librarian kind of gal. No men want me."

"I'm not too sure about that, Arianne," Mill says, "I mean look at Agent Collins. He's pretty cool. He seems interested. He's divorced. Nice. Funny. He hangs around your desk, flirting with you."

Arianne gives Mill a sidelong glance. She pats the buns carefully coiled on the sides of her head and sniffs, "He's a class clown, Mill. No proper kind of man for me. Besides, he's only over at my desk to steal M&Ms from my candy dish."

Arianne reflects for a moment and then says archly, "He has two ex-wives and no kids. He might want to dip his fingers in my personal candy dish but I bet he can't get it up. And I'm a woman that needs to be satisfied!"

At this outrageous statement, Mill peers smilingly at Arianne to see if she's serious. The mousy little woman certainly doesn't look like she'd be a demanding, passionate lover. Mill doubts if she's ever been loved at all.

Comas of laughter appear around Arianne's mouth. Mill's four-toned laugh scales up to a shout. Arianne screams with laughter, too, lightly slapping the table.

After a few moments, Arianne gasps out, "And I'd make him get it up, too! That's me--Lady Lash Moeller, Collins' dominatrix!"

The image of Arianne in fishnet and leather causes both women to howl again. People at nearby tables turn to look and smile in uncomprehending sympathy. They clearly wonder what could be so funny and hope to be that tickled tonight themselves.

When the two women calm down to mere giggles, Mill waves for the waiter. They order a large plate of nachos and another bottle of merlot.

Arianne seems to welcome the food. She makes no complaint at the additional wine.

Remembering Jake's orders, Mill resolves to pour more for Arianne out of the new carafe than for herself.

The two women chat until the nachos arrive and then dig in. For a few moments they moan over the hot, greasy, cheesy treat.

Arianne's clearly now at ease with Mill. Mill decides to try a few questions about the case.

"Arianne," she begins, "I know you were close to John O'Reilly because you mentioned that to me when I first got here. Tell me more about him. Was he a good guy to work for? Fun to be around? I'd just like to know 'cause I never met him and he sounds interesting. It could also help me with the case, I guess, even though I can't imagine how."

Arianne sits quiet for a few moments. She looks searchingly at Mill and replies with a slightly disgusted grimace, "He was a self-serving slob, if you want to know the truth. I worked for him and got along with him, but I really didn't like him at all."

Although Mill's face remains calm, she's really surprised by Arianne's words--ones that differ significantly from her seeming views of a month or so ago. Back then, Mill picked up that Arianne had been in love with O'Reilly, so strong had her feelings come across.

Now, Arianne seems to have felt nothing but contempt. Then Mill remembers the bitter glow behind Arianne's words back then. So, it hadn't been love at all...clearly...but something darker.

Her tone casual, Mill replies, "So, you sound like he was tough to work for. Did he cause you problems?"

"Oh yeth," Arianne answers, weaving slightly. Her mouth is pursed with distaste, "John always looked out for John if you know what I mean. Not a good word for anyone...anyone...unless it might get him ahead. He was always on the road, sucking up our scarce travel dollars, thucking... sucking up to somebody. I never saw his equal in that. And Sam Priest, that pompous s-steer, just chewed his cud and let John go junking...junketing off."

"My goodness," Mill responds, "Sounds like those guys were acting really crazy. How long did John run around like this?"

"All the time, M...Mill," Arianne says tartly yet with her words spaced drunkenly, "Sometimes he switched his plans two or three times...a week. I had to redo his trips...over and over again...over 'n over a-again... and his travel vouchers...he'd gouge the government for every penny he could...over and over. He was always so demanding...and...and... uncomplimentary."

Tears come to Arianne's eyes as she remembers his stinging

remarks, her hurt.

"He sounds like a real asshole," Mill responds indignantly. "What a bastard. What a prick to treat you that way. God damn him!"

"Yes," Arianne says. Her voice lowers and comes out wine-husky, grating, almost a hiss, "God damn him. I hate...hated his sorry ass. And I'm...I'm glad he's dead."

Arianne speaks as if she has almost forgotten Mill's presence. Mill waits for a moment watching Arianne's face work with emotion.

Mill asks her conspiratorially, "Don't you wish you had been there when he died?"

Arianne bows her head, her words slurring with wine and hatred, "Yesss. But they...they wwwouldn't let meee."

Mill's thoughts leap with excitement. She clamps down on those thoughts, letting nothing of her excitement show.

Arianne may have just confessed to conspiracy to commit murder of a federal agent, a capital crime. Based on that alone, Mill could read Arianne her Miranda rights and cuff her, slam bang.

But that would certainly mean that Arianne would not say anything more. And Mill wants to know more, lots more. So, Mill says to the clearly drunk Arianne in a low voice, "I'm sorry you couldn't go. Who wouldn't let you go, Sam Priest?"

"No," replies Arianne, her head sinking lower. Her voice drops and words slur even more, "Not fffffuckin' Priesht. Misssssht...Misssssshh...... Missssshhhht."

And with that sloppy alliteration, Arianne passes out, her left cheek on the table, ear in the remains of her nachos, sticky cheese goo-ing into her hair.

Mill's stunned, ideas racing if a little drunkenly. Mill hadn't been able to make out Arianne's last few words clearly. And they make no sense.

Had she been saying she had "missed" something? Missed what, killing O'Reilly?

Missed talking to the person in charge?

Missed a ride?

Missed a call, a letter, an e-mail, a tweet? What the hell, missed?

Or had she said, "mister?" Mister who?

Or "mist." Mist?

Is that someone's name? First name? Last name?

An address? An acronym? An organization?

Something about water?

What about water? O'Reilly hadn't been killed in a fog or near water.

Or had she been trying to say, "mistake?" How could she have been making a mistake by not being a part of O'Reilly's murder? And yes, killing someone certainly is a mistake but what other kind of mistake could she have committed?

Mill reaches across the table and gives Arianne a little shake, hoping to rouse her enough for another few questions. But, Arianne's body moves limply and freely...dead weight, dead drunk.

She'd had no idea that Arianne had gotten that drunk. The wine must have been coming on strong in the minutes before her startling confession.

With this level of intoxication, whatever she "confessed" would not hold up in court. But, and this is a huge 'but', Arianne has revealed at least the existence of a conspiracy. All the rest is simply a frustrating puzzle, word stew, garbage evidence. Mill knows she has to call Jake pronto.

But first, she has to deal with Arianne's drunken carcass. With the help of a bouncer, Mill gets Arianne into the ladies room for a quick cleanup and then out to Mill's government car.

Mill knows she's over-the-DUI-limit herself. But she feels her excitement pushing back the cobwebs as she motors carefully towards the address shown on Arianne's license.

As Mill drives, she glances at Arianne occasionally. Mill doesn't want her passenger's stomach full of wine and nachos all over the inside of the car. But Arianne remains lifeless, leaning against the passenger door. She looks half strangled by the seat belt and snores lightly.

Mill stops twice for directions, She finally pulls up in front of Arianne's home address which turns out to be an auto repair shop in a rundown area, closed and locked for the night.

At first Mill wonders if she's gotten the wrong address. She checks Arianne's driver's license again. The garage address is a match.

Then she takes Arianne's keys from her purse. She tries them gently in the door and the noise wakes a sleeping dog. The dog's scrambles towards Mill and barks loudly.

Adrenaline drives most of the remaining wine cobwebs out of Mill's head. Heart racing, eyes wide, she thinks, "This is no good."

Ignoring the barking dog, Mill walks around the building to see if it has a separate entrance or a second-floor walk up. It doesn't.

Mill wonders if a small house could be tucked in behind the nearby businesses and somehow shares an address with the garage. She returns to the car, starts it, and drives around the block. Nothing.

Arianne must live somewhere but not in this shabby neighborhood. Her license must be a clever fake. Or maybe she'd paid the repair shop folks to let her use their address.

Things look worse for Arianne, more incriminating evidence piling up.

Mill sits at a stop sign for a moment, thinking.

She doesn't want to take Arianne back to her own room at the Residence Inn. She doesn't want to use Arianne's credit cards to get her a strange room to wake up in.

Both actions might raise Arianne's suspicions about what they'd done or said tonight. She might wonder if Mill had tried to drive her "home" and found the fake address.

So Mill drives back to the wine bar. After circling nearby parking lots, she finds Arianne's little grey Ford Fusion. Parking next to it in the empty lot, Mill opens the Fusion, turns on the ignition, and lowers both front windows slightly. Then Mill opens the passenger door of her government rig.

She catches the slumping Arianne before she can sprawl out from under her seat belt onto the pavement. Mill unbuckles her.

With a grunt, Mill lifts Arianne and flops her behind the wheel of her car. She belts her in and tips her seat all the way back. She slips Arianne's keys under the passenger seat, out of drunken reach.

Locking the car doors, Mill gently closes Arianne's. "Sweet dreams, you murderous bitch," Mill says to Arianne silently. She steps back in her car, and drives away

A few miles away, roaring up the Turwillger curves, Mill opens her government phone. She calls Burns' secure line at home.

He wakes up with a jerk and snarls into the phone, "Meacham! What the fuckin' hell? You just ruined my only wet dream for the month. I was about to make it with Christie Brinkley—first time ever. So, God damn it, Meacham, this had better be good."

Mill's report puts Christie in second place.

———————————//———————————

When she comes into work the next day, Mill drives past the parking lot where she'd left Arianne-in-a-can.

Arianne's car's gone. A large Hummer sits where the Fusion had been.

Mill drives to the Justice Building and enters the parking lot there. As she enters, she looks around for Arianne's Fusion.

Mill doesn't see a Mist Eyes and Ears Clan warrior sitting on a bicycle, pretending to be a courier waiting for a Justice Building client.

But Ben Hicks sees her. He sends a secure text to his clan leader. The clan leader sends it on to Arrow.

Mill enters through security and rides up on the elevator. She wonders if Arianne will be in late or maybe not at all.

Mill has a 2 pm appointment at the old cathouse parlor with Burns. She hopes to talk to Arianne before then and try to sooth any concerns she has about last night's debauch.

At about 10 am, Arianne appears, looking pale and punk. Mill grimaces to her across the conference area and holds her head as if she has a major hangover. Arianne looks down, then smiles tentatively back at Mill, before hurrying into her office.

Mill works away for another hour and a half and then breaks for lunch.

She walks casually over the Arianne's office. Arianne's on the phone, talking in low tones. Mill catches her eye and points to her lunch bag and the conference table.

Arianne shakes her head painfully, looking a little pale. But after a moment, she gives Mill the "okay" sign.

Mill nibbles at her lunch for about ten minutes before Arianne drops wearily into the seat next to her.

"Did I make a complete fool of myself last night?" she asks.

"No more than I did," Mill answers, "I can't remember anything after the nachos."

"Nachos? Nachos. Oh that's what I threw up in my car," Arianne groans miserably. She shakes her head, wincing at the result, "My God, I never had that much to drink before in my life."

"Neither have I," lies Mill, thinking back to her past life in Alaska and, worse, in college, "My head felt like a well-used wrecking ball this morning. By the way, I was sorry to just leave you in your car last night. But you insisted and wouldn't let me have your keys. Did you get home alright?"

"I spent the night in my car," Arianne replies, "My neck is so kinked, I may never look to the right again. I must have dropped my keys. I found them under the passenger's seat. Thank heavens because I sure wasn't fit to drive, no matter what I said."

They look at each other ruefully, a sadder-but-wiser pair, bonded by wine, nachos, and hangovers.

"Next time," says Mill, "Let's take it easy on the wine." She looks at Arianne appraisingly, "You ever see a sweaty guy take his clothes off and shake his fanny at you?"

Arianne looks startled, "No, I have not. And I'm not about to, Miss Meacham." She pauses, "…at least not until this hangover's gone!"

They both laugh gently, headaches denying anything loud to leave their mouths.

————————————————//————————————————

About 1:30 pm, Mill slips out of the office while Arianne's on break. She catches a cab over to Portlandia. She walks two blocks to an alley entrance on a cross-street, waits near there for a few minutes checking the area and the people moving past her, then, seeing nothing suspicious, she turns down the alley to the old salon de sexe. After looking intently up and down the alley, she slips in quickly as Jake had done before.

Mill misses the Eyes and Ears warrior watching the door from an unused second-floor office across the intersection at the end of the alley.

The Mist Clan Leader, Cassi Link, adds Mill's photo to a digital album. She consults the list of task force members and finds Mill's photo, name, job and Forest Service unit. She sends a encrypted text message that reaches Arrow a few minutes later.

Link begins to web-search and dig into Mill's background.

Inside the salon, Jake flips the tiny light on. He cradles his automatic in his right hand and points at the floor. Mill looks at him, instantly tense, and points at the gun, puzzled.

He says to her dryly, "I can't shake the feeling that I'm being tailed…about the last week or two…but, don't worry…be happy…they're all butt-ugly guys, not beautiful special agents named Mill working for His Tech Lordship's Secret Service. Next week I'm going to start having one of our guys back tail me to see if he can catch any weasels workin' my scent."

He waves the Glock at the wall away from Mill, "And we can talk safe. I swept the room for bugs before you sashayed your sweet hiney in here."

She laughs. The tension drains out of the room.

"So, how was the Moeller this morning?" he asks.

She replies, "A hurtin' kitty. Clearly hung-over but ready to go alleycatting with me to see 'Bad Boys, Bare Bottoms' as soon as she recovers."

"You think she suspects anything?" he asks.

"Not that I can tell."

They spend another half hour discussing possible meanings of what Arianne had said the evening before. But they get no further in their understanding.

Burns had done a complete VICAP, Google, and Lexis-Nexis search of any name or word with "missed," "mister," or "mist" plus "environment" or "environmental." He'd gotten bewildering millions of hits as his reward.

Mill has heard nothing from Manny although, from Jake's comments, she suspects he and Suemez have been talking.

He has analysts pouring through the data with various bots and algorithms. He's not optimistic that the tech bunch would come up with anything. "I mean shit, Meacham, they got no more to go on than a pale fart in the wind. I've seen more whole cloth swinging around a stripper pole than they'll ever piece together from that web-search crap."

"There are plenty of people and organizations with 'mis'-something in their string. So far, there's nothing to suggest anything illegal or even improper, not even 'Mister Misty' a whip artist in New Orleans. She's licensed."

He laughs ruefully. "So far, it's a dead end."

"So what do you want me to do, Jake?" Mill asks.

He snaps, "What did I tell you to do?"

Mill responds in a sing-song voice, "Sniff around but don't be nosey!"

He smiles, "Fuckin'-A, smart ass. Only now I'm adding, 'Be nosey but don't get caught.' Okay?"

Mill says, "Yes," and they chat a few more minutes about security concerns before finishing their talk.

Mill leaves first. She walks at an easy pace back towards Portlandia.

Ben Hicks sees her as she leaves the alley. He's wearing a different jersey and pedals slowly past her as she heads back to the Justice Building.

Cassi records Jake's departure a few minutes later. His three trackers follow him back to the Forest Service building. They switch off the tail every two blocks to make sure he doesn't spot them.

A fourth warrior waits at the Forest Service building for Burns to return, and easily spots him walking in.

The Eyes and Ears warriors don't have much time before the Strike. They need to quickly learn as many of Burns' patterns and habits as possible.

Thursday afternoon comes. Mill and Arianne have fully recovered. They make plans to go to the Bad Boys, Bare Bottoms show on Friday night. Mill hadn't been to such a spectacle in years.

Arianne stoutly maintains that she never even considered it until Mill came along and corrupted her. Arianne seems to delight in her moral decay.

A day before, Mill called around and found out, thanks to Oregon's Constitution guaranteeing personal privacy, Portland is a pretty wide-open town.

Only four vice cops work the city. They simply try to make a dent in the violence and near slavery that's so prevalent among prostitutes. One of the weary vice cops told her that Portland offers three kinds of male shows: "gay, straight, and 'who cares'."

The cop suggested they stick to the advertised straight shows because they had much less chance of running into trouble.

"Just don't let them talk you into stripping down and going up on stage," she warned, "Somebody'll be going through your purses before you prance your naked asses up in front of the hot lights."

Sounding disgusted, she continued, "I can't tell you how many times credit card and license information gets ripped off. They're not after money. They steal your life instead. You hear society matrons bellyaching about identity theft after they've licked the sweat off those guys' balls. What the Hell did they think would happen when they went in there, true love and financial security?"

Mill and the cop talked a while longer about parts of town to avoid and then hung up. Mill picked the best of three places the cop had mentioned and then confirmed her choice with Arianne.

At 4 pm, Mill looks up to see Arianne move quickly out the door, purse over her shoulder and jacket in hand. She looks worried.

Mill knows it's early for Arianne to leave. But they aren't close enough yet to share each other's personal schedule.

Maybe Arianne's late for a doctor's appointment.

Five minutes later, Mill's government cell rings. She fumbles through her back pack and clumsily pulls it out. Hoping she hasn't missed the call, she snaps it open.

Burns voice speaks urgently, "Meacham, the lab got the video results back a few minutes ago. I reviewed them with a pack of experts. Both

Soames and Moeller hit your evidence box. We have Soames in custody. The FBI has sealed off your building. I made sure they know the skinny. I want you to have the collar! Now move and nail Moeller!"

Mill replies tersely, "Someone's tipped her. She just left. I'm on it!"

Mill snaps the phone shut and pockets it. She wishes she had a radio tuned to FBI tac channels. No such luck.

She clears her Glock from its holster even before she fully stands up.

By the time she gets to the conference room door, Mill reaches a sprint. She runs down the hall peering ahead for Moeller. The soles of her shoes squeak against the vinyl tile floors as she runs faster and faster.

Doors clatter and feet pound as FBI security teams move onto the floor where Mill searches. More feet pound up echoing staircases as others climb higher in the building. Guards take positions by each stair. Two-person teams begin a floor search, room by room.

Mill can see she'll be of little use to the well-trained pros making a systematic sweep of the building.

She stops short and asks herself, "Where would Arianne go if she got trapped in this building?" It's a big building with lots of places to hide.

An idea strikes her, "Of course, she'd be in the records room. She'd feel safe there, hidden."

Mill checks her weapon to make sure she has a round chambered. She hurries towards the advancing searchers and then swings into an alcove with three doors leading off of it.

The task force stores their records beyond the door on the right.

Mill impatiently puts her thumb down on the ID lock. At first, nothing happens. The entry indicator stays red.

Mill realizes that she's squirming with impatience, confusing the biometric reader. Listening impatiently to the sounds of the oncoming searchers, Mill presses her thumb down again, this time holding still.

The lock clicks and its indicator light turns green.

Mill raises her weapon and extends her index finger down the slide, off the trigger.

She turns the door handle and pushes the door open gently. The lights are on.

Tension gives her a little tunnel vision. She shakes it off.

Mill listens, breathless.

She hears a slight noise off to her right beyond a line of shelves.

"Arianne, this is Mill," she calls softly, "I know you're in here. I want you to come out. We'll talk. That's all. Nothing bad's happened so far, nothing that can't be explained. So let's not let anything bad happen now."

Mill waits.

No answer.

She takes two quiet steps forward.

Arianne's voice comes weakly to Mill's ears. "No, Mill, bad stuff has happened. Mill, yes…I"

Her voice trails off.

Mill hears a soft thump and rushes forward gun extended, twisting to look down each aisle as she passes.

Arianne Moeller lies on the floor in the last aisle, surrounded by her beloved shelves of record boxes and the scattered contents of her purse.

She has hiked her skirt up her right leg and stabbed what appeared to be an Epi-pen injector into her thigh, hitting the femoral artery.

She stares unblinkingly up at the bright, white florescent lights, a slightly amazed look on her face.

Dead.

———————————————————// ———————————————————

Mill, Jake, Frieda Tomlin, and Gregory Stillman sit at the small conference table in Frieda's office.

Frieda Tomlin screams with loud fury, "God damn you, Burns, I will personally fry your ass in motor oil for this…this…this phenomenal fuck up."

She's so furious she almost can't find the words to express herself. "I will have your badge, you son of a bitch. You miserable…miserable…."

Her assistant interrupts her tirade by calling on the intercom, "Agent Tomlin, the Deputy Director is on the phone from DC. Do you want me to put him through?"

Frieda pulls herself together, brushing back a wisp of hair that had come loose from her tight coiffure. She growls, "Hell yes, Alice, it's the damn Deputy isn't it?"

Used to Tomlin's gruffness, Alice simply opens the line to the Deputy.

The Deputy Director wastes no time, asking "Agent Tomlin, who's there with you?"

Frieda lists the people present.

"Fine," the Deputy continues. "First, I want to commend Officer Meacham for fine police work and for her quick reaction to orders to apprehend Moeller. How long did you perform CPR on Moeller before you were relieved, Meacham?"

Mill replies, "About 20 minutes, Deputy Director. The ambulance was stuck in traffic and the FBI EMT's were in training."

"Well, damn fine effort, Meacham. We would liked to have interrogated Moeller, but, well that can't happen. Nice work."

The Deputy says to Tomlin, "Frieda give me your sit rep."

Knowing the Deputy has a complete dossier in front of him, one that her staff completed at 4 am that morning, Tomlin gives a brief situation report, adding that the interrogation of Carrie Soames has gone nowhere.

"She claims she just did a favor for Moeller, picked up a couple of things and dropped off a file. She says she never even looked at the items. We have nothing to prove she did anything wrong other than do a favor for a friend."

"Okay," replies the Deputy, "Keep her in protective custody for the next 48 hours while we finish our background check. I have 16 agents getting us her life history. Because this might involve terrorist activity, we've invoked the Patriot Act. We've done a sneak and peek on her house, car, work space, and Y locker. We've been through every financial record she has. Our initial take is that she's straight as an arrow, but we'll see."

The Deputy continues, "Let me know if Soames gives us anything useful. And now, let's talk inter-agency cooperation, Agent Burns."

"Seems like you fucked up big-time, Burns. You didn't share important information about Moeller, such as that she might be a possible terrorist...might compromise the work of the joint task force! Are you a useless hick fuck or what?"

In reply to the Deputy's attack, Jake simply sits quietly.

After a few moments, Frieda looks at Burns narrowly, "Aren't you going to answer Deputy Director Cargill, Agent Burns?"

"Hadn't planned to," Jake drawls, "I was waitin' for His Eminence to get off the toilet and flush. You flushed yet, Billy Willy?"

It dawns on Mill that Burns and Cargill know one another, even respect one another. Jake let the Deputy vent his frustration to impress his FBI troops and assert himself.

As a friend, Jake'd stayed quiet and uncommitted until the Deputy finished. Sometimes, that's what colleagues do for one another.

The Deputy gives a snort, "Yeah I'm done flushing, you bastard. Now how did you let this thing get so fucked up?"

Jake responds simply, "We were conducting a theft investigation on another case. We didn't really suspect that they were connected until we got the results of the video enhancement. Then we found out Moeller was our girl, we went to arrest her...alerted your people. She wound up with a needle in her leg, dead as communism."

"Bill, in fact, we still don't know if there's any connection. The kicker for me that something bigger's goin' on are Moeller's drunken statements to Meacham and the weird suicide needle she gave herself. Slim pickin's, buddy."

"I mean whatever happened to the good 'ol tried-and-true cyanide capsule or a plain 'ol bullet to the head? This fancy shit's the result of the fuckin' internet, I swear! And people who have too much time to think! Maybe solar flares and the ozone layer—I just don't know!"

Burns finishes with a flourish and Deputy Cargill grunts his amusement.

"Okay, Jake," he replies, "I'll accept your bullshit explanation for now. Just know that the Bureau will investigate your conduct, back teeth to asshole—TV camera through the sewer pipe for real, guy. Your innards will be squeeky clean when we're done. Believe it!"

"And FYI, Moeller had a full background check done several years ago and checked out squeaky clean, too. That work was done by a reputable contractor. No updates since. The Bureau's going to conduct a full background on her again, from present day right back to her mother's womb. If anything turns up that could impact the Miller case, we'll let you know. Just don't hold your breath, waiting for our call."

Mill gathers from the last remark that Jake has been placed on the "time out, no need to know" list by the Bureau.

Burns would have to sit in the corner and be good for awhile until ruffled feathers smoothed and trust returned. Mill figures Jake has plenty of other sources for information, both inside and outside the Bureau.

Before the meeting, Jake and Mill had carefully scripted what they would tell the FBI, holding nothing back that might help the task force with the O'Reilly and Miller murders. But they also carefully protected Forest Service people and resources like Bill Zumo and the cathouse salon.

They didn't want the Bureau's official nose in every part of their business, shoved in places that would destroy carefully-built–up working relationships and even basic security.

The group spends another half hour kicking around conspiracy theories and ideas about Moeller's connections.

Although it doesn't seem like a promising lead, Deputy Cargill says he'd get the data miners in FBI's cyber division to start working the "missed," "mist," or "mister" angle.

The meeting ends at the top of the hour when all the big-wigs have to run to their next event.

Mill takes a moment to call Manny Suemez and tersely gives him an update. Manny's grimly concerned by the turn of events and ends the call quickly.

When Mill gets back to her office, she finds Arianne's little space empty, completely empty. Clear plastic stretches across the entrance with crime scene tape sealing it off.

Mill finds herself instantly saddened by the emptiness. A space once filled with a desk and piles of files and, more poignantly, with the energy and bustle of the little, capable Arianne is now void, lost, a vacuum.

Mill tears up for a moment.

Almost without intending to, she utters a little prayer for Arianne's soul, asking simply that she rest in peace.

Mill shakes off her sadness. Arianne had been involved in something bad...maybe murderous. Maybe she hadn't deserved to die...but she was guilty and gone nonetheless.

Mill decides she'd give the evidence a day to reach Quantico and two days to be processed. Then she'd call Chip Minor to check out what he knew.

Mill goes back to completing her full report on Moeller's death. Then, on impulse, she picks up her phone and calls Philip.

For once, he answers on the first ring.

Shocked, Mill only stammers for a moment. Then, she starts to tell Philip about Arianne's death.

First her story comes out evenly.

Then a lump rises in her throat and she chokes.

Tears run down and she can't go on.

Philip waits quietly, occasionally offering supportive and consoling words, until she simply gives up trying to speak.

After a minute or so, Philip says softly, "Milly, I know your heart hurts now. Let's meet soon and talk things through. When would be good for you?"

Mill tries to focus for a moment. Remembering Philip's schedule, she asks, "Could we try Monday again? Will you be off then?"

Philip answers, "Yes indeed. Let's try lunch this time and plan on spending the afternoon together. Would you like to visit the zoo?"

He clears his throat nervously, "I think we'll have a lot to talk about.

And I feel like maybe we ought to begin with a little fun. Don't you, Milly?"

Mill feels a little surprised at his mention of the zoo. She had actually been thinking about that location, too.

"I believe you've read my mind, Sir Philip," she smiles, sadness leaving, "I'm yours for Monday afternoon."

They chat a little more.

Mill feels better for hearing his voice.

But Philip, remembering their last visit, feels worse...guilty...wary. Crossing mental fingers, he keeps his voice cheery.

After the disaster of Monday night's dinner, he feels things could easily go badly again. Still, perhaps the worst had passed. Maybe they could move towards reconciling over the bad things in their lives, shared and personal.

Philip muses to himself, "Time will tell—it always does."

He ends the call warmly, newly hatched butterflies flapping in his stomach.

Chapter 40

Zumo's Bad Goodbye

Bill Zumo sits in his Forest Service patrol pickup, the fast four-wheeler in the rack. About an hour ago, he had answered a crackling radio call from the Lane County Sheriff's Office, asking that he come to Roman Nose to assist with a meth-lab arrest.

He'd radioed the Mapleton District dispatcher with his general destination and then headed out.

Whenever labs are found on Forest Service land, LEOs try to assist local law enforcement and be present for arrests. That way, prosecutors have the choice to try the perps under state or federal law, whichever best fits the evidence and the crime.

In addition, with severe budget cutbacks, usually only one officer from each agency can answer a call. So, federal and local cops cooperate to cover one another's backside.

Roman Nose refers to several square miles of clearcuts, old logging roads, and turnouts on top of the Coastal mountain range, just over the boundary from Lane into Douglas counties. As the name suggests, a prominent, nose-shaped rock dominates the landscape.

The isolation makes meth labs and major drug sales almost undetectable. Almost anything dropped around Roman Nose doesn't get be found for a long time, particularly if it got dumped in the early fall when the thin snow pack might cover it until the next March or April.

Over the years, chemicals from meth labs ruined the soils in spots around the Roman Nose landscape. Abandoned cars leaked oil and gasoline into the headwaters of streams. And now and then, the grisly grins of decayed, mutilated bodies had surprised spring bear hunters.

Bill doesn't get many calls from the Douglas County Sheriff, except for work on a short stretch of the south Dunes. He wonders who would be showing up. Zumo knows all the deputies that work the Dunes but figures whoever comes here might be someone he doesn't know, someone from the drug task force or Douglas County's mobile crime unit.

Roman Nose spreads out about 20 miles from the ocean. Overnight, an in flowing marine layer has trapped the mountain tops in clouds across the whole area. Drifting plumes of fog rise from the Douglas fir trees densely packed across the slopes.

Zumo hopes that the jolly Eugene weather-person was right that morning and the cloud layer would soon burn off. Otherwise, he will be cold tramping around in the cloudy, wet woods, where reduced visibility might hamper the arres or even allow the perp to escape.

A figure in a gray-green Douglas County Sheriff's uniform approaches Zumo's rig from the front and waves. In the fog, the tall man has a military bearing. His uniform looks quite squared away, campaign hat at the correct angle and belt gear in place.

Bill wonders why he hadn't come in tactical gear like most cops wore on field operations. Of course, the deputy may have been on road patrol and got diverted to the site just like Zumo.

Bill waves back and steps out of the Forest Service rig.

The tall officer comes forward and asks quietly, "Are you Zumo?" When Bill nods, the officer says, "I'm Carl Billings. I've been with the Sheriff about five years but I don't think we've met."

Zumo looks Billings over, "No, not unless you've been over on the Dunes with me."

Billings shakes his head, looking away from Zumo towards the woods. He clearly wants to cut the chitter-chat and get on with the operation.

"Okay, here's the situation," he reports, "We got a good tip that led us here. About two miles down this road, off on a spur to the left a few hundred feet, is an old Winnebago. According to our snitch, a guy we've arrested many times is cooking meth in there. I looked the place over with night vision before coming to meet you and seems like he's asleep. He has a few strings up with cans and bottles attached as some sort of half-assed alarm but no dog or lights that I can see. With me so far?"

Impressed with Billing's efficient sit rep, Zumo asks, "So is he gonna give us a fight?"

Billings shakes his head, "No, I don't think so. At least it's unlikely. He's crazy but he's never been violent before. He's pretty small—five nine and maybe 140—Caucasian, no military. If he's been into his product, he may take a swing or two at us. We'll just give him the chicken wing if he does."

With a slight smile, the tall deputy mimics to the painful arm lock two officers could put on a perp to subdue and move him.

Billings continues, "I think we can just walk in and bust him hard. We can both cite him and seal the RV up. I'll take him in, send the wrecker for the Winnebago and the hazmat guys for the site. You can get back on the road. Sound okay to you?"

310

Zumo can't think of anything else. The arrest seems routine, "Okay, Carl. Let's take him down."

Then Bill thinks of another detail, "Carl, who goes in and who stays out?"

Billings smiles ruefully, "Sorry. I knew I was forgetting something. If it's okay with you, because I've scouted all around the site, why don't you go in for the initial collar? If he rabbits, I'll do the rundown. If you get him first thing, I'll come in behind you and help you haul him out."

Zumo's excitement jumps way up. He would bust the guy—always more fun than working back up! "Okay," he smiles, warming even more to the tall officer, "Let's do this thing."

They walk quietly down the rutted dirt road to the spur, little more than an overgrown track. Bill can see that the grass and seedlings in the roadway had been mashed down by the RV. A few twigs and small branches had been broken off by the sides of the clumsy vehicle as it rolled through.

Zumo thinks to himself, "Why the Hell pick this crappy road? It's too easy to get stuck back here. Well, no reading the mind of a meth cook."

But in a less than a minute's walk down the spur, Zumo can see why the guy picked this place. After moving through the fringe of dense vegetation along the main road, the space opens up quite a bit.

Older tree plantations hem it in and overtop it on both sides but the two-track is fairly wide and easy going. And due to the plug of vegetation at the entrance, people passing by would never think someone had come back here. A great hide.

They walk on quietly, carefully.

Then, just past a low screen of brush, there in the clouds sits the old Winnebago, squat and cold looking, parked on a small landing. A few chemical containers and garbage bags stray across the site but it isn't the mess so many meth labs become.

"The cook must just be getting started," whispers Zumo, "I'm glad we caught him before the shit head did some major damage."

Meth lab sites could take thousands of dollars to clean up because of toxic chemical spills and leakage. And those dollars came out of Zumo's scarce budget. He feels glad to pinch the pennies along with the perp.

They stop for a moment while Zumo looks the site over through his binoculars. He studies the clumsy noise makers and notices that the door to the Winnebago hangs slightly ajar.

Zumo motions to the small crowbar that Billings carries to crack the door and shakes his head, pointing at the Winnebago. Billings quietly drops the crowbar to the ground.

Zumo studies the RV and the surrounding area a minute longer. Then he makes the clenched fist and pointed finger motion that signed "let's go."

The two men step forward quietly, drawing their weapons. They lift their feet carefully over the string alarm. They move low and slow until they are in position a few feet from the vehicle.

Zumo's at the front door and Billings is behind at the emergency window exit.

Bill steadies himself.

Then he leaps forward.

He rips the door open, gun raised.

Yelling "Police Officer…Freeze," he jumps into the vehicle, swinging his gun around, sweeping the vehicle from galley to sleeping area, looking for the perp.

Nothing moves.

Looking back into the rear fold-down bed, Bill sees a figure rolled up in a sleeping bag. He moves forward past the galley and tiny bath, all his attention on the figure.

He thinks to himself, "Sound sleeper. I wonder if the guy's drugged up or over-dosed?"

Zumo feels the Winnebago move as Billings steps in through the front door.

Keeping his Glock on the sleeping figure, Zumo calls over his shoulder, "I think this guy is out, Carl, maybe for good."

"Cuff him anyway," Chronos says quietly.

He raises a smooth-bore .38 revolver he'd brought from Medford and concealed by the RV's driver seat.

The sub-sonic shot rings loud inside the Winnebago.

Keeping watch down by the road, Badger can only just hear a faint pop.

Zumo down!

——————————————//——————————————

Badger and Chronos dress in clean suits, masked with filters.

They work their way through the Winnebago and the area around it, cleaning up every trace of the fake meth lab. They pile the debris into trash bags.

They deflate the blowup figure in the sleeping bag and roll it and the

312

bag up.

They clean up the few food items in the galley and tiny refrigerator.

They strip Bill Zumo's body carefully. They remove his personal items, cleaning and bagging them--wallet, keys, wedding ring, reading glasses, loose change, field notebook, pens.

Without knowing, they follow a process eerily like that used by Forest Service LEOs at a crime scene.

Chronos had shot Zumo in the neck with a frangible round, hitting his spinal cord just below his skull and killing him instantly. The impact caused the compressed-copper-powder bullet to fly into tiny fragments. The bullet choice and placement left Bill's clothes untouched and minimized blood loss.

They place Zumo's clothes in a trash bag, carry it and the bagged-up garbage down to the road, and hand the bags off to a middle-aged, War Clan warrior in an old pickup.

The warrior arrived only a few minutes after Chronos' shot. He would drop the garbage bags in several dumpsters later in the day along Route 101, the beautiful Pacific Coast Highway.

After dropping the trash, the driver would take Zumo's bloodied uniform to a late-night laundromat in Coos Bay and double wash it with mild bleach. He would then reattach Zumo's name plate and badge to the uniform and drive to Florence.

Before the ranger district office opened in the morning, someone else would smuggle the uniform back into Zumo's secure office and hang it on the back of the door.

Badger hands Zumo's keys to another warrior. He drives away and heads down back roads, making occasional, misleading calls on Zumo's radio.

Late that night, Zumo's Forest Service pickup would also be returned to the district parking lot and parked in the LEO slot, just as Bill always did. The warrior would then take Zumo's personal vehicle and drive it south to Reedsport, a half hour away.

After the two warriors depart, Badger steels herself for the last, most difficult job. The grisly part.

She and Chronos carefully remove Zumo's head, hands, and feet and place each piece in separate bags. These would be handed off to a warrior in Winchester Bay. She would take them far out to sea, weigh them down, and drop them deep into the ocean.

More than anything she had ever done, cutting up Zumo's body gives Badger qualms. She has no regret for killing the agency thug—the killers of Mother Earth deserve to die—but the grating of the bone saw as it separates head from neck…and then hands from wrists…and then feet from ankles… seems to rasp across her heart

This man, this thug, had to be killed, no doubt.

But…but…this cleaving of his body seems so beyond the necessary, so against Mother Nature herself—she who had created the whole man from his parts, grew him up from a single cell to a full human, a miracle of life.

And now, here Badger saws away, breaking the sacred bonds of cell and sinew.

Badger shakes from head to toe. She gulps down bile. She has to pause from time to time to stop her hands from shaking.

Chronos had lost his squeamishness in the first Gulf War after prying his buddy's body off the underside of a blown-up humvee's roof. He almost offers to take over from Badger but stops himself.

He respects Badger and admires the determination he sees in her leadership--how she has supported him on this Strike. So, he just waits patiently, honoring her decision to wield the saw, not offering his numb skills.

Eventually the bloody deed is done. Chronos helps her lift Zumo's torso and limbs off the floor and tumble the body on to the mattress. They carefully roll up and bag the inch or so of blood-soaked newspaper they'd put down on the floor as a pad.

Chronos takes the bagged body parts down to the stolen old jeep he had hidden in the next spur road. He would make the drop to the fishing boat in Winchester Bay. Then he'd vanish, transported by the warriors of Movement back to his home in Georgia to await further assignments.

Once she was sure his trail was cold, Badger would meet him there for his debriefing, probably a matter of a few weeks.

Badger carries the bag of bloodied newspapers out to her stolen mini-pickup. She would drive to Roseburg and dispose of them in the free landfill. She inspects the site and Winnebago again, erasing any signs that they'd been there.

Her eyes avoid Zumo's headless body on the bed.

Badger lights a short 1-inch-wide candle, drips wax onto the floor by the stove, and then sticks the candle firmly down into the wax. Stepping outside, she takes two one-gallon cans of white gasoline, tips the plastic containers on their sides, and lightly punctures them at the base with an ice pick. She sets them back inside the threshold behind the driver's and passenger's seats and tips them upright.

The gas begins to stream out...a tiny flow from each.

Badger steps clear of the vehicle and walks away a couple of hundred feet. She waits, but not long, for what she knows will come.

The twin streams quickly spread across the floor, into open cabinets, and down through cracks into the frame...then they reach the candle.

The Winnebago Warrior explodes in flames, the fire ball rising up as high as the surrounding forest and then above it, pushing up the low clouds.

Within a few minutes, the hot flames bake the nearby needles and branches of the Douglas firs. Small laddering fires run up the trees.

Many minutes later, the propane container and gas tanks blow and burning debris scatters over a quarter acre. The wet conditions rapidly squelch the fire but, for a time, a line of fire and smoke scratch and tear at the woodland.

Accepting the small risk of being discovered by someone responding to the flames or smoke, Badger stays until the Winnebago has burned to the ground, tires and all. She watches until only the bent and blasted frame remains and smoke rises from the debris and damaged trees, mingling with the drifting fog.

The scavengers would get to work on anything left of Zumo's cooked body.

Without looking back, Badger turns and walks towards the truck, feeling cold after the blooming warmth. She moves briskly, a chill of death dogging her heels.

Badger drives the crooked miles toward Reedsport. Outside of town, she meets another War Clan warrior at the BLM's elk viewing area.

The warrior had been a mill worker at Gardiner, Oregon, many years before. So, he knows the whole Oregon coast well. He now lives near Troutdale, a town east of Portland.

Although quite a bit older than Zumo, he looks a lot like him-- same height and build...similar face shape. With a ball cap pulled down to conceal a portion of his face, he closely resembles Bill.

Badger meets the warrior in the deserted elk observation gazebo. Elk mill around a few hundred feet away. Even though breeding season is months away, a magnificent trophy bull, antlers in velvet, dominates the cows and shoos off other suitors.

The two watch nature's show for several minutes. They revel in the strength of the bull and are calmed by the herd's natural flowing beauty.

Badger hands the warrior Bill Zumo's personal effects.

Back in the little pickup, she turns south and east, heading to Roseburg where she plans to spend the night. She'll visit the landfill before turning north to Portland for the next Strike.

Ekos would be in place there, waiting impatiently. Arrow would arrive soon after Badger, a comforting presence for Badger's heart.

The retired mill worker drives to Reedsport fifteen miles away, has dinner, and waits. About 11 pm, the Movement warrior who had stolen Zumo's personal rig drives up.

The two men trade vehicles. The retired mill worker drives south towards Brookings.

In Brookings, hat pulled down to hide from the cheap surveillance camera in the lobby, he checks in to the Pacific View Motel under a reservation made in Zumo's name. He pays for the room with Zumo's credit card.

In the lobby, he makes a show of his passion for a flashy prostitute who accompanies him. The woman drove up from Sacramento on the strength of a $500 retainer and the promise of $2,000 more, waiting impatiently at a truck stop until he arrived.

They bang away loudly until 4 am, drawing complaints from other guests. The night manager calls "Zumo's" room twice to tell them to tone it down and then threatens eviction when they don't. He will not soon forget the name "Bill Zumo."

In the morning, the warrior and the prostitute drive in separate vehicles to Crescent City, California. They drop Zumo's rig at the edge of the harbor's parking lot, windows open, keys in the ignition. Then they drive to Sacramento and the airport there.

Bending her over in a secluded corner of the airport parking structure, the warrior bangs her one more time before giving her the $2,000.

Smiling and satisfied, he catches a flight back to Portland. There he sleepily hands off the remainder of Zumo's personal effects and drives away in his personal car.

An hour later, Zumo's ID and credit cards go by FEDEX to identity thieves in Los Angeles. Within a day, Zumo's credit card statement looks like he has gone everywhere and nowhere, charging rooms, meals, and luxuries all over the world.

The rest of his possessions get dropped into dumpsters scattered across downtown Portland. A bum finds his wedding ring and pawns it.

Bill Zumo disappears. Forever.

Chapter 41

Mist's Grip Tightens

Raven calls Arrow early. She wakes him up before Arrow's usual alarm clock, the mean-tempered rooster that dominates his hen yard, can.

As usual, she has few words to say and her words hold great significance. "Arrow, check your secure e-mail. Mist has gained…a great advantage…over the Forest Service…pigs. I…leave matters in…your capable…hands. The Enemies Chief…would like…to talk to you… before you…act."

The phone goes quiet for ten seconds and then Raven hangs up.

Arrow shakes his head. "Typical for the Raven of Mist," he smiles as he put down the phone, "Wise like her namesake, but an oddly quiet bird. Still, one you always want to listen to."

The War Chief steps naked onto the flagstone walk that leads down to his large pond. He walks quickly down the path and onto the short dock. Taking two running steps he dives into the water.

The morning-cold water drives the air out of his lungs with a submarine whoop. Rising to the surface, Arrow churns across the pond and back. His arms stroke hard, driving his body through the water as fast as he can go to save some smidgen of warmth.

Reaching the dock, he leaps out of the pond and pads quickly back to his room to towel off.

He sets the tea kettle on his kitchen wood stove and adds several small logs to its banked fire. The fire leaps up in the firebox. Above his roof, smoke first black then white begins to pour from the stovepipe.

Water would be boiling in a few minutes. Tea would come soon. Breakfast could wait. Cancer has stolen much of his appetite anyway.

Arrow walks into his den and turns on his computer. He directs it to one of the dozens of secure web sites that Mist experts had created or had pirated for Mist uses.

One talented Mist cyber warrior had once hacked into part of a Department of Defense site, complete with access to a supercomputer and massive hard drives.

Raven had quickly closed that connection, even as valuable as it was, because of the chance of detection. After that, Mist concentrated on stealing capacity from mid-sized corporations and big-time computer gamers, believing correctly that they have far less security than the federal government.

The War Chief logs in and correctly answers the five random security questions that appear on the screen. He quickly finds a message from the Friends Chief with "MOST URGENT *** EYES ONLY" flashing in the subject line.

As he reads the message, Brixton Bragg begins to chuckle.

Then he laughs out loud, a fierce glint in his eyes and a hint of savagery in his smile.

———————————————————//———————————————————

A week before Raven's call to Arrow, Listening Clan warriors had obtained four copies of Bull Meacham's gay-sex DVD. The first copy was purchased from the man-whore, Raoul, along with the names or titles and descriptions of the other DVD holders.

The second copy came from the successful and undetected burglary of Simon Ball's home wall safe. The Deputy Chief for International Forestry had traveled to Indonesia for forest talks and trips to brothels full of teenaged oriental girls. His wife had gone to visit their grandchildren in Dubuque.

The Mist burglars encountered no problem with their home security system or the simple combination lock on their safe. In place of the Meacham DVD, they left an identically appearing one with pirated copies of Around the World in Eighty Days and Mary Poppins on it.

The third and fourth copies came from Mike Reinard. He had told Bull that he planned to send a copy to his attorney for safe-keeping and insurance purposes but unwisely procrastinated.

Two masked warriors woke him in his bed. They handed him a newsprint note that said, "Give us the Meacham DVDs now or die." The note and the silenced pistol they put to his head quickly convinced him to give up the DVDs.

He had hidden them in a lock box in his den with his collection of gay-sex magazines and explicit DVDs.

Raven later wondered if Reinard used the Meacham DVD as erotica. She made a note in Reinard's file about it.

The burglars left Reinard loosely bound so he could work himself free in an hour or so. They also left him with sore balls from a hearty kick. Another note told him they would return if he told anyone about his loss.

A few days before Raven's call to Arrow, two copies remained in circulation: Bull's and Pizzaro's. Raven didn't care about Bull's but she wanted Pizzaro's.

Mist would maximize leverage over the Forest Service Chief only if they obtained every copy except his.

Pizzaro was in Mexico on official Forest Service business. Mist burglars visited Pizzaro's DC apartment, her condominium in Los Angeles, and her associate professor's office at American University. Thorough searches found nothing.

Raven knew Mist had been lucky locating and obtaining the other DVDs so easily. She resigned herself to a longer operation to get Pizzaro's copy.

Although Raven had no way to tell, she decided that Pizzaro would keep something as valuable as the DVD at a secure site rather than leaving it for safekeeping with another person. But the secure site could be anywhere.

Some possibilities were obvious. When the burglars had gone through Pizzaro's homes and her university office looking for a safe or lock box, Raven told them to look for safety deposit box keys or receipts for long-term storage.

They found receipts that showed Pizzaro rented a storage space. Raven sent another burglar team to the dusty little room. They found nothing there except piles of books, publications, and hundreds of animal and creepy insect specimens.

Raven then knew that the likely hiding place was Pizzaro's office in the Forest Service national headquarters at 14th and Independence Avenues in DC.

She didn't want to burgle a federal facility. Raven thought of Watergate. If the burglars were caught, the cost to Mist's security would simply be too high.

Raven would wait until Pizzaro returned to extort the copy. But, a strong-arm team from the Listening Clan might be too crude.

What if Pizzaro defied them? Pizzaro held celebrity status along with the protections of federal service. Mist wouldn't willingly torture or kill the Associate Chief, not when Mist's future as a secret organization hung so precariously in the balance.

And besides the DVD itself, unlike Reinard, Raven possessed no big secrets about Pizzaro. So, anonymous blackmail would probably not work.

Inspired by the challenge, Raven had called the War Chief.

_____//_____

Unlike any other Mist chief, the Enemies Chief has a public life. He serves as an associate professor for environmental science at the University of Texas.

Among his colleagues, he holds a reputation as an adequate teacher and a mediocre researcher. He rarely publishes, so offers no threat to the tenured staff. He and Raven work closely together to make sure his public profile remains obscure.

In his disguise as an obscure professor, he legitimately moves in academic and government circles, buying drinks, asking questions, and overhearing Mist's enemies talk. Even though he has several warriors in his clan, the Enemies Chief often personally identifies the targets for Mist's character assassinations and Strikes.

Arrow calls the Enemies Chief. He catches him during his daily workout in the Texas Longhorn's Moncrief-Neuhaus Athletics Center.

Over the echoing clang and roar of weight and exercise-machines, the Enemies Chief hollers his apologies. He tells "Mr. Flecha" he will call him back in a half an hour or so. He beats that prediction by ten minutes, having kept up appearances by completing his circuit training with his work out buddy and then skipping his normal 15-minute swim.

The Enemies Chief knows Esperanza Pizzaro well enough to give Arrow some donnish advice about how to deal with her. "Pizzaro," he drawls, "Is a passionate and ambitious woman, brilliant and beautiful… almost famous…and self-made…up from the mean streets of LA."

"We studied her more and more closely as she moved up in her career. Until now, she never met enough of our criteria for us to act against her. In fact, we thought we might be able to recruit her in some way because she postured herself as a defender of the Earth and acted on her convictions directly."

He considers his next words, "Now we know her ambitions have far outrun her ethics, both social and environmental. Looking back, we probably should have seen this trait."

"But so many people are ambitious and yet innocuous, inoffensive to our Mother Earth. In fact, we love to help those burdened with ambition, but lacking intellect and skill, to take high positions in government and industry."

Arrow can hear the smile in the Enemies Chief's voice.

The Enemies Chief catches himself off-track and returns to the subject of Pizzaro, "There's never been a whiff of scandal around her, no sense of ruthlessness. Perhaps her whole image, which she has so carefully built and protected, is and always was nothing more than a sham. Still, she

320

has done some fine work academically and in the field, so we can't take that from her. Her scholarship, while limited, showed depth…."

Arrow interrupts the Enemies Chief gently, "I think we're rabbit-trailing here a little bit, my friend."

The Enemies Chief laughs ruefully, "Yes, too many years of university gossip and rationalizing has gelled my brain, I'm afraid. Where was I?"

Arrow quickly takes him back to issues about Pizzaro's flawed character, asking "What do we know about her that we could use to force her to hand over the DVD?"

The Enemies Chief thinks for a moment, "Well, I would conjecture that her image and reputation, artifacts of her life we now know to be false, possess great value for her. She might rather lose her life than to see her reputation and vanity in ruins."

Arrow laughs gruffly, thinking he personally, too, might be undone by his pride. His friend had given him some good insights into Pizzaro—they might do.

————————————————————— // —————————————————————

The next day, Arrow travels an hour to Cedar Rapids, Iowa, from his farm near Anamosa. He catches a flight to Los Angeles under an assumed name, paying cash for the first-class ticket and using nicely forged identification to pass easily through security.

Of course he gets an extra security pat down for having the boldness to buy a ticket with cash and for flying the same day as the purchase. No problem.

In major cities, Mist makes sure some Movement warriors hold jobs as cabbies. That way, Mist operators can move freely around the cities undetected and unmolested.

In LA, Arrow jumps in a commercial cab driven by a Movement warrior who already knows the destination. She will also serve as his lookout and backup.

The woman flips the flag down on her meter and guns the cab away from the terminal. Forty-five minutes later, she pulls the cab expertly to the curb on a street two blocks from the home of the gigolo, Raoul.

The cabby has placed a copy of the LA Times on the seat next to Arrow. He hefts it, finds it's quite heavy, and opens it.

A 9mm Beretta Model 92F with silencer and a weighty sap nestle there. "Nothing but bad news in this paper," the War Chief murmurs.

Looking back in the mirror, the warrior replies, 'We aim to please so please aim well!"

Arrow snorts amusement and steps out of the cab.

Raoul is not home or won't answer his doorbell. Arrow quickly picks the lock on the man's apartment. Once inside, he's unpleasantly surprised by the muddle of clothes and trash he finds covering much of the floor and by the sour smell of beer and marijuana that permeates the place.

Gingerly clearing off a chair, the War Chief moves it into the small kitchen into a position where he will not be seen when the front door opens. He settles in to wait, vigilant yet calm.

About an hour later, Raoul walks down the block towards his apartment.

The cabbie sees him turn to enter the building. She calls Arrow to let him know Raoul is on his doorstep.

Pleased that Raoul's coming in alone, Arrow stands up, puts on a ski mask, takes out the sap, and lifts his silenced automatic. He holds the sap tightly in his right hand and the automatic loosely in his left.

Raoul steps through the door with clothes on hangers over his shoulder and a small string bag of groceries in his hand. Dressed in jeans and a T-shirt, his hair in a net, Raoul doesn't expect company.

As the door closes, Arrow clips Raoul from behind with the sap. Raoul goes face down into a pile of newspapers and trash bags, limp and unconscious.

Arrow slides the man into a sturdy chair and ties him firmly to its arms and legs. He clears off a small table and sets it in front of the gigolo, setting up a tiny video recorder on a tripod. He clips a wireless microphone to Raoul's shirt.

The War Chief snaps a capsule under Raoul's nose and the penetrating odor of ammonia pushes back the stink in the room a trifle. Raoul wakes up, shaking his head and snorting to get the ammonia's biting odor out of his nostrils. His eyes widen at the sight of Arrow's masked face.

He smiles nervously. "I...I have the money," he stammers, "I mean, *madre de Dios*, I can pay you now."

He rolls his head around, testing the pain in his neck. "God damn it, you really gave me a headache, man" he whines, "Just let me go, and I'll get you the money."

Arrow brings the sap down on Raoul's knee with a snap, raising a howl from the man. "I don't want your money, Raoul," he snarls, "No, no money. Instead, I'm doing something for you. I'm going to make you a movie star...again...."

The War Chief coaches Raoul for a time. After a few taps from the sap to improve Raoul's acting abilities, they make him a movie star again.

Raoul's no actor. It takes several tries to get the story recorded convincingly. Film making over, Arrow pats Raoul on the head before clipping it again with the sap.

He unties the unconscious gigolo and dumps him over into the trash pile again. He takes a vial of costume "blood" from his pocket, drips it onto Raoul's head, and leans over the prone man to take a few photos.

_____//_____

Two days later, Associate Chief Pizzaro sits looking out through the big windows of her office at the Washington Monument past Brixton Bragg's right shoulder. She and Bragg are perched on comfortable chairs next to potted plants and a round coffee table—a cozy reception area for Pizzaro's guests. Bragg's expensive leather briefcase rests on the coffee table. They sip coffee from cups emblazoned with the Forest Service shield.

When the Forest Service headquarters building was occupied by the Treasury Department more than a century before, men with eyeshades and magnifying glasses sat in what was now Pizzaro's office, engraving the plates used for printing money.

Still perfect for engraving, the light streaming in doesn't flatter Esperanza Pizzaro. It reveals to Bragg some of the fine lines and wide pores on her otherwise beautiful face.

Pizzaro gazes over the War Chief's shoulder, bored, yet trying to seem interested and connected. She'd recognized Brixton Bragg's name when he called for an appointment. She vaguely remembers work he'd done thirty years before on the relationship between plate tectonics and climate. His work had been seminal and she'd studied it briefly when she'd worked on her doctorate.

The War Chief hadn't known that she knew of him but, once he found out, he'd traded on this work from so many years ago to get this audience with her. Now, Bragg comments politely about her career and fame and declares he's most impressed by her new position and her well-appointed office.

Pizzaro complains to herself, "Blah, blah, blah...blah, blah, blah. What the Hell does he want, I wonder?"

Finally tiring of the buzz, Pizzaro rouses herself, and meets his eyes.

She asks, "Dr. Bragg, it's wonderful finally meeting you. Is there some way I can help you? I'd love to say I'd done a favor for a man of your reputation. I have a Forest Service family meeting in about 30 minutes. I will have to go soon to get there."

The War Chief smiles inwardly at her flattery while he preens visibly for her. She's started to give him the bum's rush. It gives him the opening he was looking for.

"Well, yes," he replies a little ponderously, "I do have something you might be able to do for me and me for you. It's somewhat private. May I close the door?"

Pizzaro looks a little startled. "Sure," she says, now more interested in what Bragg has to offer because it might benefit her. Intrigued but cautious, she sets her expectations low.

Arrow walks over to the door. Closing it, he locks its well-oiled handle, shielding his action from her with his body.

Pizzaro notices nothing.

He returns to her, sits, and opens his briefcase, removing a large laptop. "I have something here I think you'd like to see."

The screen of the laptop lights up, split into two sections. On the right, the Chief Meacham gay-sex video plays without sound. On the left, Raoul's new "movie" plays with his voice quietly but distinctly audible.

Raoul earnestly explains in great detail about how the Meacham video was recorded. And then, to Pizzaro's horror, explains in equal detail about how his street "cousin" had found, recruited, and paid him for his starring role with Meacham and how Pizzaro had also directed and taped the whole thing herself.

Every time Raoul refers to Pizzaro in the video, he calls her by her full name. The gigolo must use it fifty times in his narrative. Each repetition of "Doctor Esperanza Angelica Pizzaro" comes out musically. Each time it slams her fist-hard, and the blows hit home.

Pizzaro keeps a bold smile on her face.

But Arrow can tell by the tight fix of her lips and twitching foot that she seethes with anxiety.

The two videos run out and are replaced by a NatGeo clip showing Pizzaro handling a baby ocelot, making comments about wild cat conservation and the kitten's cuteness. That clip brings Pizzaro's hard-won, and now threatened, reputation forcefully to the surface of her mind.

The ocelot clip fades into a still picture of Raoul lying bloodied and still on the floor of his apartment, apparently dead or in a coma.

When the laptop goes black, the War Chief speaks quietly, "I want you to hand me your copy of the Meacham DVD. I will check its authenticity and then I will leave. You will never see me again."

"In a week, I will send you the only copy of Raoul's confession. You may do with it what you wish. Do we have a deal?"

Pizzaro's mind works rapidly. Bragg has her back to the wall. Without speaking, she stands up and walks to her desk.

Unlocking the center drawer she takes out a key and walks to her bookshelf. Taking down a large old botany text, she brings it to the coffee table and opens it.

A slim, carbon-steel lock box with a high-grade lock lies snuggled within the book. Inserting the complex electronic key, Pizzaro turns it twice to the right and once to the left. The box opens. An integrated alarm makes a brief beep and then goes silent.

In the lock box sit several items, including an unmarked DVD. Pizzaro picks up the DVD and hands it to Arrow. She starts to close the lock box, but Bragg stops her hand.

He remarks wryly, "You were pretty hard on old Edgerton's text, Esperanza." He smiles at her and she simply stares back with hatred in her eyes.

Arrow shrugs, "Don't close the box until I check this."

Pizzaro sniffs and sits back in her chair, a grim smile on her lips, arms and legs crossed.

Arrow inserts the disc in his computer. Bull Meacham's drunken walk to the motel room door springs up on the screen. "Okay," says the War Chief, "This seems to be it."

Pizzaro leans forward to close the lock box. But Arrow has noticed several thumb drives and image storage chips in it. He stops her,

"What's on these? You didn't recopy the Meacham video, did you?"

Pizzaro's expression tightens. She hisses, "You fucking bastard. Here they are." She quickly sorts the objects and hands him two thumb drives. He checks them and, sure enough, they hold copies of the Meacham video.

Eyes narrowed, Arrow stares at her cynically, "No honor among porno-blackmailers, huh?" He pushes her waiting hand away from the lock box and removes the other electronic media.

He checks them too, one by one. Two of the camera chips hold stills and short video excerpts from the Meacham DVD.

And then something different appears on the laptop. One of the thumb drives shows a clear video of Pizzaro stretched out over the Pinchot Desk, belly and legs ivory in the evening light.

On his knees, Chief Meacham leans forward, face between her legs, giving her pleasure. The sounds of Pizzaro's enjoyment come through clearly on the video. Once she turns towards the camera and gives the lens a thumb's up.

When she's been satisfied, she stands. Meacham holds out her panties for her to put on. As she steps into them, Pizzaro slaps him lightly on the face. She says distinctly, rolling her eyes towards the camera, "Next time, you better use more tongue, Bull. We've got to work on your technique. Sloppy, too sloppy."

Arrow looks up from the video into Pizzaro's eyes. He sees rage there and, what...lust?

He holds up the thumb drive, "I'll be taking this, too, Esperanza." She stares at him, her face a cat mask on the verge of a kill, and then breaks eye contact.

"Okay," she says, huskily, eyes lowered, "I'll just make another one. I can make him do anything."

"Fine by me," responds the War Chief, "Fine by me."

Arrow rises and starts towards the door. Pizzaro says to his back, "How did you find out? How did you know?"

He just shakes his head and keeps moving.

"No," she says more forcefully, "You owe me something for all of this. Who do you work for?"

Bragg turns and looks at her, "Now that would be telling secrets. And telling secrets is naughty. Let's just say I work for an industrial concern in the west, one that wants to develop a lot of public land."

With that nail driven, Arrow turns back to the door and, hand on the handle, called loud enough for the secretaries outside to hear, "Look for my submission in the mail...about a week. Thanks again, Chief Pizzaro."

A few hours later, under yet another name, the War Chief flies west to Portland. After savoring Mist's victory over Pizzaro and her cronies, he begins to think wearily about the Burns Strike. But instead his mind fills with memories of Badger in his arms, over him, under him, enfolding him. He shoves those thoughts and feelings back. Clearing his mind, he refocuses on the Burns Strike. He begins to rehearse and re-memorize each step, each action, on the path ahead.

Nothing can go wrong. Mist's very existence hangs in the balance.

326

Chapter 42

Wary Hearts

Mill and Philip pick up their cappuccinos from the barrista in the restaurant near the entrance to the Portland Zoo. Both feel wary and awkward, afraid of more anger and hurt.

Mill still feels confused about what had happened. She has no memory of her emotional storm but she knows her emotions about the whole evening with Philip at the Greek restaurant carry an emotional tone that flashes hot and red at her.

Something bad happened. She can't be sure of what it was. She hopes that maybe today they can just put the whole mess behind them.

They begin to stroll down the zoo's many paths, confused by the signs that seem to point to everywhere and to nowhere--"Elephant House" this way and then ten feet further, "Elephant House" that way.

Mill's orienteering skills are a little rusty, but she's used to working the backcountry with map and compass. She takes out the little, colorful map she had been given with her entrance ticket and studies it.

Clearly the zoo planners intend the relatively small zoo to be park-like, with winding walkways and paths converging and parting at odd angles. The effect seems dizzying. At the same time, Mill sees how the coiling walkways make the zoo spaces seem larger, more mysterious, and full of surprises.

She peers closely at the map. She smiles, a big smile. Because of Philip's presence and this kid-ness of visiting a zoo, she has found Milly again. And Milly comes out to play.

She grabs Philip's hand, yelling "I wanna see the BUTTERFLIES."

She drags Philip into a trot. Balancing their drinks precariously, they jog down the path marked, "Butterflies." Fifty steps and there they are, a flock of butterflies, fluttering inside a large cage. Even better, Milly can go inside. They both enter and stand still, arms out in front of them, letting the beautiful insects land and fly away.

"Wonderful and even more wonder full," smiles Milly, moving slowly to keep the insects safe. She carefully reaches out and takes Philip's hand again, squeezing it hard.

Philip immediately yelps, "Ouch, Milly. Have you been working as a blacksmith?"

She says quietly, "Oh. Sorry. And, yes I have, but that's not why I'm trying to break your hand. This is great. I'm trying to break your hand because this is so great."

Philip continues to hold Milly's hand gingerly. He wonders if her touch might represent forgiveness and a re-warming of their relationship or whether…maybe…something more. Either way, he just stands there and holds on, feeling stuffily pastoral, self-conscious, and happy all at the same time.

Gradually he gets used to their public display of affection. If one of his parishioners were to come by and see him holding the hand of a beautiful woman, well…so be it. Tongues would wag...let them.

He smiles and squeezes Milly's hand a little tighter. She squeezes back and sends a smile his way.

After a ten minutes of basking in butterflies, they decide to move on. This time, they stroll hand-in-hand down random paths, checking animals and exhibits.

Philip's hopes rise and fall, rise and fall, as they walk. The warmth and tightness of Milly's touch seems to signal renewed friendship but if she has any other feelings for Philip, she gives no sign.

An hour passes. They head over to a little zoo restaurant with its cute jungle theme for lunch. Here, the walls are painted intense greens splashed here and there with bright flowers. Multi-colored leaves jump out from the green background. Animals peep at them through the painted foliage. A smiling cow elephant stands by a small stream and trumpets a spray of water over her calf.

Milly thinks the décor is perfect.

Neither one is a picky eater. Yet they still struggle to find something that isn't just kid grease. They both settle on the "Water Buff Burger" made of organic beef and Orangutan Fries made from organic sweet potatoes. Philip carries their tray with drinks and setups to the farthest table, the only one not occupied.

The platters arrive and they both dive in. Milly grins across the table at Philip, "Doesn't this remind you of those awful grease bombs at Miller's Diner in Idaho Falls? We thought we were so cool when our dads took us there. We got to eat at a real restaurant. Milk shakes and French fries like nothing at home. We were such crazies and that was so fun."

Philip grins back at her, noting an adorable smudge of ketchup to the left of her smile. He decides not to tell her about the ketchup until he enjoys it a while longer.

328

They chat over lunch, remembering old times and people. They carefully avoid discussing the members of the gang that had so badly betrayed Milly. By that avoidance, they also ignore the pain of Philip's role in Milly's betrayal.

Finishing, they bus their own table. A busy family of six zips in behind them to quickly grab their table before other people with trays in their hands hovering in the area could light.

Philip takes the tour lead after lunch. He moves them back to the coffee bar near the entrance for a couple of americanos. Then, he waves Milly over to a seating area—shady benches around a square of gravel edged by flowering bushes.

It's an area where sleeping children lie in strollers and older folks wait for their busy children and grandchildren. Public and yet private, the dense foliage in the surroundings mutes the noise of the crowds elsewhere in the zoo.

They sit side by side on the bench, sipping their drinks. Philip screws up his courage and ventures, "Milly, I think we should talk about last week. I want to apologize to you again about my role in your assault. I never intended that anything bad should ever happen to you."

More vehemently, "Never!"

Mill looks both thoughtful and confused, "Philip, I forgive you...but I have a confession to make. I really can't remember much, anything at all really, about what happened after you told me."

Now she looks both concerned and embarrassed, "I'm pretty sure I said some awful things and acted badly. Am I right?"

Philip rushes to her defense, "Milly, you got really mad and you had every right to be mad. I sold you out to protect myself. Back then, I should have told you how much of a coward I'd been. I should have warned you. I should have done something. Oh, the whole business is just so terrible."

Philip lets go of her hand and covers his face with his hands. "I never did something so despicable before then and never since. I just can't stand myself when I think of how you were hurt, degraded."

His last words come out in a rush with a sob.

Startled and concerned, Mill says evenly, "Philip, I forgive you... everything...really. No, well...I guess I'm still a little mad that you told that goon about my escape route but that's just kid stuff. You had no way of knowing what was going to happen. The...the rapist did the harm and you...you...you took care of me."

Struck by an insight, Mill's eyes open wider. Mill suddenly realizes that Philip's clumsy attempts to help her on the day of the rape, and his unfailing support in the weeks after, represented his shy, adolescent care for her, his desire to protect and help her heal. Was it puppy love? My goodness!

"Philip," Mill asks carefully, "Back then...were you...were you in love with me. I mean, in a kid way. Not now, I mean, but back then?"

Philip lowers his hands and looks at Mill's face. Her cheeks are a little red and embarrassed for asking the question.

"Yes, Milly" he said calmly, finding his own truth, "I loved the girl... and I love the woman."

He flashes a shy smile.

Mill suddenly sees the boy again--her stubborn supporter, always ready with a hug. She looks down at the ground. She can't speak.

Philip says to himself, "There, I've said it and I've blown it. She can't even look at me. Now watch her run screaming from the zoo or laugh out loud. Well, at least I've gotten my feelings out on the table."

He looks away from Milly's downturned face and up at the tree tops, irritated with himself, and with his unforgiveable candor.

He twists his head angrily. What an idiot he is!

But then his eye catches an odd sight. He sees a parrot perched on a high tree branch, an obvious escapee. But here, in the zoo's tree, the bird looks as normal as a spring robin on a wet lawn. Instantly, he begins to envy the brightly colored bird, thinking he might like to escape himself--his embarrassment, his vulnerability...his uncomfortable love for Milly.

He forces himself to look back at Milly, waiting for rejection.

Without looking up, Mill takes his hand and squeezes it, "Philip, give me...a minute or two. Okay? I think...I think...I feel...what you just said... is the nicest thing anyone, *anyone* has ever said to me."

Mill lets go of his hand. She uses her fingers to wipe the tears out of her eyes, extending her arms and shaking her fingers to dry them. She looks up and beams at him. Taking his hand again, she holds it on her lap and looks away from him.

With his other hand Philip points up at the parrot, saying, "I kinda wish I was that bird right now, a runaway and safe in a nice high tree. I think I managed to embarrass us both. If you don't have any feelings for me, I'll understand. You can just forget I said anything and we can go on being friends. I mean, really, you just can."

Mill jumps up to see the bird more clearly. The parrot startles from the tree and glides away. Philip follows the bird's flight and then looks up at Mill.

Mill sighs deeply. "Philip" she says looking down at him with a little smile in her voice, "You need to shut up now before you blow it."

He immediately answers, "Yes, Milly."

Mill sits back down. She waits almost a full minute before speaking again, "Okay, I feel like I have a lot to tell you about me, about my life, things I never told you in all those cheery little notes I sent you."

She cries a little, "If you still love me when I'm done, it will be something I can't see how I deserve. But you will be the judge of that."

Philip pats her hand and stays silent. He sits back and puts his hands on his knees, mentally drawing a protective emotional shield around himself.

He waits for her to begin.

She doesn't really want to burden him. Mill figures her truth would either propel their relationship to something higher and better or end it altogether. And she feels so ready to just tell someone everything—her hurts, her triumphs, her fears—her life.

She begins. The story mostly rushes out of her. Words sometimes tumble over others, not always making sense but conveying the essence of her experience.

Occasionally glancing at his face to look for shock or scorn or anger, Mill tells him about her life after high school--college…Sally…sex with guy after guy…Alaska…Cordova… Anchorage…booze…drugs…Tilly… becoming a LEO…recent deaths.

She doesn't hold much back, only confidential things about current investigations.

Some words come out tense, defensive, and mock-tough. Others choke out through tears.

Throughout, Philip sits stoically inside his protective shield, his face in "counselor neutral."

He'd certainly heard worse stories in his years as a pastor. But as it had at the Greek restaurant, his mind reels and recoils from the excesses of her life and the trouble her choices had brought her.

After all, Milly's story isn't about someone he barely knows. Her story's about someone he had thought he knew very well.

The rape had been something she couldn't control. But the adult Milly had made terrible, destructive choices.

Her story proves he had hardly known Milly. Could he really love this unknown person, a person very different than the youthful Milly--

someone he had idealized?

Philip doesn't feel betrayed. She hadn't lied to him. She hadn't known his feelings for her. She had concealed some things going on in her life but what normal person doesn't do that, even, or most particularly, from friends and family? The things she had done had not involved him.

Still, Philip feels increasingly uncertain. Could he love a Milly who didn't match his lofty vision of her? Until last week, he'd had her on a pedestal where no real person could stand.

Philip knows now that now, if nothing else, he will have to let her take that long step down. Would he be able to love the real Milly? She lives as a bi-sexual. Would that be her choice in the future?

Philip's concerns grow into confusion. Where would their relationship go, with so many secrets revealed?

Mill's storytelling doesn't wind down until shadows start to gather in the corners of the zoo. They watch as young families begin to tow sleepy, cranky kids home. After she finishes, Philip asks a few questions about her current life, mainly about Tilly and about Mill's work.

Then they just sit and watch the thinning crowd flow by.

After a time, without looking at her, Philip reaches out and takes her hand. After a long pause, he says with conviction, "I don't know what to feel right now, Milly...what to say, other than I'm glad I'm here with you at this moment, holding your hand. I can't express how grateful I am for how honest you've been with me. You are so brave to tell me about your life, particularly the parts you've kept to yourself before. You always were that brave, so brave."

Mill starts to speak about how much she must have disappointed him, offended him.

But he hadn't said anything like that. He hadn't judged her, just listened and said he liked being here with her.

So, Mill just squeezes his hand and gives him a shy glance, a smile, and fresh tears on her face.

She tells herself, "Don't blow it, Milly" and keeps her mouth shut.

For a moment, the quiet corner where they sit feels like Milly's young bedroom, a place where her Mom snuggles with her and they read books, one by one.

Chapter 43

Mist Forms A Noose

Badger meets the Movement Clan warriors at the drop-off point at the Safeway in Beaverton. They will make sure the stolen mini-pickup gets recycled into scrap within the week.

The young men who meet her say little. One takes her keys and drives away. The other points towards a Subaru.

"Do you want coffee or anything before we get on the road?" he asks.

She smiles wearily, "Yes, let's go in and get a cup of tea, strong tea." He smiles at her. They walk towards the door. Badger assumes he'd asked about the coffee because she probably looks like she's been up for days.

She had indeed been pulling long hours. And, when she does try to sleep, the terrible sights and sounds of cutting up Zumo's body first push sleep away and then end it early. The horror and grief have eased somewhat but not enough for more than a few hours sleep at a time.

Even after downing the strong tea, Badger dozes as the Movement warrior drives. Their destination is a safe house in downtown Portland, an artist's loft along the east side of the Willamette River.

She wakes with a start when he prods her, "We're here, Badger. This is the place." She climbs stiffly out of the car while he grabs her back-pack and duffle from the cargo compartment.

He waves at her and drives away. Feet dragging, Badger climbs the three flights of stairs to the loft. She knocks twice on the bright green door at the entrance, waits a count of ten, and then knocks five times.

Ekos' muffled voiced asks, "What time is it, Buster?"

Feeling a little silly at the word choice, Badger answers, "It's time for Easter, Eloise."

The codes and signs she and Ekos had worked on and improved after the O'Reilly Strike work. Ekos swings the door open. A small, silenced automatic and half of Ekos' face show around the door's edge. Arrow had ordered them to use every precaution. Badger feels better for Ekos' close attention to security.

Badger had voiced her concerns about the hasty Burns Strike to Arrow in Iowa.

She doesn't repeat them to Ekos.

But she knows the number of the possible Burns Strike sites alone, three, create way too many variables outside of Mist's control.

The plan has remained simple, but the open-endedness of it meant that it would involve several warriors, some observing and some carrying out the Strike itself.

Badger and Ekos would Strike Burns.

Arrow and three War Clan warriors would observe and coordinate.

Eyes and Ears and Movement warriors would support them all.

They now have only three days to scout the sites and conduct whatever rehearsals they can before the Strike itself. Quick, too quick!

Badger calls Arrow to let him know she has arrived. They set their first recon for later in the day, at rush hour, when strange cars in neighborhoods will be disguised in normal traffic.

Badger walks over to the long futon couch and lies down, arm over her eyes. She searches for sleep.

Ekos sits under the loft's large skylights, honing Skyfire, the dagger.

Chapter 44

Searching For Zumo

A red-faced Jake Burns pounds the small conference table in Frieda Tomlin's office, looking alternately between Gregory Stillman and the RSAC.

"Don't you dare tell me that Bill Zumo's disappearance is anything less than abduction or murder," he roars, "God damn it, Frieda, Zumo's a good man, a good hand, one of those rock-solid Forest Service people who make the world work. He's a good cop, not some teepee-creepin' back-seat humper. And he's the guy who's put the O'Reilly and Miller cases together. He's solid!"

Tomlin had been ready for some sort of outburst when the group convened. Even so, Burns' vehemence surprises her, drives her back in her seat a little.

She usually dishes the tough talk rather than sitting back and taking it. "Jake," she says sharply, trying to regain control, "We have no evidence of foul play. Zumo's gone and all his tracks head south with some bimbo."

"'No evidence of foul play'," mocks Burns, "Shit oh dear, we've got plenty, starting when the guy didn't show up at home, followed by when he didn't show up for work! That kind of crap, Bill Zumo just didn't do. Now, that's evidence! Somebody's laid down a red-herring trail for us and you're following."

Tomlin's face turns red. She stands and starts to lean across the table, apparently ready to slug Jake Burns.

"Okay, okay, Burns, settle the fuck down," says Stillman, worried that Tomlin and Burns would come to blows. "You too, Frieda," he says eyeing her, "I'm bigger than both of you by half. I'll kick both of your asses, if you *don't settle down!*"

He puts a hand on her shoulder and shoves her until she sits, holding hostile eye contact with Burns.

Finally she relents. "Okay, Burns," she grinds out coldly, "What if you're right and he's not off banging some bimbo in Pussyville, Nevada? What happened to him and how are you going to find him?"

Burns calms down a notch, "Let's at least get a BOLO out on him. Let's get him picked up for some crap thing, so we can at least make sure he's okay."

"Okay," Tomlin replies, "What did he do that we want all of law enforcement on the West Coast to be on the look out for him."

Burns sits back, some of his fears fading, "Last time I saw Zumo, he had a government-issued pen in his pocket and a horse-chokin' wad of government-issued keys on his handsome government-issued, machine-tooled cop belt. We officially don't know where those items are yet. So, I'd say that larcenous rascal has engaged in theft of government property. We need to apprehend him before he steals paperclips or battleships or something!"

Tomlin shakes her head, a slight smile coming to her lips even though she remains furious at Burns, "Cut the order, Gregory, we better stop that cagey desperado Bill Zumo before he steals my government-issued virginity."

An hour later, a BOLO goes out for Zumo and his personal truck.

Four hours later, a California Highway Patrol officer pulls Zumo's truck over just outside San Francisco.

A teenager had stolen it at the Crescent City harbor. He has no idea who it belonged to or why it was there. He tells the CHP officer he's headed to LA and thought the truck might like a visit to Disneyland.

The officer doesn't smile as he cuffs the kid and eases him into the back of his cruiser. If he understood the BOLO right, a cop has gone missing, maybe gone bad. The huge officer is in no mood for jokes.

A wrecker tows Zumo's truck off the highway and into custody. As the trucks roll into the impound yard, Bill Zumo's trail goes cold, really cold.

An hour after Jake speaks to the CHP officer, he sends orders down to the seven LEOs in southwest Oregon to get to Florence as soon as possible and set up a command post. He orders them to back track every move Zumo made on the day before he went missing, at least all the moves logged in the dispatch center.

They would also interview every person who might have seen him for the last week. If nothing turned up after that, they would start a grid search of all areas within a mile of his apparent travel route.

Jake Burns never lets his troops down...never leaves a man behind... never.

Chapter 45

Smokin' With Jake

After Jake sent his search orders south, he calls Mill. "Meacham," he commands, "Get your ass over to my office. We gotta make smoke together."

The joint task force office has been quiet all Thursday morning. The call from Burns comes as a welcome interruption even though his voice sounds worried and urgent.

Mill has not heard back from Chip Minor about the Moeller evidence being examined at Quantico even though she's called him several times. The FBI investigators have no new leads or theories.

Mill answers, "Okay." She scoots for the elevator, dragging her backpack, and the lunch within, in case the meeting wanders into the lunch hour.

All the way to the Forest Service building, Mill thinks about Philip. Before they went their separate ways on Monday, Philip hugged her close and kissed her forehead. He held her tightly for a long time, saying nothing.

Then he said simply, "Milly, I want to take some time before I see you again. You've been through a lot, lived a lot of things I haven't. Some of those things I can't even imagine. So, give me a chance to sort things out. Please know that I still care for you. I just don't know what that means exactly right now."

Mill has huge doubts about her relationship with Philip, too. Is it just a left-over from childhood? Does she care about him as a friend, a lover, a counselor…what? If something actually developed between them, something romantic and long-term, wouldn't she wreck it the way every one of her past relationships had come apart at the seams?

No one close ever seemed to stay a part of her life, not Mom, Dad, friends…except Philip all these years. And he hadn't been around, close, very much, since high school.

Doubts aside, she feels grateful for knowing him, for being able to work some things out with him the last couple of weeks. As always, he stood up for her and she's grateful for his steady support. She deeply respects him.

But could gratitude and respect somehow turn into love? She has no skill at love or personal things. The pain of that and the potential for losing Philip, or lousing up her relationship with him, makes her tear up a little on the way up in the Forest Service elevator.

Whatever she feels now, it can't be called "love." She would just have to wait until the confusion and distress of her recent conversations with Philip dissipate.

Maybe then some deeper feelings could emerge.

Maybe then, she could focus more on a relationship with Philip than on herself.

The elevator door opens. Mill walks quickly down the hall and into Jake's office. He looks up at her from his desk, weary and sad, something she had not seen before in the bloodhound-looking Burns.

"Close the door, Meacham,' he says flatly, "I have bad news about your boyfriend."

At first Mill thinks Jake somehow knows about Philip and that he's hurt or in trouble. She gets a little indignant that Jake had called Philip her "boyfriend." Wasn't she just having that conversation with herself on the way up in the elevator?

Wait a minute. Burns can't possibly know about Philip. She wonders who the Hell he's talking about...Stillman, Collins?

Then Burns says, "I said to close the door."

She does.

He motions for her to sit down, "That idiot Zumo's missing. He probably lost his dime for the pay potty, wandered off to take a leak, and got lost in the piney woods."

Mill's mind stops working for a moment. Zumo missing! Then a million questions flood in.

"What does 'missing' mean, Jake?" she asks, "Missing how? Missing when? Missing where?"

"Exactly what I'm asking," he replies, his mouth a grim line in his hang-dog face.

Burns gives Mill the situation report, down to the last couple of hours of non-information from the first searchers working out of the Mapleton Ranger District office. "Nothing, nothing, nothing...I keep telling those LEO peckerwoods that 'no information' is not 'information.'"

"Look, they're good cops. They've got the whole Forest Service staff doing a 'search and rescue' for him. They'll find him or information about him if they keep working."

"In the meantime, I want you to watch your unquestionably tight little ass, Meacham. I think these 'mis' people have just proved themselves dangerous...more dangerous than we figured."

338

"They may have heard that we're on to them. I just wish we knew who they are and where to find them. I'd like to send FBI hostage rescue and Delta Force recon up their asses...and I have a posse of Forest Service LEOs spoiling for a fire fight." Burns utters these last words with bitter hatred.

Mill thinks, "Whoever these unsub rats are, they better hide a long ways down in the sewer. Jake means business...and I mean business, too."

Loathing for the unsubs rises in her throat, tightens in her chest. Where's Manny? She needs him now.

Mill and Jake spend the next couple of hours going over everything they know: Miller, O'Reilly, Herrera, Mendocino Six, the FBI's data crunchers, Soames, Moeller, Zumo, the crime scene information.

Burns stands at the white board on the wall making notes. They develop a time line showing everything they know. Dates and arrows or dotted lines spread across the surface, connecting events, perps, and MOs.

They throw out theories and knock them down. In the end, they are even more convinced they're dealing with some very clever criminals and possibly a really big eco-terrorism organization--one that no one has ever heard of before.

"Cripes, Jake," Mill grouses, "How could an outfit like this go completely unnoticed? It doesn't make sense. Usually the FBI or Defense Intelligence or the state troops have these groups scoped, attend their meetings, get elected as officers."

"I mean nothing's ever really secret about these goof-ball organizations. Shit, they can't agree whether to have a meeting. They get in fist fights over the color of their flag. But dead bodies everywhere and not a word about this group on the street? No one taking credit? It just doesn't figure."

"Yeah, Mill," Jake replies somberly, "Tell me about it. Nothing about this makes sense."

They run ideas out a little while longer.

Then looking at the clock, Jake says, "Okay. I have some other news for you, Officer Meacham. I'm reassigning you back here to my staff. I called Tomlin this morning. I told her the dance was over and you were going home with me."

"She was not heartbroken. She likes you fine but she hates my guts, at least for the next millennium or two, or at least until they need the Forest Service cow cops to bail out their city-girl, candy asses again."

"Either way, the thing with Moeller and now with Zumo, they were glad to cut you loose. Besides, they're going nowhere with this task force investigation for now and they know it. Until something breaks, you'd 'a been sitting on your thumb rotatin' anyway."

First surprised at her reassignment, Mill can see the sense of Burns' move. Plus, she knows that Burns doesn't want her sitting, doing nothing.

"So what do you want me to do now, head back to the Siuslaw and help look for Zumo?" she asks, "I could do more with the employees' search and rescue thing. You know, get them better organized...do road patrols... search grids...."

Mill's face clouds up, frown deeping with grief.

"No, not yet," Burns answers, "I want you to hang out here with me another couple of weeks, at least until the background investigations come in on Moeller and Soames. Then I'll bring back our original team and we'll run through all the evidence again for O'Reilly and Miller, and now Zumo."

"After that, you're free to return to writin' tickets for people swipin' firewood and to crackin' campground drunks on the head. Nothin' better than that, is there?"

Mill smiles at his grim nuttiness, "No, nothing better 'n that!"

She'd be glad to see her house again.

Mill looks at Burns, "Jake, I have this friend...well, not really a friend...but a guy who helped me out a lot in Alaska, got me interested in law enforcement. Uh, Manny Suemez...you know, the Deputy in DC. I've kinda been keeping his in the loop...."

Mill waits for Jake to yell at her for going over his head.

Instead, Burns grins, "I'd a done the same thing. To be a good LEO, you gotta work your good networks, the right people...and Manny's both. He and I have been talking. We may be seeing him soon."

Mill feels relief flood over her. Manny's coming. Good news. And she'd expected a good cussing out instead of support.

Okay. This is okay.

They agree to meet for daily check-ins. Mill leaves Burns' office and heads for her old office by the garbage bins. She gets the space organized.

Burns had told her that, as she suspected might happen, everything but her personal stuff has been "secured" by the FBI. She would have to sign out a loaner laptop tomorrow from the computer jocks. Her backpack holds all her personal stuff anyway, so she feels no need to go back to the FBI building.

An hour later, she hits the road for the Residence Inn.

Mill actually feels relieved she will not have to return to where Arianne's stripped office sits like an empty tooth socket. It's a daily reminder of her useless death. In addition, the mysteries of how Arianne'd penetrated security, and who she'd worked for, linger in the air like malignant spirits.

The chill strikes Mill's neck again. She shudders as she leaves the building.

Ben Hicks keys a note into his Blackberry and sends it to Cassi Link.

Chapter 46

Mist Closes In

Badger, Arrow, and three War Clan warriors visit the best sites for Striking Jake Burns—his home, his favorite watering hole, and his "meet" room in downtown Portland.

Hours later, when the places are empty, Eyes and Ears burglars enter the first two locations and make quick diagrams showing the best places for concealment and ambush. They search for alarms, dogs, or motion-sensing lights that might offer ugly surprises for Ekos and Badger.

A week earlier, a slow-moving "tourist" on an historic walking tour had scanned the meet room with sensitive detection equipment disguised as a personal-carry oxygen unit. The "nebulizer" identified and mapped the motion-detecting camera and the door alarms. Soon after, Eyes and Ears defeated the systems and entered the old salon for a quick but careful search and to plant a remotely controlled and microwave-powered bug.

Before Arrow arrived in Portland, warriors spent a week watching the meet room. They used a spotting scope during the day and magnified night vision after dark. They also used the remotely controlled listening device to listen to a few conversations; but mostly they kept it's microwave power source turned off and undetectable. The room was usually empty, to all appearances guarded securely by Jake's technology.

Only Jake, a few other law enforcement people, and a couple informants met there, and then only rarely.

The Mist group photographed the few people coming and going. They identified them as far as they could and did background checks. They compiled photos, biographies, and lists of people's routines. They evaluated the threat each person represented.

They listed Mill and other LEOs as "contacts to be avoided."

Arrow has strong reservations about Strikes at Burns' home or at the bar. Too many people. He feels that other people might get hurt or interfere. Just as the Herrera killing had exposed Mist more than the Chiefs Council liked, so would any "collateral damage" on the Burns Strike.

Of the two less-desirable locations, Arrow considers Burns' home lower-risk. They might Strike Burns while his wife's off on an errand or isolate her inside while Striking him.

Still risky. Snoopy neighbors and dogs always a problem.

Back at the artist's loft, Arrow reviews all the information and makes his assessment.

Considering everything, Arrow figures Burns' meet room the best location of the three.

The alley door at the meet site has a solid but old and easily-picked lock. The security features had already been defeated.

The room itself has poor lighting. The building is nearly vacant and noise will not be noticed. They could Strike Burns there and probably attract no attention. Maybe a drunk or two would walk the alley, but no one else.

Burns' body might not be found for days or weeks. And based on evidence Arrow planned to leave there, investigators would have to assume Burns had been killed by someone he'd invited in to discuss a fraud investigation.

Arrow's finally convinced that the meet site is the best Strike location. They would try there first and use another site only if they missed.

As a precaution, the group works out final Strike plans for each site, using maps and diagrams to describe routes and movement and stopwatches to time each step. Later, they will dress rehearse each Strike location and give the plans several practical tests.

Given his rare use of the room, the key to Striking Burns there will be to lure him in at a predictable time. Once the time is known, Arrow can have Badger and Ekos in place before Burns arrives.

Getting Burns to the meet site at a predictable time is definitely Arrow's biggest challenge. Possible influences close to Burns are gone.

Warrior Moeller is dead. Sympathizer Soames has been scared off, probably permanently. And Eyes and Ears no longer has anyone inside the Forest Service Law Enforcement ranks who might trick Burns into going to the site.

However, Mist does have a Forest Service insider, the War Clan warrior on the Siuslaw National Forest. He's the person who broke in to the Law Enforcement office and removed the O'Reilly evidence. He later helped with the Zumo Strike, placing Zumo's gear back in his office after the Movement warriors brought in his Forest Service uniform and pickup.

Arrow opens his encrypted cell phone and calls the Siuslaw warrior, a handsome post-doc from OSU who recently married his pregnant fish-biologist girlfriend.

The warrior tells Arrow about the situation on the Mapleton District and the efforts to locate Zumo. The post-doc's been leading one of the search and rescue teams in the field. He tells Arrow that with all the attention and

344

action on the district, he's a little reluctant to get involved in yet another Strike so soon.

But Arrow explains all he would have to do is call Jake Burns and make an appointment to meet him privately. He would tell Burns about some evidence he'd found and weird behavior that some of his colleagues were displaying.

If Burns tells him to meet near Portlandia and gives him a time, the warrior would come up for the meet, make contact, and then just walk away. The Strike team would do the rest.

If Burns seems suspicious or wants another meeting place, the Siuslaw warrior could just wait a day and then call back to cancel. He could say that he'd been mistaken.

After more discussion, the Siuslaw warrior agrees to serve as bait.

The following morning, the post-doc warrior calls Burns, "I've been working on finding Zumo, leading one of the teams. Nothing so far but I found some of Bill Zumo's things in one of the offices here, in an empty desk, including a diary. I didn't know who to talk to about it...things are a little weird here now...."

Jake shows immediate interest, "Well Hell, did you read any of it? What does it say?"

The warrior responds, "Some of it is written in some kind of code and some in plain English, but it seems to show that Bill had taken money from some people, a lot of money. I mean I could be wrong because I don't know what a lot of it says."

Jake yells into the phone, "Drink gasoline and shit fire. No chance that Bill Zumo'd do that!"

"Well, I'm not accusing him." the post-doc retorts, "I barely knew him. I just thought someone ought to see this before it gets into the wrong hands. Do you want me to give it to the law enforcement guys who are here searching for Zumo?"

Burns shudders. "Hell no," he replies, "I want you to get all the evidence you have in here to me, overnight mail"

The warrior answers, "Okay I can do that, but, well, there's some other things, too. Some of the staff have begun to meet off site and sit in their cars on break, talking. They weren't doing that before Zumo disappeared. I have their names and everything but, well, I really don't feel comfortable talking about them on the phone. Something creepy's going on around here and I don't know who might be listening and how."

Burns replies, "I sure know the feeling. I've been looking over my shoulder for the last month like a holy-roller preacher in a titty bar. Look, any chance of you driving that evidence in here to me? Take you what, three hours or so? You could come in after work Friday and meet me downtown at a place I know. No one would see you with me. When we're done, you could grab some good food and head home. How's that sound?"

"Sounds like a great deal, Mr. Burns," the Siuslaw warrior smiles, "Can I bring my wife? I'd drop her at the mall before I come down to meet you. We just got married. There's a lot of stuff she'd like to get for our place."

"Welcome to married life, son," Jake smiles back, "And any man willing to make as big a mistake as getting married can call me 'Jake', so please do."

"Sounds good," the warrior responds, "See you Friday...uh, Jake. Where should we meet?"

Jake replies, "I'll be standing under Portlandia's ass, reading the Whore's-a-groanin'-again newspaper. Just come up and say 'Zumo' and I'll tell you what to do. It may seem cloak and dagger but it's simple. You know like walking and shit like that."

The warrior laughs, "Even though I'm a married man, I can still walk."

"Not for long, son...not for long," says Jake and hangs up.

As soon as the Siuslaw warrior hangs up with Jake, he calls Arrow and tells him that Jake has asked him to meet him under Portlandia's ass at 8 pm on Friday. Arrow thanks him and tells him he has done extremely well.

Arrow's team moves out to rehearse as invisibly as possible at the three deserted sites on Portland's north side near the Columbia River.

Chapter 47

Changes in the Fog

As soon as he ends the call with the post-doc on the Siuslaw National Forest, Jake Burns calls Mill. "So, Meacham," he says, explaining his contact, "You know this guy? I mean is he legit?"

Mill thinks for a moment, "Yes, I think he is. I never worked with him but he's been around the forest for awhile doing research, well-liked. I think we hired him permanent, full-time, recently. And he knocked up one of the staff, according to Zumo, and they were thinking about marrying."

Burns replies, "Well, all that checks out. It seems odd to me though that Zumo's stuff would just show up like that at the Mapleton District office. You know what I mean? A plant maybe...to throw us off? 'Cause it seems borderline strange that Zumo'd keep a diary in addition to his log, and one that incriminates him to boot. Well, that just doesn't seem like my ol' buddy."

"Shit, that boy left school in the fourth grade. He couldn't even read street signs until I showed him how." Burns pauses, remembering that Zumo might be in real trouble or dead. "Sorry, Meacham," he murmured gruffly, "I guess I get carried away."

Mill gulps a little, "No problem, Jake. I have to think of him as alive, too, until...well, you know."

"Yeah," Jake replies softly, "I know."

Jake goes on, "Anyway, Mill, if it's okay with you, I want you to back me up on Friday night. You know this guy. You know the area and the security drill, except you'll do the wait-and-watch for me before I get to the alley with the kid in tow."

"Once we go in, no hanging around playing super-spy. You don't have to tail me or conduct surveillance like those pansies at FLETC *didn't* teach you how. Just grab dinner down there close somewhere. Keep your eyes open and watch my back trail. I'll call you if I need you. Would that be okay?"

Mill says she couldn't be happier than to watch a pro like him in action.

"Meacham," Jake retorts, "You can kiss my ass until its rosy red, but I'm still going to like you. So, what's this goofy, overeducated college boy look like?"

Mill gives Jake a full description of the engaging fellow and they end their call. Jake picks up the phone and calls Oregon Department of Motor Vehicles. A few minutes later, the post-doc's photo pops up on Jake's cell phone screen. He has all he needs to ID the guy on Friday.

Late on Wednesday, Mill calls Philip and, as almost always, gets his voice mail. She leaves a brief message, neither cheery nor sad, and asks for a call back.

An hour later, Philip calls, complaining he'd been in a budget meeting with the church finance committee. "I'd rather be boiled in oil," he says ruefully, "than deal with the church budget. But, truthfully, it's so important I make myself like it--kinda like liver and onions. Somebody in the congregation serves me liver and onions, first I pray it'll taste like chicken. Then I eat it."

Mill laughs, "Has it ever tasted like chicken?"

"No, Milly" Philip replies, "But God has a sense of humor. And, I'm pretty sure until I approach the gift of a liver dinner with the right attitude, I think it will still taste like liver. And once I get my attitude straightened out, it'll no longer matter. That's God's sense of humor. All of a sudden you realize He's played 'gotcha' on you *again*. If you listen closely, you can hear His belly laugh."

Mill suddenly has a mental picture of a naked Santa-looking guy up in a bunch of clouds pointing down at Philip and slapping his godly leg. "Yikes," she thinks to herself, "So God's a practical joker. I hope he's not aiming one at me."

Then another thought strikes her--maybe He already had! How many? Damn! More to think about.

Chasing away thoughts of that mystery, Mill laughs again, "So, there you go talking about God again. If we're going to hang around together, will I get an earful of God all the time?"

"No, Milly," replies Philip, "Only if you want to. But, someday, maybe...uh...you'd come hear me preach?"

Another absurd vision has filled her mind--Philip in long, black robes hovering over his congregation, showering them with golden words. Mill almost laughs out loud.

She smiles broadly into the phone, "Sure, if you promise not to wear your long black robes."

Philip pauses for a moment, thinking of the times he'd preached in shorts or jeans and a polo-shirt, "Black robes? Pink is my color, Milly, pink with orange stripes."

Now they both laugh.

"Philip," Mill goes on, "Could we get serious for a moment."

He replies a little warily, "Sure."

She continues, "Okay. Look, I know I hit you with a lot of bad stuff about my life, some of it really weird, particularly to someone nice and normal like you. I want you to know that I'll be fine if we never talk about all that again."

"Whatever happens between us, I just want to make sure we stay friends. You're my best and longest friend. I don't want to lose you over old, crazy stuff in my life." Mill has decided to avoid any talk of "love" between them...for now...until maybe...if...Philip mentions it again.

Philip doesn't reply for a long time. Mill can't be sure whether he's upset or waiting for her to add more comments. Finally fear of losing him begins to wash over her. Her arms and knees feel a little weak.

She asks, her voice a little panicky, "Philip, are you okay? Did I say something that flipped you out or made you mad? Please say I didn't! I tried so hard to get it right!"

"Milly, Milly," Philip replies softly, "We'll get through this... together. I'm still sorting out all my feelings. You surprised me the other night. I've always idealized you. Now I know you're a real woman with a real life, a real history. I'm grateful for knowing you in this new way."

He gulps a little, thinking of some of the things she'd done and about her lesbian relationships.

"I just haven't sorted out what my new way with you will be. Don't give up on me, okay? Trust your old friend, Philip, Milly. I won't leave you no matter what."

Mill feels like young Milly again. Philip's hugging her after the assault. She's warm and numb at the same time.

And he had said clearly, "I won't leave you no matter what." Those words fall on her like water on a parched plant.

Mill feels her confidence swell. Her fear recedes, and her strength returns.

She answers simply, "Okay, Philip, I'll be ready to talk when you are."

When she finishes her call with Philip, Mill calls her home number. She has not heard from Tilly the entire time she was in Portland. At this hour, Tilly will be at work. Mill intends to leave a voice message asking Tilly to call with the schedule for her move.

A gruff male voice answers, "Uh, Corcoran residence."

Surprised, Mill asks, "Who's this, please?"

The man answers, "I'm Jack with the moving company. We're packing Ms. Corcoran's stuff."

Mill feels both pleased and sad. She's also a little miffed at Tilly for letting people into Mill's home without telling her in advance.

"Thanks, Jack," Mill replies, "This is Mill Meacham, the owner of the place. When do you expect to be done?"

"Well," he answers, "Pick up is tomorrow. So, we should be gone by noon."

"Thanks, Jack," she says softly, then adds, "Safe trip. Okay?"

"Okay, Ma'am," says Jack, "Nice talking to you."

Mill hangs up in a rush of feelings about Tilly. Then she lets go of those feelings.

Till and Mill have definitely fallen all the way down to the bottom of the hill.

Chapter 48

Mist Hits the Bull's Eye

Bull Meacham looks up from the Pinchot Desk. There's a shapely figure back-lit in his office door.

Strange. The hour is 6:30 am and he usually has few visitors before 8 when the staff comes in. Most mornings, he's at the office before six and stays until three in the afternoon. With this schedule, he can avoid the worst of the DC Beltway traffic and have evenings free.

Power people around DC have figured out he's just a figurehead, so he gets few invitations to meetings of the powerful and influential. Out of the spotlight, he picks from among four or so lesser receptions a week and goes to them to suck free drinks and gobble up eats.

Occasionally, Pizzaro or Reinard order him to one event or another. He goes, gritting his teeth. Irritation aside, at these official receptions, he finds he can console himself with good talk and occasional pussy.

As he'd predicted, being a hollow Chief isn't so bad when you add the high pay and perks to the low job requirements.

So, on this morning Bull looks at the figure at his door and asks himself, "Who would want to see me at this hour? Pizzaro isn't in town and my meetings don't start until 9."

He motions to the person to come in, "Some way I can help you?"

A tall woman in a severe business suit walks in. She looks quite attractive in a tough Beltway-lawyer way.

Bull stands up and walks over to shake her hand. As he gets closer, he scopes out her breasts which peep at him over the top of her plain, white vee-neck blouse.

"Butter creams," he thinks to himself, distracted.

"Chief Meacham?" she asks, noting the direction his eyes have taken.

Finally making eye contact, Bull answers, "That's me." He waves her towards the chairs in the corner with the best view of the Washington Monument, "Please, over here," he says, now watching her backside as she walks easily ahead of him.

Before sitting, she offers him her hand, "I'm from the Aquasis Foundation. I have something for you."

He shakes her hand in the weak way east-coasters did, "I confess

I've never heard of the 'Aquasis Foundation' before. I'm wondering how an upright lady like you got into this place so early in the morning. Also, what did you say your name was?"

"Chief Meacham," replies Raven's emissary, "Who I am and how I got in aren't important today. As I said, I'm an attorney representing the Aquasis Foundation, an organization dedicated to restoring a verdant, pure world. I have something for you that I believe you will be delighted to receive."

With that, the Listening Clan Leader removes a DVD player from her large purse and turns it on. Instantly, the image of the drunken Bull leaps onto the screen. Bull goggles at the screen, "Well, uh...."

The Mist representative stops the DVD player, "I think you know what the rest of this DVD represents, egregiously poor choices on your part and equally bad faith on the part of others. When we at the Aquasis Foundation found out about this grotesque breach of discretion and faith, we immediately went to work to obtain all copies."

She nods encouragement to the incredulous Bull, "We now possess every copy except yours. We also took receipt of some additional copies and still images made by your Associate Chief, Esperanza Pizzaro. Moreover, we got a video confession from the male prostitute. His statement fully implicates Associate Chief Pizzaro. Here they are."

She holds out a small, bulky package to Bull who sits thunderstruck, staring at her.

Bull's mind swings wildly from hope to bitterness. This is too good to be true!

Who the Hell're these Aquasis people? Why the Hell had they gotten involved in his humiliation? Are they out to get him, too? Do they want money; would this be blackmail for cash, influence, what?

He looks at the Mist representative narrowly. Have they sent a beautiful woman to rub in the insult of him being caught on tape with a man? Do they know how stupidly he'd been trapped by Angie's wiggling ass?

The woman seems to understand everything running through Bull's mind. She smiles tightly at him, "Chief Meacham, we spent over a million dollars and hundreds of work hours getting these horrible images for you. They are yours. Because of our investment, we will continue to own one copy."

She looks him in the eye and smiles even more severely, "And, of course, because of our generosity and your certain desire to thank us, we demand a commitment from you. When asked, you will do what we require—no questions."

"You will probably not hear from us very often. When you do, you must, and I emphasize *must,* do what we say immediately. The person representing us will show you a symbol identical to this one. That will be proof of their authority."

The woman hands Bull a complex green cloisonné leaf, as long as his thumb and half as wide as his palm. Intricate engraving and glass work formed a realistic and complex leaf pattern over gold.

"The leaf is genuine gold, another token of our esteem for you. But remember, when our representative presents our leaf, you must do what we ask, when we ask it."

The woman looks into his eyes again and holds them, "Do we have a deal, Chief Meacham?"

Bull sits back in his chair, letting her words sink in fully. He considers their importance.

If he agrees, he'll be free to be a full–power, full-steam-ahead Chief except for rare "musts' from Aquasis. He'll be able to stick it back to Ball and Reinard. And, most of all, he'll have Angie Pizzaro under control, even under his belly when he chooses.

He says to himself, "I wonder what Angie's mouth will look like on the head of my cock before every morning staff meeting?" He savors the thought for a moment.

Refocusing on the intent face of the Aquasis representative, Bull asks, "So will you be asking me to break the law?"

"Perhaps," she replies levelly, "But not in the criminal sense. What we will most often want from you is simple, accurate information about people you know, or know about. We may ask about government contracts or proposals. Your work for Aquasis will be essentially risk free although it may not always be without consequence."

Bull thinks a little longer. "You have a deal," he says, grinning. With that, the Mist clan leader stands up and holds out her hand. He shakes it, a strong western-style grab.

"Then I'll be going," she says.

"You sure you wouldn't like to get together for dinner or a drink sometime?" asks Bull.

With a faint smile and a twist of her face, she answers, "No, Chief, not after what I saw on that video." And then she disappears through his door.

As the Mist Clan Leader walks to the elevators, she turns off the microchip video camera and audio recorder expertly concealed in her large purse.

Mist has the complete record of the bribe, including the Chief's handshake sealing their deal. Meacham doesn't know it yet, but Mist will be dictating his major decisions from now on.

Bull sits for a time, shuffling through the discs, thumb drives, and photo cards. He isn't sure what half of this crap does, but he'd see it all smashed and burnt before the day ended, except for Raoul's confession. He has an immediate use for that.

He pushes the pile into his brief case, locks it, and sets it inside the Pinchot Desk. He locks the drawer for additional safety.

At 8 am, his secretary arrives. He tells her, "Set up an appointment for me with Associate Chief Pizzaro for 6 pm Monday. I know we'll be staying late, but I have a couple of ideas to put to her."

He chuckles and walks back into the Chief's Office, beginning to imagine the humiliation he would wreak on Pizzaro.

Bull has a quirt at home that he uses when riding the rental horses at Prince William Park. He begins to think a few bright red stripes across Angie's white, wiggling backside might be just the way to start out Monday evening.

Angie would be a special, long-term project.

And then, of course, Bull is challenged by what he will do to Ball and Reinard.

He has some ideas. More would come.

Bull savors the moment.

They *will* feel his heat.

Chapter 49

Ekos Burning

At 4 pm on Friday, Arrow leaves Badger and Ekos at the loft. He takes the other warriors downtown to the Portlandia area. War Clan warriors move into their positions to help Badger and Ekos if called. Movement warriors begin driving the area with the Eyes and Ears warriors, scouting for police presence or other suspicious signs.

A Movement car will come for Badger and Ekos about an hour before Burns is scheduled to meet the Siuslaw Warrior and take them to the meet room.

Badger and Ekos go over the diagrams and schedule, step by step, again and again. The plan inside the room is simple enough. Ekos will kill Burns with Skyfire as soon as he enters the room and closes the door. Badger will help Ekos and minimize any commotion.

They have thought out several ways to keep the noise down. The best plan is for Badger to kick Burns in the throat as Ekos thrusts Skyfire into his heart from behind.

Badger will have to appear suddenly and instantly kick.

Ekos will have to coordinate the thrust with Badger's kick.

Although both moves are simple enough by themselves, together they present a bigger challenge, particularly timing. So, for more than half an hour, the two spar and choreograph their moves.

Time after time, using a karate dummy, they spring forward from concealment and end with Badger's foot buried in the dummy's neck and Skyfire buried eighteen inches below in its heart.

They also practice several other moves, including Badger disarming Burns if he was able to draw his weapon before Skyfire killed him.

Ekos practices aikido against Badger's black belt in tae kwon do. Both use force but not full force to test reach, reflexes, and precision.

After their workout, they take quick showers. They go through their weapons and tools one more time. Finally, everything nests in the right place, ready to draw and use.

They slip on their gear—body suits in deep, non-reflective grey, deep, slim pockets on front and sides of legs, tools nestled within, some secured with small bits of Velcro. Ekos slides Skyfire into a forearm scabbard and tightens the scabbard's straps snug. Badger slips a sap into her waist sash and slides a six-inch push-knife with a wide handle into a leg sheath. They both fold ski masks and gloves into small bundles and tuck them into the top of their right-side cargo pockets.

Dressed and equipped, they put on baggy and nondescript street clothes to provide cover as they move to the Strike site. Badger looks out the window to see if the Movement car has arrived yet but it has not.

"Nervous, Badger?" asks Ekos, "It's not like you."

"No, not really, Ekos," she replies, "I'm ready to kill this thug. There's just a lot of moving parts on this Strike, more than both of us are used to dealing with."

"Sure, but its no big deal," Ekos answers, "We Strike. We go. No one will touch us. No one ever does."

Badger walks over to Ekos. "Ekos," she whispers, "We're not... you're not infallible. We are two women doing something against the laws of this country. Our cause is just and right. Our actions are absolutely necessary. But people will hunt us down if they know where to find us. The Burns Strike will drive federal law enforcement into a feeding frenzy. Make no mistake, we must leave no trace of Mist tonight."

Badger holds Ekos at arms' length and shakes her a little, "Do you understand?"

Ekos shakes her head angrily. She pushes Badger back a step, "This is easy, Badger, no sweat. What's the matter with you? I'll kill this fucker alone if you're turning yellow. You've gotten to be such a nervous bitch lately. If you can't handle the work, get out."

Badger begins an angry response but a muffled honk sounds out by the curb. Badger looks out the window and sees the Movement car.

"Let's go," she orders, teeth clenched, "We're going to Strike Burns tonight. We can settle this later."

Badger is having some serious concerns about Ekos' stability. No Mist assassin had ever talked so carelessly about Mist security. Ekos' blood lust and arrogance seems far ahead of her judgment.

They walk silently out to the car. Once in the car, Badger fumes and worries until they get dropped off about three blocks from the alley. There, she refocuses her mind on the Strike.

Badger calls Arrow and asks for a situation report. Arrow simply tells her, "All clear. Strike hard."

Pocketing her muted cell phone, Badger moves down the street and into the alley with Ekos. They walk quickly to the door and open it, then step in quickly. The lock had been picked moments before.

Badger quickly locks the door and flicks on the tiny light. Both women take off their street clothes and put them in a trash bag. They pull on their ski masks and adjust them until their eyes glint through tiny slits. They put on their gloves and flex them to make sure the gripping surfaces fit snugly against their palms and fingers. They check each other's gear one last time.

Badger moves to the little alcove. She opens the door and puts the trash bag of clothes into the space full of cleaning supplies. Closing the door, she moves as far back as she can, well into the alcove's shadows.

Ekos checks to make sure Badger is effectively invisible in the dim light. She calls softly, "Okay."

Ekos slips back to the side of the stack of chairs farthest from the alley door. She kneels down and then curls up, spreading a dark grey silk shroud over herself.

Badger walks over and makes a small adjustment in the shroud. She whispers, "Okay" and steps away.

She turns out the tiny light and re-hides herself in the alcove by the beam of a small flashlight. She snaps out that light. Everything goes dark and silent.

The Mist Strikers wait, coiled.

A few minutes later, Burns walks up to Portlandia. He opens a copy of the Oregonian. A rather nerdy looking young man steps away from the side of a nearby building and approaches. "Zumo" he murmurs quietly.

Jake gives him a quick once over. The man is not as tall as he had expected but has the kind of good looks Mill described and matches his DMV photo as much as anyone does. He looks like some guy who spends most of the year indoors and the summers getting baked and bug-bit.

Jake says to him, "Follow me, but not too close. Do what I do." With that, Burns steps away and walks briskly down the street. He looks back once and sees the young man well back, keeping pace. Good.

Jake reaches the alley. Quickly checking his back trail, Jake turns and goes down the alley to the door.

Jake slips his key in the lock. Inside, the two women are instantly alert. In this moment of great tension, they use calming techniques to relax their bodies and control their breathing. The two steel themselves against making noise.

Jake opens the door and steps in. He stands silently for a moment, listening. He hears only muffled noise from the Chinese kitchen two walls away.

He hears a tiny noise. He almost reaches for his sidearm but instead decides it must be a mouse, common enough in here. Okay.

He steps across and turns on the tiny light. Lit by its dim radiance, the dark and shadows recede only slightly.

Jake turns to check the door-camera video screen, his head moving away from Ekos' hiding place.

Ekos launches her attack.

Jake catches sight of her movement in his extreme left peripheral vision. He throws his left arm out defensively and reaches for his gun with his right hand.

He never sees Badger as she whips out from the alcove and drives her foot into the center-right side of his neck.

As Badger's foot lands, Ekos thrusts Skyfire under Jake's left arm and into his chest. Her thrust was supposed to be body-center. But now, because Skyfire is too short to reach Jake's heart from that direction, the dagger only pierces his left lung and does not kill him.

As Badger's kick drives Jake towards Ekos, Ekos moves lower to hold on to the dagger.

Jake pivots across Ekos' grip and falls down to the floor, gun skittering away. He moves feebly, bleeding out in his lung.

He tries to yell.

Badger leaps to Jake's side and pulls the push knife from its sheath. She jams it to the hilt in his right eye.

He dies instantly.

Angry that she didn't make the killing stroke, Ekos pulls back on Skyfire only to find it's caught in Burns' clothes.

"Shit," she yells, "God damn it. The fucker's stuck."

She turns on Badger, saying, "This was my Strike. I wanted this thug. He was mine, Badger, and you took him instead."

Behind the mask, Ekos' eyes squint and gleam.

With a powerful twist, Ekos pulls Skyfire free.

Whispering hoarsely to Ekos to "quiet down," Badger braces herself for a fight with the young woman, possibly to the death.

————————————————//————————————————

A few minutes earlier, Mill was seated at an outdoor restaurant a couple of blocks away from the alley. She saw Jake go by to his rendezvous at Portlandia and watched him come back again to go down the alley.

After a minute or two, she saw the Siuslaw post-doc guy go by. He walked well behind Jake at about the same pace. The fellow reached the entrance to the alley and looked down it for a moment. Then he kept walking along the street, now at a faster pace, and got into a car which sped away.

As the car disappears, Mill feels the hair go up on her neck again. Something's way off about this. Why would Mr. Post-doc walk past the alley and drive away? Had he gotten cold feet? Was this a set up for Jake?

Bad shit, either way!

She jumps up from the table.

Across the street, a young Mist warrior who's been watching her casually from a park bench gets up and edges towards the alley entrance. The warrior has strict orders to watch and distract anyone covering Burns but not to harm them.

Mill throws a twenty dollar bill down to cover her coffee and hors d'ourves. She races across the street and somehow collides with a teen-aged girl who's appeared out of nowhere.

They go down in a heap, the girl striking her head and crying out. "Blood" appears on her head.

Delaying for a moment to help the girl up and over to a bench, Mill charges around the corner and down the alley, pulling her gun.

Arrow sees Mill coming. He radios Badger and Ekos, saying "Meacham's coming fast down the alley, armed."

At first, because Badger is focused on a possible fight with Ekos, she doesn't comprehend what Arrow has said. Then it sinks in with a shock, "Meacham" would be Mill Meacham, Zumo's assistant and Burns' investigator.

Badger quickly says to Ekos, "No time for this now. Mill Meacham is headed this way. We have to go out through the hallway and escape."

Badger quickly walks to the alley door and locks its solid lock. The door would not hold long but maybe long enough for them to get away. Then she walks to the hallway door and unlocks it.

Ekos slips off her mask and glares, snarling, "You got Burns, I get Meacham."

Badger turns on her, "No Ekos, not possible. Meacham's not the target of this Strike or any Strike. She's the Forest Service Chief's daughter. We absolutely can't risk harming her. We've got to GO."

Badger points to the hallway door, beyond which was the front of the building and freedom. "Go now," Badger orders.

Ekos spits at her and waves Skyfire, "No," she utters slowly, thickly, "Meacham is mine."

"No," Badger tells her, "If anything, she's mine. Do not kill her!"

At that moment, Mill rattles the door knob. She calls quietly, "Jake, are you in there? Open the door, it's Mill. Something weird's going on with this meet."

Lightening fast, Ekos reaches out and douses the light.

Nearest the door, she unlocks it and moves quickly behind it.

Mill comes through the door into the darkness, Glock held high. She figures Jake's turned off the tiny light as he did before so that no one can see the door open and close. She waits momentarily for him to turn the light back on.

Instead, a powerful blow hits her gun and it sails away.

"Jake," she yells, ducking away from the impact, "What the Hell...!"

Ekos sends Skyfire towards Mill in an overhand stab. But Mill's ducking away. So, rather than hitting her neck, Skyfire only rips shallowly across her right shoulder.

At that moment, Badger turns on the tiny light.

Caught by surprise, Ekos rocks back on her heels. She lowers Skyfire for a thrust at Mill's mid-section.

Mill instantly drops into horse stance. She hits the off-balance Ekos in the chest with a full-force eagle-beak punch, breaking her sternum and hurting her like Hell.

Mill's blow would have felled most opponents because of heart shock but Ekos stays up. Ekos staggers back into an aikido *uke* miga-hanmi position. Skyfire droops towards the floor in her right hand. Her left hand and arm protect her broken chest.

Mill steps in and throws her next punch, a half-closed fist aimed at Ekos' throat.

Balanced again, Ekos drops Skyfire and uses her right hand and Mill's force to spin Mill forward. She twists Mill's arm to dislocate it and throws her head first into the nearby wall.

Mill's forehead makes a dent in the old wall.

Small bits of plaster shower down.

Mill goes down with them...lands hard, out cold.

Skyfire had been kicked over to the hallway door. Ekos spots the dagger and goes to retrieve it, clutching her chest, bent over with deep pain.

She says bitterly, "That bitch can punch!"

She coughs convulsively.

When she turns with the dagger in her hand, Badger stands between her and Mill. Badger says simply, "I told you she was mine and I meant it."

Ekos scoffs, "Like Hell. I put her down. Now, she's my kill."

Attempting to brush by Badger, Ekos lurches forward.

But Badger blocks Skyfire with her right hand and drives her left fist into Ekos' damaged chest, knocking her unconscious with heart shock.

Ekos falls flat on her back and slides a few feet in the plaster dust.

Badger takes Skyfire from Ekos' hand.

After a moment's hesitation, she drives it into Ekos' heart.

Ekos' body twitches violently, then stills.

Badger stands up wearily...bone tired.

She wipes at the tears that started to flow as soon as she killed Ekos. "Mist daughter...Mist daughter," she sobs, "You gave me no choice. I loved your fierce warrior ways. But you gave me no choice! Damn you!"

Badger stands over Ekos, letting the tears flow for a time. She's exhausted by weeks of stress and now by profound grief.

For a moment, she feels dizzy. She almost falls down next to the two woman warriors who lie with their feet touching.

And then, with great effort, Badger refocuses on the Strike scene. Mist security demands she get Ekos' body and herself out of there. Now!

Someone might have heard the commotion. Urgency drives out her gathering grief and fatigue and makes her act.

Badger walks to Mill's Glock and disarms it, tossing the pieces around the room. Then she walks back to Mill and kneels beside her. She brushes plaster and dust from her face and hair.

Testing the dislocated shoulder, she takes Mill's arm carefully in hand. She gives it a sharp twist, putting the socket back in alignment. Until Mill gets to a doctor, there'd be no way to tell if she has permanent damage. But Badger's action might spare Mill some pain and further injury.

Badger almost calls Arrow. Time is running out. Arrow will be worried. But, Badger knows she can't call, at least not yet. Not when she's this close to...to....

Badger takes out an ammonia capsule. She snaps it under Mill's nose. At first, Mill makes no response. Badger holds the smelly cotton object closer under her nose. She pinches the space between Mill's index finger and her thumb, pinches hard.

After a few more seconds, Mill rouses blearily, concussed from the impact with the wall and almost immobilized by the pain in her shoulder, head, and neck. Her right eye has swollen shut.

She's a mess.

"Milly," Badger says distinctly, "It's your mother. Wake up! It's your mother, Rebecca Theophile, wake up, dear."

Mill reacts drowsily, the voice sounding familiar and yet a far-off memory. Is it time to get up? Time for school? No, that isn't right!

Suddenly much more awake, Mill grabs Badger's arm strongly. "What the fuck," Mill grits, looking at a masked face.

Mill drops Badger's arm and pulls back for a feeble blow, "You're not my mother."

Rebecca Theophile Meacham replies, her masked, alien face in shadows, "Yes, Milly, I am. I love you. I always have. Today I saved you. That felt good. But I have to go now. And you have to rest. I will be in touch with you soon. Say nothing of me to anyone, my beloved."

She gently touches Mill's bewildered face with her gloved hand.

Taking out her radio, she calls Arrow, "Ekos is down. Meacham killed her. She's out. I need the team."

Badger gets up and walks to the tiny light. She turns it out.

In less than a minute, a darkened Movement vehicle pulls up in the alley. Two masked War Clan warriors carefully bag Ekos' body and place it in the van. Badger gathers up any Mist materials, including Skyfire, the faked fraud evidence, and the bag of clothes in the utility room. She walks out the door and pulls it closed behind her.

Mill tries to move but the pain in her head and neck is too great. Alone in the darkness, she weeps for a time for the pain and for...losing her mother...again...mother? She must be crazy...hallucinating.

Mill spins back into unconsciousness.

The van speeds off. Badger uses her cell phone to call 911.

She orders an ambulance to the little room in the alley where lies her only daughter.

An hour later, the Mist Strike team scatters in every direction, back to their hide-aways.

Badger goes to ground at the safe house in Portland.

She has more to do...on her own business, not Mist's.

Chapter 50

Mill Rests

A minute after the Mist van leaves the alley headed north, a dark blue Suburban roars into the same alley from the south. Manny Suemez leaps out before the driver can bring the big vehicle to a stop.

He hits the door to Jake's meet room and bounces off. Gone are the days when there was no wooden door that could stand in his way.

Behind him, a huge FBI entry-team member runs up with a 60-pound battering ram. Two blows at the hinges and the door collapses into two pieces and crashes inwards.

The entry team member goes in first with Manny on his heels.

Manny quickly scans the room. God damn it!

Burns is clearly dead with a frightful eye wound.

Mill is down, not appearing to breathe.

"*Dios mio*," Manny groans inside, "Two of the best...dead."

Angry tears start in his eyes. He brushes them away angrily, appalled at how law enforcement had underestimated the terrorists.

He gets a grip. This is no time for his weakness for others to bring him down.

Then Mill stirs; one arm moves. In the distance Manny hears the sound of ambulances wailing and weaving through traffic, their engines roaring all out.

"Come on, you bastards." he roars inside, "Get here, damn it, now. This is my *nina* here."

————————————//————————————

Mill Meacham gains and loses consciousness frequently over the next week. Because of her head injury, she has 24-hour nursing at the Oregon Health Science University Trauma Center's Intensive Care Unit.

Beeping monitors check pulse, respiration, and blood pressure continuously, sending data to a central nursing station. Mill's head, neck, and shoulder get X-rayed, CAT scanned, and MRIed repeatedly to give the ER, neurology, and orthopedic doctors windows into her body.

They see the damage Ekos had done to her and they watch her heal.

Mill initially has a small bleed and some swelling in her brain. So, the neurologist keeps her in a drug-induced coma for the first 48 hours, and a brain surgeon stands by in case she needs to drill into Mill's brain case and relieve pressure.

As the nurses and aides haul her back and forth for tests and imaging, she responds to them no more than a sack of potatoes might have.

As drug levels go down, Mill almost wakes before more drugs slide her back into oblivion. Each time she nears consciousness, she begins to struggle against bizarre dreams and hallucinations.

In their grip, she groans and moves, grabbing monitor lines and IV tubes. Watching her on video monitors, nurses come in and restrain her hands until the narcotic they pump into her takes her back under.

In different ways and in different dreams, Mill keeps seeing a dark grey face, human but cat-like, with slitted eyes and a flattened nose. The face says, "I'm your mother, Milly, your mother...your mother."

Mill thrashes and says, "No, no, no, you're not. My mother's gone... gone...dead." The listening nurses only hear the whimper sound of a small child, lost in the dark.

On the third day, the doctors withdraw her breathing tube and stop the narcotics except for on-demand morphine for pain.

Mill wakes up four hours later. She lasts ten minutes before she drifts back to sleep and then, over the next twelve hours, gradually stays awake for longer and longer periods of time.

Doctors come and give her various tests. They report the status of her condition and recovery. Their voices are soothing, but she can't remember what they said five minutes after they leave.

On the morning of the fourth day, they move her out of intensive care and into a private room. They wheel her bed down the hall and into a room.

The slightly dizzy Mill notices a uniformed police officer outside. She asks the aide, "Why's he here?"

Her words slur slightly and they are barely audible over the roaring in her ears. The young man answers, "Just for your safety, Officer Meacham. I don't know much personally, but people will be in to see you soon. You should ask them."

They settle Mill in bed. She's so tired from her travel, she drifts off to sleep immediately. An hour later, shoulder pain forces her awake. She hits the button on the morphine pump without opening her eyes.

From a few feet away Frieda Tomlin's voice says, "Meacham, God damn it. Cut the joy juice! Wake up! We need to talk!"

Mill's eyes shoot open. Where the Hell had Tomlin come from? Is this another terrifying dream?

But a real, solid Frieda Tomlin stands over her bed, wearing a tight smile, "You almost got yourself fuckin' killed, Meacham. And who ever kicked your ass knew what they were doing. Didn't they teach you cow cops how to fight or at least call for back up?"

For all her tough words, Tomlin actually looks more like a concerned sister than her drill-instructor bluster suggests.

Mill grins crookedly. Along with her right eye, half her face is swollen tight as a balloon. Now, the balloon presents puffy red, yellow, and purple flesh to the world.

"Fuck you, Frieda," Mill mumbles, "I was Jake's back up. Give me more shit and I'll put you in an even smaller flight suit next time!"

Frieda smiles, narrow eyed. "Ah," she retorts, "You finally confess. For someone who looks as bad as you do and is flat on her ass, I wouldn't be pissing me off any more. I could thump you and no one would see any new bruises on your shitty lookin' face. Besides I have something here for you."

Frieda Tomlin takes a dark blue four-by-six inch hinged velvet box out of her purse. She opens it and shows its contents to Mill. A small, beautiful bronze medal glows against the velvet.

Suddenly emotional, Frieda clears her throat, "This is the FBI's Distinguished Service Medal. I'm giving it to you for valor while engaged on an FBI case. You were a dumbass to go in without back up, but you showed true bravery when your partner's life was threatened. There's a lot more blah, blah, blah in my commendation request. You can read it later; half of it's even true."

With that, Tomlin takes the medal out of the box and pins it to Mill's pillow.

Groggily remembering something about government awards, Mill asks Frieda, "Frieda, thank you. I'm overwhelmed...but...so, how did this commendation go through so quickly? I mean they told me I have been out for four days or so. Nothing could come through that fast."

Tomlin looks a little embarrassed, "Yours is on its way. This medal's mine. I got it after I took a round in a bank robbery shoot out six years ago. My partner and I walked into an ambush. He was killed. I capped three of them before going down. Fuckin' Wild West show, I swear. I wanted to give you this before all the other shit starts. You can give it back when yours shows up."

Deeply touched by Frieda's gesture, Mill is also instantly concerned by her remark about upcoming trouble.

"What 'other shit' are you talking about?" Mill asks.

Tomlin looks at her with a wry smile, "You are about to go through the grinder, sister Mill. There's at least four law enforcement agencies waiting to take your statement. Then there's the press. Then there's your old man, the Chief of the whole fuckin' Forest Service—what a piece of work he is. The docs will let them at you starting tomorrow morning. Be ready. With tomorrow in mind, I'll move along now and let you rest."

Tomlin starts to move towards the door. Mill suddenly remembers something important, really important. She asks Tomlin, "Frieda, it was an ambush. What about Jake? How is he? Did he make it?"

"No, Meacham," Frieda whispers, her voice husky, "That pain in the ass Jake Burns got himself killed."

She could say no more. Shaking her head, Tomlin walks out the door, angrily wiping away tears.

Mill closes her eyes and sobs quietly, "Oh Jake...."

The sobs send daggers of pain through Mill's neck and shoulder. She presses the morphine injector repeatedly until it no longer beeps or dispenses. In less than a minute, all pain disappears.

She sleeps, tears drying on her cheeks.

An hour later, Manny Suemez comes into Mill's room. After admiring the medal pinned to her pillow, he gently wakes her, "Mill, it's Manny. Come on, *chica*, wake up."

With great effort, Mill wanders out of the grip morphine and grief have on her. "Manny," she says, "How did you get here. I mean when...oh, I don't know."

Manny looks at her with compassion, his mouth drawn into a tight line of concern, "I was doing routine back up for you and Jake with an inter-agency team...we had no intel about a possible attack, just a precaution. We were sitting a about six blocks away when our point man saw you run into the alley drawing your piece. He had orders to wait for us and it took us several minutes to plow through traffic. By then...well, it was over. But, *chica*, I want you to know that the information you gave us allowed us to capture that guy from your forest, the doctor guy."

Mill looks amazed, "I can't remember giving you anything...saying anything."

"But you did, *chica*," Manny says with a grim smile, "In the ambulance you kept saying, 'the post-doc set us up' or words like that. It

366

wasn't hard to figure out who that was...and, Jake a photo of him on his computer and on his phone. We grabbed him at the bus station in Olympia, dressed like a hobo, headed for LA. God knows where he would have gone after that. Left his new wife and baby...what a prick."

Suemez smiled a rare smile, "I just wanted you to know about the collar."

They talk a little more but Mill begins to drift off again. Manny prepares to leave.

Mill mumbles, "Manny, thanks for you know...me...everything...." She feels his comforting hand on her arm and then falls asleep, grief and good news making a gentle, healing blend in her dreams.

———————————//———————————

Over the next two days, Mill answers questions for the Drug Enforcement Administration, the FBI, the Forest Service, and the Oregon State Police. She goes over her Portland assignment in considerable detail, prompted by notes and materials her questioners bring with them.

Her memory of the night of Jake's death remains spotty, although repeated interrogations help her get back some memories. They pop up oddly. One memory triggers another unexpectedly, randomly, almost like the way bits of grass and bark tumble up in a flooded stream.

Mill really doesn't remember much about her fight with Ekos or her supposed contact with her mother. In fact, she intuitively withholds the idea that one of Burns' attackers might be her once-gentle mother.

Her justification is simple—she never saw the woman's face and she can barely remember what the woman said. Mill's memory holds an impression only--an emotional coloring lost in extreme pain, nausea, and disorientation--a reaction to the woman's voice. Mill's experience only suggests that the woman might be her mother, Rebecca Theophile, rather than offering proof that she was.

Besides, the woman said she would "be in touch." Better to wait and sort things out more if and when that "touch" happened...if it ever did.

The next day, Bull storms into her room. With him comes Sam Priest, an entourage of Bull's DC toadies and national press.

Under her breath, Mill says to herself, "Just shoot me now." She figures coma would be better than this. Didn't her Dad and Priest understand how she looks and what she'd been through?

She gives the morphine pump several jabs. Her outlook improves.

Bull's communications director quickly arranges the media so they can record Bull's words to his hero daughter. The next few minutes are agony for Mill who has no love for any spotlight. It's tolerable only because Bull does most of the talking after relegating Priest to the verbal sidelines with a gesture.

One of Bull's answers stands out in Mill's mind. A Fox News reporter asks Bull, "Chief Meacham, has Milly's mother been in to see her?"

Bull answers, "We divorced years ago. She hasn't been in touch even with Milly being so badly injured. Says a lot about the kind of person she is."

Mill thinks, "Leave it to W. A. Meacham to bad mouth my Mom on national TV when he hasn't seen her for twenty years."

When the last question has been asked and answered, everyone files out except Bull. He stands looking at his daughter. "God damn, Milly," he jokes, "You look like shit. You doin' okay?"

"I've been better, Dad, "she replies wryly, "Looked better, too."

W. A. laughs, "Isn't that the truth, Milly. Your face looks like a baboon's backside, all swole and purple."

He laughs again and then looks at his watch. "Okay," he says, "I have to get goin'. Got a plane to catch up to Missoula to grab and grin for the Forest Service Museum fund raiser tonight. Get better, Milly. There's a new assignment comin' your way soon, gal!"

With that, W. A. Meacham barges out of his daughter's hospital room.

Mill says to the empty room, "Hi, Dad. Bye, Dad. Thank God you're gone, Dad. What 'assignment?'

Christ!"

Chapter 51

But Still Unrest

When Mill gets discharged from the hospital, Philip drives her home.

Security had kept him out of her hospital rooms. So, on her release, she'd accepted his help for "a couple of weeks" until she could operate pretty well on her own again.

Philip won't be her only helper. Once they get back to Florence, a female FBI special agent posing as a nurse will "look in" on them several times a day to secure Mill's house. An FBI "watch team" will keep guard from Mill's neighbor's hastily rented-out home. Local police will provide inconspicuous street security.

It's all a low-key trap set for the killers if they should decide to make another try at Mill.

Mill wonders what the whole thing might be costing. She gives up when her calculations reach thousands per day.

She says little during the drive to Florence, two FBI tail cars leap-frogging them and annoying Philip with the need to pass them only to have the pass him again.

He doesn't grumble audibly at the car ballet; he just lets Mill rest. Still groggy and hurting, Mill alternately sleeps and wakes. Waking, she remembers Zumo and Burns…and Arianne. Their deaths were such a waste—inexplicable really.

And her mother! She wonders where her mother fits in the whole picture. Is she one of the "mis" people? Her mind wanders down into the questions and then orbits away from them…no answers and none in sight.

Respecting her silence, Philip only asks questions about her comfort. He knows she will tell him what she wants to in good time.

All through the three-hour drive, Philip wants to tell Milly how much she had scared him, about his feelings for her. Now that he's almost lost her, he's clear about this feelings. But he remains silent until she's stronger and waits for when they can talk and look at each other at the same time.

They arrive at her house. Everything in and around the house is quiet and orderly. Mill feels the kindness of normalcy, known things in their place.

Yet Mill also feels a pinprick of loss. Movers have taken everything of Tilly's out of Mill's house. Tilly's spaces are empty. Tilly has not left a note or even a forwarding address.

Mill muses to herself, "So little after so much." She angrily swallows a small lump in her throat.

Philip helps Mill stiffly into her bedroom. Because her right arm is immobilized and her neck is in a soft cervical collar, it falls to him to help her take off her going-home clothes and dress her in a nighty and oversize bathrobe.

His face red with embarrassment, Philip removes Milly's hoodie and sweat pants, dropping them to the floor.

She's surprisingly, shockingly naked before his eyes.

He wonders what he thought he would find when he took off her clothes, nun's garb? What an idiot he always is!

Now he can't help himself. He looks briefly at Milly's strong back, the swell of her hips, and the line of her bottom. His face gets redder.

Looking away, he tries to drop the nighty over her without looking. But, afraid his clumsy tugs will hurt her, he turns his eyes back. Before the cloth drops, he sees the gentle slope of her breasts, her nipples, her stomach.

His cheeks glow brighter. He helps her get her good left arm into the sleeve of the bathrobe and settles the bathrobe around her.

She holds the robe closed in front with her good hand while he works his way around her to tie the belt.

Mill almost kids him about ogling her.

But, seeing Philip's red face, she says lightly, "I've never had a maid before. This is nice. You can help me anytime."

Philip merely gulps, "Glad to...glad to help."

After she's all tucked into the robe, Philip pulls a surprise for her out of a shopping bag--fuzzy, bright yellow, Oregon Duck slippers.

Mill chuckles her appreciation, "I never had my foot up a duck's butt before. You're spoiling me. Keep it up."

He stoops down and helps her put the slippers on. She steadies herself on his shoulder with her good hand. Her touch feels wonderful to him.

Philip walks Mill into the living room. He settles her on the oversized couch, propped up with pillows, a light throw over her legs. He goes into the kitchen and makes tea. He takes out some of the fruit and light snacks he'd bought on the way to Mill's house.

While he boils water and clatters plates, Mill probes her feelings about the night she'd discovered Tilly's infidelity on this couch. The pain of it has gone although some of the anger has not.

Philip comes back to the living room, places a tray on the coffee table, and puts Mill's cup within reach of her left hand. He sits down across from her in one of the overstuffed chairs.

"This place is great, Milly," he says smiling, "A place to be happy."

Mill responds, "Yes, it is. And thank you for making everything so easy for me."

She pauses and then says seriously, "Philip, I don't want to shock you or upset you but we need to talk about your stay here."

He looks apprehensive as she continues, "We're going to be here together for the next two weeks or so. You're going to have to help me shower, change clothes, all that…at least to start with. So, I'm going to give you permission to look at me…naked or parts of me naked."

His face flames red. She almost laughs but she can see how acutely uncomfortable he's become.

Mill goes on gently, "I know this is hard for you. I respect this might not be something you want to do."

Philip holds up his hand and exclaims, "Milly, this isn't something I don't want to do. The problem is it's something I want to do very much, maybe *too* much. I'm not really a prude but…but…you're so attractive. And me…well, I'm so *attracted!*"

"I know you've been in relationships with both men and women. That fact confuses me but doesn't make me want to run away. It makes me hesitate to move closer. I don't want to offend you…or…or…presume… well, you know."

Mill finally understands his hesitation. "Okay. I hear that you're worried I might be offended if, as a lesbian, you make advances towards me. Is that right?"

Philip nods somewhat miserably.

Mill continues, "Well, I'm not a lesbian, at least not what all that label implies. I'm not even bi-sexual as I understand that term. I just get attracted to different people, not caring so much about their gender. I look for people to be kind, and supportive, and accepting of me. Most of all, if they become a part of my life, I want them to stay. I want them to stay…to *stay*…even when they could go, maybe even *should* go. Stay, just to be with me. *Me, me alone.* Understand?"

She'd never been clearer with herself about her desires than today, talking to Philip.

Maybe it takes a blow to the head, or almost dying, to provide clarity…whatever…it had come.

Philip looks calmer but puzzled, "Okay. I think you are saying that you might be interested in me if I was the right kind of person. True?"

Mill laughs gently to prevent shaking her bruised body, "Yes, silly, that's right. And, although I didn't realize it until the last couple of weeks, everything I know about you seems to say you are the right kind of person, the best kind of person."

Mill looks at him kindly, almost lovingly.

Then her face turns sad, "But, Philip, I've messed up every relationship I've been in so far. I can't seem to tell the difference between someone who wants me, promises to stay with me, and then leaves me one way or another. And maybe I'm jinxing everything by wanting too much, holding on too hard. Maybe I just don't know anything about intimacy... can't ever get it right."

Mill turns her eyes away and tears spill down her cheeks.

She's angry at her weakness but she has more to say, "So, I'm afraid, Philip, that if I start a relationship with you, I'll do something dumb and you'll leave me. My best friend would be gone then, along with my lover, and I just couldn't stand it. I wouldn't lose just another one, I would lose the best one of all."

Tired and sad, she closes her eyes.

The next thing she knows Philip is kneeling by the side of the couch. He puts his arms around her gingerly. He carefully presses his lips against hers.

They kiss very gently for a long time.

Finally, Mill laughs through the kiss, "See, silly, I'm too banged up to bite you."

Philip ponders this for a moment, his lips still lightly against hers, "And too banged up to bang me, too."

She chuckles deep in her throat, her lips again gently busy on his.

————————————// ————————————

Three days later, after the "nurse" has done a security check all around the inside of the house and departed, Philip is helping Milly out of one of the living room chairs on her way to bed.

They hear three quiet knocks on the back door. Both tense at the sound. Philip instantly retrieves her Glock from the rack by the front door.

Mill has shown him how to operate her handgun. He carefully chambers a round and holds his trigger finger along the slide as he moves toward the kitchen.

"Should we call for backup?" he whispers.

Mill shakes her head, "No." "Could be a cop...anybody," she says, "I have this in case it's a bad guy."

She raises the "panic button" she was given by the FBI team in her good hand, "Push it and they'll bust down the door in less than a minute."

Mill had given Philip instructions about home security. So, he turns off the hall light to keep from being silhouetted and moves through the kitchen along the shadows by the counter to the back door.

Staying well clear of the door itself, he snaps on the back porch light briefly and then shuts it off. The flash of light tells him that a tallish woman in a hoodie stands on the porch with nothing in her hands held out from her sides.

"It's a woman...alone," he says to Mill.

Mill's heart beats harder. Woman...Mother...could it be?

She grips the panic button, looks at it for a second, then slides it into the big pocket of her robe.

She has to know...and if it's Rebecca Theophile...know everything. She gestures to Philip with her now-empty hand.

Philip steps backwards into the dining room. He hides himself behind the door jamb and aims the Glock at the back door.

"Who's there?" he calls loudly.

No answer.

"I have a gun," he calls more loudly, "and I'll use it."

His hands start to shake and he steadies the Glock against the door jamb. He hopes it won't clatter against the wood the way his teeth have begun to chatter in his head.

Remembering Milly's bravery, he steadies himself again. He wills himself to act more like her.

A quiet, woman's voice speaks from beyond the single-pane glass, "I'm not armed. I want to talk to Milly Meacham if she's here. I have a message for her."

Philip calls softly to Mill, "Let her in or not? It's up to you."

Mill's heart had leaped when she heard the soft voice say "Milly." Now she says distinctly, "Let her in, but keep the gun on her."

Philip edges carefully over to the door and turns the dead bolt. Then he walks swiftly backwards to his former position behind the jamb.

"Come in," he says firmly, gripping the Glock in shaky hands.

The door opens slowly. The woman steps into the kitchen.

"Stop," Philip tells her, "Now, close the door. Reach to your left and turn on the kitchen light."

She closes the door. Her left hand fumbles around the light switches, first turning on and off the porch light, and finally flipping on the kitchen light.

She stands in its glare with her hands at her sides.

By now, Mill has made it to the kitchen door from the living room. She leans against the jamb and stares at the woman. "Keep the gun on her, Philip," she grits. "Ma'am, reach back and lock the door."

The woman fumbles again until she finds the dead bolt and it clicks.

"Okay," Mill says, "Now I want you to start taking off clothes until I tell you to stop. Slow, easy movements. Once you've removed an item, hold it out at arms' length and drop it. Make a pile."

The woman reaches up slowly and unzips the hoodie. She carefully removes it and holds it out towards Mill, dropping it to the floor. Under the hoodie and her loose-fitting jeans, the woman appears to be wearing a thin wet-suit.

As the hoodie drops, Mill listens for a thump, perhaps signifying a weapon. No thump comes from the garment as it hits the floor.

Looking at the woman's odd under-clothing, Mill tells Philip, "Point your weapon at her head."

Then she asks the woman, "What's that you have on, body armor?"

"No," the woman answers softly, "It's what the military calls a 'cool suit'. Keeps my outward heat signature at air temperature. Got me past the thermal and motion sensors law enforcement must have all around your place. Works on batteries..." Her voice trails off.

Mill says, "Get it off. Now."

The woman begins to unzip the parts of the suit and slip out of it. Her face becomes clearly visible in the overhead kitchen light.

As he sees the woman's face, Philip gasps, "Milly, I think it's your *Mom.*"

Mill looks at her sharply and says with a little bitterness, "Maybe, maybe not."

"It *is* me, Milly, your mother," said Rebecca Theophile calmly, "Is this really necessary?"

Mill studies her grimly, "My memory of the night Jake Burns was murdered is faulty but I remember something about you being there. You were not on my team, so I can only surmise you were working for the bad guys. So, I'm very skeptical. You get checked."

Rebecca droops her head, "Okay, I understand. I'd do the same."

Mill continues with the inspection, "Okay, finish taking off your clothes. And, Philip, keep the gun on her."

Rebecca smiles, "It's okay, Philip. It *is* Milly's little friend, Philip, isn't it? I mean you were seven or eight when I saw you last."

The tops of Rebecca's now-naked breasts gleam in the overhead light, undersides in darkness. She bends to remove her treadless shoes. Then the jeans and shoes drop to the floor.

"Yes, Mrs. Meacham…I mean Theophile," he says, eyes avoiding her arching breasts and blushing as the lower part of the cool suit slides down. She removes it to drop. His eyes follow the naked line of her belly involuntarily.

"It's definitely me, Philip," she answers, voice soothing.

Before the words are out of her mouth, Rebecca moves so quickly that he can barely see her. Her hands close on the Glock. She twists it out of his grip.

Mill starts into the kitchen but Rebecca tells her distinctly, "Stop there, Milly. Nothing bad's going to happen unless you make me use this on Philip. I just needed to disarm him. I wasn't sure he knew which end of a gun goes up. I didn't want him shooting me or you by mistake. And, I have to leave in a few minutes. I can't be slowed down."

She waves them into the living room with the Glock, "We're moving in there, away from windows. Once we get there, turn out all but one light and sit down on the couch. Keep your hands where I can see them at all times."

Badger picks up her clothes and the cool suit. She moves towards them.

Philip helps Mill back into the living room and turns off all but one lamp. They sit down together on the couch. Philip's right arm goes around Milly protectively. She smiles nervously, elated at his touch, but scared of what her bloody-handed mother might do.

Rebecca quickly dresses one-handed, Glock in the other, finally buckling her belt. She takes one of the chairs a few feet away from them. She sits down looking at them intently, the gun held in both hands pointed at the floor between them.

"Looks like you two are a couple," she says with a warm grin. "Nice. I hope you last. I've never known what that's like."

Her face turns grim, "Milly, we have a lot to talk about, you and I, but that can't happen tonight. There's a police cruiser parked down the street

375

several blocks, so I know people are still concerned about you and...the organization I am a part of."

Taking a chance, Mill interrupts. "Would that be one called 'missed?'" she asks.

At Mill's question, Rebecca's eyes widen with surprise. Before she can stop herself she asks, "Where did you hear the name 'Mist,'" Milly?"

Covering, Mill replies, "Oh, different places, Theophile." Mill spits the words out, angry but not wanting to reveal anything to her criminal mother.

"Well, I guess it really doesn't matter, Milly," Rebecca sighs wearily, struggling to contain the damage her slip had caused. "I've been a part of helping to keep our Mother Earth safe for the last twenty years, since soon after your father made me leave you. I suppose someone would hear about us sometime...just a little group, really...doesn't do much."

Mill ignores the 'father made me leave you' statement. She asks acidly, "So, Theophile, why does a nice environmental organization go around killing people, lots of people, good people?"

Rebecca looks surprised, "That's not what I came here to talk to you about tonight, but who says lots of people have been killed? We don't kill people."

Mill eyes her narrowly, decides to push, "The FBI, the Congress... little groups like that. So, why has your Mist murdered lots of people?"

Rebecca stares at her daughter. Her mind screams, "The nightmare has started. Mist is revealed. Important people know about Mist...have known maybe for a long time. Federal law enforcement thugs might be chewing their nasty paths through Mist's guts *right now!*"

Badger can't just sit here. She remembers Raven's words from the cave, "*All lost....*" She has to get the news to Arrow and Raven as soon as possible. She struggles to keep her face neutral.

She rises slowly to her feet, every movement casual "Milly, we do what we do to protect our Mother, the Earth. That's all. No killing. Agent Burns was killed by someone else. I just happened to be there to try and stop it. Look, here's my message. Mist believes *you* killed one of our people. But you are not a target for revenge, at least not now. I will try to keep you safe but it's mostly not up to me."

She peers out at the darkened night, "I shouldn't be here, shouldn't ever have come. It's wrong...betrayal. But...but...you're mine...always. I have to go now. Remember...be careful."

She reaches out to touch Mill but her daughter pulls back, "Don't touch me. I see the blood of my friends on your hands."

Rebecca looks at her hands. She nods, face drawn and ashen, and moves to the kitchen door. "I'll be in touch again soon, my beloved," she calls softly. Then, with the click of the latch, she's gone.

The back porch stairs creak. The Glock thumps the roof above the back door.

Mill turns to Philip, "Please go get my gun. There's a ladder in the garage. But before you go, get my cell and speed-dial Frieda Tomlin. I have a few things to tell her."

He nods grimly, "Shouldn't we call the watch team in...get her picked up?" He searches her eyes, sees the war within her, love for her mother against the hate...the anger...the questions.

"In a minute," she whispers, "Just a minute...."

Philip retrieves the phone. Walking to the back door, a deep, cold anger over the threat to Milly's life climbs up his stiff spine. Once outside, he stares fiercely into the green-black night, willing invisible enemies to appear out of the light mist that lays on the land.

Before the call connects to Frieda, a large fist pounds on the front door. A big voice yells, "Police, open up!" The pounding continues.

Mill ends the call and moves slowly to get off the couch and over to the door. Philip comes in from the back porch and helps her cover the last few feet.

He snaps on the front porch light. They see a big Oregon State Trooper on the porch dressed in field gear. He has a Remington tactical shotgun slung over his shoulder.

Philip hurriedly opens the front door. The big man peers in. "Sorry to bother you folks," he exclaims, "But I was watching your place with a starlight scope. I saw someone leave, heading out past your garage. I figured I'd better check with you and see if everything's alright."

Mill squints inquiringly at the officer, "Could you tell who it was?"

"No," he answers, "The person looked middle-height, slender, dressed in a hooded sweatshirt or coat. At first I thought it was your guy here, but then he shows up at the door to the garage. That's when I came over."

Mill smiles slightly at the mention of Philip as "her guy," then says, " I was just calling the FBI when you knocked. We had a visitor. Maybe a bad guy. Nothing happened. Scared him off with lights and, of course, I had my weapon. Where did he go?"

But there's no reply from the trooper. He steps away from the house and unslings the shotgun. Cradling it in one hand, he calls his partner on the radio, "Call for Lane County back up. Make sure they send a K-9 unit. We have a possible bad guy in the area."

Nodding to Mill and Philip, he turns on the high-intensity flashlight on his shotgun and walks carefully towards the garage and the creek beyond.

Without saying anything, Philip seems to understand why Milly didn't reveal the truth about her mother's visit. "Time enough to discuss that issue later," he tells himself.

A moment later, a member of the FBI watch team walks up rapidly. He gets the low-down and steps inside the house to check security before leaving to follow the big trooper out into the yard.

An hour later, after finding no sign of the bad "guy," the county units leave. The big trooper and the FBI agent come to the front door. The trooper says, "Sorry we didn't catch the bastard, Meacham. We'll get him if he shows up again."

With that, turning down the offer of coffee and a snack, he turns and heads back to his unmarked cruiser parked in their driveway. Gunning the vehicle back to the street, he motors back to his observation post.

The FBI agent looks at Mill and Philip, "I can't figure why our sensors didn't pick the guy up...doesn't make sense...."

"Beats me," replies Mill, "A gap some place maybe...guy got lucky. I don't know."

The agent shakes his head, "Yeah, I guess so...I got a tech team on their way here now...about an hour away. They'll try not to wake you up when they check things."

He looks around Mill's property, "Okay, I'll head back next door. I bet that we scared 'em away permanently, but we'll stay on the job until we get ordered out. You'll know if that happens. It's almost midnight. Get some rest, you two."

He smiles, turns, and walks away.

Mill wearily asks Philip to finish retrieving her Glock from the porch roof. He heads to the back of the house. As soon as he's gone, Mill eases her way out the front door. She carefully walks to the garage.

The K-9 unit had gone over the whole property, finding a hot trail down to the creek. The trail ended where the creek flowed through a large flat-bottomed culvert under Route 101. The police speculated that the bad guy had stashed a rubber raft there and simply floated away unobserved.

Mill thinks their theory is a good one. It would be just like this Mist outfit to be that thorough, that careful. But, she still wonders if the cops hadn't overlooked something, maybe something not too obvious. So, she works her way into the garage and turns on the lights.

Looking high and low, at first Mill sees nothing, just the garage with her car and all her junk in it. Then she notices something odd. High up, where the rafters meet the ridge at the end of the garage, at the point furthest away from the entrance, she sees what can only be described as a shadow.

No, it's more a visual blank spot.

Mill walks to the work bench and picks up a flashlight. Shining it upward at the blank spot, she sees that the spot has a shape.

"Mother," she calls softly, "Come down. I can see whatever you are hiding behind. I'm not armed and the police have gone...for now."

Mill does not know if she can trust her mother but she has increasing confidence that her mother has not come to harm her or Philip. After all, she'd gained the power hand in their previous encounter and didn't shoot either of them.

Just the same, she puts the flashlight back on the bench, slides her hand into her robe pocket, and grips the panic button, thumb poised.

The blank spot moves. A piece of cloth flutters down to the floor near Mill. Even on the floor, it seems to absorb light, a dark pothole in the concrete.

Two quick moves and Rebecca lands softly next to Mill like a cat, steady and ready. She blinks at her daughter and smiles a little shyly, "You weren't supposed to catch me, Milly. I was just going to wait up under your high, high roof and make my escape in an hour or so."

Instantly angry, Mill spits vehemently, "Theophile, this isn't a game. You're a murdering bitch! Turn yourself in! Let go of this crazy group you're a part of and rejoin the rest of the human race."

Rebecca looks sadly at her daughter, the cool suit hood oddly framing her face. "Milly, that can't happen. Maybe once long ago, but not now. I have to go soon before that goofy boyfriend of yours retrieves your Glock and shoots me with it."

The thought strikes both women so absurd that both laugh. Their laughs twine musically. Suddenly Mill remembers their laughter's love, the kindness of her mother's arms, their endless hours of play...of touch. Her heart hurts, shoulders droop.

"Mom," she whispers, tears glinting in her eyes, "Why did you leave me? I mean, I never knew...no word...you know...Dad said...."

Rebecca's face changes instantly, first to compassion then to malevolent rage, "That son of a bitch sent me away after hurting me so badly...told me he would kill us both if he ever saw me again. I believed him...look at these scars."

Rebecca rolls up her sleeve and unzips the cool suit's zipper from her wrist to her elbow.

Mill sees the purple-pink scars on her mother's forearm, "W. A." She reacts blankly and then with horror. "You're saying he did this?" she asks, incredulous.

"Yes," Rebecca hisses, "He did this and worse. I will tell you the whole nasty business some day but not today. I must go...*really* must go."

Mill's head spins. She doesn't know whether W.A. had inflicted that harm on her mother or whether her mother might have done it herself. By why would Rebecca Theophile, blue-blood PhD, hideously mutilate her arm? It makes no more sense than her Dad doing it.

At that moment, Philip calls from the house, panic in his voice, "Milly, Milly, where in Hell are you?"

Both women hear the sound of his feet approaching, no doubt attracted by the lights coming from the garage.

Mill turns towards the door just as Philip enters.

"What in Heaven's name are you doing out here, Milly? I've been looking all over...why didn't you answer my call?"

As explanation, Mill turns to point at her mother.

But there's no one there.

Rebecca Theophile is gone, the piece of cloth with her.

Mill looks back at Philip and says, "Doesn't it just figure. Every time I turn around my mother disappears."

Philip stares and then hurriedly checks the garage. Rebecca is indeed gone, out the back window and into the mist still touching the land and water nearby.

Philip puts his arm around Milly. He murmurs, "Yes, your mother's gone, but I'm here...with you...." and gently leads her back into her house.
Home.

END

Thinking and Talking About the Book

Principal Characters

Armando "Manny" Suemez - a tough, experienced Forest Service Special Agent in a powerful position and Mill Meacham's law enforcement mentor

Clarence "Bud" Miller - a tough and generous long-term Forest Service employee who believes in "industrial forestry"

Ekos - an arrogant, fiery Mist assassin with no known background

Mill/Milly Meacham - a dependent, endearing, and self-reliant young woman with a painful background, a 5th generation Forest Service employee, and a new Law Enforcement Officer

Bill Zumo - a Forest Service Patrol Captain and Mill's exacting boss, well connected throughout the agency, later killed by a Mist assassin

Matilda/Tilly Corcoran - Mill's charming and seductive lover who lives two lives and who betrays Mill to support her ambitions

Philip - a caring, if slightly confused pastor and Milly's life-long friend and devoted supporter

W.A. "Bull" Meacham - Mill's father, Chief of the Forest Service, a tough, ruthless narcissist driven by his lust and career ambitions

Rebecca "Badger" Theophile Meacham - Bull's ex-wife and Mill's mother and an angry, aristocratic Mist Clan Leader in charge of assassins like Ekos

Hammond "Ham" Hoggett - Bull's sycophant, a burdened, enduring, power-hungry man given to backstabbing and behind-the-scenes deals

Esperanza Angelica "Angie" Pizzaro - a talented and charming woman who seduces and betrays Bull to gain autonomy and power

Mike Reinard - a powerful Congressional staffer who betrays Bull to gain power

Simon Ball - Forest Service Regional Forester who betrays Bull to gain autonomy and sexual gratification

Brixton "Arrow" Bragg - Mist's careful and strategic War Clan Chief and Rebecca's lover

Raven - Mist's terse Listening Clan Chief, expert gatherer of information

Golden Eagle - Mist's impetuous Money Chief

John O'Reilly - an overly ambitious Special Agent killed by Ekos

Sam Priest - a Regional Special Agent in Charge who talks a lot and says little and who is Jake Burns' boss

Arianne Moeller - a sensitive, withdrawn Forest Service secretary and Mist agent

Carrie Soames - an over-focused, industrious Forest Service secretary and Mist sympathizer

Jake Burns - an eccentric, gifted Special Agent who leads the hunt for Mist and for Zumo and who is killed by Badger and Ekos

Frieda Tomlin - an ultra-tough but generous FBI Special Agent in Charge

Gregory Stillman - a calm, precise FBI agent who works in tandem with Frieda Tomlin

Questions About the Characters

Who did you identify with most? Why? Which characters changed, grew, or developed? Which remained the same? Why?

Which characters held secrets? How did secrecy affect their lives? Make them vulnerable? Help them grow?

Did any of the characters represent "good" or "evil" in a pure sense? Why?

Which characters cared most about the environment? How did they show this caring? Was their expression of caring constructive or destructive?

Plot

A Deep Green War has a basic plot that 1) pits the underground, murderous environmental group Mist against Forest Service law enforcement and 2) describes Bull Meacham's attempt to rise to power and dominate the Forest Service.

Who wins? Who loses? Why?

How are the Mist Clan Chiefs and Bull and his supporters alike? How are they different? What role does secrecy play in their values and behaviors? How does the story deal with the conflicts among characters? Are the conflicts resolved? How?

Sub-plots

A Deep Green War also has several sub-plots and themes: 1) Mill's family history and the relationships among Mill, Bull, and Rebecca, 2) Mill's love life and her relationships with Tilly and Philip, 3) Milly's rape, the mystery of her rapist, and importance of her recovery, 4) Mill's post traumatic stress disorder and how it affects her life, 5) Mist's history, culture, and actions, 6) Rebecca's relationship with Arrow, 7) betrayals, 8) sex), 9) relationships and culture within the Forest Service, and 10) relationships among the Forest Service, BLM, and FBI.

Who is in love? With whom? What kind of love? How do the love relationships work out?

Who wants to control nature? Control other people? How does that desire for control affect relationships and outcomes?

The gold coin and cloisonne leaf are Mist's bait intended to bring about the destruction of Forest Service employees. How does the story deal with gaining treasure from the forest? How does nature treat non-treasure hunters, like Ekos and Milly, who enter the forest for other reasons?

Do sex and sexual relationships mirror other aspects of characters and how they support, control, or dominate others.

Is rape or sex a substitute or symbol for power and control? For love? For commitment? A contract? What roles do sex and violence combined play in defining characters or outcomes?

How about the idea that how people treat other people reflects how they treat nature? What does it mean when a character like Bull treats both people and natural resources as objects to be used to further his career? Is Mist's treatment of people and resources different than Bull's? How? Does Mist's behavior suggest anything about modern environmentalism as a movement or its strategies, tactics, or impacts on people and communities?

Organizations have cultures and insist that new employees adapt. Naive new employees may be betrayed and victimized by more experienced workers. How does Milly's rape fit the pattern of new-employee treatment within large organizations such as federal agencies? Does this treatment clash with agency ideals such as "fair treatment" or a corporate "family?"

How does Tilly's betrayal of Mill reflect how agencies deal with one another? Can trust and commitment develop between agencies with hidden agendas and false intentions?

What crimes are committed? By whom? How are the criminals punished or how do they escape punishment?

Crisis

At a certain point in *A Deep Green War* life changes for Mill and other key characters such as Bull and Tilly. When do these changes occur? What happens that means the characters will never be the same again? How are these changes like adaptation in nature?

Satiric Elements

Satire uses mockery to reveal and denounce vice or folly. *A Deep Green War* has satiric touches including names, behaviors, and concepts. First names and nicknames such as "Millicent" and "Mill," "Tilly," "Bull," "Ham," "Ekos," "Badger," "Arrow," "Raven," and "Golden Eagle" have both direct and implied meanings. Some, like "Millicent," evoke ideas ("innocent") and may speak to feelings or an emotional state. Others, like "Mill," speak to behavior or character traits like persistence or tenacity. "Philip's" antonym "fillip" refers to "excite by tapping with a finger," something Philip did to Mill at the Greek restaurant with profound results.

How does the nick name "Tilly" fit with Tilly's behavior? The name has a certain cute, casual charm to it. Does the charm disguise anything? What?

What about the rest of the names on the list?

Last names also contain satiric elements. These include: "Meacham" (me), "Theophile" (God lover), "Hoggett," "Pizzaro" (adventurer), "Reinard" (fox), "Ball," "Bragg," "Priest," "Moeller" (mole), and "Burns." Names like "Bud Miller" (two brands of beer) combine to make other satiric elements.

How do the names on this list reflect the behavior of the characters or the character of the individuals? How do they emphasize conflicts or influences over outcomes?

The Forest Service has a strong culture with many admirable characteristics. Straight talk, hard work, and strong personal relationships are among them. *A Deep Green War* introduces the idea that some elements of the Forest Service culture are less desirable. So the satiric elements of a Green Creed developed and forced on others by agency aristocrats, the Legacies, are an essential part of the book.

What effects on morale and performance might grow out of an aristocratic culture in which favoritism, privilege, and advancement are a birth right for a few people? Does the presence of an aristocracy affect who can be promoted? Rewarded? What role might retirees play in promoting or defending such an aristocracy?

How would the existence of unstated public policy such as the Green Creed affect agency performance? Relationships? While it could reinforce tradition, how would a Green Creed help define the agency's future? Help it react to changing times and leadership?

Humor

A Deep Green War describes some pranks, jokes, and teasing. These include pranks such as Zumo painting Mill with a yellow smiley-face, jokes such as Mill and Arianne mocking Agent Collins as Moeller's lover, and teasing such as Mill's interaction with the other LEOs when she "needed a jump."

How does such basic and often transparent humor support the plot? Does it reflect culture? Teamwork? How does it disguise conflicts or secrets? Does it bring people together or separate them? Build trust or defeat it?

Word Play

The novel contains occasional word play in the form of chapter titles, unusual word mixtures, people's names (for example, "Ham Hoggett"), and the use of certain punctuation such as the ellipse (...). Some characters use colorful figures of speech as Jake Burns does. Others, like Pizzaro, make occasional puns.

How does word play contribute to the story? To our understanding of the characters? To their approach to life or other people? For example, puns are inherently competitive and intellectual. Colorful figures of speech reveal a lot about a character's approach to others and may serve to disguise their true feelings. How do those ideas fit with certain characters?

Thanks for reading!

Look for more about Mill's life and

experiences in Alaska and the Rockies!

A Deep Blue Abyss

and

A Deep Brown Crucible

The First and Third Mill Meacham Stories

Carson A. Pierce Novels

Available Now

www.ingramcontent.com/pod-product-compliance
Lightning Source LLC
Chambersburg PA
CBHW070732180626
46818CB00007B/2814